Praise for
*...traordinary Circumstance*

"Weylyn Grey is enchanting. . . . Each bittersweet story shows our capacity to accept people who are different." —*Real Simple*

"This exquisite and adventurous book will remind you of classic fantasies that you read as a child." —*Bustle*

"This tale feels comfortable and familiar, imitating Lewis Carroll's casual, everyday description of magic and starring a sympathetic, mature boy with Peter Pan–like abilities. Original and imaginative, especially in its multifaceted exploration of one extraordinary person, Lang's novel is a lovely and fascinating feat of magical realism." —*Booklist*

"This enchanting title mixes magical realism with romance, humor, and adventure, delighting readers who enjoy strong fantasy populated with quirky characters and events." —*Library Journal*

"*Beasts of Extraordinary Circumstance* by debut author Ruth Emmie Lang will grab you by the hand and thrust you into a world complete with animal whisperers, supernatural occurrences, and people who search their whole lives to find what's right in front of them." —*Bookreporter*

"Ruth Emmie Lang's debut glitters with the glow of fireflies, explodes with the force of fantastically strange events, and warms with the love of a man who has so much possibility contained within him it overflows in miraculous ways. Skeptics who shun magic on page one of *Beasts of Extraordinary Circumstance* will be converts by the end."
—*Shelf Awareness*

"I read this book on the first of September and it has stayed with me all month. The story is whimsical and gorgeous. The writing is just beautiful. And it made me smile the entire time." —Kate Krug, *Book Riot*

"This wonderful, whimsical, warm-hearted novel is filled with subtle and not-so-subtle nods to the books I loved as a child. . . . Reading this book is so comfortable and uplifting, you almost feel as if you could conjure a herd of fireflies to get through a power outage, or a field of daffodils to celebrate a loved one's birthday. *Beasts* is exactly the book I needed right now, and it made me so happy I wanted to howl at the moon." —Steph Opitz, *Marie Claire*

"Ruth Emmie Lang's prose has the earthy warmth of a campfire story, best enjoyed in the woods and under the stars. Her contemporary spin on the American folktale, *Beasts of Extraordinary Circumstance*, bristles with charm and curiosity, and its oddball hero, Weylyn Grey, will make you want to follow him into the forest." —Winston Groom, *New York Times* bestselling author of *Forrest Gump*

"A wholly original and superbly crafted work of art, *Beasts of Extraordinary Circumstance* is a masterpiece of the imagination. Intelligent, witty, and brave, Ruth Emmie Lang takes us on an uplifting and unforgettable adventure of love, magic, friendship, and fate. An extraordinary work of fiction by a truly gifted author." —Lori Nelson Spielman, *New York Times* bestselling author of *The Life List* and *Sweet Forgiveness*

"Ruth Emmie Lang dazzles with her inventive and magical debut. Told with brains and heart, *Beasts of Extraordinary Circumstance* introduces a protagonist who is both mythical and relatable. Weylyn Grey leaves a lasting impression on everyone he meets, and he will on readers, too." —Michelle Gable, *New York Times* bestselling author of *A Paris Apartment* and *I'll See You in Paris*

"*Beasts of Extraordinary Circumstance* is a brilliant button on the coat of American magical realism. Think *Charlotte's Web* for grown-ups who, like Weylyn Grey, have their own stories of being different, feared, brave, and loved." —Mo Daviau, author of *Every Anxious Wave*

# Beasts of Extraordinary Circumstance

## Ruth Emmie Lang

 ST. MARTIN'S GRIFFIN  🦋  NEW YORK

*To Max*

*and a lifetime of wandering this world together*

BEASTS OF EXTRAORDINARY CIRCUMSTANCE. Copyright © 2017 by Ruth Emmie Lang. All rights reserved. Printed in the United States of America. For information, address St. Martin's Press, 175 Fifth Avenue, New York, N.Y. 10010.

www.stmartins.com

Designed by Steven Seighman

The Library of Congress has cataloged the hardcover edition as follows:

Names: Lang, Ruth Emmie, author.
Title: Beasts of extraordinary circumstance / Ruth Emmie Lang.
Description: First edition. | New York : St. Martin's Press, 2017.
Identifiers: LCCN 2017024873 | ISBN 9781250112040 (hardcover) |
    ISBN 9781250112057 (ebook)
Subjects: LCSH: Paranormal romance stories. | Magic realism (Literature) |
    GSAFD: Fantasy fiction.
Classification: LCC PS3612.A5548 B43 2017 | DDC 813/.6—dc23
LC record available at https://lccn.loc.gov/2017024873

ISBN 978-1-250-30666-1 (trade paperback)

Our books may be purchased in bulk for promotional, educational, or business use. Please contact your local bookseller or the Macmillan Corporate and Premium Sales Department at 1-800-221-7945, extension 5442, or by email at MacmillanSpecialMarkets@macmillan.com.

First St. Martin's Griffin Edition: December 2018

10  9  8  7  6  5  4

*prologue*

HOLBROOK, MICHIGAN

1968

## DR. DANIEL FOUST, OB/GYN

I have delivered over a thousand babies in my career, but one in particular stands out in my mind. Weylyn was by all outward appearances a healthy baby boy: eight pounds, two ounces, all the necessary parts accounted for, and a wail that could shatter good china. He fit perfectly in the crook of his mother's arm and watched her with one eye, carefully, as she was still a stranger to him. I would have forgotten all about this seemingly ordinary child if it hadn't been for the storm.

The moment Weylyn took his first bewildered gulp of fresh air, it began to snow. Not just a few flurries, but buckets of the stuff, tumbling through the sky and belly flopping on the ground outside the hospital room window. By the time the nurses had him cleaned and swaddled, there was a good six inches on the ground.

It was June 29.

The child turned one eye on me, then opened the other like a backward wink. His irises were molten pools of solder that had not yet set, and for a moment I thought I could see a fire behind them, keeping them liquid.

"He's a healthy baby boy," I told the mother, trying my best not to sound unnerved.

Weylyn's eyes closed peacefully, and the snow melted almost as quickly as it had fallen, leaving shimmering gray puddles on the sidewalk below.

*first interlude*

## WILDWOOD FOREST, OREGON

2017

## ROARKE

"A betting man can lose a dollar. It's the man he bets on that can lose an eye." My mother would say this with a confidence that suggested there were no other possible outcomes, that there were thousands of one-eyed boys out there apologizing to their mothers for not taking their advice.

I, remarkably, still had both my eyes despite my impulse to hurl myself off things that were often a generous distance from the ground. Some of my other hobbies included running with sharp objects, lighting fires, and lighting sharp objects on fire and launching them into the sky with my slingshot. So, naturally, when it was my turn in Truth or Dare, my friends never had to ask.

"Dare!" I hollered and head-butted a tree.

The other kids laughed. That was my favorite part.

"I dare you to . . ." Mike looked around the forest for something I hadn't yet climbed, eaten, or peed on. One time, he puked after I made him eat a worm, so I ate ten worms and a beetle just to make him look like a baby in front of pretty Ruby S.

"This'd better be good," Ruby said as she perched herself on a tree stump like it was box seats at the opera, pointing her candy heart nose at the ceiling as she admired the crown molding.

Mike thought for a moment longer, then flashed me a wily grin. "Did you hear about the thing that ate Gretchen's dog?"

"Again?" I scoffed. Mike's cousin Gretchen was always making up stories. Her most recent string of lies featuring beloved family pets meeting strange and untimely demises. She was pretty weird.

"This one's real!" Mike insisted. "Charlie got off his leash and started sniffing around this old cabin by the creek. She tried to call him back, but he wouldn't come. Then like a minute later, she saw this half-man, half-spider thing looking back at her through the window, and she bolted."

Ruby gasped and leaned forward on her stump. "She just left Charlie there?"

Mike nodded and continued, "She showed me the place. It's creepy. Covered in cobwebs and stuff. I wanted to look inside, but Gretchen started crying 'cause she didn't want me leaving her there by herself. She's scared of spiders."

"I think *you're* the one who's afraid of spiders," I said, wiggling my fingers like they were eight hairy legs.

Mike didn't take the bait. He leveled his gaze on me and said, "I dare you to touch it."

"What? The cabin?"

Mike nodded, searching my face for signs of fear. "What d'ya say? Truth or—"

"Dare."

"That's it." Mike pointed to a ramshackle cabin made of splintered, gray wood. The windows were dark and shrouded by cobwebs. It appeared no one was home.

This was going to be easy. "So, I just have to walk up and touch it?" I asked.

Mike hesitated, clearly thrown off by how unfazed I was. "Yeah . . . but you have to keep your hand on it for at least twenty seconds."

I almost laughed. This was weak, even for Mike.

"Guys, look," Ruby said, pointing to a small flock of sparrows that had settled on the roof of the cabin.

"What is it?" I asked, failing to see what was so interesting about a bunch of birds.

"Just watch," she said.

One by one, the birds beat their wings, but none of them lifted off. It was as if something was anchoring them by their tiny wishbone feet. They furiously flapped and chirped for help as their heads jump-cut from one angle to the next, searching the sky for hawks or eagles.

"Poor birds!" Ruby cared enough to exclaim, but not enough to do something about it. She turned to me. "You have to save them."

"Yeah, Roarke. Save them." Mike nudged me forward.

For the first time in my life, I hesitated. I didn't hesitate when I drove my uncle's truck when he left it running in the driveway, or when I caught that snake and wore it like a necktie. But something about this was different. My heart fluttered; my pulse raced. I was . . .

"What's wrong? Scared Old Man Spider's gonna eat you?"

"No!" I sounded more defensive than I'd have liked. I could see the other kids doubting me, Ruby doubting me.

I head-butted the nearest tree, took one last look at Ruby's candy heart nose, and ran to my almost certain doom.

I slowed to a stop within spitting distance of the cabin—twenty-three feet, my personal best. I made sure the coast was clear before I pulled myself onto the branch of a sagging elm and shimmied over to the eaves of Old Man Spider's roof. Then I realized what was keeping the birds from leaving. Most of the cottage's roof was missing, and in its place was what looked like a tarp made of spider's silk. I carefully placed my weight on one of the several rotten two-by-fours that remained of the original roof and went to work freeing the birds with my Swiss Army knife, cutting the threads that bound their tiny feet while being careful not to step on the sticky stuff myself.

I could see Ruby from where I was, so I decided to make a show of it. I leaped from board to board, bird to bird, cutting them loose and throwing my arms in the air as if I had performed some kind of magic trick. Ruby's lips were moving, probably saying something like, "Oh! Did you see that? Roarke is so brave." When all the birds were free, I took a bow and wondered if I'd get a kiss later. Then came time for my final trick: the Disappearing Act. Like a trapdoor, the board beneath my feet gave way, and I fell.

I braced myself for the landing I had nailed a hundred times before from the tops of trees, roofs, and bridges, but it never came. I found myself cradled in a hammock of spider silk not three feet from the ground. I had fallen into Old Man Spider's trap.

I struggled to break free but only succeeded in making myself more tangled. Where was my knife? Not in my pocket. I eventually spotted it suspended several feet above me from a single thread of silk. I could see the webbing had caught the blade, not the handle, so all I could do was wait as gravity cut through the thread and hope it didn't land on any part of me that contained a vital organ.

As my eyes adjusted to the dark, my surroundings revealed themselves. The room itself was spartan—the only pieces of furniture were a kitchen table and a sofa bed with springs sticking out of the mattress. It was what was above eye level that was cluttered. Spoons, toothbrushes, socks, tweezers, tennis rackets, and other household miscellany hung suspended in long, sticky tendrils that dangled from large sheets of cobweb on the ceiling. It was as if all those items had gotten stuck at some point and whoever lived here just hadn't bothered to cut them down.

I heard a shuffling noise behind me. My heart raced as I imagined a giant half-man, half-spider pinning me down with its hairy arms as it prepared to devour me headfirst. Luckily, the thing that found me was no mutant human-spider hybrid, but entirely man: two legs, two arms, two eyes, hair mostly concentrated on his scalp. He also had two pant legs and two sleeves—both of which were soiled and frayed—and a long, salt-and-pepper beard that he most likely used as a napkin from the amount of food particles that were nestled in it. I guess he wasn't so much *old* as he was dirty, although I could see how it might be hard to tell from a distance.

"What's this?" His look of surprise suggested he had never seen a child before.

"Get away from me!" I shouted and struggled against the webbing that bound me.

"You'll pardon my asking, but this is my house. Why do you ask that *I* remove myself from it when *you* are the one dropping in unannounced?"

"I'm not scared of you!"

The man once again looked surprised. "And why should you be?"

"Because! You . . . you're a villain!"

"A villain?"

"You trap animals in your web and eat them!" I said bluntly.

"I think you have me confused with someone else. Have you tried Myra Oswald on South Street? She's an odd one."

"What about . . . kids?"

"Of course not! Eating children is a ghastly business."

My muscles relaxed a little. "Then why do you live in this creepy place?"

"Because I needed a place to stay and it was available. The roof needed some patching-up, so my eight-legged friends offered to fix it for me. Would you like something to eat? Cheese? Watermelon?"

I liked both cheese and watermelon, and Old Man Spider didn't seem so bad, but I wanted out of that web. "No, thanks. Could you help cut me out? My knife got stuck."

He gazed up at the hole in his ceiling. "What were you doing up there, anyway?"

I told him about the birds, the bet, and Mike.

"I tell them not to land on the roof, but they keep doing it. You could say they're a little *flighty.*" He paused like actors do in sitcoms after they've told a joke, only I had no idea what the joke was. "Never mind," he added flatly.

"Can you get me outta here or not?"

"Of course, of course!" Old Man Spider went to work untangling my mess. "This might take a while. As you can see, when things get caught, I usually just leave them where they are."

I glanced at a cheese grater hanging not ten inches from my face and wondered if he just stood in the middle of the living room to grate his cheese.

"What is your name, young man?"

"Roarke."

"Roarke, Roarke . . ." The man ran off and rummaged through a kitchen drawer. He pulled out a leather-bound book and flipped through it. "Rachel, Randy, Reginald, Ronald. No Roarke. You're the first!" He excitedly scribbled something in the book. "I try not to repeat names. You don't know how many Johns I've told to skedaddle! My goal is to know one person of every name. I haven't met another Weylyn, yet. That's my name—Weylyn Grey," he said, shaking my hand. His name suited him. He had gray eyes that shone like fish scales in the light.

The web was starting to make my skin itch. "I really gotta go home."

"Of course. My apologies." Weylyn got back to work.

I hoped my mom had bought more chocolate milk. Maybe she'd let me have some after she made me try on that eye patch again and asked me how I'd like to have one of my own.

"So, what's a smart boy like you doing climbing on people's roofs? You could've hurt yourself."

"I've done much crazier stuff than that."

I told him some of my best stories: the one about the sewer and the train tracks and the neighbor's dogs. Weylyn seemed unimpressed.

"What? You got something better?"

Weylyn smiled. "I was young once, too."

*book 1*

## THE WOLF BOY

## TIMBER HILLS, MICHIGAN

1979

# 1

## MARY PENLORE

It was the morning of my eleventh birthday, and as usual, my dad had failed to notice. It wasn't that he didn't care; he had just never been one for party planning or affection in general. That had been my mom's job. Still, a card would have been nice.

Instead, he gave me my order for the day. It was 5:00 A.M., and he handed me a postcard. "It's all one order. The directions are kind of confusing, but I'm sure you'll figure it out." Without another word, he walked back into the freezer and shut the door behind him.

On the front of the postcard was a picture of a dormant volcano with steam rising from its peak. In bright orange text, it read, *Aloha!* I flipped it over and found directions on the back. They were confusing, mostly because there wasn't really an address. It read:

*W.*
*The Howling Cave*
*Twelve Pines Forest*
*Timber Hills, MI*
*United States*
*Enter from the southwest corner of the forest. Follow the path for a half a mile, then follow your nose.*

I hitched my icebox trailer to my bike and set out just as the sun began to outline the jagged tree line.

Five minutes deep into the forest, all I could smell were pine needles and the first of the season's bee balm. I love the smell of bee balm. My mother used to tie a bundle to the clothesline upwind of the laundry as it dried, so my sheets would come out smelling like fresh air and mint. She had an elevated sense of smell like a blood-hound, so half her day was spent sniffing out odors and concocting perfumes from things she found in the woods behind our house: pine and juniper for bathroom odors; lemon and sage for smelly drains; a cocktail of water, dandelion, and crushed peach pits worked great on upholstery; and a towel tumble-dried with cinnamon sticks was a surefire cure for a wet dog.

Breakfast was her favorite time of day. Every morning, I would find her in the kitchen in a state of euphoria as her nostrils gulped the scents of bacon, eggs, and syrup. I even caught her drooling on her apron a few times.

Watching her eat was even more fun. Every bite she took was fol-lowed by a series of *mmmm*s and *I've outdone myself*s, even when all she had made was buttered toast. Her food was usually underseasoned for my tongue, so I'd sneak a dash of salt when she closed her eyes, something she did when she swallowed so she could concentrate on the blooming of every taste bud. I once joked she should wear ear-plugs, too, and was then asked if I could pick some up for her next time I was at the store.

Her condition wasn't all syrup, bacon, and eggs, however. I once forgot to take the trash out, and one whiff of it caused my mother to pass out on the kitchen floor. I quickly got rid of it and revived her with an orange peel. When she had her stroke last year, I tried basil, lavender, ginger, garlic, anything I could find until the doctor told me to stop.

For her funeral, her friends brought bouquets of not only flowers but also dried herbs, soaps, fruits, sandalwood, and other sweet-smelling things. When I looked at her in her casket, I pretended she had just closed her eyes for a moment so she could take them all in at once. I hid a piece of orange peel behind her right ear.

I stopped my bike and smelled the air. It would have helped if I knew what I was supposed to smell or whom I was meeting or *what*.

Then it hit me like the punch line of a bad joke, every foul-smelling particle of it. I opened my mouth to cough, and my tongue absorbed it like a sponge. I stuffed my mouth with mints fluffy with pocket lint and looked for the source of the smell. It didn't take long to find the carcass of a dead raccoon half-hidden in the bushes beside my feet.

*Is this some kind of prank?* I thought. Had I been dragged out into the woods at 5:00 A.M. just to smell a dead raccoon and go home? If I had, that would have been the time for the comedian to jump out from behind a bush and shout, "Gotcha!" so I could run him over with my bike.

"This is dumb," I muttered to no one and steered my bike back the way I came. My pedals had only completed one full rotation before I stopped again. Another smell overtook me: smoke. Someone somewhere had a campfire going. It was the only thing I had to go on, so I left my bike on the path, unhitched the trailer, and followed my nose through the brush.

I was surprised when I found the campsite. Not that I thought it didn't exist but that my sense of smell led me right to it. My mother would be proud.

At the mouth of a narrow cave, there was a clearing. In the center of the clearing was a crackling fire, but—as far as I could tell—no one to tend to it. In fact, there was very little that suggested anyone had ever been there, aside from a cast-iron pan and a single sock half-buried in the dirt.

"Hello? Is anyone there?" No response. Whoever it was, was

probably gathering more firewood or relieving himself behind a tree, something totally ordinary, not the things my brain was telling me he was doing, like putting the finishing touches on his booby trap.

Then I heard something my brain had not prepared me for: a low growl. I turned slowly toward the sound and met the eyes of a terrifyingly beautiful gray wolf. Her ears were back, and her fur formed a serrated crest along her spine. Her fangs were long, and her claws were sharp. I'm sure she had many other worthy qualities, but the dangerous ones were all I could concentrate on at that moment. I closed my eyes and pictured my mother making bacon for me in her new kitchen.

"Ma! No!"

I snapped out of my daydream to find a boy, a human boy about my age, jumping between the wolf and me.

"It's okay, Ma. I invited her here. She's brought us breakfast." He gestured toward the icebox. The wolf snorted and shot me a warning glance before lazily collapsing next to the fire.

"Sorry 'bout that," he said as he turned his attention to me. He had a silly smile. The kind you paint on a clown, wide and red. "She's not used to people. 'Cept me."

He was filthy from head to toe with a wild crop of brown hair and silvery-gray eyes. His clothes were damp and smelled like wet dog. I desperately wanted to throw them in the dryer with a cinnamon stick or three.

"You're W.?"

"Yeah. I know it's far, but we bought out all the other butchers."

"You live here?"

"Yep. That's my mom."

The wolf grunted.

"Well, not my real mom. She's dead. My dad, too."

"Oh."

He shrugged. "Yep."

After a few seconds of awkward silence, I said, "I'll get your order."

I started unloading the meat from the trailer. The boy insisted on helping and gave me a quarter for my trouble. How he got the quarter and how he had been able to pay my father for thirty pounds of meat I didn't ask, but something else was bugging me. "So, why do you have to buy meat at all? Can't your . . . mom just hunt her own food?"

The boy looked troubled. "Not anymore. Our pack can't steal livestock 'cause the ranchers will shoot if they hear so much as a moo. I lost two cousins that way."

"What about deer?"

"Deer have moved out. Don't know where they went, but they're not here. We kill rabbits and squirrels, which are fine for me, but for my family, they're not more than a snack."

The wolf groaned.

"Comin', Ma!" The boy grabbed a raw steak and tossed it to her. She gobbled it up in a matter of seconds and flopped back on the ground, pleased.

"What's your name?" he asked. "I love hearing what different people are called. Someday, I'd like to meet someone by every single name."

"My name's Mary."

"That's a good one."

"I guess." If it hadn't been my mother's name, I wouldn't have thought so. Most people think she named me after her, but I was actually named after Mary Tyler Moore, her favorite actress.

"I'm Weylyn, which I like okay. I think it'll look good on a business card."

"Sure."

"How old are you?"

"Eleven . . . today."

"Today is your birthday?"

"Yeah." I didn't mean to say it, but maybe I was just tired of pretending it wasn't true.

"Happy birthday! You have to stay for breakfast. Unless you have other plans?"

I pretended to think about it and said my other plans could wait.

Most girls celebrate their eleventh birthdays with a few of their friends from school. They eat cake and ice cream off paper plates and sit and gossip about the girls who couldn't make it. They talk about articles they read in magazines stolen from their older sisters, using phrases like *second base* and *frenching* without actually understanding their meaning.

I spent my birthday with a pack of wolves.

They were very welcoming, allowing me the best spot next to the fire and licking my face clean after I had eaten. Even Weylyn's mother warmed up to me after a while, inviting me to scratch her belly and ears.

Weylyn also proved to be better company than I had had in a long time. He told stories about life in the pack: stories about friendship, long winters, the hunt, and being hunted. He even told me about his parents (the human ones).

"Our house backed up onto the woods," he said, gazing over my shoulder as if the house were right behind me. I nearly turned to look, but stopped myself.

"It had a fire pit where me and my parents would roast hot dogs and marshmallows and stuff. One night, this wolf came sniffing around," he said, nodding at Ma, who was curled up by his feet. "I was scared at first, but my mom told me it was okay. She said the wolf was just hungry and threw her a hot dog. After that, Ma would show up every time we lit a fire. At first, it was just 'cause she wanted hot dogs, but then I think she liked being around us." Weylyn ran his fingers through the scruff of Ma's neck. The wolf sighed contentedly.

"There's a picture somewhere of Ma and me on a trampoline, but I don't know where it is," he continued. "It's probably with the rest of the stuff I left behind when my parents died. It was a snowstorm, you know."

"What was a snowstorm?"

"That's how they died. In a car accident. That's what the lady from the government told me, anyway, when she came to get me."

I wasn't used to talking about death. My dad and I avoided the topic as much as humanly possible. During my mom's funeral, he mostly just sat in the corner of the room, humming to himself. When people offered their condolences, he asked them why, as if he hadn't yet heard the news. It made some of the mourners second-guess whether they were attending the right funeral.

"So . . . how'd you end up out here?" I asked awkwardly. "In the woods."

"I just ran away," he said, shrugging, as if it were that easy. "My parents kept emergency money under their mattress, so I grabbed that and some other things that were important to me and snuck out through my bedroom window. Ma must've known something was wrong 'cause she was waiting for me at the edge of the woods."

"Do you ever miss them? Your parents?" I asked.

"Yeah. I do," he said, his bottom lip quivering slightly.

"I know how you feel. I lost my mom."

Weylyn's expression shifted gears. I could tell, even before he spoke, that he had drained his mind of his own sadness and replaced it with empathy for mine. "I'm really sorry," he said, and meant it.


It was almost noon. The fire was dying, and the wolves were all napping in the sun. Weylyn and I licked the last of our meal off our fingers and were ready for a nap ourselves. "This is the best birthday I've ever had," I said with a full belly and a full heart.

"It's not over yet. You can't have a birthday without a gift."

Weylyn jumped up and ran into the cave. I heard him rummaging around; then he came back out with both of his hands behind his back.

"Close your eyes," he said, giddy.

I closed them, and he placed something in my hands.

"Now open."

It was a postcard. On it was a picture of the ocean during sunset, fiery orange and pink with text over it that read: Wish You Were Here.

"I took my dad's collection of postcards with me when I left, dozens of them from all the places he'd been. This one's my favorite. I don't know where it is, but it's pretty. I thought maybe you'd find it pretty, too."

I did. When I got home, I placed it on my nightstand. It was the first thing I saw when I woke the next morning.

2

# NELSON PENLORE

It was Sunday afternoon, usually my busiest time of the week, but today, I was fishing. I closed my doors at ten that morning because my freezer was completely empty. I'd never had an empty freezer in over twenty years. Even on Easter, Christmas, and Thanksgiving, there was something left: gizzards, necks, feet—the parts that weren't festive-looking enough for a holiday table—but this W. guy had ordered everything, down to the bucket of entrails I keep by the slop sink. I stuck a note to it warning that it might make him sick, but what he did with his own guts was his business.

The fish weren't really biting, probably because there were no fish left. My disgruntled customers occupied every square inch of the bank.

"Margaret was planning on making pork chops tonight," grumbled Fred Toomey. "I love pork chops."

"Then give me a pig, Fred, and I'll chop it up for you. Otherwise, you're just gonna have to wait until Tuesday when I get my next shipment."

Fred muttered something under his breath, packed up his gear, and left.

I caught two small trout, enough for Mary and me. I didn't usually cook, but it was Mary's birthday, and her mom always used to cook something nice on her birthday. She also used to make big meals on Sundays right after church because, as she said, "praying made me hungry." I'm not sure what she prayed about. In fact, she never once talked about her beliefs during our marriage. During service, she sat studiously, both hands in her lap, listening to the sermon and nodding occasionally. I was able to piece together a few of the things she thought were important from the timing of those nods: first, she cared about the poor; second, she seemed to be behind the notion of forgiveness; and third, that yes, she would like to join the rest of the congregation for cookies and punch in the activity room. She would also nod once or twice on her way to the car, as if putting check marks next to her list of lessons learned for the week. I admired the personal nature of her spirituality, even if I only kind of understood what it was.

The mosquitoes were nipping at my ankles, a sign that it was getting late. I packed up my kit and took a shortcut home—I wanted to beat Mary there so she wouldn't make herself a sandwich before I got the fish going. We didn't eat together much, partially because neither of us liked to cook. Didn't talk much, either, but I never talked much to anyone, including my customers. It only got worse after MaryAnn died. My wife once said she'd had a better conversation with a donkey, but she agreed to marry me, anyway, because I was a good listener and was slightly better looking.

It's true. I could probably tell you every word my wife ever said. Mary, too. Most people remember their child's first word, but I remember her first twelve: *Ma, Da, yes, no, me, you, now, Cheerios* (pronounced "chee-momos"), *ball, bear, kiss,* and *love.* But the more words I stuffed into my brain, the less room I had for other information. I'm pretty sure the lyrics to every song I've ever heard now occupy the part of my brain that once controlled speech. Maybe that's why MaryAnn got so mad whenever I was late because my first instinct was to sing "Time Is on My Side" by the Rolling Stones.

It was nine o'clock by the time Mary came home. "Oh. Did you make dinner?" she said as she looked at the two plates of food on the table. One was nothing but bones and a crushed wedge of lemon. The other was covered in tinfoil.

What I wanted to say was, *I went fishing so I could make you a nice dinner like Mom used to.* But instead, I just said, "Yeah. Trout."

"Thanks, Dad, but I already ate," she said and put her plate in the fridge.

I opened my mouth to wish her *Happy birthday,* but ended up mumbling The Crests' "16 Candles" too quietly for her to even hear.

## 3

### MARY PENLORE

Weylyn became my father's best customer. Every Sunday, he'd clean out his entire stock, down to the last gizzard. My father even had to turn away some of his regular customers. "Maybe come by on Saturday next week," he'd tell them.

"Who says I'll be coming back at all?" was a common response before they stomped home to their Sunday tables dressed with potatoes and no meat.

This didn't bother my father. He was the only butcher in town, so unless the whole village decided to go vegetarian, he wasn't going to lose any business over it. In fact, business was booming. My dad must have chopped up every piece of livestock in the county. He was so busy that I had to help with the butchering, a task that I hated even more than mopping up the blood.

Every time I started on a new animal, I laid a dish towel over its face so I wouldn't have to look it in the eye. "It's not going to haunt you, ya know," my father would say in his usual droll tone, then punctuate the end of his sentence with a loud chop.

I let him believe I was scared. It was better than admitting that the dish towel was the only thing stopping me from crying.

I loved Sundays. I loved waking up with the birds, smelling the cool air, and riding the forty minutes to Twelve Pines. Most of all, I loved being greeted by a warm fire and a hot meal courtesy of Weylyn.

On this particular Sunday, Weylyn had made warm berry syrup to top the sponge cake I had brought. "I think I remember liking cake," he said the week before, "but it's been so long, I can't be sure."

"This is the best thing I've ever tasted!" he said, his chin stained pink with berry juice. "Mary, you're the best cake-maker in the whole world!"

My cheeks, chest, and arms broke out in hot, pink patches—my mom had called it my shy rash. As Weylyn gobbled up the last of the crumbs, I picked up my cake tin to leave.

"You're leaving already?" Weylyn looked disappointed, his face covered in berry juice.

"Oh. Well . . ." I'd told my dad I'd help with chores that day. "I don't know. Am I?"

"It kind of looks like it."

I stared at the cake tin in my hands, wishing I had a table or a counter to set it on so I didn't have to keep awkwardly holding it.

"You wanna hang out?" He looked up at me eagerly.

"Yeah."

"So, why're you still holding that tin?"

I chucked the tin into the bushes.

Weylyn grinned mischievously. "You ever ridden a horse before?"


"This is way more fun than any horse," Weylyn assured me as he helped me onto the back of a large gray wolf called Arrow. He must have seen the terror in my eyes because he said, "Don't worry. He's only ever thrown me off twice."

Before I had a chance to back out, Arrow jolted forward. I screamed and grabbed hold of his fur as he shot through the trees. I could hear Weylyn laughing behind me.

"First one to the hill wins!" he hollered and shot past me on Moon, a white she-wolf.

Arrow sped up, and I buried my face in the fold of his neck.

A few bumpy minutes later, I was brave enough to lift my eyes from Arrow's fur and feel the breeze on my face. Trees raced past us at an astonishing speed, but Arrow's breath was calm and even. Moon was right alongside us, Weylyn perched confidently on her back, his long hair whipping itself into plaits. He looked over at me. "There you are! How's it goin'?"

"Good." I was grimacing.

"Just good? Then you're not going fast enough!" He let out a howl, and the wolves went faster. I hunkered down into the safety of Arrow's shoulder blades.

We stopped at the crest of a hill. Weylyn pried my stiff fingers out of Arrow's fur and helped me off his back. I willingly crumpled to the ground and waited as my muscles unlocked themselves.

"You're missing the view." Weylyn sat on the edge of a cliff, facing the sun. I crawled over to join him. Twelve Pines sprawled out beneath our feet, the treetops gilded by late afternoon light.

"This is where I come when I'm sad . . . or happy. It's where I come to *feel* is what I mean."

I was still trying to regain feeling in my face.

"You know, you're the first girl I've seen in a long time. I'd almost forgotten what a girl looks like, then I met this hunter in the woods, and he told me that girls are prettier than boys, which, I'm not gonna lie, kind of hurt my feelings. Then he showed me a picture of this pretty lady in a magazine, and I understood what he meant."

I scrunched up my nose and felt it tingle. "We're not all lucky enough to look like the girls in those magazines."

"You must be lucky, then. You look just like her."

Some people have a knack for accepting compliments. I get defensive. "No, I don't!" I pictured my body in my head. There was either too much or too little of every piece of me, like I had been molded by an amateur artist in a beginning pottery class. "I'm sorry the first real girl you've seen in five years had to look like me." I was always doing that, apologizing for the way I looked as if the world were somehow suffering from it.

Weylyn looked at me like I was crazy. "If you're the only girl I ever see, Mary, I can't say I'd be sorry for it."

Mary. It felt nice to have a boy call me something other than a pronoun. My shy rash burned.

We sat there for a long time, watching the sun sink into the valley like butter melting on toast, or at least, that's what it looked like at first. The longer I stared at it, the more it looked like the tree line was reaching up into the sun, not the other way around. "Do you see that?" I asked.

"See what?"

"The trees look like they're growing."

"They *are* growing."

"No, I mean, faster than normal."

Weylyn squinted into the sun, then shrugged. "They look normal to me."

I looked again. The sun had set, and the trees stood perfectly still, like trees are supposed to do.

"I have to tell you something," Weylyn said, his expression suddenly grave.

"Is something wrong?"

"I'm out of money. I used up the last of my parents' emergency money on meat, and now I have nothing left."

"What're you gonna do?"

"We have to find new hunting grounds. We have to leave."

Moon and Arrow howled. Then Weylyn. Then me.

# 4

## NELSON PENLORE

On Sundays, Mary was usually gone all day. I didn't used to worry about how long she was gone because she usually had a lot of deliveries to make, but not lately. Not since W. had been buying up my stock. She made her 5:00 A.M. delivery to him; then I didn't see her until nine or ten at night. I asked her what she did all day, and she said she and her friends rode bikes together. I tried to imagine her with other girls her age riding around town with a meat cooler hitched to the back of her bike. She was probably lying, but she would come home smiling carelessly like kids are supposed to, the way she had before MaryAnn died, so I didn't ask questions. I did silently count any bruises she had, just in case they multiplied.

Mary didn't really need me to protect her. She's way smarter than me. Once, when she was eight, I took her on a bike ride in the woods, and we got lost. After I led us in circles for an hour, she noticed a crow she had seen feeding its young on our way in. We followed it to its nest, and she led us the rest of the way. That girl has great instincts.

It was almost midnight, and she still wasn't home. I tried reading a book, a forgettable mystery novel that my wife must have bought. Every time I picked it up, I had to reread the previous three pages just to remember who died last. I sat in my chair in the front room so I would hear Mary when she came in.

I must have fallen asleep because the next thing I knew, it was three in the morning. Mary wasn't in her room, and her bike wasn't in the garage, so I did something she would probably hate me for: I called the police. I waited on the front steps, gulping fresh air and trying not to throw up. I pictured Mary following that crow and sang "Bye Bye Blackbird" to myself until the cops showed up.

## 5

MARY PENLORE

I ran away from home.

It's hard to say exactly why. I was a kid, and kids do stupid things sometimes. What I do know is that Weylyn made me feel good in a way that I hadn't felt since my mom died. He talked to me. He made me laugh. I had never kissed a boy before, but I imagined what it might be like to kiss him. I pictured us sitting in the boughs of an oak tree, barefoot, watching a light summer rain stir the leaves.

He'd kiss me gently, just once; then I'd close my eyes and imagine when our next kiss might be. I suppose if I'm being honest, I ran away because I liked a boy.

So I packed a few things I might need: a change of clothes, a few of my dad's knives, some books, and a magazine cutout of Scott Baio—I *was* eleven, after all—and I met Weylyn at the Howling Cave.

"If you're gonna be part of the pack, there are a few things you're gonna have to learn," Weylyn said as we started our journey north.

"That's okay. I'm a fast learner." In school, I was a year ahead in math and English, but somehow, I didn't think he was going to ask me to solve any equations or write a poem.

"Mostly, you just gotta know when you're in danger and the best way to get out of it."

"What kind of danger?"

"Wolves aren't the only things in the forest that bite, Mary Jane."

Jane wasn't my middle name. I think he was thinking of the kind of shoe.

Suddenly, he stopped me with his arm. A fierce-looking snake slithered past a foot ahead of us.

"Copperhead. They don't like it when you step on them."

Snakes. I hadn't thought about snakes. Why hadn't I thought about snakes? Or bears? Or mountain lions? I imagined myself being mauled to death by a lion and decided that it wasn't my imagination but the first premonition in my short-lived career as a psychic.

Weylyn must have seen the fear in my face, because he said, "Don't worry. Most of the time they won't bother you." I think he thought the word *most* would offer me more comfort than it did.

For the rest of the morning, I kept my eyes on my feet.

We went searching for rabbit holes, which turned out to be easier than I thought it would be. I used to think that rabbits burrow in fields, but Weylyn explained that they make their dens by trees where the earth is soft enough to dig and elevated enough not to flood. They also live under thorny blackberry bushes, which are harder for predators to maneuver through, and they provide a delicious snack.

None of the dens we found had any rabbits in them. Either they were abandoned, or the rabbits were all out to lunch. I hate to say it, but I was kind of relieved. I had helped my dad butcher hundreds of rabbits and had no desire to do it again, but I knew that was something I was going to have to get used to if I was going to be part of the pack.

I had a pet rabbit when I was five. Lucky, I called him. He had escaped a crate of rabbits that had been delivered to my dad from Dietrich's Meat Supplier. There was some mix-up, because the rabbits were supposed to already be dead, and while my dad had no issue with hacking off their limbs, he wasn't in the business of breaking their necks. So he sent them back, except for Lucky, who hid in a box of saltines until I found him later that day.

My mom got a crate for him that she lined with newspaper, and although it was thoughtful of her to give him reading material, I thought he'd appreciate the fresh air more. When my mom and dad were at work, I tethered him to the leg of a chair and let him hop around the vegetable garden. I'm sure my mom noticed the bite marks in her lettuce leaves, but she never said anything. It was a rabbit's paradise, so what prompted Lucky's escape attempt, I don't know. All I know is that I should have measured the rope before I tied him to it, because when he jumped the fence, it was neither short enough to stop him nor long enough for him to stick the landing on the other side. Needless to say, I found him too late and never asked for another pet.

Arrow eventually caught a wild turkey, and I lent Weylyn my knives in place of the sharpened piece of stone he usually used to skin the meat. We built a fire and threw the drumsticks on a spit for Weylyn and me while the wolves fought over the rest.

"So, how does it feel?" Weylyn said with a mouthful of turkey.

"How does what feel?"

"This." He waved his turkey leg, but I knew he meant more than just what I thought about lunch.

"I feel like . . . before, I had one way of looking at things, and now, I have a million possibilities, and I get to choose."

Weylyn cocked his head slightly to the side. "You talk like a book."

I couldn't tell whether he was making fun of me or not—the turkey in his mouth took all the subtleties out of his intonation—but I took it as a compliment. I had brought one book with me, my favorite. "It's called *To Kill a Mockingbird*," I told Weylyn as I pulled it out of my backpack to show him.

"Why would you want to kill a mockingbird?" he said, confused. "There's barely any meat on them."

"It's not about killing birds. It's a metaphor." Weylyn didn't know what a metaphor was. He barely knew how to read. He remembered learning a little in kindergarten but had forgotten most of it. That's why he signed his orders with *W*, because he was only 60 percent certain that his name had a *Y* in it, and he didn't want to go through the humiliation of spelling his own name wrong.

"You spelled just fine on that order you sent my dad," I said.

"I had help with that one. A jogger. He mailed it for me, too."

"That was nice of him."

"Yeah. I wish I could have done it myself, though. I have this dream sometimes that I'm in school and the teacher asks me to read out of a book and I'm really bad at it and everyone is laughing," he said as he traced the letters of my book with his fingers. For someone who had only spent four months in kindergarten, he had painted a pretty accurate picture of public school.

"I'll teach you," I said.

"How?"

"With this." I pointed to the book.

Weylyn looked skeptical. "I don't know . . ."

"Just think about it."

He nodded and threw his bone to Moon for her to gnaw on.


North. That's the direction we were traveling, and when I asked, "Why not south? Or east? The settlers seemed to think west was a pretty good idea," Weylyn shrugged.

"We had to pick one," was his answer.

"So, we're not following tracks or a scent or anything? We just head north and see what happens?"

"If there was a scent, we missed our chance. The deer disappeared almost three months ago, and we waited too long. It's my fault. I didn't wanna leave."

I could tell Weylyn was homesick. Twelve Pines had been his home for five years, and his parents' house lay just on the edge of the wood. To me, one tree was just as good as any other, but I didn't tell him that. At that moment, I wished I had my mom's sense of smell, so I could at least get us going in a deliberate direction.

Some of the wolves had lost a lot of weight. Arrow's shoulder blades looked like they could cut glass. Weylyn sometimes gave up his portion for them. "It's okay. I'm still stuffed from breakfast." He had only a handful of berries that morning. "I wish we still had some of that cake left."

I wished the same thing. I had only been living in the woods for two weeks, and I had never wanted something so badly in my life as I wanted cake. I had a dream where I licked the batter from a wooden spoon the size of a Cadillac while Weylyn bounced on top of the finished sponge cake like it was a trampoline.

Cake wasn't the only thing I missed. I missed showers—senselessly long with water so hot it was almost uncomfortable. And soap! Dense, bubbly, wonderful soap. I made do with a paste of crushed alyssum flowers and sunflower seeds that I rubbed under my arms and feet. Mom once used it as a deodorant when we went camping together and had forgotten hers at home.

I bathed in rivers, but the water was cold, and I had no way of drying myself. Weylyn dried himself the old-fashioned way. He would strut around, naked and unashamed, until the last drop of water had evaporated from his skin. I, on the other hand, would hide behind a bush and clumsily pull my clothes over my wet body like ground sausage trying to squeeze back into its skin, then walk five miles in squishy shoes. "You're gonna give yourself blisters," Weylyn said as he walked beside me, naked as a newborn.

"No, I'm not." I already had two on my heels and one on my big toe.

"Why are you so scared to take your clothes off?"

"Because I'm a girl!"

"So?"

"So . . . it's embarrassing."

"Why is it embarrassing?"

"Because you're not supposed to see a girl naked until you're married."

Weylyn considered this. "That's stupid."

"You're stupid." My shy rash spread like wildfire. I was glad I wasn't naked because I was pretty sure it was on my butt, like a baby with diaper rash.

"That was mean." Weylyn's big smile made for an even bigger frown. "Is it because I'm a bad reader?"

"No!"

"Just because I'm not any good yet doesn't mean I can't learn."

"I'm sorry. I didn't mean it like that."

Weylyn stopped and started putting his clothes back on. I turned away while he changed, a completely unnecessary courtesy, seeing as I'd just seen him naked. When he had finished, he said, "I want to learn how to kill a mockingbird."

I was one of those freakishly smart babies, the kind that spoke in full sentences at the age of two and was able to craft convincing lies as to why I was going through Mommy's kitchen cabinets. My mother compared it to talking to a tiny alien whose ship had crashed on Earth, and who was now trying to reconstruct it with her pots and pans.

Some of my mother's friends found it unnerving. I wasn't even three yet and my mom's friend Cynthia was babysitting me when, in her most patronizing voice, she asked me if I'd like Tater Tots for lunch. I said, "I'd like to hear the specials first." Of course, I had no idea what that even meant. I'd obviously heard my mom say it at restaurants and was just mimicking her, but it scared poor Cynthia so much that she never babysat me again.

Needless to say, I was a natural when it came to learning to read. My kindergarten teacher even sometimes let me lead story time while the other kids gawked at me and picked their noses. I thought I was the queen of the English language until my first lesson with Weylyn.

After one day, Weylyn was able to read the first chapter of *To Kill a Mockingbird* aloud. I told myself most of that was just memorization, but I knew it wasn't. "Is that good?" he asked. "For a beginner?"

I swallowed my pride along with a dandelion I had been reluctantly munching on. "It's really good. For anyone."

He closed the book and held it out to me.

"No." I pushed it back toward him. "You keep it."

"Thank you," he said, holding the book against his heart, his face beaming with gratitude. "I need to give you something in return."

"You don't have to get me anything," I insisted, but Weylyn didn't listen.

His gaze darted around the forest floor. Eventually, he spotted a barely bloomed daffodil peeking out from behind a mossy rock. He plucked the flower from the wet earth and handed it to me. Then he leaned his back against a tree, opened his book, and read out loud, "Chuh-ap-ter . . . two."

I carried that flower around with me for days. It didn't wilt or turn brown. A week later, it still looked as fresh as the moment it was picked. Tiny roots began to sprout from the bottom of its stem, so I replanted it in a grove of maple trees. As I packed dirt around it, I remembered the day Weylyn and I watched the sun set on the hill. I remembered how the tree line had seemed to rise like dough under the hot sun, and I could swear that from the time I placed that daffodil in the soil to the time I walked away, it was taller by at least two inches.

Reading lessons helped distract us from the hunger. Even I was aware of the hollowness of my belly. The acoustics were great. Every growl sounded like it was echoing off the walls of Carnegie Hall. Between Weylyn and me, we had a crude symphony.

We hadn't seen one deer since we left Twelve Pines, and it was seeming less and less likely that we ever would. If only we had gone west, I thought, where the buffalo supposedly roam. I remember the first time I asked my dad where babies came from. He dodged my question and instead sang that song, "Home on the Range." Between the ages of four and seven, I thought cowboys delivered babies to their parents on the backs of their horses.

"I can read!" Weylyn announced as he finished the last chapter of *To Kill a Mockingbird*. The dance that followed was free of influence from any sort of cultural context, which made it strange but extremely genuine. Ma grunted, unimpressed, and relieved herself on the alphabet I'd written in the dirt. I guess she didn't have the same appreciation for education as we did.

I couldn't blame her. The hungrier I got, the less I cared about the outcome of Tom's trial and the more I thought of home. I wondered if my dad had noticed I was gone or whether he had been mistaking the coat rack for his daughter for the last few weeks. I pictured him going to hang his coat up and muttering, "Sorry, Mary. Didn't see you there," and throwing it on the back of the armchair instead.

The silence in that house was painful, but I had begun to realize that half of it belonged to me. Maybe my dad would have liked nothing better than for his daughter to bake *him* a birthday cake, but I never had. I didn't even know what day his birthday was. I suddenly felt hot with shame.

Weylyn started singing a song that didn't exist and probably shouldn't have existed. I lay down in the sun with the rest of the pack and hoped the warmth would soothe the aches out of my belly.

# 6

## NELSON PENLORE

"So. Let me make sure I have this correct. You sent your daughter to deliver large quantities of meat to a man with no official address and only one initial?" the officer said, deadpan.

"Well, when you put it that way . . ."

"Sir, I'm not putting it one way or another. I'm just reading your own answers back to you."

I gritted my teeth.

"How did this Mr. W. place orders? By phone?"

"No. He sent a postcard."

"A postcard?" Sometimes it takes hearing your own words from another person's mouth to realize how strange they sound.

"Yeah. I thought it was from one of my relatives on vacation. Then I flipped it over and saw the order."

"Do you still have it?"

"I think so."

I went inside and came out with the postcard. "That's his address on the back."

The officer plucked it from my hands with tweezers and dropped it into a plastic bag. "Evidence," he mumbled. I could tell he hated his job, probably because he was always helping idiots like me solve entirely preventable crimes. "Are there any more?"

"No. All other orders went through Mary."

He nodded and scribbled something in his notebook—probably a doodle of me getting hit by a car.

"What's next?" I babbled. "Are you gonna go talk to W.?"

"We'll take it from here." He flipped his notebook shut. "We'll call you once we've found something."

"I can't just sit here. I have to do something."

"Wait for her here. Half the time they just show back up on their own."

"And the other half?"

"We'll call you with any news."

As soon as his cruiser was out of sight, I jumped in my truck and headed to Twelve Pines Forest to find my daughter.

I had only been walking for five minutes and I was already lost. I tried to "follow my nose," per the instructions on the postcard, and had wandered off the path because I smelled what turned out to be bear scat, which was fine until I smelled what turned out to be a bear. Before it could see me, I ran as fast as I could without thought to the direction I was going and ended up losing my bearings completely.

*Follow your nose?* I wanted to grab W. by the collar and punch him in his nose so hard that he never smelled again. If MaryAnn were here, she'd be darting around like a dog, smelling every tree, bush, and rock until one of them smelled like Mary. If there is a God, it would have made more sense for him to take me instead of MaryAnn; then both of them would have been safe, and I could finally retire.

I found it by accident. No smells preceded it. I just tripped on something and looked down, and there it was. MaryAnn bought that cake tin shortly after Mary was born. She said that now that we had Mary, there were a million more reasons to celebrate, and a million more cakes to be baked. I don't think she ever hit one million, but it had to be in the hundreds somewhere.

Sometimes, she would make a cake just because it was a sunny day. I probably put on a good twenty pounds by Mary's first birthday.

I opened the tin, but there were only crumbs. If only Mary had left a trail of crumbs or something for me to go on. Then I noticed the prints. Huge paw prints that looked like they belonged to a giant dog or maybe a wolf. Next to them were a set of footprints, small, like Mary's. There was no blood, no signs of struggle. It was possible they weren't even there at the same time. Maybe it just looked that way.

I convinced myself of these things, that she was alive and that I was going to find her that way. So, I followed her footsteps, bringing the tin with me so we could bake a cake when I brought her home.

The sun had just come up when the rangers found me. I had walked all night following tracks I could no longer see and was three miles from the road.

After the rangers took me home, I threw the cake tin as hard as I could across the living room, breaking a vase that belonged to Mary-Ann's late mother. My body trembled with anger and utter hopelessness. I had failed Mary. All I could hope for was that the police were better at their jobs than I was at being a father.

I couldn't stand being alone in that house another second, so I cleaned myself up and went to work. I spent the whole morning deep-cleaning the freezer—something I hadn't done in months—and sharpening my knives. The pipe under the slop sink was leaking, so I fixed it, and the wall was cracked, so I fixed that, too.

By four o'clock, I had run out of projects and took the long way home, the one with plenty of red lights. I spent the evening waiting for the phone to ring, and when it didn't, I waited for sleep. It was five in the morning when it finally came, just in time for me to miss the sun illuminating Mary's perfectly made bed.

## 7

## MARY PENLORE

I've never liked the word *desperation*. It reeks of melodrama and people falling on swords, neither of which I was particularly fond of. I couldn't fathom a single reason that was worth sticking yourself with a sword over, especially not family honor or obedience to some mentally ill warlord or love. Love was the worst reason of all. Romeo barely even knew Juliet before he was willing to drink poison to be with her, and Juliet had to one-up him and use that dagger. I never liked the word *desperation* because I never understood it—that is, until I was slowly starving to death.

Like a lion, I squatted silently behind a bush, watching every twitch of the rabbit's ears. He was happily munching on a dandelion, cute as can be, but all I saw was him roasting on a spit over an open flame.

My stomach growled. Loudly. The rabbit paused for a moment and looked around. I held my breath. Once he went back to his lunch, I pulled my hamstrings taut, leaped forward, and crashed down on top of the patch of weeds. I looked up just in time to see the rabbit's cotton ball tail disappear into the brush.

"You let him get away!" I looked up at Weylyn and barely recognized him. The muscles of his face were mushy with exhaustion, but

I could tell he was angry by the way his silver eyes burned. "Why'd you do that?"

"I'm sorry," my voice gargled as I forced my tears back into my throat. Girls cry. Wolves don't.

Weylyn's left arm started wagging slowly at the elbow like wolves' tails do when they're angry. "You should've come and got me! Now we're gonna starve for sure!" he shouted and pulled his foot back to kick a birch tree. I braced myself for the moment of impact, the moment when he screamed as the bones in his toes shattered like porcelain, but it never came. As his foot arced toward the trunk, a strong gust of wind tore through the forest, knocking Weylyn to the ground. I felt the sting of hundreds of pine needles whipping past me as I covered my face with my hands and waited for the wind to pass. When it finally stopped, I shook the needles off me before turning to Weylyn, who was still prostrate on the ground.

"Are you okay?" I said, placing a hand on his shoulder. I don't know why I did it. My mother had taught me to never put my hand in a wild animal's cage or I might get bitten.

Weylyn recoiled. "What're you doing?"

"I-I don't know . . ." I retreated and sat back on my haunches, watching blood pool in the corrugations of my scraped knees.

Several minutes passed before he finally spoke. "That rabbit was fast. I probably couldn't have caught it, either." He wasn't a very good liar, probably because he didn't have human parents to practice on.

Weylyn helped me up, and we headed back toward camp. On the way, we were taunted by the mooing of cattle in a nearby pasture. Weylyn paused by the gate to watch them as they grazed. His body language was relaxed, serene even, but traces of alarm still lingered in the corners of his eyes. Flaxen grasses hissed softly as they carried a breeze across the field toward us. Although the air was warm, Weylyn shivered.

That night, the woods were velvet. I folded myself into them and listened as the trees spoke in hushed tones about matters that could wait until morning. *She's hungry and tired. Let her sleep*, they seemed to say. "I *am* tired," I whispered as my eyes lolled shut.

I dreamed that I was Scout Finch and Weylyn was Boo Radley. He was inside his house, peering at me from behind a pair of faded curtains, and I was gesturing for him to come outside and play even though there were storm clouds gathering overhead. Boo (Weylyn) let go of the curtain and slipped deeper into the house, obscuring him from view.

It started raining heavily. Drenched and frustrated, I was about to give up on my reluctant playmate and walk home, when the front door creaked open. Out jumped not Weylyn but a vicious-looking wolf. The beast stalked toward me, its lips peeled back from its sanguine gums, exposing an impressive set of fangs. As I backed away, I noticed Weylyn at the window, watching me with a helpless expression on his face. Then the wolf lunged.

I jerked awake and realized my clothes were damp. The stream I was sleeping next to had risen and soaked the lower half of my body and all my belongings. I grabbed my soggy rucksack and emptied its contents. Luckily, I had sealed my photographs in a plastic bag. Everything else would dry out just fine in the sun the next day. There was, however, something missing: my knives.

I looked around for Weylyn, thinking maybe he had them. I found him once, using my paring knife to whittle a turtle out of wood. I got mad at him for dulling the blade, and he reluctantly handed the knife back, whining that the turtle only had three legs. He was probably off carving that fourth leg or using my cleaver to split a log for a new creation. You can't sneak up on Weylyn, so I decided to stay awake and catch him in the act as he tried to slide my knives back into my bag.

An hour later, Weylyn had still not come back. I began to think he wasn't whittling after all, that something was wrong. I grabbed my bag and quietly tiptoed around the sleeping wolves until Ma blocked my way. She stared at me, knowingly.

"I think I know where he is," I whispered. Ma stepped aside to let me through so I could lead her to her son.

Wind howled across the pasture, rolling over the cattle's broad, heaving shoulders as they slept. Ma's jowls overflowed with saliva as she anxiously paced in front of the gate. Even I was salivating, and I had always preferred pork to beef.

Gathering storm clouds had blotted out the stars and moon, leaving me very little light to see by, but eventually, I spotted a small figure bent over one of the sleeping beasts, holding a rope in one hand and my paring knife in the other.

"Weylyn! Stop!" I hissed.

He looked up, surprised. "What are you doing here?"

"Stopping you from doing something stupid." There was a light on in the farmhouse at the other end of the pasture. Someone was awake. "Please. Come back with us."

"I can't!" he shouted and looped one end of the rope around the cow's neck. It mooed, annoyed.

"Weylyn, be quiet! Someone will hear you."

Weylyn's volume didn't change. "You have to take Ma back to camp. If anyone sees her—"

"What about you?"

"I'll be fine."

"You're gonna get caught!"

"No, I'm not. Now get out of here!"

Thunder clapped. A strong gust of wind knocked Weylyn off balance, and he nicked the cow's hide with my paring knife. It hollered and scrambled to its feet.

Before we had a chance to move, a shot rang out, and the cow bolted. I could see the shadow of a man marching toward us, rifle cocked and aimed.

"Weylyn!" I reached out to him, but he ran in the opposite direction, leading the man with the gun away from me. "Weylyn! No!"

Another shot. Ma whined and backed away from the fence.

Weylyn darted through a frenzy of panicked cattle. If the bullets didn't kill him, surely the stampede would.

The man with the gun took aim at Weylyn again, his hands steady. Then Ma jumped the fence.

The next shot didn't miss. The man with the gun wheeled around just in time to see Ma leaping toward him, her fangs catching the moonlight as they made for his neck.

She crumpled like laundry. I screamed and clambered over the fence. The man took aim at me, then lowered his weapon. "Whoa! Hey, little girl!" he shouted.

I ran to Weylyn, who was collapsed on top of his mother's body, shielding her from the rain that had just begun to pour.

"Ma? Ma, wake up." His voice was thin. Ma's eyes held a blank stare, and her jaw hung slack, tongue lolled out to one side.

"I said wake up!" he screamed as he smacked her on the snout. She hated that.

When she didn't bite back, when she didn't even flinch, a high-pitched whine escaped him. It was the saddest noise I've ever heard.

Only rain, not tears, ran down his cheeks. He wasn't a real boy, after all. He was a wolf, and he cried like one.

I wasn't. So, I let my tears run until my cheeks were crusty with salt.

## 8

## NELSON PENLORE

Three and a half weeks after Mary's disappearance, there was a knock at the door.

"Nelson Penlore?" Two cops stood on my doorstep. One of them was holding my daughter's hand. She was all there. Every finger, toe, eye, and hair. She had no bruises, only a couple of scraped knees and dirty clothes. She looked skinny. And small, smaller than I remembered. She was so mature and independent that I had thought of her as full grown, five-foot-six with a woman's frown, but she barely stood above my elbow. Her ears and feet were the only things that had stopped growing.

When she saw me, a look crossed her face that I hadn't seen since she was a little girl: need. She needed me, her dad, and for the first time in years, I scooped her up in my arms.

Her voice wavered. "I'm sorry, Dad."

"It's okay, sweetheart," I said, holding her tight.

The officers gave us a minute before getting back to business. "Mr. Penlore, could we have a word with you in private?"

"Sure," I said, reluctantly letting my daughter go. She gave me a kiss on the cheek and ran inside.

The officer with the red hair cleared his throat before beginning.

"Mr. Penlore, the Potter's Creek Sheriff's Department picked up your daughter on a local rancher's property. Allegedly, she was stealing cattle with a homeless boy about her age."

"Cattle? Why would Mary need to steal cattle?"

The officers exchanged a glance that I couldn't read. "They said they were hungry. Your daughter and the boy had been living with . . . wolves."

"Allegedly," the other officer piped in.

"There *was* a wolf with them," the red-haired one continued. "The rancher shot and killed it."

*Wolves?* I didn't know any songs about wolves. Maybe that was for the best. I'd already spent too much time in my own head.

Later that night, I asked Mary to tell me the whole story over the "Welcome Home" cake I baked for her myself.

She began, "Well, his name is Weylyn Grey . . ."

*book 2*

# RAINMAKER

## PARIS, OKLAHOMA

### 1980

## 9

## LYDIA KRAMER

Out of the five prettiest girls in Paris, Oklahoma, my mama made four of them. This was according to the *Paris Gazette*, which features a yearly column on the Miss Paris Competition. There's only one winner, but the paper lists the top-five favorites, and that year, four of the Kramer girls were on the list.

First, there was Caroline, who won the 1979 Miss Paris crown. She had the bluest eyes and the longest legs of anyone in the county. Twenty boys asked her to homecoming, so she let all of them take turns dancing with her. Her favorite color was Barbie pink.

The runner-up was Sarah, the oldest. She had boobs the size of volleyballs and went to school to be a teacher, but flunked out and moved back in with Mom and Dad. Her hobbies include narcissism and auditioning for *The Dating Game*.

Emily came in third thanks to her silky red hair and that darling laugh that sounds like a baby bird chirping. She was a ballerina and a pathological liar, and her favorite food was celery.

In fifth place was Angelica, who thought she was ugly because she hadn't come in fourth. She also thought Chinese people came from a place called Chinasia. Her favorite movie was "the one where John Travolta wears those tight white pants."

And then, there was me. I didn't make the top five. I probably wouldn't make the top fifty, and I loved it because it drove my mom bonkers. She would say, "You have such a pretty face. Stop hiding it under all those doughnuts."

And I would say, "Then why don't you cut off my face and let some skinny girl wear it as a mask?"

"Don't be macabre, Lydia," she would say, then tell me to wash that gunk off my arms. The "gunk" she was talking about was my art. I loved to draw, but I didn't like my drawings tucked away in the folds of some sketchbook where no one could see them. So I drew on my arms, feet, and ankles. I drew people, places, anything I saw that looked interesting to me. Sometimes I drew things that didn't exist—alien monsters or vampire donkeys—those were my favorites.

Later in the shower, my creations would disappear down the drain, but it was somehow better that way. The ones that mattered would find their way back to me when I next picked up my pen.

Anyway, Mama and Daddy had five girls, four of them pretty. Daddy always wanted a boy. I think he figured since I was the plain sister that I'd end up a tomboy, so he'd try to get me to play catch with him. He never said anything, but I could tell he was disappointed when I wasn't any good. That's why I wasn't at all surprised when he decided to foster a boy.

We were at the dinner table when he told us. Said the boy was a lost soul and he needed our help. He didn't tell us that the boy's mama was a wolf and that she was murdered in front of him. I'd find that out later.

My sisters were horrified. "A *boy*?" Caroline screeched. "Daddy, you're letting a boy live in our house?"

"Have you forgotten that I'm a boy?"

"No, Daddy. You're a man of God. This boy has probably never been to church!"

"I don't know whether he's been to church, but if he hasn't, wouldn't it be nice to take him to his first service at St. Agnes?

Sarah, you could teach him the hymns. Emily, you could help him find suitable clothes."

The girls looked at each other with disgust.

"I'll help him," I said. "With hymns and clothes and stuff."

"Thank you, Lydia! I knew I could count on you." Daddy winked. He *could* count on me. I was the only one who gave him presents at Christmas that he actually wanted, usually wrapped in the socks and ties that Mama and my sisters had gotten him the year before.

Mama hadn't said a word since dinner started. She had this look on her face that was the same as the one Angelica had when she hadn't been asked to the homecoming dance. Mama hadn't been asked about this. Not really, anyway.

Weylyn. That was his name. I went with Daddy to pick him up from social services even though I was supposed to be in school. Daddy said it was okay because I was doing so well, and one day wouldn't hurt. He hardly ever let my sisters stay at home when they were sick, never mind play hooky.

I liked that kid as soon as I saw him. He had no suitcase or shoes, just the thrift store clothes on his back and an old book tucked under his arm. I could tell he was sad because of the way he blinked—slow, like he didn't want to look at the world more than he had to—but the corners of his mouth still curled up slightly like a handlebar mustache. *Maybe sometime I can convince him to let me draw one on his upper lip,* I thought. *When he's feeling better.*

"Hi, Weylyn. It's nice to finally meet you. I'm Reverend Thomas Kramer. You can call me Mr. Kramer." Daddy extended his hand. The boy looked at it, confused. "It's all right. We'll save that for another day." He noticed the book Weylyn was holding. "Do you like to read?"

He nodded.

"When we get home, we'll get you a library card, and you can borrow as many books as you want."

Weylyn smiled slightly.

"Well, I don't know about you guys, but I'm getting kind of hungry," Daddy said, putting his arm around Weylyn's shoulders. "How about we grab some lunch on the way home?"

Mama never let me have hamburgers or fries or soda. She said they had too much fat and gave you zits. Daddy didn't care about fat or zits, so he took us to McDonald's. "And what would you like, son?" he asked Weylyn.

Weylyn perused the illuminated menu. "Um . . . hamburger."

"Excellent choice. You want fries, too?"

Weylyn looked confused but nodded, anyway.

"That'll be three burgers and three medium fries, please," Daddy told the cashier. "Oh, and Cokes, too."

Daddy and I sat down at a table with our trays, and Weylyn sat on the dirty carpet, cross-legged, with his tray in his lap. "You don't want to sit up here with us?" Daddy pulled out a chair for him.

Weylyn shook his head and pulled the burger patty out from between its buns.

"Weylyn. In our family, we sit together during meals," Daddy said sternly.

Weylyn looked up at him, uncertain.

"So, come on now. Scoot over." Then my daddy, the most respected man in Paris, sat on the floor of the McDonald's. "You too, Lydia," he instructed, and I scrambled off my chair. I could feel people staring and whispering, but I didn't care, and neither did Daddy. I only wished Mama and Caroline had been there to see it.

When Mama met Weylyn, she was as sweet as syrup, which didn't surprise me because she was raised in the Deep South, where hospitality is only second to Jesus. She used to live in one of those huge, white plantation homes that was musty with old money.

When Grandmama died, she left half her fortune and the Syca-more Estate to Mama, and we all flew to Mississippi to pick the stuff we wanted before Mama auctioned it off. As my sisters looted the crystal, I found a rusty, old harmonica with the words SOMEONE LOVES YOU inscribed on the underside. I showed it to Daddy, and he said it probably belonged to a Confederate soldier—a gift from his sweetheart. At the Sycamore Estate Luncheon and Historical Auc-tion, I told Mama's Mississippi friends I was going to learn how to play the harmonica so the soldier's ghost could hear it and it would reunite him with his long-lost love. Mama told them I was ill and sent me outside so I wouldn't scare any more guests.

Weylyn was her guest, even if he was a little "rustic," as she put it. When we arrived home, there was a feast waiting for us: pork shoul-der, creamed spinach, biscuits with cinnamon butter, potatoes au gratin, and three different kinds of pie. Daddy looked at me and put his finger to his lips. I wouldn't say anything about McDonald's, but I couldn't promise I'd be able to fit any more food inside me.

Mama had her apron on for show—we knew Lizbeth, our maid, had cooked everything. It was part of Mama's humble persona that she tried to cultivate after marrying a reverend, but it was never quite genuine enough to stick.

"Hello, Weylyn!" she cooed, dripping with buttery Southern charm. "We're so glad you're here!" When Daddy went over her head like this, she pretended like it was her idea. It was the only thing she could do to feel in control. She looked Weylyn up and down. "Heav-ens! You look like you're swimming in those clothes! Come with me."

When they came back downstairs, Weylyn had on a blue blazer, bright white shorts, and fancy leather loafers. He wriggled with discomfort. "Doesn't he look handsome?" she announced.

I snickered. Daddy shook his head. "What were you thinking, Clara? Buying white shorts for a twelve-year-old boy? He'll get them dirty in two seconds."

"My mama used to say, 'There's no better way to teach a boy manners than a pair of pressed, white slacks,'" she said evenly.

"You were an only child. What boys was she talking about?"

"Remind me to take your white shirts to the dry cleaners, Thomas. They're in a ghastly state," she said pointedly, then dragged Weylyn into the dining room, where he promptly grabbed a piece of pie, plopped onto the floor, and decorated his white shorts with gobs of gooey cherry filling. I watched a knot form in the middle of Mama's face as Daddy roared with "I told you so" laughter.

I may have had some positive memories of my mother. Maybe she took me to the zoo or taught me to ride a bike, but if those memories existed, they were in some dusty, yellowed volume in the back of my mind along with everything I had learned in piano lessons.

Secretly, I hoped I was adopted. I imagined my real mom—a doughy, sarcastic woman who drank her booze out of coffee mugs and let dogs lick her face. She operated a forklift at a factory and earned a modest living. Her house was small, but she had worked hard to afford it and only filled it with things that were special to her. She had never been married, but she had so many friends that it didn't matter. Her socks had holes in them, her white shirts had stains in the pits, and she never, ever flossed. Her flaws were in plain sight, not buffed out with salt scrubs or hidden under layers of Mary Kay.

When she gave her baby up for adoption, she didn't pretend she was okay. She cried in front of the nursing staff until her lungs ached.

I knew she wasn't real. I had an exact replica of Mama's tiny, up-turned nose that reminded me of it every day. Someday, I'd have a surgeon replace it with a Cyrano de Bergerac–esque honker, and I could pretend that somewhere, there was a chubby, sweaty, wonderful woman that had a nose just like it.

Daddy gave Weylyn the room next to mine. It used to be Mama's sewing room until she had a meltdown over one of Caroline's pageant dresses. After that, it was used for storage, then became a sewing room again after Mama promised not to attempt any more silk chiffon. I was personally thrilled when Daddy moved Weylyn in there because it meant I wouldn't have to turn the TV all the way up to hear it over the incessant whirring of that goddamn machine.

After Weylyn had turned in for the night, I found Daddy curled up in his armchair reading the Wandering Wizards series. We had started it together—he was on book four, and I was on five. It followed a young wizard named Finneas Frog who saved the world from a race of evil dragons. The series had been banned from schools by the same group of troglodytes that called Dr. Seuss a heathen, folks my dad felt sorry for because they had no sense of wonder.

"Hi, Daddy," I said, sitting on the leather ottoman by his feet. "Shouldn't you be in bed?"

"I thought parents told their kids to go to bed, not the other way around." Daddy laughed and placed the receipt he was using as a bookmark on the page he had open. "You're right, though. I am tired."

I waited for him to head upstairs, but he continued to sit with the book open in his lap like a napkin at a fancy restaurant. He was clearly avoiding something.

"Mama's mad about Weylyn, isn't she?"

Daddy stared past my shoulder at nothing in particular. "She's . . . adjusting."

*Adjusting*. That's the word he used anytime Mama took issue with a decision he'd made. The problem was, she never really adjusted to any of them.

"What about you?" Daddy asked. "What do you think about Weylyn staying with us?"

"I like him," I said. "He's weird, but in kind of an awesome way. What happened to him, anyway? For him to end up here, I mean."

"His parents died when he was little. Since then, he basically lived on his own out in the woods. The social worker said she had no idea how he was still alive." Then Daddy frowned, strangely. "He says he lived with a wolf pack."

"Whoa." Suddenly, Weylyn's odd behavior made perfect sense. "Did he?"

"Probably not. It's more likely that his story is some kind of coping mechanism that helped him deal with the death of his parents," he said sadly, and he glanced out the window. "He must have been really lonely out there."

No wonder the kid was messed up. It was also no wonder why Mama didn't want him sitting on the "good" sofa. "Poor Weylyn," I said, mostly to myself.

Daddy finally closed *Wandering Wizards* and placed a hand on my shoulder. "I'm counting on you, Lydia. He could use a friend." It felt good being the one my dad turned to in times like these. I could tell it was important to him.

I said good night to Daddy and headed upstairs. On my way to my room, I paused in front of Weylyn's door and listened, half expecting to hear him whimper like a dog as he slept. Instead, I heard a funny squeaking noise, like something scraping against the window. It only lasted ten, fifteen seconds at the most; then everything went quiet. *It's probably just a tree branch*, I thought, even though I was imagining a wolf running its long claws along the glass.

I had once asked my dad if he believed in magic. He'd said he believed in "possibilities." That year, Weylyn Grey showed us all just what kind of things were possible.

The next day was July 4, also known as George Washington's birthday, according to Angelica. It was the most important secular holiday in the Kramer household. Our house had a perfect view of the fireworks, so every year, Mama would invite practically the whole town to picnic on our lawn. Every able-bodied Parisian man would bring his grill, and we'd pig out from sunup to well after sundown. It was my favorite holiday, because it was the only time I could eat five hot dogs in front of Mama without a commentary track.

"You'll like this 'cause you get to sit on the ground while you eat," I told Weylyn, who was busy watching the fish in my aquarium, holding that book of his like a teddy bear. The outfit Mama had laid out for him that morning was a navy-blue polo with brown plaid shorts, the perfect shade to hide any stains from the chocolate cake she—or rather, Lizbeth—was making. He still hadn't said a word since he arrived at the house, and I was getting bored just listening to him breathing.

"Weylyn? Hello! Don't you know how to talk?"

He pressed his nose against the glass, his eyes crossing as he tried to focus on a guppy hovering on the other side.

"It's okay if you don't. My friend Doug didn't learn to talk till he was seven. 'Course, he wasn't all that smart to begin with."

Weylyn twitched.

"I like you all the same. Even if you are dumb—"

"I'm not dumb!" he shouted. The guppy zipped back into its pirate ship.

"Then why don't you talk?" I shouted back.

Weylyn pouted and rested his chin on the book that was clamped between his crossed arms and his chest.

"What's that book you're always carrying around, anyway?"

"*To Kill a Mockingbird*," he said warily.

"Never heard of it. Must be one of those books they banned from the schools."

"Banned?"

"It means it's against the law. I'd hide it if I were you, before someone burns it or something." His eyes widened with panic. "You can hide it under my bed if you want. That's where I keep the stuff I'm not supposed to have. See?" I pulled a box out from under my bed that was lined with VHS tapes. "Mama would have a fit if she saw these! I'm not a big reader, but I love movies. Copied most of 'em from the TV, so they have commercials and stuff, but I can fast-forward through those parts."

Weylyn cautiously approached the box and picked up a tape labeled *Land of the Lost*. "That's my favorite TV show," I said. "It has dinosaurs in it."

Weylyn looked confused. "What's a dinosaur?"

"This!" I popped the tape into my VCR and pressed Play. On the screen, Will and Holly were being chased by Grumpy, the tyrannosaur.

Weylyn's jaw dropped. "Is that . . . real?"

"No, it's fake. But they were real millions of years ago. The school board doesn't want you believing that 'cause of the Bible and stuff."

Weylyn nodded like he understood, then hesitantly handed me his book. "Somewhere safe?"

"The safest," I assured him and tucked the book between *Willy Wonka & the Chocolate Factory* and *Young Frankenstein*. "No one will find it there."

Weylyn nodded and went back to watching the fish. I sketched him on my arm, staring down a giant guppy. "So, what's your story? Where're you from?"

"The woods," he said.

"What woods?"

"Twelve Pines."

"Never heard of it."

"Then I must be pretty far away," he said, distant.

I gave him some shading under the eyes to make him look sad. "You wish you were back there?"

He nodded, tracing his finger across the glass of the aquarium. The guppy followed, its little suction-cup mouth opening and closing.

"With the wolves?" I added. I know Daddy said it was probably just a story he had made up to make himself feel better, but it didn't seem like that to me.

A small, involuntary whine escaped Weylyn's lungs. I drew a wolf's tail and ears on the cartoon of him and held out my arm. He smiled at me for the first time.

Weylyn had one of those maniacal smiles that could make a person nervous, especially if that person was one of Mama's book club friends. It was ten in the morning, and the party was already in full swing. Mama's friends had taken over one of the picnic tables for their gin rummy and were tipsy on Bloody Marys and gossip. They weren't talking about books—they never did—but were making up their own scandalous fiction about the people they knew.

I tried to hurry Weylyn past them but was paralyzed by a familiar yodel. "Yoo-hoo! Lydia!" It was Bonnie Grace Campbell. We called her the Town Crier, because she liked to run through town telling everybody's business. Bonnie Grace was Mama's best friend and helped organize the Miss Paris Competition every year. She's the one the girls of Paris have to thank for the contestant weight requirement and the unspoken virginity rule. There's no hard evidence, but all I'm saying is that Shay McNeil was a shoo-in for Miss Paris two years ago before prom night. After that, she mysteriously rescinded her candidacy.

"Miss Lydia! Who's that handsome boy you're with?"

I reluctantly approached the table. "Hi, Mrs. Campbell. This is Weylyn."

"Oh, yes! The poor soul your mother took in. The one who was savagely taken hostage by wolves!"

So, not only was Mama taking credit for it; she had also turned it into one of her party stories.

"It's nice to meet you, Weylyn!" Bonnie practically screamed.

"He can hear you fine, Mrs. Campbell."

"Does he speak dog?" she said earnestly. "Ask him if he can tell my Buster to stop getting up on the couch."

I could hear a very faint growl coming from Weylyn's throat. "I don't think so, Mrs. Campbell."

"I suppose he doesn't speak much at all after the trauma, poor thing." Bonnie's chorus clucked, "Poor thing," as they fanned themselves with playing cards.

"Nice to see you, Mrs. Campbell. Ladies." I tugged Weylyn by the arm, and we made our escape.

"Sorry about that," I said as we sat under the shade of the giant oak, eating cake with our shoes off. "She's had a lot of Bloody Marys . . . and she's a bitch."

"Wolves and dogs don't speak the same language," he said defiantly. "It's like a person trying to talk to a frog. It doesn't work."

"So, you *can* talk to them?"

"Who?"

"Wolves."

"Sort of." Weylyn chewed while he thought. "We just kind of . . . understood each other. I don't really know how to describe it."

"That's so cool! The closest I've got to a wild animal is my sisters at a shoe sale. They're avoiding you, by the way." I pointed to a large group of girls sunbathing by the pool. "Emily is convinced you're going to chew her new Pucci pumps. I told her *Poochi* sounds like a shoe for dogs, anyway, and she threw her curling iron at me. It was totally worth it, though. My favorite person to mess with is Mama. It's just so easy. Well, you know that already."

Weylyn stared back at me blankly, chocolate smeared all over his face. Just then, Mama came running around the side of the house chasing a fat raccoon with a broom. "Shoo! Git! Filthy animal!"

"That's Marcel. He lives in the chimney. I gave him a chicken bone once, and he keeps coming back for the buffet. Mama hates him."

Then I had an idea. A good one. "Hurry up and finish your cake, Weylyn. I need your help with something."

Mama had joined the other hens at the picnic table and was dealing new hands when Weylyn walked up, scratching his scalp furiously.

"What's wrong, sweetheart? The mosquitoes get you?" she said with insincere kindness.

He shook his head and continued to scratch.

"He must have allergies," she explained to the other women. "Do you want some cough medicine?"

Weylyn shook his head.

"Hey, Mama!" I flanked her on the other side, also scratching my head.

"Lydia? What's wrong? Why are you and Weylyn scratching like that?"

"Weylyn said he's always itchy. Now, I'm itchy, too."

Bonnie Grace Campbell started scratching her head, also. "Now you mention it, I've been kind of itchy today."

Mama's perfectly lined eyes went from round Os to almost straight lines. "Lydia, what are you up to?"

"Nothing, Mama! I'm just so itchy."

The women at the table started scratching phantom itches, too. Then Bonnie Grace gasped, "The boy lived with wolves. He must have . . . fleas!"

The women jumped out of their seats. Cards and Bloody Marys went flying. "Fleas! Fleas! Fleeeeas!" they screeched and nearly wriggled out of their housedresses.

Mama's face was as red as her favorite lipstick. She grabbed both of us under the arms and dragged us toward the house. "Both of you are going to your rooms!"

"It was just a joke," I protested.

"That's the problem!"

Mama escorted us to our rooms, making a point of slamming our doors behind us. Once I heard her footsteps descending the stairs, I opened my window and leaned on the sill. I was laughing at Mama's friends checking each other for fleabites when I saw Weylyn open the window next to mine and lean out into the sweaty, summer air. He didn't look as amused as I was. In fact, he looked genuinely disappointed. Here I was, supposed to be making him feel welcome, and instead, I had ruined his first Fourth of July.

I was about to call out to him and apologize when his face suddenly fell into shadow. I turned and saw that the sun had been blotted out by a dark mass of cloud. It moved with astonishing speed, polluting the blue sky with roiling gray plumes that sagged with rainwater. Seconds later, the cloud burst and heavy rain was wreaking havoc on the party below. The flames that flickered beneath Daddy's pineapple-glazed chicken wings were snuffed out. My sisters ran screaming into the house, holding magazines over their heads and slipping on the wet grass. Mama tried in vain to rescue a water-logged potato salad before giving up and following the rest of the partygoers into the house.

I looked over at Weylyn, who was still leaning out the window, blinking heavily as rain ran into his eyes. A bitter smile crossed his face, as if he knew I was watching him; as if he were answering the question that was on the tip of my tongue: *Did you do this?*


It rained for the remainder of the day and into the night, forcing the city to cancel the fireworks show. "The forecast said it was supposed to be clear," I overheard Daddy saying to my mother in the hallway. "It's like it just came out of nowhere."

*That's because it did come out of nowhere*, I thought. Maybe I had just read too many Wandering Wizards books, but I couldn't fight the feeling that Weylyn had had something to do with the rainstorm. I knew my ridiculous theory was most likely the product of boredom combined with three cans of Pepsi, but I just couldn't shake it. If I was going to get any sleep that night, I'd have to ask Weylyn myself.

After I heard my parents' bedroom door click shut, I opened mine slowly and padded barefoot into the hall. I was about to knock on Weylyn's door when I saw something move in the darkness. Whatever it was, it was small, no bigger than a chipmunk.

As it came closer, I saw that it actually was a tiny brown chipmunk with a piece of tinfoil in its mouth. It scuttled toward me, then turned sharply to the left and darted under Weylyn's door.

*How'd that little guy get in here?* I wondered. Then I heard a strange squeaking sound through Weylyn's closed door, the same one I had heard the previous night. I leaned in to listen through the door and heard other sounds as well: shuffling, clacking, grunting, and Weylyn speaking in hushed tones. I tried the doorknob. It was locked.

Weylyn—and whatever else was in there with him—must have heard me because there was a sudden scrabbling sound. I ran back into my own room and looked out the window only to catch a furry flash of tail vanishing into the darkness.

## 10

## MRS. MEG LOWRY

"Those who can't do, teach." I hated that saying because it made teaching sound like it was just a fallback career for the runners-up of the world, like being a good teacher wasn't a goal in itself. It implied that all you had to do to be a teacher was be smart enough for a child not to notice when you were wrong.

I had wanted to be a teacher ever since my first day of school. I wanted to learn everything about everything so I could be the best teacher ever, but I ran out of time and ended up settling for knowing a little bit about everything—which is probably why Principal Evans asked me to take over the general education class.

At first, I was crushed. I had spent the last ten years teaching freshman biology, and I had finally gotten the hang of it. I knew what labs my students would respond to, what experiments yielded the best results, what silly rhymes would get them to remember mitosis and which ones would later be mocked in the cafeteria. I wasn't a great scientist myself, but I brought out the best in the students who were, and to me that was *doing* something. That was doing a heck of a lot.

I taught in Suffolk County, a perfectly square patch of prairie land in rural Oklahoma with a total population less than the average city high school. I lived in the town of Paris, where most folks didn't even know there was a city in France by the same name, and the ones that did thought we came first. Only half the population graduated high school, a handful graduated college, and almost 25 percent of the kids were homeschooled.

What prompted the mass exodus of students from Paris schools was the reintroduction of dinosaurs back into the science curriculum—the subject had been previously removed in 1972 due to the volume of parent complaints. I heard from the other teachers that the homeschool parents got together and wrote their own textbook. Janet Crabtree—American history—got her hands on a copy and called it "the kind of book you'd find in a Cracker Jack box: completely devoid of substance and slightly racist."

Eventually, some of the parents got sick of their kids and reenrolled them. Academically, they were behind where they needed to be, but rather than holding them back, Principal Evans came up with general education, or the dummy class as the kids called it. The curriculum covered a broad scope of subjects: geometry, literature, biology, history, art, and so on. For one teacher to substantively cover all these subjects was hard enough, but with kids from seventh through twelve grade, it was nearly impossible. It's no surprise that most general ed teachers lasted only a year, then moved to places as far away as Alaska.

As soon as I heard the news, I immediately started applying for positions in other counties, other states. That was in April of that year. Three months and no offers later, I started prepping for my first year as a general ed teacher.

"I don't even know where to start!" A dozen textbooks lay on the kitchen table in front of me, covering everything from physics to physical education. My husband, Nate, peered over my shoulder. "Phys ed? Did you tell them the softball story?"

Five years ago, Nate and I signed up for an adult softball league. In one season, I set the record for number of outs, foul balls, and times traveled around the bases in the wrong direction. "I think I'm just going to have them run laps while shaking tambourines. Kill two birds with one stone."

"They're making you teach music, too?"

"I have a box of kazoos in the car."

"That's crazy! You can't possibly teach all this in one year!" Nate was a good husband, the kind that knows how to program the VCR and does the laundry without being asked. But he was also a good man, which is harder to be, I think. Nate never did things just because they were easy. "I'm gonna talk to him."

"Talk to who?"

He was pacing now. "Evans."

"No, you're not."

"I'm gonna go down there and shove a kazoo up his you-know-what!" He went for his shoes. I kicked them out of his reach.

"You want to get me fired?"

"Well, no, but he can't treat you like this."

"He didn't call me names or punch me in the face. He reassigned me. It happens all the time."

He finally stopped pacing. "No word from the other schools?"

I shook my head. "Maybe this will be good. A new challenge, at least."

"You'll be great." He kissed me on the forehead. "Those kids are lucky they're getting a second chance with a teacher like you."

"Thanks."

"I'm guessing you can't use the D-word?"

"No dinosaurs."

"That stinks. Dinosaurs are the coolest."

I opened the book nearest to me, chemistry, and scribbled notes in the margins while Nate made hot chocolate.


Nate and I got married in our forties, too late to seriously think about having kids, so we collected dogs—seven so far. With our friends, we joked that they were kind of like trading cards, we needed one of each breed to complete the set. They laughed out of pity, then invited us to their kid's birthday or soccer game or recital, so we could get a taste of what real parenting was like and maybe we'd stop letting our dogs eat from the table.

The summer after Nate and I were married, I babysat my friend Anita's son, Jasper, while she and her husband vacationed in Italy. Jasper was as tightly wound as a yo-yo and would run in circles around the coffee table for an hour before passing out on our chocolate Lab, Milo's, doggy bed. He carried one of his mom's old purses with him everywhere he went and stuffed it full of treasures: rocks, leaves, pinecones, bottle caps, coins, and so on. At the end of the day, he would dump everything he collected in a pile on the sidewalk and just walk away. I picked out the coins and kept them in a jar for him.

One day, he decided it was Halloween and walked right up to strangers at the outlet mall, holding out his purse and shouting, "Twick or tweeeeat!"

"They don't have any candy because it's not Halloween," I explained and bought him a Milky Way. Jasper put the candy bar in his purse and later dumped it on the sidewalk along with some paper clips and a Chinese take-out menu.

I was a little heartsick after he left. I spent the following day browsing adoption pamphlets and trying to picture myself pushing a stroller alongside moms half my age. In Paris, it's normal to be a grandmother in your forties. You usually see all three generations together at the grocery store. Mom and Grandma arguing over something pointless while the baby screams in the shopping cart. After a trip to the store to get some milk, I threw away the pamphlets and took my dogs on a walk.

The next day, however, I dug those pamphlets out of the trash and laid them out on the kitchen counter for Nate to find. I broached the subject with him several times, but every time he just shrugged and said, "I have you, and that's more than I thought I'd get. I'm happy with the way things are." The first time he said this it was sweet. The second time it was disheartening. The third time I almost wept and shouted, *I want a baby! Don't you get it?* After the fourth time, I gave up and never mentioned it again.

## 11

## LYDIA KRAMER

Weylyn was the inspiration for Daddy's sermon this week: tolerance. He read a passage from Romans 16:17, "Watch out for those who cause divisions and create obstacles contrary to the doctrine that you have been taught." Then, with emphasis, "Avoid them."

Weylyn was quiet and attentive, sitting like a yogi on the red carpet, an act that didn't go unnoticed by the rest of the congregation. Out of the general rumble, I picked up words like *blasphemous* and *disgraceful*. Mama insisted he sit on a pew, but when that failed, she made her rounds, apologizing for Weylyn's *unchristian* behavior. When Daddy quoted Romans, I could feel some of his flock slipping away. A dozen or more wouldn't be back next Sunday, but it was a risk I was proud he took.

Mama was in tears when we got home. She said she had never been so embarrassed. Daddy looked her square in the eye and said, "Me, too. Don't ever speak to my congregation on my behalf again," then disappeared into his study and didn't come out the rest of the night, even for dinner.

That night, after several days of weird sounds coming from Weylyn's room, I decided to solve the mystery once and for all. I figured that whatever creatures were making those noises were coming and going from Weylyn's window and were probably climbing the tree outside to get to it. So I did what all clumsy, athletically challenged teenagers should do once in their lifetime: I climbed a tree.

To an outsider, it would have been akin to watching a cow attempting the same feat. I'm not saying I'm as big as a cow, just that I have the agility of one. My hands might as well have been hooves because my grip was shockingly inadequate, and I wasn't limber enough to get footholds on the higher branches. Needless to say, it was a slow process.

I finally reached the branch that armed out to Weylyn's open window and peered inside. What I saw wasn't wolves but nearly every other native species gathered around Weylyn: raccoons, squirrels, chipmunks, opossums, mice, birds, and moles, just to name a few. I even spotted the striped tail of a skunk.

In front of Weylyn was a pile of what looked like trash: candy wrappers, foil balls, bottle caps, and broken glass. A raccoon I could swear was Marcel was holding something glittery out to Weylyn with his tiny black paw. Whatever it was, it wasn't trash. Weylyn looked uncertain but took the gift, anyway, and put it in his pocket. The raccoon sat back on his haunches, pleased.

I shifted my weight, and the branch beneath me creaked. Weylyn and his friends looked at me all at once.

"Hey . . . ," I mumbled awkwardly, then screamed as the animals clambered out the window and down my back to the branches below. I nearly fell, but Weylyn reached out the window and put a hand on my shoulder to steady me. I looked up at him sheepishly. "Sorry. I didn't mean to ruin the party."

"It's fine. Here, let me help you." He held out his hand and pulled me inside. I looked around Weylyn's room for any furry stragglers, but it appeared that I had scared them all off. Before I could address the elephant in the room, Weylyn beat me to it. "Those are my friends. They only visit after Mrs. Kramer has gone to bed because they're scared of her."

"Aren't we all?" I said. "So, you can communicate with other animals, too? Not just wolves."

"Kind of," he mumbled, fussing with a pile of shiny garbage on the floor.

I sat cross-legged on the floor next to him. "Can you do anything else?"

"Like what?"

*Summon a rainstorm?* "Oh, I don't know . . . stuff that normal people can't do."

Weylyn looked back at me, blankly.

"Forget it," I said, feeling stupid. "What's with all the trash?"

"It's not trash," Weylyn said crossly. He pulled out one of Mama's empty hatboxes from the closet and began transferring the garbage into it.

"Did your friends give you this stuff?"

"They bring me things they think I'll like." He placed the last piece of trash in the box, then put his hand in his pocket and wrapped his fingers around the gift Marcel had given him.

"What's that?" I prodded.

Weylyn hesitated. "Something I'm probably not supposed to have." He pulled the item from his pocket and showed it to me. It was a tennis bracelet, diamond, the one Mama gave Emily for her sixteenth birthday.

"Holy shit! That's Emily's." I giggled gleefully.

Weylyn's eyes went wide with panic. "Oh no. What do I do?"

"Throw it in the box with the rest of your stuff. Hide it. We'll put it back in the morning, and she'll never know it was gone."

It sounded simple. It should have been. What I hadn't accounted for was Mama's keen snooping ability. She wasn't a casual snoop, one who checks sock drawers now and then for drugs or condoms. She was more methodical than that. She could tell when and where to look based on what you ate for breakfast that morning. I once ate oatmeal, and she raided my backpack for candy. Sure enough, she found three candy bars and a bag of chips. I thought a healthy bowl of oatmeal would put her off my scent, but it only attracted her, like a moth to a flame.

It was the hair that tipped her off. Weylyn's hair was usually a mess, but that morning, it was neatly combed. She found the box in less than three minutes and the bracelet inside. "Weylyn! Would you care to explain what this is doing in here?" She held the contraband in the air like a witch holding your own heart up for you to see.

Weylyn froze and opened his mouth to reply, but no sound came out. I jumped to his rescue. "We didn't want to get Emily in trouble."

"Emily?" she scoffed.

"Yeah. We found it on the lawn. She must have lost it playing volleyball at the barbecue. Weylyn and I were going to put it back in her room without her noticing." It was a clever pitch, but Mama was sharp. It was hard to get things past her. It felt like a full hour before she replied.

"I told her not to wear it outside." Her expression went from severe to stern as she turned back to Weylyn. "There's still the matter of the trash in my sewing room."

"Weylyn's room," I corrected her.

A new fire flared behind Mama's eyes. "I'll be back in twenty minutes. If this garbage isn't gone by then, there will be consequences."

Weylyn reluctantly threw away his all treasures, save one piece of green glass. But there were consequences, anyway. Mama sent him to some kind of "gentleman training" camp in Marble Heights for the rest of the summer—the kind that teaches boys how to mix a proper martini and groom the facial hair they don't have yet. Unless that camp also taught boys how to refrain from speaking to animals and controlling the weather, Mama was unlikely to get her money's worth.

When Weylyn returned a month later, he handed out business cards printed with nothing but his name in plain black type.

"What are they for?" I asked. "You don't have a job or a business."

"I will someday," he said proudly as he topped off Daddy's martini with an olive. He had passed every test with flying colors, except he still wouldn't sit in a real chair. Sir Priestley—not a real knight—said he tried everything he could, but the boy flat-out refused. So, despite his otherwise stellar performance, Weylyn would not be earning his graduation bowler this year.

"Well, I'm proud of you, anyway," Daddy told Weylyn at the dinner table. Daddy had found him a crate he could sit cross-legged on so he wouldn't have to eat off the floor.

"What's he going to do when he goes to school?" Mama objected. "He won't have any crates to sit on there!"

But Daddy ignored her, as he usually did. It was easy to take Daddy's side in those days, but since then, I've sometimes wondered if he ignored her because she acted out or if maybe she acted out because she was ignored.

The next day was my first day of junior year, and Weylyn would be starting the seventh grade. He would put on the clothes Mama laid out for him and eat the lunch she pretended she'd made for him. He would find out what teenagers were willing to do and say to each other to fit in. He might try to do the same, but probably not, so he'd get left behind. They'd laugh at him, I was sure of that. They'd call him Wolf Boy and howl at him in the hallway, but he'd get used to it. I redrew the picture of him with a wolf's ears and tail—on paper this time—and added a pair of fangs. That morning, I tucked it into his pencil case for good luck and hoped he wouldn't need it.

## 12

## MRS. MEG LOWRY

It was the first day of class and I was already exhausted. I had spent the last month shoveling facts into my brain like it was a landfill for useless knowledge. I would never tell my students that most of what I taught them had no practical application—they would find that out once they entered the workforce—but I was a firm believer in knowledge for knowledge's sake, even if it was the gestation period of a sloth.

Students began to filter in, looking bored already and I hadn't even said anything. A girl wearing a yellow halter top looked at my map of the United States on the wall and actually rolled her eyes. I'd call on her first.

Five minutes before the bell, Mr. Rash, the school counselor, poked his head through the doorway. "Mrs. Lowry? Can I speak with you a moment?"

"Sure." I joined him in the hallway. George Rash was a nervous little man who wore sweaters every day, regardless of the season, and always carried a number-two pencil. "What is it, George?"

"I just wanted to give you a heads-up about one of your students."

"Which student?"

"Weylyn Grey. Parents died years ago. Moved in this summer

with his foster parents. Mrs. Kramer, his foster mom, said he can be . . . peculiar."

"Peculiar how?"

George hesitated. "He was raised by wolves."

"He was *what*?"

"I know it sounds crazy, but it's true. He was caught trying to steal cattle. The wolf that was with him nearly took the rancher's head off."

"Well, that's a first."

"I just thought you should know."

"Yeah, sure. Thanks, George." Maybe he was just yanking my chain, although George wasn't really the type. His idea of a joke was writing weird things in Sharpie on his brown-bagged lunches like "Killer tomatoes. Do not touch!" or "Human tongue. Don't ask." He brought beans once and wrote, "Air quality alert 12:00 P.M. Enter lounge at your own risk." When George took his lunch break, he found an empty bag with a note written in grape-scented marker that read, "I found this at 11:55. Not sufficient enough warning. You'll find it on the front lawn." George found his beans and ate them on the lawn, but the aftershocks were felt for hours.

The bell rang, and I returned to my classroom. "Good morning!" I was greeted with twenty blank stares, two groans, and one middle finger disguised as a nose scratch. "I'm Mrs. Lowry, and I will be your teacher for this semester's general education class." I scribbled my name on the board in chalk.

"Now you know my name, I'd like to know yours." I took out my attendance sheet and was about to start reading names when I heard a voice, "My name is Weylyn Grey!"

I turned and saw the boy sitting, not in his chair but cross-legged on top of his desk in the front row by the window. He wasn't what I had expected—feral, long-haired, snarling through rotten teeth—but rather the exact opposite: mint condition, white tablecloth, dry-clean-only down to his pleated khakis and perfectly parted hair, the kind of kid that should be on a yacht somewhere eating crudités and driving golf balls off the deck.

Weylyn pulled a small white card out of his shirt pocket and held it out to me. I walked over to him and took the card. It was plain aside from the name *Weylyn Grey* printed in black text.

"I left the bottom blank so I can fill it in when I get a job," he said. The class snickered.

"First you have to go to school before you can get a job, and while we're on the subject, will you sit in your seat, please? This isn't a drum circle."

"Beg your pardon, ma'am, but I haven't sat in a chair since I was six, so I'm pretty sure I'd stink at it."

The other students got a kick out of that one. I could feel my control over them slipping away. "Don't worry," I said through gritted teeth. "It's just like riding a bike. Once you learn, you never forget how."

"A bike is just a chair with wheels. Would you like to use a different metaphor?" he said so politely I could have punched him in the mouth.

"I'm sorry, but if you don't sit, you can't be part of this class. I suggest you go to the principal's office."

"Wonderful! I haven't had a chance to introduce myself to him yet," Weylyn chirped as he slid off his desk.

I ignored that last remark and handed him a yellow slip. "Give this to the secretary when you get there."

Weylyn headed toward the door, and I continued with the attendance. "Mara Andrews?"

"Here," the girl in the yellow halter mumbled.

"Dylan Atkins?"

Before Dylan could answer, Weylyn chimed in, "Excuse me, Mrs. Lowry?" He had his hand on the doorknob, grinning back at me like the Cheshire Cat.

I sighed. "Yes, Weylyn?"

"I'm not very good with doors, either. I never know when to push or pull. Which kind is this one?"

The class roared with laughter.

That was it. "All right, smart guy. That's detention, too!"

Weylyn beamed. "Is that where all the smart kids go?"

"No. It's where the kids who talk back to their teachers go."

The boy looked confused, then tried pushing open the door, but it didn't budge.

"Pull! It's a pull," I snapped. Weylyn pulled the door open, thanked me, and left the classroom.


I had just sat down to lunch when I was called into Evans's office myself. "How's the first day of class going?" he said while gobbling a cherry danish.

I fantasized about the microwavable brownie in my lunch box that I would probably have to wait until tonight to eat. "Good," I said unconvincingly.

"Yes, it must be relaxing seeing as half your class has ended up in my office."

I looked into the hall where almost a dozen of my students were seated. Weylyn was sitting cross-legged on the floor. "Is there a problem?" I said.

He pulled out a yellow slip with my handwriting on it and read, "Ms. Garber was chewing her gum in an exaggerated way."

"I could see the whole wad every time she opened her mouth," I said meekly.

He sighed. "Mrs. Lowry, I picked you for this class because I thought you could handle it. Now, if I'm going to have to do all your disciplining for you, maybe I need to find someone else."

"No! I can handle it."

"Are you sure?"

"Yes. Positive."

"Just don't let it happen again."

I stood up to leave when he stopped me. "Oh, one more thing. Weylyn Grey—"

"Yeah, um . . . he was sitting on top of his desk. I asked him to sit down—"

"If he wants to sit on top of his desk, let him."

"What? Why?"

"He's living with the Kramers."

I shrugged.

"Reverend Thomas Kramer. St. Agnes."

"Oh. Sure." I had seen his name on a pamphlet. I found it tucked in my screen door inviting me to a bake sale with a cutesy name like *The Batter, the Bun, and the Holy Toast*. I remember wondering if they were actually selling toast.

"The Kramers are pillars of this community and personal friends of mine, so we're going to do whatever we can to make Weylyn feel comfortable." Evans was always sucking up to folks with bigger houses than his so they would invite him to their parties. He would roll up in his leased BMW and the same tux he got married in and spend the next four hours telling made-up stories starring people he had never met. No one knew where he lived, but Mr. Hagerty—geometry—postulated that it probably had wheels.

"Sure. If that's what you want."

"Good. Now, could you send Weylyn in? I might have to do some damage control."

*Damage control?* I had asked him to sit in a desk, not pushed him down a flight of stairs.

When I left the room, Weylyn looked up at me with that silly grin of his.

"Weylyn. Principal Evans would like to see you in his office." I noticed his shoes were gone. "What happened to your shoes?"

He shrugged. "I dunno."

As I walked away, I could hear Weylyn pulling the door when he should have been pushing.

———

"Maybe you should give him a break. The kid's obviously been through a lot," Nate said as he filled up the watering can in the kitchen sink.

"I know. But I also can't let the behavior of one kid allow the entire class to descend into anarchy. I'm gonna have a hard enough time getting these kids to understand photosynthesis as it is with this thing as an example," I said, poking at the yellowing ficus that I was supposed to be using in a class demonstration the next day. With all the papers I'd been grading over the past week, I had neglected to water it and was honestly considering spray-painting the leaves green.

"I'm just saying. Sometimes you can be a little . . . severe."

"Severe?" I tightened my grip around one of the plant's stems, bending it in half. "Shit . . . I guess you're not totally wrong."

Nate handed me the filled watering can. "Maybe you should talk to him. One-on-one. Find out what's really going on before you rush to judgment."

Nate was a grief counselor at the local hospital. He could take Greek-tragedy kind of pain and use it as fuel for extraordinary displays of love. Everyone he counseled had different beliefs, and he adapted to their needs. For those who believed in God, death was only the end of the first act of their story; for those who didn't, it was up to their loved ones to write the epilogue.

When we first started dating, I asked him which one he believed. He said he didn't know, but he wasn't going to spend the precious moments he did have agonizing over which was which. I was guilty of agonizing now and then, of letting my uncertainty sabotage my chances at happiness. I mourned for things that hadn't happened, things that never would. So much of life is marked by birthdays, graduations, weddings, births. I'd had my fair share of birthdays, graduated twice, and married a man I loved. Without children to experience those same things, time seemed to stand still. The selfish years of my teens and twenties were long gone, and now, it didn't seem like enough to just take care of myself.

Nate cared for other people all day. Maybe taking care of a kid on top of all that was just too much for him to handle.

"I'll talk to Weylyn tomorrow," I said, fruitlessly pouring water over the sad, neglected houseplant. Nate was right (as usual). The boy had been through a lot. Despite losing his parents, he managed to survive in the wilderness and not get eaten by wolves. It was admirable, really. I just had to be patient—something I admittedly wasn't very good at—and help Weylyn navigate what was probably a strange and scary new world.

"And what gives plants their"—I tentatively pointed at the mostly yellow plant sitting on my desk—"*green* color?"

"Chlorophyll!" Weylyn shouted with more enthusiasm than I was prepared for. He still sat cross-legged on top of his desk, a quirk I was willing to let slide for today.

"Yes. Thank you, Weylyn." He had done the reading and was actively participating. I scanned the other students who were either asleep or in the middle of doodling. I suddenly felt ashamed of my behavior the day before. He was a good kid—eccentric, but good.

The end-of-the-day bell rang, startling the napping teens in the back. As the students filed out of the classroom, Weylyn lingered by my desk, bending over to inspect the sickly ficus.

"Good job today, Weylyn," I said as I packed up my things.

He beamed. "Thank you, Mrs. Lowry."

"Do you mind if we talk for a minute?"

"Sure."

"So. This is your first time in a school?"

"I went to kindergarten for a few weeks, but all we did was glue macaroni to stuff."

"Well, I have to say you're a very fast learner. Where did you learn to read?"

"My parents taught me a little. And my friend Mary. She's really smart. She gave me a book."

"What book?"

"*To Kill a Mockingbird*."

"That's one of my favorites. How do you like it?"

"I like it very much," he said excitedly. "At first, I thought it was about birds—you know, 'cause of the title—but I didn't care that it wasn't really about birds because it was a good story. I'd like to read some books about real birds, though. Or wolves. I like wolves, too."

"Have you heard of *Julie of the Wolves*?"

"No. Is it a book?"

I nodded. "Tell you what. Tomorrow, I'll let you borrow my copy if you sit in a chair like the rest of the students." I instantly cringed at my own words. Bribing a student? With *books*? Clearly, I was still in need of some sensitivity training.

Weylyn frowned. "Mr. Kramer got me a library card. They let me read on the lawn."

"Oh. That's nice of them." This conversation wasn't exactly going the way I'd planned. I tried to think of something Nate would say in my situation. "Look . . . I know starting a new school can be hard, so if you ever find yourself worried about something, I hope you know you can talk to me."

Weylyn shouldered his bag, lumpy with book corners, and smiled. "Thanks, Mrs. Lowry. I'll see you tomorrow."

"See you tomorrow, Weylyn," I said as he headed toward the door. I stuffed a stack of essays on the fall of the Roman Empire in my satchel, then turned to grab the potted ficus.

I froze. The plant I had effectively left for dead minutes earlier was now a vibrant green with full, hardy leaves, just like the day I bought it. I prodded a leaf to make sure I wasn't imagining things, and sure enough, it bounced back like a healthy leaf should.

I jumped out of my chair and ran to the door just in time to see Weylyn's overstuffed backpack disappearing around the corner at the end of the hallway.

## 13

## LYDIA KRAMER

"Do you think you have to be seventeen to read *Seventeen*?" My best friend, June, had stolen one of the magazines from Caroline's room and was now flipping through it at the kitchen table, unimpressed.

"No, but you apparently have to be in the seventeenth percentile in intelligence." I didn't read those kinds of magazines, mainly because I didn't need one more person telling me I was too fat.

"Did you know that a sense of humor is 'in' this season?" June continued.

"What?"

"It says, 'A sense of humor is making a comeback this season with sexy lady comedians making the A-List. Try out some of your favorite jokes on your friends or sign up for an improv troupe. Or take your crush to an open mic night and impress him with your best Nixon impersonation.'"

"A Nixon impression? That's the funniest thing they could think of?"

"Apparently," June said flatly. She had been my best friend since the seventh grade when we were picked last and second-to-last, respectively, in kickball. June had twenty pounds on me, and even though I had thirty pounds on my heaviest sister, she still called me skinny. She was of Polynesian descent with skin the color of rawhide, and had a tiny heart tattoo by her left eye that her crow's-feet would later crinkle like crêpe paper.

She was apathetic about almost everything, including herself. The only thing I ever saw her get excited about was when a tornado swept through our school with us inside. Everyone else took shelter, but June stood at the window, cheering as the tornado tore out the stadium goalpost. Eventually, I managed to drag her into the hallway, where the rest of the students quivered with books over their heads. As they cowered, June eagerly watched the ceiling and listened to the building groan as the twister tried to pry it off its foundation.

"So, does that mean taking yourself too seriously is out? If so, your sisters should read this." June tossed the magazine at me, nearly landing it in my bowl of Lucky Charms.

"I'd kill to see Caroline attempt improv as her 'talent' in her next pageant." I then did my most nasal, breathiest impression of Caroline to date. "Soooo, what's the deal with lighting in department store dressing rooms? Are they trying to get us to *buy* the clothes or donate them to *charity* for ugly people to wear? Am I right or am I right?"

The kitchen door swung open, and in walked Caroline on a pair of strappy wedges that had steeper inclines than most ski slopes. She wobbled over to the fridge without so much as a hello, pulled out a jar of peanut butter, and started eating it with a spoon.

June watched her. "One hundred."

"What?" Caroline snapped, then ate another spoonful.

"Two hundred."

"What are you doing?"

"Nothing." June went back to her magazine. Out of the corner of her eye, she watched Caroline scoop herself another helping. "Three hundred."

Caroline slammed down the jar. "Okay. What are you doing? Lydia! What is she doing?"

I shrugged.

"I'm counting," June said.

"Great. You can count. Now shut up!"

"I'm counting the number of calories you're eating."

"Calories?"

"It's the stuff in food that makes you fat. At least that's what *Seventeen* says."

"You're lying."

"No, I'm not. See?" June turned the magazine so Caroline could see it. Sure enough, on the page was a picture of a peanut butter jar with a big *100* stamped next to it in bold type. "Every spoonful of peanut butter is one hundred calories. You just ate three hundred calories in less than thirty seconds!"

Caroline, horrified, dropped her spoon and stormed away, leaving the peanut butter open on the kitchen counter.

"You're mean." I laughed.

The door opened again, but this time it was Weylyn carrying the world's heaviest backpack. "Hey, Weylyn. How was school today?" I asked.

"Good!" he said and dropped his bag like a ton of bricks. "I learned what makes plants green. Chlorophyll!"

"Cool," I said, feigning interest. "Make any friends yet?"

"Mrs. Lowry."

"Your teacher?"

He nodded.

"Teachers aren't your friends," June corrected. "Most of them are aliens in disguise."

Weylyn looked confused. "What's an alien?"

"Monsters from other planets that only eat boys."

His eyes went wide with horror. "But . . . *I'm* a boy!"

I smacked June on the head with the rolled-up copy of *Seventeen*. "Don't listen to her, Weylyn. She has issues."

"My therapist's writing a book about me," June added.

"I love books!" Weylyn said. "Can I read it?"

June snorted. "He's a trip. I bet your mom hates him."

"She doesn't hate him—"

"Yes, she does," Weylyn said matter-of-factly. I guess he was more aware than I gave him credit for. He didn't look bothered by it; in fact, he looked very slightly amused.

"Welcome to the club," June said and winked at him. "Or pack. Whatever you wolves call it."

I had yet to tell June about the animals in Weylyn's bedroom or the rainstorm the night of the fireworks. Not because she wouldn't believe me, but because I knew she would. June was into all things hocus-pocus. She was always trying to talk to the dead or lay curses on girls she didn't like. When that tornado hit our school, she convinced herself that it was because she had tested out a new spell the night before. If I told her about Weylyn and the rain, she'd harass him until he agreed to help her flood the gymnasium the night before prom, or worse: she'd blab about it and ruin whatever social life he may have had. There was only one person I could talk to about Weylyn, only one person who might take me seriously.

I found Daddy in the garage—or at least I found his feet. The rest of him was hidden underneath his baby-blue '75 Ford Thunderbird, or the midlife crisis as Mama called it.

I squatted down and waved at him. "Hi, Daddy."

"Oh. Hi, sweetheart," he said, rolling out from under the chassis. "You're back from school early."

"It was a half day. Parent-teacher conferences."

"Oh, that's right. Your mother mentioned something about it."

I fiddled with the zipper on my jacket, unsure of how to say what I wanted to say next. Daddy noticed. "Is there something you want to talk to me about?" he asked, sitting up and wiping his hands off on a rag in his pocket.

I nodded. "I'm just worried you won't believe me."

"Why do you think that?"

"Because what I'm about to tell you is completely nuts. If Mama found out, she'd have me committed."

Daddy frowned with concern. "Should I be worried?"

"No, no. It's just . . . who do you think controls the weather? God?"

"I'd say he sometimes has a hand in it, yes. Why? Has June been saying she started that tornado again?"

"No. Well, yes, but that's not why I'm asking." I took a deep breath and continued, "I think that Weylyn can do things that other people can't."

I instantly regretted saying it. By the look on Daddy's face, you'd think I'd just told him I'd been abducted by aliens. "Not like God or anything," I backpedaled, "but not exactly normal, either."

Daddy studied me. I could tell he was trying to give me the benefit of the doubt. I had always been the sensible daughter, the practical daughter, the daughter who understood the difference between truth and fiction even though I spent more time doodling monsters on my arm than studying. Most important, he knew I would never lie to him.

"I agree that Weylyn doesn't quite fit into the world we're familiar with," Daddy said, choosing his words carefully. "He's a strange boy, but in a wonderful sort of way. Maybe that's what you're picking up on."

My cheeks flushed hot with embarrassment. "Yeah, I guess you're right. Thanks, Daddy," I said quickly, then hurried out of the garage.

## 14

## MRS. MEG LOWRY

I couldn't sleep. I kept thinking about that stupid ficus: dead one minute, alive the next. I tried to come up with any semiplausible explanation that would stop me from believing the impossible one, but I couldn't. *Occam's razor*, I thought. *Can the simplest explanation also be the most absurd?*

Eventually, I gave up trying to sleep and carried the zombie plant down to the basement where I kept my old microscope. I hadn't used it in years, so the plastic cover was dusty, but the microscope itself was in reasonably good shape. I carried it by its base to Nate's woodworking bench where I had set the ficus.

I clipped off a tiny piece of one of its leaves, placed it between a glass slide and a wetted coverslip, adjusted the magnification, and looked through the eyepiece. What I saw was, by all accounts, a perfectly normal clump of plant cells with healthy membranes. There was no evidence that this plant was dead or had ever been dead. In other words, what had happened to it wasn't zombification so much as it was resurrection.

I must have drifted off at the table because when I woke, I had a glass slide on my face and it was already 7:44, seconds before the first bell was supposed to ring. I wiped the drool off my face and ran my fingers through my hair. Twenty minutes later, I stumbled through my classroom door with the same panic I had seen on the faces of dozens of students.

I wasn't surprised to find that all the students but Weylyn had left. I *was* surprised, however, to find ten piglets chewing the tennis balls I had attached to the feet of the chairs to keep them from scraping the floor. Weylyn stood next to an empty wooden crate with a crowbar in one hand. "Hi, Mrs. Lowry."

"Hi . . . ," I said, my brain still playing catch-up with my mouth. In my exhausted haze, I had forgotten about the pigs. The day before, I had spent an hour on the phone arguing with the school's supplier of dissection specimens. After twenty minutes on hold listening to self-indulgent saxophone runs, I hung up and called the only other place I could get a pig on short notice: Dietrich's Meat Supplier. The customer service rep told me I'd get ten pigs first thing the next morning. She hadn't specified, however, how alive they would be.

"They were crying, so I let them out. I hope that's okay." Weylyn scratched one of the piglets behind the ears.

Finally, the reality of the situation sank in. "Shit. There are pigs in my classroom!" If Evans found out, I'd be applying for a job at McDonald's by the end of the week. "Help me get them back in the crate."

"Sure, Mrs. Lowry."

Weylyn and I spent the next ten minutes chasing after squealing piglets as they skidded across the linoleum. We successfully got nine back in the crate and looked around for number ten.

A soft snorting noise came from behind my desk. Weylyn crept toward it, and when he bent down, a confused *hmph* escaped his lips.

"What is it?" I asked.

"This pig is . . . different."

I joined Weylyn and looked inside my trash can to find a runty brown piglet chewing on an apple core. "Look at his forehead," Weylyn said. I looked closer. On the pig's forehead was a small, bony stump. "What do you think it is, Mrs. Lowry?"

"It looks like a horn," I marveled.

"That's what I thought." Weylyn sat back on his haunches, thoughtfully. "What are you going to do with them?"

"Send them back, I guess."

He looked grave. "Will they be killed?"

"I suppose they will." I watched the little pig happily munching on the soggy, brown apple flesh, and something inside me stirred. "But I'm open to suggestions."

Weylyn looked at the heavy crate. "We can't move them all at once." He pulled the little horned pig out of the trash and put him in his backpack. "Can I have a hall pass, Mrs. Lowry?"

All ten pigs made it out of the building without attracting too much suspicion. One of the piglets wailed like a banshee when Weylyn caught its tail in his zipper, which caused Freddy, the custodian, to poke his head in the door and ask if everything was all right. We were fine, I assured him, in a gluey, nasal voice that allowed him to believe the snorts he heard were a side effect of my sinus infection. I gave Weylyn my keys, and he deposited the pigs in the covered bed of my truck.

I was on my way out to meet him when I ran into Principal Evans. "Mrs. Lowry? Shouldn't you be in class?"

Out of panic, I continued my stuffy-nosed charade. "Ib was. But all ob my students were absent today."

He looked doubtful. "All of them?"

"Yes. Which is a coincidence, 'cause Ib was feeling a bit under the webber, anybhow."

"That *is* a coincidence," he said suspiciously. Beads of sweat tickled my temples. "I hate to say this, Mrs. Lowry, but I think you've been the victim of a prank."

"Sobrry?"

"Your students planned this."

"Ohb," I said, exhaling a little too forcefully. "A prank."

"You can send them all to my office tomorrow."

"No. Thankb you. I'b prebfer to discipline them myselb."

"Are you sure?"

"Yes. They neeb to understand that I won't tolerate that kind of behabior."

Evans nodded, pleased. "I couldn't agree more. Now, go home and get some rest. You sound like my daughter did when she had the flu."


Weylyn insisted on keeping the pigs company in the truck bed while I drove. Every time I hit a bump in the road, I heard a collective squeal and one loud "Ouch!" When I turned, I heard a scrabbling of hooves and Weylyn's laughter as the pigs knocked each other over like bowling pins.

He helped me ferry them inside the house and agreed to stay for a mug of hot chocolate. "Are you going to keep them?" he asked.

"I don't know." I put the kettle on to boil. "I might see if an animal rescue will find them a home. Somewhere safe with lots of apples."

He nodded in approval, then scooped up the little horned pig, "I want to take this one home."

"Do you think the Kramers would let you keep him?"

"Mr. Kramer might. Not Mrs. Kramer. She hates animals."

"That must be hard. After where you came from," I gently prodded.

"Yeah. Sometimes it's okay, but most of the time I just wish I had my wolf family back. I'll probably never see them again." The pig nuzzled Weylyn's chin with his snout. Weylyn smiled.

I stirred cocoa powder into mugs filled with hot water. "I'm sorry. I wish you didn't have to go through that."

Weylyn shrugged. "Me, too. But I've got this philosophy . . ."

The corners of my mouth began to curl. I folded them back into a straight line. "What philosophy is that?"

"Don't cry over the same thing twice. Get it all out the first time, even if it's loud and messy. Then it's over."

"That's a good philosophy."

I put a giant handful of marshmallows in his hot chocolate and sat it down in front of him at the kitchen table. I nearly did a double take. Weylyn was actually seated at the table! I casually joined him with my own cup. "So. Any theories as to what that horn might be for?"

The pig was now wandering on the tabletop, chewing the corner of my music theory textbook. *Go ahead, pig*, I thought. *I don't want to teach it, anyway.*

"Defense, maybe?" Weylyn suggested. "But that doesn't seem necessary."

"Boars have tusks."

"Yeah, but this breed looks—what's the word? Domesticated."

"Then what else could it be?"

He considered this for a few moments before shouting, "Magic!"

"Magic?"

"Maybe the horn is magic. You know, like a unicorn. Lydia let me borrow her *Wandering Wizards* book, and the unicorns in there grant wishes."

This was getting a little off track. "Unicorns don't exist." *And plants don't spontaneously come back to life, either*, I reminded myself.

"You said last week that humans still know very little about the universe."

"Well, yes—"

"What if magic is a part of that?"

I hesitated. I had no proof that unicorns didn't exist on some nauseating planet where they granted wishes and pooped rainbows. I had no logical explanation for what had happened to my ficus, either, but I wouldn't call it magic—unexplained phenomenon, maybe, or a curious coincidence. However, I knew one thing for sure: this strange boy had piqued my curiosity.

"I don't really believe in magic," I said, "but I've seen things in my life that I couldn't really explain, this pig being one of them." Although, at that moment, it wasn't the pig I was watching closely.

Weylyn, satisfied with my answer, held out his mug to the little horned pig and said, "I'm going to call you . . . Merlin." The pig grunted and slurped up what was left of his hot chocolate.

When Nate came home, he was greeted by nine pigs, seven dogs, and one bewildered-looking cat. He and the cat shared a moment before he noticed me feeding a piglet with a baby bottle. "Let me guess. Agricultural sciences?"

"No . . ."

"Are we having a hog roast I don't know about?"

"God, no!"

He looked at the baby bottle again, and his tone was suddenly solemn. "Are we about to have that conversation again?"

"What conversation?" I gave the pig a kiss on the snout.

"Meg . . ." He looked tired.

I set the pig back on the ground. "It's not like that. They were going to be killed."

"And you had to bring them here?"

"Where else was I supposed to take them? The slaughterhouse?" I was standing now and probably yelling from the look on Nate's face.

He started pacing, piglets darting in between his strides like an obstacle course. "I don't wanna have this argument. Not again."

"What argument?"

He looked me square in the eye. "The one where I tell you I don't want kids and you say you don't, either, but then you get sad because you really do. You want kids."

"How'd you get there from a bunch of pigs?"

"You're feeding it a bottle!"

He was right. I knew I had a choice to make, but I couldn't seem to come to terms with the consequences of either.

"I love you, Meg. You're all the happiness I need, but if you need more than you can get from just me—"

"You *do* make me happy . . ."

"But do I make you happy enough? Am I *enough*?" The room filled with an unbearable silence. I couldn't hear any of the nine pigs, seven dogs, or one cat. All I could hear was the hiss of air between two people who had nothing more to say to each other.

Nate and I first met at the dentist's office. I was getting a root canal, so I had to be sedated, but I had forgotten to arrange for someone to pick me up. As I stumbled out of the office, my cheeks stuffed fat with gauze, I bumped into a man I thought was the Swedish Chef. Apparently, "Herdy gerdy floop" meant "Do you need a ride?"

By the time I got home, the man's eyes had wiggled out from behind his bushy eyebrows, and his nose had shrunk to a believable size. He even spoke English. "Are you going to be okay here by yourself?"

I gurgled in affirmation and passed out on the couch. The man sat in his car at the end of the driveway until I finally woke up and gestured for him to come inside. "You didn't have to sit outside like that," I said.

"I didn't know if you'd remember me when you woke up. I didn't want to scare you."

I couldn't eat solid foods, but we didn't want to wait to have dinner together, so we went out for milk shakes the next day. He surprised me with a bouquet of neon curly straws and a bottle of painkillers. After nine months, I wanted to marry him, and I found out later that he already had a ring after six. He held on to it until our one-year anniversary, when he proposed to me at the same ice cream parlor where we'd had our first date.

That was five years earlier. In the years since, I often wished I could go back to that first date and tell him I wanted kids, not nodded and smiled when he said, "I never really saw myself as a father." To borrow words from my husband, he was more than I thought I'd get. The only difference was, I still wasn't happy.

## 15

## LYDIA KRAMER

"Lydia! Lydia! Get up! I have to show you something!" Weylyn burst into my room without knocking. I had fallen asleep trying to watch *Jaws* for the third time. So far, I hadn't made it past the part where Brody tells Quint he's going to need a bigger boat. In my dream, I was on the boat, too, showing them the scar on my knee that I got from falling off the monkey bars in the third grade.

"Shark!" I jolted upright in bed.

"Shark?" Weylyn said, confused.

"Weylyn! What're you doing in here?" I looked up at the TV just in time to catch the last of the credits crawl up the screen.

"I need to show you something."

"Show me what?"

"Come with me and you'll see!" Weylyn tugged on my shirtsleeve.

I batted him off. "All right, all right. Gimme a sec." I wasn't in the mood for playing games today. Mama had been at my throat all morning for leaving a ring on her cherrywood buffet, and all I wanted to do was finish my movie in peace. I dragged myself out of bed, shuffled my feet into the sandals Mama calls hobo shoes, and followed Weylyn down the stairs.

Weylyn led me out the back door toward the carriage house that was tucked in a grove of birch trees at the edge of the property. It was a beautiful little cottage with white gingerbreading and a miniature front porch that only had room for a single rocking chair. Mama used it as a dumping ground for stuff she considered too tacky to keep in the main house: hand-me-down furniture, clocks that make animal noises, tchotchkes from various U.S. tourist traps, holiday decorations, and Daddy's fishing gear. I felt at home there with the other misfit toys, all the things Mama had pretended to like, then rejected. Last year, I tried to convince my parents to let me live in the place, but Mama refused, saying that she didn't want the neighbors thinking she had some troubled child locked up in the back house. So, I cut my hair into a shaggy mop and spoke only in riddles for two days. Ironically, I was grounded and sent to the carriage house so I wouldn't frighten her Mississippi relatives who were staying for the weekend.

As we approached the house, I wondered what Weylyn could possibly have to show me. I secretly hoped he was finally going to come clean about the rainstorm on July 4. Maybe he had his magic rain machine stashed inside the wicker laundry hamper shaped like a penguin.

Weylyn paused at the front door. "Before I show you, do you promise not to tell anyone?"

"I promise."

"Especially not your mom."

"You're kidding, right?"

We stepped inside, and Weylyn's eyes darted around like Ping-Pong balls. "Where is he? Merlin!"

"You're hiding a wizard in here?" I laughed.

Weylyn got down on his hands and knees and started poking his head under furniture. "Merlin? Merlin, where are you?" Eventually, he emerged out of the bathroom carrying a brown piglet with a weird bump on his forehead.

"*This* is Merlin?" I was impressed. Not even I had tried something that gutsy under my mother's watch.

"Mrs. Lowry helped me rescue him. He's magic."

"Magic?"

"Yeah. See his horn?" I looked closer. It was a horn, all right, no bigger than a candy corn. "That's where all his powers come from," he explained.

"What powers?"

Weylyn shrugged. "I don't know. He hasn't used them yet."

*That's because he's a pig*, I thought. *He doesn't have powers.* "Are you sure it's the pig that's magic?"

He frowned. "What do you mean?"

Either Weylyn was trying to fool me or he was fooling himself. Maybe imposing magic powers on a pig was his way of dealing with it, his way of diverting attention from the real magic pig in the room. Regardless, I wasn't falling for it.

"Look. You and I both know something weird is going on with you. You don't need to keep hiding it from me."

Weylyn looked stunned for a second, then angry. "I don't know what you're talking about."

"Yes, you do. What about the rain?"

"What about it?" Weylyn said, indignant.

"I know you had something to do with it."

"No, I didn't."

"Fine! Be that way," I snapped back. "Have fun with your pig. I'm gonna go see how *Jaws* ends." I turned sharply and yanked the front door open.

As I stormed away, Weylyn shouted after me, "The shark explodes!"

Weylyn and I avoided each other the rest of the day the way kids do when they don't want to admit they're wrong. By the next morning, however, we were back to acknowledging each other's presence, and by the afternoon, we were friends again. After school, Weylyn and I sneaked over to the carriage house and found Merlin sleeping inside a wicker basket filled with scraps from Mama's unfinished quilting projects.

"I feel bad waking him," I said, not wanting to interrupt whatever adorable pig dreams he was having.

"He won't mind. Especially once he smells apples," Weylyn contended.

Our neighbors had a small grove of apple trees on the back of their property. As kids, they told my sisters and me to feel free to wander over and pick apples whenever we liked. As far as I knew, the invitation was still good, although I'm not sure it applied to stowaway pigs.

Weylyn picked up the basket with Merlin in it, and we walked to the apple grove, keeping careful watch for Mama and her many spies—namely, my sisters. Once we were safely out of sight of the house, Weylyn sat the basket down on the grass under one of the trees. Merlin's snout popped out from beneath the fabric scraps as he sniffed the air furiously. A split second later, he leaped from the basket and began looting the trove of rotting fruit that circled the base of the tree.

"He's hungry," I said.

"Me, too." Weylyn reached up and plucked one of the few amber-colored apples that were still attached to the tree's branches. "Want one?" he said, offering it to me.

"No, thanks."

Weylyn shrugged and bit into it, not bothering to wipe the juice off his chin as he chewed. We sat cross-legged on the ground, the brittle, yellow grass prickling our legs, and watched Merlin greedily scarf down mushy apple after mushy apple.

"Where do you think he came from?" Weylyn asked as he tossed his apple core over his shoulder.

"A pig farm, I guess," I said. From the unimpressed look on Weylyn's face, I realized he'd hoped I'd whip up a more whimsical origin story. I thought for a moment, then added, "Or maybe he's from the future."

Weylyn nodded approvingly, so I continued, "A future where pigs have evolved to shoot laser beams out of horns in their foreheads."

"So, it's a weapon?" he asked, playing along.

"It can be, but they also use them to slice apples."

"Yeah, that makes sense. But how'd he end up here?"

"Because of the Great Apple Famine of 3026. He traveled back in time to gather apples so his family wouldn't starve."

Weylyn looked accusingly at Merlin, who was busy stuffing his face. "He's not doing a very good job of 'gathering.'"

"The time travel gave him amnesia. He doesn't remember that he has powers or that he has a family back home or even where home is."

At that moment, Merlin lifted his head and gazed wistfully into the distance as if my silly story had triggered a memory. Weylyn burst out laughing, and so did I. It occurred to me that our time-traveling pig story was no more ridiculous than one about a wolf boy who controls the weather—aside from the fact, of course, that I had seen the latter with my own two eyes.

A few days later, an old truck pulled up to the carriage house. I watched from my window as a middle-aged woman climbed out of the cab and started unloading boxes with words like *kitchen* and *books* written on them in marker. She looked sad, an unashamed, nobody's-watching kind of sad. Tears spilled over her lower lids like a tub overflowing and puddled in the crevices of her nose and upper lip. She exhibited all the symptoms of someone who had just gone through a breakup. Based on her age, I guessed it was probably more like a divorce. As the woman picked up another box, the bottom fell out, and something glass smashed on the concrete below. If this were a movie, I thought, it would be something symbolic like a cake plate she got as a wedding gift. She would bend over to pick it up, and as she did, she would catch her pained reflection in a hundred jagged pieces. But it wasn't a cake plate, just a lightbulb, and the woman barely acknowledged it had broken.

"You need any help?" I said as I walked up the drive. The woman jumped with surprise and clumsily knocked tears off her cheek with the back of her hand, "Oh. Sorry. I didn't know anyone was home." The skin of her face was raw, and her eyelids were plump with salt water. She was wearing a stained SCOOTER'S BARBECUE shirt that most people would have retired to the pajama drawer, and her wedding ring bit into her finger like a tourniquet. I figured she was only still wearing it because she couldn't get it off. "Are you moving in?" I asked.

"Yeah. Reverend Kramer, your . . . dad?"

"Yeah."

"Your dad is renting it out to me temporarily."

"You're Weylyn's teacher, aren't you?"

"Yeah. Ms. Lowry. Meg." She grabbed a potted plant from her passenger seat and headed toward the door. Without invitation, I followed her inside.

She hadn't brought much, just a few boxes and trash bags full of clothes. I opened the box that read, VIDEOTAPES and shuffled through her collection. They were classics mostly: *Funny Face*, *His Girl Friday*, *A Streetcar Named Desire*. I held up her copy of *Casablanca*. "Can I borrow this?"

Ms. Lowry—Meg—shrugged. "Sure." She set the plant down on the kitchen counter, grabbed a bottle of wine by the neck, and poured some into a plastic cup. It was noon.

"I know it's none of my business, but why were you crying?"

Meg took a long gulp to give herself time to think. "I left my husband."

I nodded like I knew what she was going through. "That's rough."

"Yeah."

"Why'd you leave him?"

Meg slumped down in the ugly, plaid armchair that Mama's

uncle Ben had given her as a housewarming gift. It hadn't been allowed to thaw her backside for more than twenty minutes before she banished it to the carriage house. "We wanted different things."

"You still love him, though?"

"Absolutely," she said and pulled off her shoes. Her socks had gray soles, and the right one had a hole that left her big toe completely exposed to the elements. I was so exhilarated by the unceremoniousness of it that I almost whipped off my own shoes. I wanted to dig my toes into the spongy, cream carpet, then spill a whole bottle of grape juice on it and watch as Meg shrugged like she did when that lightbulb had broken. "It's only a carpet," she'd say. Mama had removed all the carpet from the house because she didn't trust us not to ruin it.

"Sorry. I didn't get your name," Meg said.

"Lydia."

"Lydia, I'm usually not like this. I'm pretty embarrassed."

"I don't care. If you were puking or something, that would be different."

Meg shared one "Ha!" with me. Two is customary, but she was going through a divorce, so I cut her some slack. "Oh, and you know you're sharing this place with a pig, right?"

She nodded. "I think he's in the bathtub sleeping."

"His name's Merlin, and he likes tomatoes."

"Noted."

"Well . . . I guess I'll get out of your hair," I said and headed to the front door. I was about to grab the doorknob when I turned back to face Ms. Lowry and said, "Weylyn thinks Merlin has magic powers."

Meg's eyes flitted to the plant she had left sitting on the kitchen counter. "Do you believe him?" she asked. Something in her voice made it seem like she was angling for a particular response.

I hesitated. "About the pig?"

"No . . . not exactly," she said expectantly. Had she seen something, too? Had Weylyn made it rain in the cafeteria because they were serving cold frittatas again? If he had, I think I would have heard about it.

I wanted to tell her everything, but I couldn't. I had just met this woman, and now she was my neighbor. If she didn't believe me, I'd have to leave for school every day with a bag over my head. "I'll bring the movie back tomorrow," I blurted and ran out the front door.

Two weeks later, I wore a coat to school for the first time that year. Fall had made its presence known in the form of wet, earthy smells and shivering tree limbs shedding leaves in various shades of exotic cat. I walked to school that morning, listening to the crisp sounds that punctuated each one of my footfalls and the honks of geese flying overhead. I found it strange that there could be so much beauty in the death of all these living things. Maybe it was only beautiful because we knew they would be resurrected next spring. I don't think I would enjoy fall quite as much if I knew there was an eternal winter to follow.

By then, Ms. Lowry had settled into her new home. After school, Weylyn and I would help her rake leaves or plant bulbs, and then we'd sit on the porch and drink hot chocolate, watching the steam draw treble clefs on a gray sheet of sky. She had done a lot of work inside, too, somehow managing to arrange the garage sale furnishings in a way that made them look almost intentional. Even Uncle Ben's bedbug habitat looked vintage with the right throw pillow. She removed the more heinous knickknacks from the shelves and replaced them with her huge collection of antique books. I helped her organize them alphabetically and was browsing the titles when she said, "I only buy a book after reading it twice. If you can enjoy it more than once, you know it's a keeper." I couldn't imagine how long it must have taken to read every one of those books twice. It took me four months to read book three of Wandering Wizards.

Mama hated it when I went over to Meg's. "I don't want you

spending all your time with a lonely divorcée," she said. "It's not healthy."

I wanted to mention that her loveless marriage wasn't exactly healthy, either, but instead occupied my tongue with a large mouthful of mashed potatoes. I could only imagine how she would react if she found out there was a pig living there, too.

Daddy had no issue with my friendship with Meg. "Ms. Lowry's a teacher. She could help Lydia with her studies." Mama looked as sour as month-old milk, but nodded the way her mama taught her to when her husband made a suggestion.

On school nights, Weylyn and I would do our homework at Meg's. She would help me with mine, but Weylyn had to fend for himself. "I assigned you that homework. What kind of teacher would I be if I gave you all the answers?" she said, then leaned over my shoulder to explain functions to me for the umpteenth time. He didn't really need help, anyway. Weylyn was doing great in school, and not just for an orphaned wolf boy. His grades were better than mine, and I had eleven years of schooling that should have proved otherwise. Maybe he was only asking for help to make me feel less stupid. If that was true, he never let on.

Sometimes Meg and I would catch each other watching Weylyn, the object of our mutual curiosity, but we never spoke about it. I would go back to my homework, and Meg would go back to grading papers as if nothing had happened. I suppose nothing had, really.

June would come over some nights, but did very little actual studying. In fact, I think Merlin learned more of the French language from sniffing the pages of her textbook than she did. "How do you say *pig* in French?" June asked as Merlin used her French dictionary as a scratching post.

"Why don't you look it up?" I grunted as I drew a covalent bond in my chemistry notebook.

June, Weylyn, and I were seated cross-legged on the floor with our books and binders piled in the center like we were going to have a bonfire later. It was December 20, our last chance to study before first semester finals.

June yanked her dictionary away from Merlin and flipped to the Ps. She ran her finger down the page. "Pig, pig, pig . . . *le cochon!*"

Merlin snorted, unimpressed.

"Do you think there's a French word for unicorn-pig?"

"No."

"I guess you guys did kind of discover a new species. Are you gonna sell him to the zoo or the circus or something?"

"No!" Weylyn snapped. "He isn't going anywhere."

June looked surprised. "Sorry, man. I was just joking . . . kind of." Weylyn deemed her apology good enough and buried his face back into his history book. "What do you think it's for, anyway? The horn?"

It had grown. It was now the size of a mini golf pencil and was brown and slightly curled like the fingers of women who grow their nails too long.

"I'm guessing it doesn't do anything. It's probably just some piece of bone that ended up in the wrong spot," I said in a distracted tone that would kill most conversations.

"I bet it's magic," June continued.

Weylyn poked his head out from behind his textbook. "You do?"

"Yeah. Have you ever tried making a wish?"

"No."

"Can I?"

"Sure." Weylyn sounded apprehensive.

June cleared her throat and put a hand on Merlin's horn. "I wish for Brandy Sweeney to turn into a frog!"

I'm not sure if pigs can roll their eyes, but I was pretty sure I saw Merlin do just that. There was something odd about him, something ironic, like there was a joke he should be laughing at but didn't know how (like the one about the pig that all the dumb humans thought was magic).

"There's something wrong with you, June," I said impassively.

"You should try. Turn Caroline into a frog. Here." She pulled a tiara from her book bag and held it out to me. Caroline's Miss Paris Crown . . .

I gasped, "June! Where'd you get that?"

"Duh. Her room."

"If she finds out it's missing . . ."

"She won't care if she's a frog." June placed the tiara on Merlin's head and shouted, "Presto chango!"

"You have to put that back," I said, unamused. "I don't want to get in trouble trying to sneak it back in. Didn't work out so well the last time."

"Relaaaax. I will." June grabbed the tiara off Merlin's head and placed it around her own black nest of hair. Coupled with her heavy eyeliner and red lipstick, the crown made her look like a Disney witch. "Just let me have tonight before my carriage turns back into a pumpkin. Pleeeeeease?"

I reluctantly nodded and went back to my homework. Weylyn had stopped his work and was staring at Merlin intently.

"I want to make a wish," he said. He placed his hand on Merlin's horn, then closed his eyes.

After a few moments of silence, June interrupted. "Well? What's your wish?"

Weylyn hushed her and closed his eyes again. Seconds later, I heard what sounded like a dog howling in the distance. Merlin darted out of the room, and Weylyn looked as though he'd seen a ghost.

"What's wrong?" I asked. He ignored me and ran out onto the porch. We heard another howl, but this time it was Weylyn. I watched him from the window as he paced and panted, his left arm twitching like an agitated dog's wag. As he let mournful vowels escape into the night air, the porch lamp backlit the first lonely drops of rain.

## 16

## MS. MEG LOWRY

It would have been a very white Christmas had the temperature been below freezing, but it had been an unseasonably warm week with highs in the midfifties, so instead, it was just wet. The less rational part of my brain thought that maybe I had Weylyn to thank for the balmy weather after what I had witnessed on my front porch the week before.

By that point, I had managed to shake my obsession over the zombie plant and had chalked it up to stress and possibly a low-grade fever. Weylyn and I had grown close since the Great Pig Escape, and life in general had been mostly uneventful until that night. Something must have upset him, because Weylyn was out on the front porch whining and howling like a wild dog. I asked Lydia what happened, but she just shrugged. Then without warning, it began to pour. I wouldn't have thought anything of it—it was just rain, after all—other than the fact that, a few minutes earlier, I had been stargazing through the skylight in my bedroom. As far as I could tell, there wasn't a cloud in the sky.

Reverend Kramer had invited me to join him and his family for Christmas dinner, but I pretended I had plans with family in Litchfield. On Christmas morning, I parked my truck two blocks down the road and snuck in around back so I wouldn't run into Thomas or his wife. I made a roast chicken and ate it while watching *The Odd Couple* reruns on TV.

Nate and I had always gone to his parents' house in Indiana for Christmas. The Lowrys had been married and lived in the same house for over fifty years. For dinner, they had various birds served Russian doll–style and made everyone wear silly hats. Afterward, we'd play charades, and Mr. Lowry would act out the same movie he did every year, *It's a Wonderful Life.*

"You have to pick another movie!" his wife would shout.

His reply was always, "Well, I couldn't think of a movie that better sums up the life I've had with you, my dear."

As corny as it was, it always made me want to cry. Knowing that he'd do it again and I would miss it made me actually cry.

Merlin watched me from Uncle Ben's chair with an expression that resembled empathy. "I'm sorry, Merlin. I must be ruining your Christmas." His face was sticky with apple juice, and his eyelids lolled dreamily. He was having a fine Christmas.

At nine o'clock, I was about ready to throw in the towel for the night when there was a knock at the door. I peeked through the closed blinds to see who it was, then opened the door.

"We've got pumpkin pie," Lydia said as she and Weylyn scooted inside. "Man, it's really coming down out there."

"How'd you know I was here?" I asked.

"I saw your truck parked on Oakland. Don't worry, my parents don't know." Lydia collapsed her umbrella and hung it on the coat rack.

"I wasn't trying to be rude. I just didn't feel that . . . festive."

"Don't worry. I totally get it. We snuck out after the talent show started."

"Talent show?"

"For Mama's Mississippi relatives. Caroline was playing 'Silent Night' on the piano when we left, and Aunt Corinne started singing."

"She sounds like a goat," Weylyn chimed in.

Lydia made herself comfy on the sofa and peeled the foil back from the half-eaten pie. "Want some?"

"Sure. I'll get forks," I said and headed to the kitchenette.

"We brought my *Twilight Zone* box set if you wanna watch."

"Sounds good." I was grateful they hadn't brought any Christmas movies. If I had to watch *It's a Wonderful Life*, I probably would have had a meltdown.

I passed out plates and forks, and we divvied up what was left of the pumpkin pie, including a small slice for Merlin, who wasted no time devouring it. Weylyn came in a close second. "I had no idea Christmas was this delicious," he said as he licked chunks of pumpkin off his fingers.

"I guess this is the first Christmas you've had in a long time, isn't it?"

"Yeah. I kind of remember Christmas with my parents," he said thoughtfully. "Not with the pack, though. The only holiday wolves celebrate is the full moon, and there's no pie or anything. It's mostly a lot of howling."

I swallowed to stop myself from laughing. I was still getting used to Weylyn's strange anecdotes.

"There's gonna be a full moon soon. You should teach us how to howl!" Lydia chimed in.

"It's not that hard," he said. "You just have to use the back of your throat. Like this." Weylyn tilted his head back, formed a loose *O* with his lips, and let out a long, doleful howl. Lydia immediately responded in kind.

After a brief moment of hesitation, I joined the chorus, and we all howled at a waxing moon we knew was there but couldn't see.

## 17

## LYDIA KRAMER

One of my favorite *Twilight Zone* episodes had just started when we heard the scream. It was Caroline, and she must have had her window open because I could hear it as clear as day, even over the storm. Ms. Lowry, Weylyn, and I ran out onto the porch. Through her window, I could see Caroline pacing back and forth and shouting. At first, I couldn't make out what she was saying because of the rain, then I heard her scream, "Crown!" and look out the window at the three of us watching her from the porch.

Shit. I had forgotten all about the crown. June said she would put it back, but then again, she hated Caroline. At that moment, Caroline's most prized possession was probably nestled between the shaggy ears of Coconut, June's fourteen-year-old mutt with the balding tail that made it look like a sewer rat.

"What's wrong?" Ms. Lowry asked.

"Caroline's crown. It's missing."

"She's going to think I took it," Weylyn said soberly.

Ms. Lowry put a hand on his shoulder. "Don't worry, I'll talk to her if it comes to that."

"Me, too," I said reassuringly, and we went back inside to await the wrath of Mama. Five minutes later, there was a pounding at the door.

Ms. Lowry answered it, and Mama and Caroline stormed inside without acknowledging her. Daddy trailed in behind them and gave Ms. Lowry an apologetic shrug.

"Where's Weylyn?" Mama demanded, then spotted him sitting in Uncle Ben's chair, back straight like a man on trial. "There he is! Where *is* it?"

"Where's what?" Ms. Lowry answered.

"The little thief stole my crown!" Caroline shrieked hysterically. I could tell she had been crying because her eyeliner had puddled in ghoulish shadows under her eyes.

"Why would Weylyn take your stupid crown?" I spat back.

"He took Emily's bracelet!"

"No, he didn't! And even if he had, Emily's bracelet is diamond. Your tiara is cheap plastic and rhinestones."

Caroline growled and lunged at me, but Daddy held her back. "Caroline! Stop!"

Weylyn was silent, but his fingers dug into the upholstery so hard I was sure it would rip.

Ms. Lowry stepped in and spoke evenly to Mama. "Do you have any proof that Weylyn did what you're claiming?"

Mama's lips pinched together to form a hard beak. "I don't need proof. I know."

The gentle patter of rain on the roof became a harder, clicking sound. I followed Weylyn's gaze out the window and saw small pellets of ice bouncing off the surface of the glass. Mama and Ms. Lowry were yelling now, but all I could hear was the *click click click* of that ice. Weylyn's left hand twitched in time with the sound.

Then Daddy spoke.

"Clara, be reasonable. It's Christmas," he begged. Daddy never got angry on Christmas, and I could tell that right now, he was trying really hard not to.

"I don't care what day it is! I'm sick of you siding with that boy over your own family!"

*Clack clack clack!* The ice was now the size of marbles. I met Weylyn's gaze, but he quickly looked away.

"Don't make this about him!" Daddy had finally had enough. "This is about you! I asked you to open your heart to Weylyn, but you won't even try. You're only a Christian when it's convenient for you."

"And what about stealing? I guess that's *conveniently* not a sin to you anymore?"

"No, it's a sin." The anger in Daddy's voice had turned down to a low simmer. "But I would sooner forgive a thief his sins than I would forgive you your coldness."

Mama staggered back like she had just been struck.

Weylyn stood up, his whole body quaking with anger. "I'm not a *thief*!" he shouted.

The room fell into a stunned silence, but it didn't last long. The vacuum soon filled with the discordant wail of tornado sirens.

What happened next was like something straight out of the movies. The villain says something terrible, and there's a flash and a *boom*! The lights flicker, and everyone in the theater screams. I didn't scream at the noise because I'd seen enough movies to know what to expect. Only this wasn't a movie. This was real.

## 18

## MS. MEG LOWRY

We Oklahomans are all too familiar with hail and the promise it makes and almost always keeps. That night was no exception.

At first, I assumed it was an ice storm, but when I opened the door, I was greeted with a warm, humid breath of air. Sirens wailed above cracks of thunder that sounded like giant bones breaking. Merlin's ears perked up, but he didn't appear spooked like my dogs would have been. *The dogs!* I hoped Nate had taken them with him to his parents'.

The anger in the room was broken by the apocalyptic chorus outside, and a new, fearful tension started to sink in. Lydia switched on the TV news. The meteorologist had the same bewildered look on his face as the rest of us did. He was wearing a Rudolph the Red-Nosed Reindeer tie, and his collar had a small pink stain on it that looked like cranberry sauce, a remnant of the Christmas dinner he had been pulled away from. He pointed to a nasty red blob that was getting ready to chew through the city of Paris, his voice crackling with panic. "A tornado has touched down two miles west of Paris and is headed east. If you have a storm shelter, go there immediately." Then he added, probably for his family at home, "Please . . ."

"But it's Christmas," Mrs. Kramer muttered in disbelief.

Thomas turned to his wife. "Clara, you get the kids to the shelter. I'll get the girls and your family."

A still-stunned Mrs. Kramer nodded obediently, and Mr. Kramer ran out into the rain. Clara turned to face us. The angry fog that had been clouding her eyes cleared as she looked into her children's scared faces. "Follow me, girls. Hurry," she instructed and ran out the door.

Lydia and Caroline followed, but Weylyn didn't move. He had a far-off look in his eyes and clutched Merlin tight in his arms. "Ms. Lowry," he whispered. "I have to tell you something."

I desperately wanted to hear the rest of that thought, but first, I needed to get him to safety. "Later. Come on." I grabbed his hand, and we stumbled out into the storm.

Rain hammered on the back of my skull as I struggled to move myself through it. The sky had turned an eerie shade of dark green, and the clouds twisted and contorted like phantoms. My ears filled with a roaring sound, but it wasn't the train noise that most people describe tornadoes sounding like; it was more like I was standing at the foot of a giant waterfall. A set of Christmas lights was ripped from the house and tried to wind itself around my feet. I let go of Weylyn's arm while I shook them loose and searched the sky for the twister I could hear but couldn't see.

Then a brilliant flash of lightning illuminated the monster lurking in the dark. He was a big boy and hungry. I watched in horror as he swallowed the neighbor's barn whole and spat out the bones. I ran faster.

I could see Mr. Kramer guiding the rest of Lydia's family into the shelter a hundred feet ahead. *Almost there*, I thought as I felt the drag of the wind on my back.

We reached the shelter, and Mr. Kramer helped the girls inside. First Caroline, then Lydia, then Mrs. Kramer, but no Weylyn.

"Where's Weylyn?" I shouted to Thomas over the noise of the storm. He was looking at something, mouth agape. I followed his gaze and saw Weylyn and Merlin halfway between the carriage house and the shelter, staring down the storm.

"Weylyn!" we yelled at the top of our lungs, but he didn't look back.

Lydia scrambled up the stairs of the shelter and tried to run after him. I grabbed her, kicking and screaming, and pulled her back inside.

When I ran back up to the top of the stairs, I saw Weylyn in the distance, resting his hand on the pig's head and standing perfectly still. The twister kept advancing, looming over Weylyn like a God sent to ruin him, but he didn't flinch.

Thomas turned to me. "I'm going to get him. If I don't come back, close the door and bar it shut."

I nodded. Thomas sprinted out of the shelter. His wife screamed in protest, then recoiled against the concrete wall and started sobbing, her makeup running in zebra stripes down her cheeks. Lydia wrapped her arms around her mother, and they cried together.

Then, all at once, the rain stopped and winds calmed. Mr. Kramer's sprint slowed to a hesitant walk as the twister looked like it had been put in slow motion. The debris it carried bobbed around in a circle as if on a carousel, and the clouds swirled gently like a cotton candy machine. Slower and slower it churned until it was almost stationary, a photo in a *National Geographic*. Then it simply fizzled away, dropping five tons of debris and leaving a curtain of blinking stars in its wake.

Lydia and I rushed out of the shelter.

"Daddy!" Lydia exclaimed and wrapped her arms around him. Reverend Kramer started laughing. "What's so funny?" she asked.

Merlin casually grazed on the grass beneath his feet as if nothing had happened, and Weylyn made his way slowly toward us, looking dazed and confused but generally unharmed. I looked him up and down just to make sure he wasn't hurt. "Are you okay?"

Weylyn nodded slowly, then smiled. "I told you he was magic."

Then he kneeled down next to Merlin and patted him on the back of the head. The pig looked up at me, knowingly.

I guess I knew less about the universe than I thought I did.

There was a nervous energy among the congregation that filed out the wooden double doors of St. Agnes's Church the following Sunday. Some headed straight for their cars, but many lingered on the sidewalk, murmuring to each other and periodically casting apprehensive glances at the gray clouds overhead. As I wove my way through the crowd, I caught pieces of their conversations that individually sounded like nonsense, but together, they told a story:

> . . . *the Kramers' house was almost destroyed* . . .
> . . . *my son is friends with his daughter, and she said it just vanished into thin air* . . .
> . . . *I heard it was the pig* . . .
> . . . *you know, the wolf boy* . . .
> . . . *he just stood there like nothing was wrong* . . .
> . . . *I knew there was something weird about that kid* . . .
> . . . *it's a miracle.*

I walked inside the empty church and found Reverend Kramer sitting alone in one of the pews in the back row, bathed in reddish light from the stained glass window. He looked deep in thought as I suppose most clergymen are on a Sunday afternoon.

I sat down in the pew in front of his and turned around. "Hi, Thomas."

"Meg," he said, smiling gently. "Thanks for meeting me here. I thought it best not to get Clara involved in all of this."

"Sure," I said, although I was unclear on his meaning. "So, what is it you wanted to talk to me about?"

Reverend Kramer glanced down at a pocket Bible cradled in his hands, then back up at me. "I've been praying a lot over the last few days, asking God for guidance because I had an important decision to make." He took a deep breath and continued, "I don't think I'm going to be able to take care of Weylyn anymore, and I was hoping you would."

"Oh," I replied, taken aback.

"I'm sure it comes as no surprise to you that my wife and I have been having . . . problems, and not just since fostering Weylyn. It's been going on for years. That tornado reminded me there are greater things in this world than our petty arguments. Maybe the storm was God's way of reminding me that my family comes first. As far as Weylyn's part in all of this . . ." Thomas trailed off as if hoping I'd finish his thought for him so he didn't have to say it out loud.

I obliged. "He *complicates* things."

He looked me in the eye and nodded soberly. "Am I crazy?"

"No, you're not crazy, and neither am I. I can't speak for your congregation, though. One of them thought the pig caused the tornado."

Thomas guffawed and cringed slightly as his laughter echoed off the walls of the church. "It's good to know there's at least one person crazier than we are."

I glanced out the front doors at the chattering churchgoers. "It would probably be best if Weylyn left Paris. He could use a fresh start."

"I agree," Thomas said. "Are you sure you're okay with that?"

"I was thinking of moving, anyway. I've already bumped into Nate twice since we split up. This town is just too small."

"It can be, yes . . . You know I'll help in whatever way I can."

"Thanks. I appreciate it."

"Maybe I could stop by tomorrow evening to work out the details?"

"Yes, that's fine."

Thomas smiled despite the otherwise doleful look on his face. "Weylyn's a special kid. I just wish my wife could have seen it, too."

"He is special," I said, standing up. "I promise I'll take good care of him."

I turned to leave, but the reverend held out his hand, signaling me to stop. "Oh, Meg," he said, his voice thick with remorse. "Will you tell Weylyn I'm sorry? I plan to tell him myself, but he'll probably be too hurt to believe a word I say. Will you tell him again for me? Once the dust settles?"

I would tell him. I would also tell him how, as I was leaving, I saw Thomas wipe a stray tear from his cheek.

## 19

## LYDIA KRAMER

"It's important you know that we still care about Weylyn. He just won't be a part of our family anymore," Daddy said reassuringly.

I couldn't believe what I was hearing. My parents were kicking Weylyn out for the "good of the family." Weylyn *was* part of our family. If they were going to send anyone away, it should have been Caroline. She's the one who started a fight over a stupid tiara.

"You can't do that," I fumed.

"I know this is hard, Lydia, but it's the best thing for all of us." Daddy placed his hand on my shoulder as if that would comfort me somehow.

I squirmed out of his reach. This had nothing to do with Weylyn. My parents were using him as a scapegoat for their failing marriage. I expected this kind of response from Mama, but not from Daddy. I thought he was better than that.

I choked back tears. "Don't act like you care about Weylyn! You only care about yourselves!"

I turned to Mama, who at least had the decency to look contrite. She'd finally gotten what she wanted. It must have taken a lot of self-control not to break into gleeful laughter.

"I hope you're happy," I said pointedly and ran out of the room before she could see me cry.

In the days leading up to Weylyn's departure, I avoided my parents by spending evenings in the carriage house. It was too cold and wet outside to do anything other than watch TV, so I brought over my entire library of VHS tapes and asked Weylyn to pick ten movies he couldn't leave without seeing. After blackballing *The Brady Bunch Variety Hour*, I stacked the tapes he'd selected on the TV stand. One by one, we fed them into the black maw of the VCR and watched in silence until there was only one tape left in the stack, *The Wizard of Oz*. I had saved it until the end because it seemed fitting for Weylyn's last night in town. The tornado was a little on the nose, maybe, but I thought he'd enjoy a story about adventure given that he was about to start a new one of his own.

When Dorothy clicked her ruby slippers together and wished she were home in Kansas, I looked over at Weylyn and saw that he was tearing up. "Sorry . . ." I paused the tape. "Do you want to watch something else?"

"No, it's okay," Weylyn said, blinking away tears. "I like it. It's just . . . it was nice to have somewhere I could call home. Now I have to start all over again."

"I know. It's bullshit," I said, fighting back tears of my own.

"I'm not stupid. I know my being here has caused some problems, but I thought Mr. Kramer liked me."

"He does. They're just taking their problems out on you. It's not fair."

Weylyn cast his eyes down. "Do you think they're scared of me?"

"I don't think so. I don't even think they believe you had anything to do with what happened."

"What about you? Are you scared of me?"

"Ha. No way," I said, squeezing out a smile. "I'm more scared of Merlin than I am of you."

Weylyn laughed and looked down at the little pig napping in his lap. "He is pretty scary, isn't he?"

"Terrifying. Is he coming with you to Alabama?"

He nodded. "I couldn't leave him behind."

We sat in silence for a few minutes, listening to Merlin's gentle snoring and the muted percussion of sleet on the windows. "You can always call me, you know," I said. "Or visit. I mean, even if you live someplace else, you're still my brother."

Weylyn brightened. "Really?"

"Of course."

He smiled and turned to look out the window. A small break in the clouds revealed a perfectly full moon. "Look! The moon! Will you come outside with me?"

I nodded and joined him on the front porch without my coat. I should have been cold, but strangely, I wasn't. The moonlight was slightly warm like sunshine tempered by clouds, and the precipitation that bounced off my skin felt more like a summer shower than sleet. It was as if the moon had been waiting for us.

"Ready?" Weylyn said, his eyes catching the moonlight and shining like newly polished silver.

"Ready."

Our howls reached the moon just in time. A few moments later, the clouds returned, and our wolf song slipped behind them with the moon, the stars, and the rest of the night sky.

## 20

## MS. MEG LOWRY

You don't really know whether you'll make a good parent until you are one. I wasn't perfect. I let Weylyn stay up late on school nights and track mud into the house. He repeatedly forgot to brush his teeth because I forgot to remind him, and I let him eat cake for breakfast multiple times the week following his birthday. To be fair, I was thirteen years behind where most parents are by that point. I was just grateful I never had to change any diapers.

Weylyn and I moved back to my hometown in Alabama and into our own little apartment. It wasn't much, but it had a patio out back where Weylyn would plant tomatoes in the summer. Every day, he'd bring in bowls of ripe, juicy tomatoes even though I never saw him water them once.

Lydia would visit during breaks from school, and we'd watch movies or make hot chocolate or both. It wasn't long before she left for college and not so long after that before Weylyn left, too. I guess I only really had five years as a mother, but it was five more than I ever thought I'd get.

And I spent them with Weylyn Grey.

*second interlude*

WILDWOOD FOREST, OREGON

2017

# ROARKE

"Pssht! I could take down a tornado," I said dismissively as I swung from a ropy tendril of cobweb like it was a jungle vine and I was Tarzan. "I'd just throw rocks at it. Or kick it like this. Hiiiiya!" I pumped my legs, forcing my body into a swing and kicking the air.

"I wouldn't do that if I were you," Weylyn said as the rotten joists overhead creaked ominously.

"I'm flyyyying!" I squealed. "I bet you can't do that, can you?"

"No, I can't fly," he said, irritated. "Now, stop before you take the rest of the roof down with you."

"You're no fun." I relaxed my legs and let my body slow to a stop. "If my dad heard your stories, he'd say you're full of—" I stopped short when I felt hot, wet breath on the back of my neck. I spun around and came face-to-face with a huge, white wolf. Screaming, I hid behind Weylyn.

He laughed. "Boo won't hurt you. He's as soft as a peach. Aren't you, boy?" Weylyn scratched him behind the ears. The wolf leaned into his fingers, jaw slackening into a dopey pant.

"He was trying to eat me!"

"Nonsense. He *could* eat you. Unfortunately, I've spoiled him so much that he barely remembers how to hunt. His favorite is grilled cheese."

Boo ambled a few steps, then collapsed lazily onto the dirt. "I never had any kids, but I suspect that if I had, they'd be as doughy as this one."

I inched out from behind Weylyn and patted the wolf's huge head. Boo's tongue lolled happily out the side of his mouth. "I can't wait to tell Mike I saw a full-grown wolf!" Or won a fight against one, whatever sounded good at the time. "The only time I've seen a wolf is when the lady from the zoo brought a wolf puppy to class."

"Really? What kinds of things did you learn?"

"The wolf peed on Mike's backpack!" I snorted.

Weylyn didn't seem to find it as hilarious as I did. "Well," he said as he put down his knife, "looks like you're free to go."

The sun had set, leaving behind a forest of dark-blue, deep-ocean shapes. My mother probably already had the FBI on the phone, so I'd have to hurry if I didn't want my face on the back of a milk carton.

I felt a drop of rain land on the back of my head. Weylyn must have felt one, too, because he looked up at the hole in his ceiling and frowned. "I have an umbrella around here somewhere. Ah! Here it is!" He reached for a black umbrella that was tangled in a nest of cobwebs over the fireplace. After several hard tugs, Weylyn yanked it free, and it popped open, sending dust motes flying like dirty confetti.

"Here," he said, coughing, and handed the umbrella to me. A spider dangled from its lip by a thread of silk. The tiny creature seemed to return my gaze for a moment before rappelling down to the floor below.

Weylyn looked up at my knife that was still suspended from the web. "Sorry about your knife. Once it falls, I can mail it to you."

"Nah. It's okay. You keep it." My mom told me if she saw me with it again, she'd introduce me to her friend who accidentally cut his own thumb into a pot of potato soup. I opened the front door.

"Oh, Roarke . . ."

"Yeah?" I said, turning back.

"I could use some help patching the roof if you're free tomorrow. I've already used up all my favors with the spiders."

The hole was kind of my fault. Plus, it could earn me a few more brownie points with Ruby if I told her I had not only escaped Old Man Spider's lair but I had also returned for a second round. Maybe if I was super helpful, I could even convince Weylyn to stage a fight with me and let me win. "Sure," I said. "It's Sunday, so I don't have school."

"That would be great. Thank you."

"Sorry again."

"It's okay. I've done crazier things to impress a girl," he said, knowingly.

I blushed despite myself. "What girl?"

"When I heard you clomping around up there, I looked out the window and saw her watching. Can I give you a piece of advice?"

I shrugged, unsure of whether or not to trust the romantic wisdom of a hermit.

"Don't try so hard," he said; then he set out a bucket to catch the rain that had started puddling on his kitchen table.

When I arrived at Weylyn's the next day, he was already on the roof, but I couldn't see a ladder. "Use the tree!" he shouted down to me, then darted out of sight. I gave him credit. Most old people I know are terrible at climbing things, my dad especially. I once had to run and get help when he "got stuck" in my tree house.

I dropped my backpack, shimmied up the branches like I had the day before, and joined Weylyn, who was sitting on a rickety wooden beam, his legs dangling over the edge of the hole. I peered into the kitchen below, expecting to see puddles and soggy furniture, but the room was surprisingly dry.

"Ready to get started?" Weylyn hopped to his feet, the board beneath him groaning under his weight.

"Sure."

"Mud or straw?"

I must have looked confused because he pointed to a bucket of mud sitting next to a pile of straw. "Mud, I guess," I said, unsure of what he wanted me to do with it. Usually, when one of my friends pointed to mud, it was because he was daring me to eat it.

"Good choice!" Weylyn dropped the bucket at my feet. Mud sloshed over the edge and onto my sneakers. I groaned as the wet muck soaked through to my socks.

"I'll place the straw, and you pack it with mud," Weylyn instructed and began laying straw bundles across the opening in the roof. I sank my hand in the bucket, pulled out a goopy wad of mud, and slathered it across the layer of straw. "Like this?"

Weylyn nodded. "Excellent. The messier, the better."

I smiled. I was good at messy.

After we had finished the first layer, Weylyn said we needed to let it dry before adding a second. I glanced up at a wall of dark clouds that were rolling in. "But what if it rains?"

"Don't worry. It won't," Weylyn said as he lowered himself off the edge of the roof and onto a tree branch.

"But what if it does?"

"It won't," he insisted. "Do you want a grilled cheese while we wait?"

"Yes!" I was starving. My mom had made meatloaf the night before, and all I had eaten was my side of green beans and a chocolate milk.

We climbed off the roof, and Boo greeted us at the front door. "Hey, Boo!" I crouched down next to the wolf and tousled the scruff of his neck.

Weylyn went to the fridge and pulled out a stack of cheese slices and a loaf of bread. "How many pieces of cheese do you want? One or two?"

Boo's ears perked up at the word *cheese*. "Three," I said.

Weylyn dropped a pat of butter onto the cast-iron pan sitting on the stovetop. "Three slices, comin' up!" Boo licked his jowls and whined. "Don't worry, Boo. I haven't forgotten about you," he said and tossed a slice of cheese to the wolf, who caught it in midair with an audible *chomp*.

When the butter began to sizzle, Weylyn placed two sand-wiches on the skillet. I sat down at the kitchen table and accidentally kicked over a bucket, the one Weylyn had pulled out the night before to catch the rain falling through the roof. It was empty. "Why is the room so dry?" I asked.

"What do you mean?"

"It was raining last night. Why isn't everything wet?"

Weylyn gave a perfunctory glance around the room. "It stopped just after you left."

"No, it didn't," I protested. "It rained all night." Or that's what Mrs. Kutschbach said when she told me I couldn't play basketball at recess because the blacktop was flooded.

Weylyn dished the grilled cheeses and sat down across from me at the table. "Yes, but it didn't rain here."

"That doesn't make sense."

"Remember that tornado I told you about?"

I nodded.

"Well," he said, taking a bite of his sandwich, "I can say from per-sonal experience that the weather doesn't always do what's expected of it."

*book 3*

## STORM SEEKER

### LITTLE TURTLE, MISSISSIPPI

1997

## 21

## BOBBY QUINN JR.

I was the first student council president of Little Turtle High to ever be impeached. My fellow officers held a secret meeting in the cafeteria after school and unanimously voted me out. I heard my treasurer pretended her jelly doughnut was me and stabbed it with her pencil, and everyone laughed as I bled sugary red goo. I'm not saying I didn't deserve it. I did hire a magician instead of a DJ for the winter formal. But for them to go behind my back like that, and for my treasurer to stab a perfectly good doughnut, well, that was just plain rude.

I didn't even want the job. My dad, Robert Quinn Sr., made me run for student council in an attempt to get me to follow in his footsteps. He was mayor at the time, and the only reason I won was because he promised the student body he'd waive their speeding tickets if they voted for me. Traffic violations went up 20 percent the week of elections. I got rear-ended by a fourteen-year-old kid with a VOTE FOR BOBBY bumper sticker. Most of the kids who voted for me didn't even know my name. They just wrote "mayor's son."

My dad was mayor of Little Turtle for forty years. His dad was mayor for fifty, and his dad, well, let's just say he dropped dead cutting a ribbon with a comically large pair of scissors. A dynasty, that's what we were. It was easier that way. We were a small beach town whose citizens were mostly students from the local college who would rather be surfing than voting, anyway, so there was usually only ever one name on the ballot and only a few dozen people who bothered to fill it out. I usually forgot, which drove my dad crazy. "Why does it matter? You're gonna win whether I vote for you or not," I'd gripe every four years.

"Because someday you'll be the one who no one votes for, and I want you to understand what that means," he'd growl as he knocked the sand out of his loafers. If there was one thing my dad couldn't stand, it was the beach. He built our house as far inland as he could within city limits. We couldn't see the beach, but we could still smell the salt water. Mom called Little Turtle well seasoned. I don't think I ever saw my dad use a saltshaker.

I'm sure my dad would've liked to win an election the old-fashioned way. He once tried to goad his friend Howie into running against him. Howie worked in the governor's office for thirty years, then one day up and left to open a taco stand on the boardwalk. Howie refused, but my dad was mayor, so he put him on the ballot, anyway. It was a tight race, sixty-six to sixty-eight. My dad won.

That night, he took the family to Crableg Joe's for a bucket of lobster tails. Howie was there with some boardwalk buddies and a pitcher of margaritas. Mom told Dad to be a good sport and go over there. I saw him shake Howie's hand, but I couldn't hear what they were saying. I'm pretty sure Howie never realized he was on that ballot.

Twelve years later, my dad had his first stroke, and without warning, it was my turn to run. The first person I ran to was Howie. I begged him to take my place, but all he said was "Sorry, kid," and handed me a taco with extra sour cream as if I wasn't sour enough already. I was thirty-seven, and the only real job I'd held was renting surfboards to tourists who should have been renting canoes—all they did was float and paddle around on them, anyway. I knew nothing about being a mayor—or an adult, for that matter. I had promised my dad a long time ago that I'd take his seat someday, and after trying everything I could think of to get out of it, I entered the special election for mayor. Even though I was the only candidate on the ballot, I still only got twenty-nine votes, and I didn't deserve any of them. My dad wasn't shy about reminding me of that fact.

"Would it have killed you to wear a goddamn tie?" he said when I arrived at city hall for my swearing-in ceremony. His near-death experience hadn't softened him one bit. In fact, it had only made him surlier—due in part to the wheelchair he was now confined to. The only arguably positive thing that had come out of the whole experience was that he now had a legitimate excuse for not going to the beach.

"I couldn't find mine," I lied. I had one tie, and it was currently the only thing stopping my trunk from flying open when I drove.

"You should have called me. I would have let you borrow one of mine." Now he was lying. If I had called him asking to borrow a tie, he would have said, *You're an adult, Bobby. Adults buy their own ties.*

"Can I borrow one now?" I asked, nodding at the navy striped tie around my father's neck.

"You want me to take off *my* tie and give it to *you?*" he asked, incredulous.

I shrugged. "You kind of offered."

He smoothed out his tie, making a show of not removing it. "There are photographers here, Bobby. I'm not showing up in tomorrow's paper looking like a waiter on his cigarette break."

I looked down at my rumpled white dress shirt and black slacks. It was the same outfit I'd worn as a busboy nearly twenty years earlier. "I'll see if they have any ties in the lost-and-found," I muttered, reluctantly taking the back of my dad's wheelchair and pushing him up the disability ramp.

My dad hadn't wanted to resign. My mom and the doctors had made that decision for him. If it had been up to him, he would have kept chugging along until the day he died like his grandfather had. He had always talked about me carrying on his legacy. I just think he hoped he wouldn't be alive to see it happen.

We passed through security and into the lobby of city hall, a two-story atrium that had marble floors with a bronze inlay of the state seal in the center. Standing on the seal waiting for us was city council member Teddy Mitcham, a roundheaded man with a dense, tweedy mustache that eclipsed his upper lip. An old-school conservative, he knew exactly how much money was in the treasury at all times. He once made an aide of his fill out an expense report for the penny he left in the Take-a-Penny, Leave-a-Penny dish at the gas station just to make a point about fiscal responsibility.

"Robert!" Teddy said, clapping my dad on the shoulder. "It's good to see you out and about."

"Well, I wouldn't dream of missing my son's big day," my dad replied with a smile. The man could be affable when he wanted to be.

"Ah, yes," Teddy said, turning to me. "Congratulations, Bobby. If you're anything like your dad, I'm sure we'll get along swimmingly." I detected a note of sarcasm in this voice. After all, he knew me as the kid who TPed his house in the spring of 1973.

Before I had a chance to answer, my dad cut in. "So, how's the levee project coming?"

"Still in permit purgatory, I'm afraid. Also, I'm guessing you heard about the public works bill?"

"Landlocked bastards. You know if they moved the capital here, we'd have it funded in less than twenty-four hours." Before his stroke, Dad had been in talks with the U.S. Army Corps of Engineers to build a levee but was waiting on funding to come through. Little Turtle didn't have enough in its piggy bank to pay for the construction, so he'd applied for aid from the state of Mississippi. The whole plan was largely dependent on a bill that would allocate more resources to public works projects on the Gulf Coast, the same bill that had just failed in the state senate.

Teddy and my dad continued to grouse about the idiots in Congress as if I wasn't even there. After five minutes of being completely ignored, I interrupted them. "So, what's the new plan?"

They looked at me, clearly stunned that I had taken an interest in what they were saying. "What do you mean?" Teddy asked.

"I mean, now that the bill has failed, what's the plan for the levee?"

Teddy gave my dad a sideways glance. "Well, there's another bill that's going to the house. It's not as comprehensive, but it's better than nothing."

"Won't that take a while?"

"These things always take a while," he said, chuckling to himself.

"But hurricane season's already started. Can't we do something quicker?"

My dad's face went pink with embarrassment. "That's not the way government works, son."

"Don't worry, Bobby," Teddy said, his words reeking of condescension. "We'll take care of it." In other words, he and the rest of the council would continue to run the town while I pretended to. I should have been relieved. I was getting a decent government salary for effectively doing nothing, but it didn't feel right. I had always been a little lazy, but never at anyone else's expense. This felt like cheating, and with a baby on the way, I was trying to be a better man.

Lacey and I had hooked up in the bathroom of Crableg Joe's while she was on her lunch break. I was there for the all-you-can-eat soup and salad when this gorgeous waitress asked me if I'd like extra Parmesan. I'd never seen anyone look so sexy grating cheese. Three months later, Lacey calls me and tells me I'm gonna be a dad. She said she didn't want anything from me other than what she was legally entitled to. I agreed and hung up the phone.

Then on the day of my swearing-in, something inside me shifted. As I stood in front of my constituents in the Santa Claus tie I'd pulled out of the lost-and-found bin and my left hand on the Bible, I felt a pang of pride. I decided that I didn't want my colleagues stabbing jelly doughnut effigies of me behind my back. I wanted to eat that doughnut in a meeting where I said important things and other people nodded in agreement. I didn't want to just cut ribbons and make appearances in commercials for Not-So-Little Turtle Motor Homes. I wanted to sign documents and know what they said.

I wanted to make my little girl proud.

I caught up with Lacey before she left for work. Her stomach was now the size of a Thanksgiving turkey, and her work apron was tied beneath her bulge so low it looked like a loincloth. "So, you want a relationship with the baby?" she said, distracted. She was camped out on her couch, watching *Mythological Mysteries*, one of those documentary-style shows that uses blurry camera footage and canned sound effects to convince people that crap like Bigfoot and aliens really exist.

"Well . . . yeah," I said, awkwardly hovering next to the TV. "I can take care of you and the baby."

"And how are you gonna do that?"

"Because I'm the mayor."

She finally took her eyes off the TV. "You're the mayor? Of *where*?"

"Of . . . here. I have an office and health insurance. I even have a 401(k). Look." I handed her the newspaper from the day before. The headline read, BOBBY QUINN JR. ELECTED MAYOR OF LITTLE TURTLE.

Lacey didn't look as impressed as I'd hoped. "I didn't know there was an election."

"Well, there was, and I won," I said, chuckling nervously.

"Says here you only got twenty-nine votes."

"I know, but—"

"And you were the only person on the ballot."

"Because everyone was too scared to run against me?" It was

supposed to be a statement, but my insecurity made it sound like a question.

Lacey looked thoughtful for a moment, then handed back the paper. "Okay," she said. "We can figure something out."

"Really? That's awesome. Thanks," I said, grinning like a moron.

Lacey nodded dispassionately and turned her attention back to the TV. A tornado appeared on-screen, chewing through a small prairie town. "You see that?" Lacey pointed at two small figures moving toward the funnel.

"Yeah. That guy picked the wrong time to walk his dog."

"It's not a dog."

I didn't bother asking what she meant. I was too engrossed in what was unfolding on-screen. The man and his dog had stopped right in the path of the twister. It looked like they were trying to get themselves killed because they showed no signs of backing down. "Run, you idiot!" Lacey barked, but the man didn't move. Seconds later, the twister's rotation slowed to a stop and *poof*! Like someone popping a balloon-shaped tornado, it was gone.

"Holy shit," I said. "Did you see that?"

Lacey squinted at me. "You don't think that shit's real, do you?"

Normally, I didn't buy into that kind of stuff, but this was way too realistic to have been faked, not even by the best Hollywood effects house. Against my better judgment, I now had an idea for how I was going to solve Little Turtle's hurricane problem.

The TV picture dipped to black, and a title card popped up that read:

*Do you have a mythological mystery you'd like to share?*
*Call our hotline at 1-800-BEL-IEVE.*

There was one thing I knew for sure. If I was going to do this, I had to make sure my dad never found out.

## 22

# MARY PENLORE

## July 13th, 1997, 10:47 CST.

*Oxygen readings (see data) indicate hypoxia in water column. Morning tow produced higher* Chaoborus *(glassworm) density in epilimnion than hypolimnion.*

*Haven't eaten breakfast yet. Had doughnut in bag, but escaped through opening in pocket membrane. Assimilated into ecosystem with help from squirrel.*

## July 13th, 1997, 14:29 CST.

*Diet analysis findings worth noting: Calanoids comprise 71 percent of* Chaoborus *diet. Cyclopoids largely made up remaining 29 percent.*

*Not hungry anymore. New thesis: studying bugs suppresses appetite.*

# July 13th, 1997, 22:11 CST.

*Eight percent increase in* Chaoborus *density in epilimnion. Supports theory that they forage at night when predation risk is low.*

*Also supports theory that they are lame. What is not lame: wolves. A wolf could eat fifty glassworms and not realize it. New experiment: throw wolf in epilimnion and see how many glassworms he eats by accident. First, going to Taco Bell.*

"Do you want me to go on?" Professor Rubin—or Hugo as he liked to be called—looked up from my field notes with an expression of disappointment usually reserved for moms whose daughters got their ears pierced out of the back of a van. I shook my head. I really didn't want him reading the August 14 entry that *may* have described my work as a "black hole for research dollars."

To be fair, I thought these notes were private. The thesis I was working on didn't describe the work I was doing as "lame," and there wasn't one mention of wolves. I had made the mistake of leaving my notes on the boat, and Hugo had no reason to believe their content would be anything other than scientific.

"If it's a diary you wanted, you should have got one with a lock," he said as he handed the notebook back to me. I wanted to apologize, but I knew it was too late for that. "Maybe now you can study wolves like you really wanted."

He was right. I had wanted to study wolves, but the programs were very competitive. Three researchers in the whole country had spots available when I applied, and even though I was a good student, I apparently wasn't quite good enough. I didn't have enough practical experience, they said. I should have volunteered at a zoo. *I lived with wolves!* I wanted to scream. *I hunted rabbits and howled at the moon. I watched one of my pack die in front of me. I am a wolf!*

My first application essay was a heartfelt retelling of that month I spent with Weylyn and his family, but my undergraduate advisor wouldn't let me submit it. "Your essay shouldn't be a work of fiction," she said. I was mad, but she was right. No one would believe me even if I did tell the truth.

I wasn't accepted into any of those programs, but apparently I was a hit with all the swamp things and creepy-crawlies: frogs, turtles, mudpuppies, crayfish, and of course glassworms, a particularly boring kind of freshwater larva. Frogs would have been more interesting, but I chose glassworms, probably because I wanted to punish myself for not getting into better programs. *I don't deserve frogs*, I thought. If it showed up as a character in an animated movie, it was too good for me. You'd never see a glassworm getting kissed and turning into a prince, that's for sure.

And Hugo had been so enthusiastic. For whatever reason, he thought these larvae were worth dedicating his life to. I admired his commitment to something that most people wouldn't consider important. His research would never make him rich or famous, but it would buy him fifteen hundred square feet in the burbs and a trip to Myrtle Beach every other year. And it made him happy. I imagined him as a boy, clawing through clods of mud in the schoolyard, oblivious to the squealing kids chasing each other in circles around him. He liked quiet, so he chose friends that didn't speak: earthworms, beetles, and centipedes. They'd never make fun of his hair or his clothes. The worms didn't even have eyes.

I had let him down in the worst way possible. I had suggested that his worms, his life's work, didn't matter. I was rotten and thoughtless.

"No, you're not," said Quan, my boyfriend. Quan was also a Ph.D. student. We had met eight months earlier at one of those awkward student mixers. I was stuck talking to this guy who wouldn't shut up about his research. He was a microbiologist and had made some world-changing breakthrough that he was paranoid his professor would steal. "So, I'm applying for a patent," he said pompously.

At this point in the story, my friends would ask, "Did Quan save you from that guy?"

"No," I'd say. "That guy *is* Quan." That would leave them looking confused and disappointed. I'm not sure why I tell the story that way. It would be easier to just say, "I went to a party and met this interesting guy. He's applying for a patent, you know!" But I couldn't. It's like I didn't want anyone to have unreasonable expectations of Quan before they met him. I wanted him to grow on them like he had grown on me.

Of course, I would never tell it that way when Quan was around. If an acquaintance asked the both of us how we met, I let him tell it. Apparently, I was the most beautiful, interesting girl in the room.

"Look at it this way. Now you can apply for that fellowship," Quan said distractedly. He was halfway through a book on patent law. Preparation, he said, in case he ever had to take his professor to court. I'd met Professor Hutchins. He called me darling and sang in the church choir, not the sort of man you would peg as an intellectual property thief.

"Did you know the plaintiff can be awarded compensation for attorney's fees in federal court?"

"Why would I know that?" I asked.

Quan shrugged and continued to read. I took another sip of my coffee and let the warm liquid steam on my tongue before letting it trickle down my throat.

It was a typical Saturday. On Saturdays, we'd wake up at eight, walk the five blocks to Ubiquity, order cappuccinos, and bury our faces in our books like all the other students that frequented the shop. We lived in Little Turtle, a small college town that also happened to be minutes from the beach, making Brewster College one of the least productive universities in the country. Most students took six years to get their undergrads, if they didn't drop out to become full-time beach bums.

I had only been to the beach twice in the ten months since I'd moved there. Most of my time was spent in the Okchamali Wetlands twenty miles northeast of town. "Wanna go to the beach today?" I asked Quan.

He looked at me like I was deranged. "The beach? Why?"

"I don't know. It might be fun."

"I have to go into the lab today. You can go without me, though."

"Oh. Yeah, I might."

"You should work on that essay. I can help you later tonight if you want."

"It's not ready for anyone to read yet." I hadn't even started it. To get the Canis Fellowship was the dream of every zoologist: spending three years observing gray wolves in Mammoth National Park, Montana. It was given to only one person every year, so I frankly didn't like my chances.

"You should get a jump on that," Quan said in that fatherly way that made me momentarily repulsed by him.

I abruptly gathered my things and stood to leave. "I'll call you later."

He studied me for a moment before plunging back into his paranoid courtroom fantasy.

I hadn't told Quan about Weylyn and the wolves, not only because he wouldn't believe me—that much was obvious—but also because even if he did, he wouldn't appreciate it. He would watch me as I spoke in the measured, critical way of a professor judging a thesis defense. When I was finished, he would refute, argue, try to convince me that it never actually happened. Everything would change between us after that. It was better that he didn't know, better for both of us.

The ocean sparkled like millions of flashbulbs at a red carpet event. Soon, the afternoon sunbathers would show up and pollute the air with top-forty anthems, but for now, the only sound I could hear was the hiss of waves dragging across the sand.

I reached into my bag and pulled out the postcard that had been given to me by Weylyn all those years ago. The beach on the front of the card looked almost exactly like the one in front of me. I pulled my notebook out of my bag and wrote:

*Canis Fellowship Admissions Committee,*
*My name is Mary Penlore, and I lived with wolves.*

## 23

## BOBBY QUINN JR.

After some serious digging, a hundred phone calls, and a little flirting with a seventy-year-old county clerk, I found the guy from the tornado video. His name was Weylyn, and he lived four hours north near Tuscaloosa, Alabama. I asked him to meet me at the Kitchen Sink on Route 10 at 11:00 A.M. Normally, I wouldn't go to the Kitchen Sink sober—the food was only palatable beyond a certain blood alcohol level—but I could count on not running into anyone I knew that early in the day. My buddies and I would sometimes stumble here on Saturday nights, scarf down three pounds of bacon between us, and flirt with Darla, our favorite waitress, who referred to us as the Duke Boys. "That makes you Daisy!" I'd say playfully.

"You're only saying that 'cause you're drunk," she'd say as she refilled our coffees for the third time that night.

I picked a booth by the window so I would be able to see Weylyn when he arrived. I ordered my usual bacon and hash browns from a waitress who wasn't Darla and nervously sipped on my coffee while I waited for him to show. Several excruciating minutes later, I began to have second thoughts. This was by far the most harebrained idea I'd ever had. If my dad found out, he'd probably have another stroke. On the other hand, if it worked, I might finally be able to get him to admit that I wasn't a total screwup. I didn't even need him to be proud of me, just a simple *maybe you're not hopeless, after all* would suffice.

It was almost 11:15 when I saw a man climbing out of the passenger side of a badly dinged Honda CR-V in the parking lot. He must have hitchhiked or something, because he pulled a duffel bag out of the trunk, then walked back around to the front of the car to thank the driver. I guessed it was probably Weylyn by his white T-shirt. No one wore white to the Kitchen Sink because the booths were covered in a shiny, gray film of lard grease.

The man I thought was Weylyn stepped inside the diner and lingered by the entrance, scanning the room. I caught his eye and waved to him. He waved back and headed in my direction. He was con-man handsome with shaggy black-coffee hair and a huge set of carnivorous white teeth. I stood to meet him, and he shook my hand. "Hi. Weylyn Grey. It's nice to meet you."

"Bobby Quinn. Mayor." People usually laughed when I introduced myself that way, probably because most of the time I was wearing a T-shirt with the sleeves cut off. That day, I was wearing one of my relatively more respectable flannel shirts with the sleeves rolled up to my elbows. Weylyn sat across from me in the booth as the waitress brought me my plate. She turned to Weylyn. "Can I get you anything, hon?"

"Just water, thank you. I'm Weylyn. What's your name?"

"Gail."

"Gail! That's pretty. I've never met anyone by that name before."

"That so?"

"It's nice to finally meet a Gail, and I can tell you're one of the better ones, so I don't suppose I need to meet another." He flashed her a smile.

Gail blushed and said, "I'll get you that water," then hurried away.

Weylyn grabbed a pen and a napkin and wrote *Gail* on it. "You gonna ask for her number, man?" I asked.

"No. Just the name will do."

Seemed like this guy had a screw loose. Then again, I was the one who'd believed the ludicrous story he'd told me over the phone, the one about his magical pet pig that controls the weather.

I thoughtlessly took a big bite of bacon and said, "Where's the pig? I didn't see him get out of the car."

"His name is Merlin." Weylyn pointed out the window to a small pig nosing through an overturned trash can. When he popped back out with an apple core in his mouth, I noticed the horn on his forehead.

"Most places don't let me bring him inside. I tell them pigs are cleaner than most humans, but they tend not to believe me."

"Maybe because they saw him digging through their garbage."

"Touché," Weylyn said, doffing his imaginary cap to me. "Luckily, Merlin doesn't mind the rain." It had been spitting all morning, one of the downsides of living in a near-tropical climate.

"Well, I do. I was planning on going to the beach today," I grunted and scowled out the window at the murky, gray sky. "So, how does it work? Merlin's . . . powers or whatever you call them?"

"Well, I don't exactly know. It's still a bit of a mystery to me. He's gotten pretty good at stopping and starting tornadoes. Snow is tricky, though."

"Wait. I thought you said he *stopped* storms, not started them."

"Yes, but sometimes the opposite happens. Not intentionally, of course."

*Well, that makes me feel better,* I thought.

"I have to say, I was surprised when you called me. I didn't think you got tornadoes this close to the coast."

"We don't," I said. "I'm talking about hurricanes."

Weylyn frowned. "Hurricanes? Merlin doesn't have any experience with hurricanes."

"Yeah, I figured. Do you think he would be willing to try?"

He didn't answer right away. Instead, he stared anxiously out the window for several seconds. "I'm just worried, you know?" he finally said, not yet looking back. "It takes a lot out of him. I don't want him to get hurt."

"I don't want him to get hurt, either, but a lot of other people could get hurt, too, if a hurricane hits."

Weylyn turned back to me, his brow furrowed with worry. "I wouldn't want that." He fiddled with his fork while he mulled it over. "Okay. We'll do it. We'll try to help you, but I make no guarantees. Like I said, this is new territory for him."

"Understood."

We shook on it and worked out some of the finer points of the deal—compensation, lodging, and so on—then Weylyn handed me his business card. It had his name printed on it in plain black type and the words *Assistant to Mr. Merlin, the Storm-Taming Pig!* scribbled beneath it in pencil.

"I'd better be going," he said. "I think Merlin is getting antsy." Sure enough, the pig was staring at us through the window, squirming impatiently.

"Wait," I said as Weylyn stood to leave. "How do I know this is, you know . . . real?"

Weylyn smiled. "I guess you'll just have to trust me," he said, then left the diner the way he came.

A minute later, I heard a knock on the window. I looked up and saw Weylyn on the other side of the glass. His voice was so muffled I could barely hear him, but it sounded like he said, "Looks like it might clear up." As he walked away, the rain clouds outside suddenly evaporated, exposing a perfectly blue swatch of sky.

I couldn't stop staring at that sky. It just didn't seem real. It was too . . . *blue*, like someone had taken a regular sky and cranked up the saturation. I looked around me to see if anyone else was as confounded as I was, but no one else seemed to notice. They just continued to sunbathe and play Frisbee like it was any other day at the beach.

Weylyn had made his point. I was convinced. Now, I just needed a cover story that wouldn't tip off my buddies at the city council—namely, Teddy Mitcham. It was obvious my dad had instructed him to keep an eye on me, so I had to be particularly careful what I said around him. If I so much as farted, my dad was sure to find out about it.

"You're not supposed to incur any new expenditures before we finalize a budget, Bobby," said an exasperated Teddy at our meeting that afternoon.

"Sorry," I said, trying to keep my cool. "I would have run it past you guys first, but it was kind of an emergency."

"An emergency?" Councilwoman Maria Flores piped in. Her mustache was almost as thick as Teddy's. "Did your car get towed from Taco Bell again?"

The other council members snickered.

"No, *Maria*. It's for the levee project. I secured funding."

The reaction from the room was mixed. Some of the council members looked mildly impressed, while others, like Teddy, looked doubtful. "Then why is money going *out* and not *in*?" he pressed.

"Because I had to hire an engineer. The money is contingent on plans that prove the project would be eco-friendly since the grant came from a green energy company."

Teddy raised an eyebrow. "Oh? And what company is that?"

"The Green Energy Company." Okay, so it wasn't the greatest name, but I thought the rest of my story sounded pretty convincing.

The council members looked at each other and shrugged, but Teddy was clearly still suspicious of me. "I'll need to see the paperwork."

"Yeah, sure. No problem."

"In the future, Bobby, don't go spending money before it's been approved."

They all thought I was a joke—and maybe they were right—but the way I saw it, I had nothing to lose. We didn't have the money to build a levee, anyway, so even if Weylyn turned out to be a fraud, it would be no worse than if I had done nothing. Well, except losing a thousand of the city's dollars to pay for an "engineer" who was really a pig. Maybe my dad would find it funny or, more likely, he'd lose me in a tragic boating "accident."

## 24

## MARY PENLORE

I'm not sure how I ended up at the beach. I just remember waking up with no plans and a ravenous craving for sunshine. The past three weeks had been difficult. Without work to keep me busy, I felt utterly useless. I could feel Quan getting frustrated with me, too. The first week, he came home every day to find me still in my pajamas. The following Monday, he laid out a shirt and jeans for me on his side of the bed. I left the outfit where it was so when it was time for bed, he had to move the clothes to pull the covers back. We never spoke about it. The gesture itself had said everything.

I folded my legs on the sand, closed my eyes, and let my breath empty me slowly. When I had fully exhaled, I lingered in that dark, airless place and tried to imagine the rest of my life. I thought maybe a little oxygen deprivation would help clarify things, shake out the cobwebs. But my mind didn't take me forward; it took me back, back to that summer with the wolves. Before I knew what was happening, a melancholy howl escaped my lungs. I looked around me, acutely aware of how foolish I must seem, but no one paid me any attention.

I nearly jumped out of my skin when I heard a howl in return. I thought it was my imagination or some teenager mocking me. I scanned the beach for the latter and saw something move out of the corner of my eye. I whipped around to face a runty, old pig with a crooked brown horn poking through his fleshy forehead. I stared at him, aghast. The pig peered back at me with an alien calmness, his glassy black eyes motionless behind fat, whiskered lids. I bent down until my face was level with him. Up close, I could see that his eyes were not completely black but freckled with browns and golds. His brow bowed into a curious arch, and he grunted the way my dad did when he had just read something confusing in the paper. I grunted back as if to say, "You and me both."

"Mary Jane?" said a voice. I didn't need to look up to know who it was. My eyes lingered on his feet, bare and muddy, shadowed by an awning of dirty rolled-up cuffs.

"Where are your shoes?" was the only thing I could think to say.

Weylyn laughed strangely—strange in that it had the timbre of a man, not the boy I had met seventeen years before. His body clearly belonged to a man, too, although his long limbs gave him a lanky, adolescent quality. His face was as I remembered it, only with fewer round edges. In my subjective opinion, he was objectively handsome.

He offered his hand to help me off the sand, and as I grabbed it, my heart gave one hard thump. My head was swimming with questions, so I just started spitting them out like a frantic game show contestant. "Howareyou? Whatareyoudoinghere? Doyoulivehere? Isthisyourpig? Whereareyourshoes?!"

"I don't wear shoes on the beach. His name is Merlin, and he's my business partner. I'm renting a place nearby because I'm helping out the mayor for a bit, and I'm doing just fine," he said evenly. I nodded as if this information were completely normal and expected. "What about you?" he asked.

I hesitated. I thought about that T-shirt and jeans flattened out on my bedspread like a paper doll and the way Quan had silently folded them and placed them back in my drawer. "Not so good," I admitted.

Weylyn studied me, not with pity but as a problem that needed to be solved. "How can I help?"

"What's a *Chaoborus*?" Weylyn asked as we sat on a bench, eating the ice cream cones we'd purchased from a nearby cart with a striped canvas awning. As we ate, we watched students wearing backpacks zip by on bikes and Rollerblades and families wait in line for tacos while their off-leash dogs scavenged for discarded popcorn on the boardwalk.

"It's a type of larva. Basically, a freshwater worm."

Weylyn stared at me quizzically. "You're right. That does sound boring," he said, oblivious to the ice cream that was melting down his forearm. Merlin, however, was closely monitoring the situation and was lapping up the raspberry-flavored puddle at Weylyn's feet.

I stared down at my own plain vanilla cone, wishing I had chosen something more interesting: mint chip, maybe, or lemon sorbet. Hell, even cookie dough had the added thrill of potentially contracting salmonella. "I guess that makes me boring, too," I said glumly.

Weylyn shook his head. "How could you be boring? You ran away from home to live with wolves. That fact alone disqualifies you from ever being boring."

"That was a long time ago. I was a kid."

"So what? Just because you're old now doesn't make you a different person."

While I tried to decide whether to take offense at his quip about my age, Weylyn continued, "If you don't like studying water worms, study something else. Bears or alligators or something else with lots of teeth."

I smiled to myself, thinking about the letter I had written to the Canis Fellowship. I was tempted to tell Weylyn about it—out of all the people I knew, he would appreciate what an amazing opportunity it was—but at the same time, I didn't want him getting his hopes up on my behalf. It was a long shot, after all. The only reason I had told Quan was because my getting accepted would affect our living arrangements.

"You're right. I do need a change," I conceded and tossed Merlin what was left of my vanilla cone. "Although, it probably won't be as crazy as running away with a boy I barely know and a pack of wolves."

Weylyn flashed me a winsome smile. "Even I thought you were crazy."

"Really?" I laughed.

"Yeah. I thought to myself, *This girl has a house and a family and she wants to run around in the woods with* me?"

I looked away, embarrassed. He was right. I had a home and a father who loved me, and Weylyn had neither of those things. I suddenly felt ashamed for not seeing that before. "I'm sorry. I never thought of it that way."

"No, no. Don't be sorry!" he said, placing his hand tenderly on my arm. "I'm glad you did, and I'm *really* glad we ran into each other again."

The warmth from his hand radiated up my arm, and my cheeks began to burn. "Me, too."


When Quan came home, I was watching an episode of *Mythological Mysteries*. He sighed disdainfully as he threw his man-purse on the kitchen table, but I barely even noticed. I was engrossed in the events unfolding on the screen in front of me. A huge tornado was barreling down on Weylyn and Merlin; then, like a disappearing act at a magic show, it was gone. The woman behind the camera gasped and thanked Jesus. "You should be thanking the pig!" I said.

"Why should I be thanking a pig?" Quan had taken his socks off and was inspecting his athlete's foot.

"I was talking to the TV." *Now he thinks I'm lazy* and *crazy*, I thought. And maybe I *was* crazy, because I had a B.S. and a year of Ph.D. studies under my belt, and yet, I was still considering the possibility that a pig could stop a tornado with his mind. The video defied everything I had learned in Physics 101, but it appeared to be authentic. It was so popular that it had even inspired a parody video on *The Tonight Show* depicting other barnyard animals fighting natural disasters: a goat stopping an earthquake; a chicken putting out a wildfire; cows launching themselves into space to deflect an asteroid. These were comped together with the help of green screens and cheesy, generated effects. The video of Merlin was too realistic to have been doctored, not without the help of a Hollywood effects house.

It wasn't just the video that had me questioning my better judgment. I believed Weylyn, or at least, I wanted to believe him. The story he told me that day on the boardwalk was sad and strange and no less than extraordinary.

*After the tornado, Meg and I moved to Alabama. I studied hard and got a scholarship for college. Meg paid for my books, and Mr. Kramer covered my room and board. Meg got sick while I was in school, and I asked her if she wanted me to move home, but she said no.*

*Merlin came with me, of course. My roommate and I hid him in a file cabinet whenever the RA came by. His name was Gordy, my roommate. He saw ghosts and said that our dorm room was haunted by the spirit of a boy who had fallen out the window throwing water balloons at coeds twenty years earlier.*

*So, there were four of us: me, Gordy, Merlin, and Joe—that was the ghost's name. Sometimes Joe would spell out messages with the magnetic letters on the mini fridge. "Hands off my Froot Loops!" and stuff like that. We never had any Froot Loops in the room, so we could only guess that that was what he had for breakfast the morning he died. Aside from that, he was pretty amenable.*

*I found out through Joe that Meg had died. I came back from my chemistry final and he had spelled her name out on the fridge. Maybe it was coincidence— her name only had three letters, after all—but it was only a few minutes later that I got the call from the doctor saying she had passed. I imagined her and Joe hanging out, sharing a box of Froot Loops, and Meg chastising him for throwing water balloons at other ghosts.*

*After school, I joined a crew that rebuilt houses that had been destroyed by tornadoes. Three days into my first project, another storm came—or maybe it was the last one returning to finish what it had started. I hadn't seen a twister since that one Christmas. I'd tried to push it out of my mind like a bad dream, but here I was again, standing inside the partially built frame of a house and a crew of people clinging to the support beams, hoping their handiwork was good enough to withstand the winds. Then . . . well, the rest is on video . . .*

When I snapped back to the present, Quan was hovering over my shoulder like an annoying parent checking on the progress of my homework. "Have you finished that application yet?"

"I already turned it in."

"You should have let me look it over first."

"It didn't need looking over," I snapped and stormed out of the room.

I crawled into bed and let my duvet form a fluffy mold of my body. Within minutes, I was deep inside a dream.

In the dream, I was standing in a barren field with a tornado barreling down on me. I didn't try to run. It was too late for that. I closed my eyes as the winds began to wrap around me. Then I heard Weylyn's voice say, "It's never too late."

I jolted awake and looked over to see Quan drooling on the pillow next to me.

## 25

## BOBBY QUINN JR.

He said we should go out to "celebrate." Those were his exact words. I hung up the phone and tried to swallow the lump that was growing like a tumor in my throat. Teddy had filled my dad in on the levee funding and the engineer I had hired, and now he wanted to take me out for lobster tails so we could "catch up." I knew this was going to happen, eventually. I had just hoped I would be able to avoid him for long enough that he would give up, but he tricked me by calling from the phone inside the bait shop. I thought they were calling to tell me the lures I wanted were back in stock.

That night, I met my dad at Crableg Joe's. Fortunately, Lacey wasn't working. The last thing I needed was two awkward conversations in one evening. The hostess sat us at a table underneath a hanging fisherman's net filled with plastic crabs, and my dad ordered a pitcher of pale ale for the table. I hated pale ale, but at least it might take the edge off what was bound to be an uncomfortable dinner.

"Soooo . . . Mr. Mayor," he began.

I winced. It was possibly the most condescending thing I had ever heard my dad say, and he had once told the governor of Mississippi to "go make yourself useful."

"Teddy tells me you funded the levee project all by yourself."

I took a generous swig of my beer and nodded. "Mm-hmm."

"What was it called again? The nonprofit who offered to fund you?"

I reluctantly swallowed and said, "The Green Energy Company."

The father-knows-best frown on his face told me one of two things: either he knew I was lying or he thought I was too stupid to know that I was being lied to. Thankfully, it was the latter. "That's what I thought. You should know that I did a little research, and there is no 'Green Energy Company.' Son, you've been scammed."

I stared back at him, dumbfounded. While I was crafting this lie, I figured my dad would take it upon himself to second-guess its legitimacy. I just never thought he would peg me for the victim. "What do you mean?" I asked.

"Con men like that prey on small communities like ours, promising to fund projects, then taking the money and running. It's lucky you only gave them that engineer's fee. They could have stolen thousands, maybe millions!" He illustrated his point by grabbing a generous handful of complimentary ketchup packets from their caddy and dumping them in the middle of the table.

My dad had unknowingly given me the out I needed. I tried not to smile when I said, "I can't believe they would do that! I mean . . . the guy seemed so nice . . ."

"That's their game. They act like your friend; then they take you for everything you've got."

I hung my head. "I feel so stupid."

"Well, at least you learned a valuable lesson," he said in that infuriatingly superior tone of his. "Next time, talk to me. I might be able to save you a lot of trouble."

I had learned something. I learned that my dad thought he was still the one running this town. I couldn't wait to prove him wrong.

## 26

## MARY PENLORE

I took Weylyn with me to Okchamali and saw the marsh with new eyes. For the first time, I didn't view it as something to be studied, collected, or measured. I saw it in terms of colors, shapes, light, and shadow, like an artist would if she were sitting down to paint.

"I don't believe in magic," I said resolutely, like a jury member declaring a verdict. *We hereby find the defendant . . . not magic!* The defendant was Merlin, of course, Weylyn his attorney.

"What makes you so certain?" Weylyn was knee-deep in the lake, searching for the "bugs" I studied. I told him he wasn't going to find any in water that shallow during the day, but he still held up every insect he could find to ask me if it was the right one.

"Because there are no scientific laws that support stopping weather with the human mind, let alone a pig. And no, not it." He had a dragonfly larva by its hind leg. He let it go, and it jetted through the water, an action achieved by a rapid expulsion of air through the anus, I explained. Weylyn shrugged, unimpressed.

"These laws . . . weren't they all considered hocus-pocus until someone proved them to be true?" he continued.

"Yes, but it takes years, sometimes decades of experimentation.

This . . . correlation between Merlin and the weather, I'd like to get to the bottom of it."

"How? With experiments?"

I could feel Merlin's wary eyes on me. "No! I just want to . . . observe."

"Observe?"

I pulled out my notebook. "See? No machines. No needles. Just me and my notebook." Merlin lost interest and began investigating a patch of wild mushrooms.

"And what if you observe something you can't explain?"

"Then I keep observing until I can explain it."

Weylyn looked amused. He scooped something up in his hands and held it out for me to see. "What about these little guys?" Sure enough, swimming around in his cupped palms were dozens of tiny translucent glassworms.

"Yeah, that's them," I said with disbelief. "They shouldn't be in the shallows this early in the day. They usually only come to the surface at night."

"I can think of a word for it," Weylyn said. "I'll give you a hint. It starts with an *M*."

"Malfunctioning air sacs? 'Cause if they were overinflating, they wouldn't be able to dive—"

"Why do you do that?"

"Do what?"

"Take something beautiful and vandalize it with skepticism?"

"Because without beauty, we'd be bored. Without science, we'd be dead." I realized then how miserable I must sound. I thought of Quan's and my first date, and how we'd spent the whole night talking about the things we disliked and found that we had a lot of those things in common. Our list of common "likes" was much shorter: coffee, National Public Radio, and hypoallergenic dog breeds. Quan isn't allergic but has an aversion to stray hair. He once shaved his head when he discovered a bird had used some of the clumps of hair from his hairbrush to build a nest. That's how I felt right now, like someone who'd rather shave off all her hair than risk another creature enjoying it.

Weylyn must have seen me cringing at my own words because he didn't even argue. "I know you're the scientist, and I don't have a fancy notebook or anything, but can I ask *you* a question?"

"Sure."

"Are you lonely?"

"No." I looked around as if I were surrounded by friends that would prove otherwise. "Why? Do I look lonely?"

"No. You sound it. Something in your voice."

"Well, I'm not. I have a boyfriend. We live together."

"I know."

Suddenly, I was furious at him, mostly because he was right.

"Sorry. I didn't mean to upset you. I was just making an observation."

"I guess you're a psychologist, too, huh?" I snipped.

"Or maybe I just care about you." Weylyn dipped his cupped hands back in the water, and the tiny creatures flitted out from between his fingers, leaving behind a starburst-shaped wake.

"You're right," I said. "I am lonely."

Weylyn glanced up at me, then looked back down at his still-cupped hands under the water, waiting patiently for something new to fill them. "Me, too."

### September 5, 1997, 13:18 CST.

*Location: Okchamali Wetlands*
*Temperature: 89°F*
*Cloudy skies*
    *Subject (pig, "Merlin") doesn't appear to be under physical stress.*
*Posture relaxed. Demeanor calm.*
    *Clouds begin to evaporate. Still no indication of stress on the subject.*

*Skies now mostly clear. Rainbow to the south. Subject rubs head against tree. Unclear as to whether this behavior is related to weather or whether he is just scratching an itch.*

*Weylyn has been watching me this whole time. Not the clouds that inexplicably evaporated, but me! I asked him why, and he said I looked so serious he thought I must be in the middle of a great discovery. But that doesn't explain why he was watching me while I ate my lunch. Maybe I had something in my teeth.*

## September 7, 1997, 15:56 CST.

*Location: Okchamali Wetlands*
*Temperature: 94°F*
*Clear skies*

*Instruct subject to generate cloud formations. Several small cumulus formations materialize. Subject does not acknowledge the event. Suggests that he is unaware of his control over it or—more likely—that it is mere coincidence. Without physical changes in the subject, it is hard to attribute the climatic changes to him. Maybe mere observation isn't going to provide the answers I'm looking for.*

*Weylyn has moved on from just watching me to writing as well! He brought a notebook of his own and has been scribbling in it all afternoon. I asked him what he was writing, and he wouldn't tell me. I threatened to seize it from him, but he just laughed and held it in the air, well above my reach. Maybe it's a diary. I wonder if there's anything in there about me . . .*

## September 10, 1997, 11:33 CST.

*Location: Okchamali Wetlands*
*Temperature: 90°F*
*Mostly cloudy skies*

*The weather is crummy, and the subject is taciturn as usual. There was a rain shower, which the subject may or may not have anything to do with.*

*Weylyn left his notebook alone while he stepped away to use the bathroom. I opened it to find that half the pages had been ripped out, leaving only blank ones except the corner of one page that didn't rip out clean. On that tiny triangle of paper, in ballpoint pen, is my name: "Mary." I find myself desperately wanting to know how the rest of that sentence reads. I would even settle for a punctuation mark because at least then I could make an educated guess. I know it's none of my business, but I can't help it. Weylyn is a mystery to me. A strange, intriguing, oddly charming mystery . . . but I digress.*

"Made any conclusions yet?" Weylyn lay mostly facedown in the grass. I had been studying Merlin for ten inconclusive days, and I could tell he was losing interest. So was I. My skepticism had turned chalky, something a swift wind might carry away at any moment. "No." I threw my notebook on the ground. "I'm stumped."

"So, no explanation? No scientific theories or formulas to rub in my face?" he said with a trace of glee in his voice.

"I do have one theory."

"And what's that?"

"You need a hobby. Then you wouldn't be watching me all day."

"I could say the same thing about you."

"I don't stare at you."

"No, but you started this whole observation charade so you could spend time with me," he said knowingly.

I blushed a little. "No, I didn't . . ."

"I'm just saying, we don't have to have some pretense for spending time together. We could just hang out."

"And do what?" When Quan and I "hung out," it usually involved studying for something.

"Anything!" Weylyn put his hands firmly on my shoulders. "It's time you had some fun, Mary."

I half expected—or rather, hoped—he was going to kiss me, but instead, he grabbed me by the hand and yanked me toward the car. "Where are we going?"

"The beach!"

We were two of only a few people on the long stretch of sand that straddled Fish Gutter's Pier and Gator Tooth Cove—I think it's safe to say the founders of Little Turtle weren't poets. On calm, cloudy days like this, the beach belonged to the gull-billed terns and oyster-catchers that used the opportunity to prey on mollusks that would normally be hidden by beach towels and beer coolers. Sea stars, urchins, and cucumbers lay soaking in tide pools that rippled like tiny spas. The air moved as it always does across the ocean, but delicately, like fingers moving across the strings of a harp. I'm no poet, but if I had found this place three hundred years ago, I would have called it something like Lullaby Beach, a name that would become increasingly ironic with the invention of plastic and pop music.

"Do you like surfing?" Weylyn asked, grinning.

"Isn't the tide a little low?" I said as I watched rolls of waves unravel onshore.

"It'll pick up. Won't it, Merlin?" Merlin was busy pulling a half-eaten submarine sandwich out of the sand. He looked up at Weylyn and grunted.

"I'll get the boards," he said and ran toward the boardwalk.

Minutes later, the wind did pick up a bit, and the waves swelled. I observed Merlin closely—every twitch of his ears, every flick of his tail—but nothing seemed out of the ordinary. "You have no idea what's going on, do you?" I said to the pig, who seemed to shrug with his eyebrows.

Weylyn came running back with two shortboards, one for each of us. I looked at them nervously. "I've never surfed before."

"Neither have I!" Weylyn whooped before running full tilt toward the water. He had stripped down to just his boxer briefs, and the lean muscle on his back and calves shuddered as he ran. He belly-flopped atop his board and paddled into the oncoming waves.

I nervously thumbed the hem of my shirt, considering my options, then grabbed the fabric in both fists and pulled it over my head. I yanked off my jean shorts, grabbed the board, and sprinted toward the waves that were rushing at me.

Water crashed across my chest, nearly knocking the wind out of me, but I powered through it. Eventually, I made it onto my board and paddled. As I crested each wave, I could see Weylyn in front of me, straddling his board while he waited for one to carry him to shore. Then I saw him being lifted like he was on the back of a great whale. I watched in awe, but what I didn't see was the massive wall of water that arched above me. The next thing I remember was my body spiraling out of control and an intense pressure in my chest. I drifted deeper, suspended like a marionette with its strings cut. Tendrils of seaweed snaked past me, and I tried to grab them in hopes they would carry me upward, but they didn't. The sun grew thinner, the water murkier.

Then there was blackness.

My eyelids fluttered open, and for a moment, the world stuttered like the frames of an old piece of film. Weylyn was bent over me, his face wrinkled with concern. Beads of seawater clung to his lips, then fell onto mine. I could taste the salt on my tongue. He turned me on my side, and the rest of the water spilled from my lungs into a puddle that was almost immediately absorbed by the sand. He stroked my wet hair. "You're okay. You're okay."

Years later, I would barely remember the way my lungs burned, but the feeling of Weylyn threading his fingers through my hair would stay with me forever.

I sat up slowly. He wrapped his shirt around my shoulders. "I'm sorry. I shouldn't have made you do that. It was too dangerous."

"No," I said, turning to face him. I thought about the hundreds of hours I had spent over the last year staring at bugs and cataloguing them; about how small my world had become: the wetlands, the coffee shop, the apartment, Quan. I imagined myself looking at Earth through a microscope and having to crank up the magnification to 1,000,000 × to be able to see the five-mile radius that I called home. Even geese fly north for the summer. I was less adventurous than a goose.

"I wanna try again!" I tossed Weylyn's shirt off my shoulders and picked up my board.

He looked uncertain. "Are you sure?"

"I promise not to drown this time," I said and made for the water, kicking up sand as I ran.

When I got back to the apartment, it was nearly seven o'clock and my clothes were soaked and gritty with sand. Quan was throwing a frozen brick of something in the microwave when I arrived. "What happened to you?"

I had no intention of lying, but when I opened my mouth, I didn't recognize what came out. "I was walking on the beach and my foot got tangled in some seaweed and I fell into the water."

Quan nodded, accepting my explanation, and punched in his cook time.

"I'm gonna take a shower," I said and scurried out of the room.

I felt exhilarated. I had another life, a secret one that I didn't have to share with Quan. I already had to put my toothbrush in the same cup as his. What was wrong with having something that was just mine? *Someone* that was just mine? Plus, I wouldn't have to field awkward questions like, *How do you guys know each other?*

*I lived with Weylyn and his wolf pack for a month when I was eleven.*

*And what's he doing here?*

*He and his magic pig are going to stop a hurricane.*

He'd have me committed, and the last thing I wanted was to be locked up now when things were just starting to get interesting.

I took a long shower, threw on an oversized sleep shirt, and microwaved my own frozen block of something. I ate my dinner on the couch while Quan played some first-person shooter game on his computer. Normally, I would hide in my room during one of his gaming marathons, but tonight, I wasn't even annoyed by his frustrated grunting. I stayed up until one in the morning, playing my own game in my head. In it, I'd wipe out again and again, and each time, Weylyn would lean over me, our noses almost touching, his breath hot on my face.

## 27

## BOBBY QUINN JR.

Everyone in Little Turtle has a hurricane story. They share them over beers with friends who've heard them a thousand times, who then chime in with their own stories that place them on top of roofs, holding their beloved child or pet in their arms. There's always a note of pride in their voices. They survived an act of God, after all. I guess that would make anyone feel powerful.

I never told anyone my hurricane story. It was too embarrassing. My family was the kind that evacuated before there was even a drop of rain. My dad was a University of Texas grad, so we'd get a hotel room in Austin and make a vacation out of it. When my friends were watching water creep up their stairs, I was watching Hank Williams Jr. on the *Austin City Limits* stage. Dad called them our "secret vacations." As far as folks in town were concerned, we were stranded in our house that was thankfully a good five miles from most of theirs.

The only hurricane story I have took place a week after Hurricane Nancy. I was fifteen and still buzzed from the UT versus Alabama game my dad managed to get us tickets to. He bought me a bright orange foam finger with a longhorn printed on the side. I loved that finger and wore it the whole ride home, not even taking it off when we stopped at Denny's for lunch.

Our house had very minor damage. The basement was a little damp, but we never kept anything of value down there, anyway. It was over one hundred degrees out, and my dad's Oldsmobile had leather seats, so I was desperate to cool down as soon as we pulled into the driveway. I stripped down to just my boxers and foam finger and ran straight to the pool. I didn't look before I jumped. I should have.

When I came up for air, I realized I wasn't the only one who decided to take a dip that day—so had an eight-hundred-pound alligator. I panicked and started screaming and thrashing, which only got his attention. Before I knew what was happening, he clamped his jaws down on what he thought was my bright orange finger. Luckily, all my real fingers were safe inside the foam fist. As he yanked the souvenir from my hand, I scrambled up the stairs to safety.

I guess I could have told it in a way that made me sound like a hero, not a dumb kid home from vacation, but I didn't. Truth was, I thought it was karma, God's way of punishing me for not facing his storm like a man. Karma or not, that didn't stop me from fleeing every storm since, until Hurricane Jolene.

She was still a tropical storm brewing off the coast of the Cayman Islands and was expected to make landfall in twenty-four hours. Suddenly doubting every decision I had made, I called Weylyn's room at the Mermaid Motel. He didn't answer, so I left a somewhat frantic, rambling message on his machine. When he called me back an hour later, he reassured me that everything was going to be fine, but I could hear the same doubt in his voice, too. I hung up the phone not feeling any better than I had when I picked it up.

Teddy Mitcham called an emergency council meeting. I contemplated skipping it because he was still angry with me over the phony Green Energy scam. At every meeting since, whenever anyone brought up projects that were in progress, Teddy passive-aggressively pretended we were exactly one thousand dollars short of being able to complete every one of them. Apparently, my error had cost the town two crosswalks, new uniforms for the high school marching band, and toilet paper for the library bathrooms. "I guess people will just have to wipe with the books," I said, trying to lighten the mood. Unsurprisingly, no one else found it funny.

I got there twenty minutes late—thanks to the Conch Street Taco Bell, who towed my car again, forcing me to walk to city hall—and by that time the damage was done. I was barely in the door when I saw both Weylyn and my dad sitting at the conference table. Merlin sat in Weylyn's lap, sniffing a plate of doughnuts that was just out of his reach. Horrified, I nearly turned around and ran the other direction when Teddy called to me, "Bobby! Weylyn was just introducing us to his *magic pig*. Why don't you have a seat?"

I sank down into the seat opposite Weylyn, trying not to make eye contact with my dad. I shot Weylyn a "what the hell are you doing here?" glance, and he returned it with a polite smile and a shrug.

"So. Bobby . . ." Teddy sounded like he might choke on his own manners. "Weylyn here tells me you didn't try to hire a levee engineer. You hired a pig to stop the hurricane."

"That's correct," Weylyn answered and smiled at me as if he had just done me a favor.

Finally, my dad spoke. I didn't need to see his face to know how angry he was. "Bobby? Is this true?"

"I don't know what he's talking about," I muttered.

Weylyn frowned. "You came to us last month and asked us to help you. I assure you that we have every intention of keeping our promise. Merlin and I are men of our word." Councilwoman Flores almost snorted her iced latte out of her nose. Weylyn didn't seem to notice.

I fixed my gaze on the plate of doughnuts to avoid having to face my dad. "I don't know what this is about. I've never met this guy before."

Finally, my dad lost his temper. "Teddy has signed checks in this man's name that prove otherwise, Bobby. You're in serious shit, you know that? Some folks would call that fraud. I bet the voters might if it comes to a recall election. Then again, if the council brings it to the state legislature, which they're considering, you might be impeached. You know what impeachment is, Bobby? It's a trial. You'll have to swear on the Bible to tell the truth, so you might as well fess up now and save yourself the public humiliation of admitting you believe in a magic pig."

I didn't know what to say. I just sat there, staring stupidly at that plate of doughnuts and thinking about what I'd tell my baby girl years from now on Take Your Daughter to Work Day. *You don't wanna watch your daddy scrubbing toilets, darlin'. Why don't you go to work with Mommy instead? Least there you get free soda and crab legs.*

I was so lost in my own thoughts that I barely realized what I was doing. Before I could stop myself, I had smashed the plate of doughnuts with my hand, squirting red globs of jelly on both Teddy and Merlin, who licked it off his snout with sticky delight. Teddy wasn't so pleased. It had gotten in his mustache, and I could only imagine how hard that thing was to keep clean. He'd probably have to shave it off.

Before my dad could continue his tirade, I bolted. When I was safely outside on the sidewalk, I took a moment to catch my breath. A minute later, the front doors opened and out walked Weylyn, carrying Merlin in his arms. He spotted me and shook his head. "I don't understand, Bobby." He looked hurt—on the inside, I mean—although he might have got some jelly in his eye. "Why didn't you tell them about us?"

"Did you not see what just happened in there?" I shouted. "Why couldn't you have just lied like a normal person? Now they all think I'm insane!"

Weylyn's eyes darkened like the storm clouds gathering overhead, and his left arm started swaying back and forth at the elbow. "You expected me to lie for you?"

"Yes! That's what people do. They lie. They don't go around telling people their pigs can magically stop hurricanes. That's *crazy*."

"You don't believe me, either, do you?" said Weylyn bitterly. I felt the first drops of rain on the back of my neck.

"No . . . maybe. I don't know." I slumped onto a stone bench and put my head in my hands. At this point, I wasn't sure what I believed. Weylyn was so sincere, and I wanted to believe him, but my dad had a talent for making me feel stupid. It almost didn't matter if Merlin's powers were real or not. I would never be able to convince my dad that I had done the right thing, and if I was being honest with myself, that's all I had really wanted, anyway. The best thing I could do now was wait for the hurricane to drown my sorry ass.

Weylyn sat down on the bench beside me. "You're right," he said patiently. "This whole thing does seem crazy, but I promise you, it's not. I wouldn't tell you we could help you if we couldn't. I've seen firsthand what Merlin can do. I've seen storms evaporate into thin air. I've seen the relief on people's faces when their homes are saved. You have no real reason to trust a word I say. I know that. But Merlin and I would still like to help if you'll let us."

I lifted my head sheepishly. "Really?"

"Well, jelly doughnuts *are* his favorite." The pig was still working the rest of the jelly off his snout with his tongue.

The way I saw it, I had nothing left to lose. "Tell him to be safe out there," I said, nodding at the choppy ocean on the horizon.

Weylyn followed my gaze and inhaled deeply like a diver coming up for air. "I will," he said before submerging once more.

## 28

## MARY PENLORE

It was all over the news. Jolene was on track to reach category-four status by the time she made landfall. I had an idea what that looked like. While I was getting my master's degree at the University of Michigan, I traveled to Florida over spring break with Habitat for Humanity and mucked houses that were destroyed by Hurricane Andrew. I shoveled muddy children's toys out of broken windows and lingered on family photos before adding them to the pile of refuse on the front lawn. I saw the markings on the doors, an inventory of the number of dead that waited inside for loved ones to come by and give them names. I had seen what a storm like that could do, so I didn't take the decision I was about to make lightly.

"How long before it makes landfall?"

"Tomorrow afternoon." Weylyn and I had been surfing all morning as the waves geared up for the next day's storm. We were sitting in the sand under the dock, Weylyn's new home since he was kicked out of his motel. I offered him Quan's and my couch, but he politely declined, saying the sound of the waves helped him sleep.

"They didn't believe me," Weylyn said as he chucked a seashell across the sand. "And Mayor Quinn denied even knowing me."

"Are you surprised?"

He shrugged. "It's not the first time I've been laughed at."

I thought hard before saying what I said next. "This isn't some cute trick, Weylyn . . . people could die."

"You don't think I know that?" he said, indignant.

"Only you know if what I've seen so far is coincidence or not. I just hope you know the difference."

He looked me square in the eyes. "Even if I said I did, like everyone else, you wouldn't believe me."

We had nothing left to say to each other, so I started my walk home. I had a decision to make, too.


Quan already had our bags packed when I got home. "You packed my bag?" I said sharply.

"I figured it would save time if I packed for you. We should leave as soon as possible." He was already grabbing his keys.

"Wait a second. Can we talk about this?"

"Talk about what?"

"I didn't ask you to pack my bag."

"I know. You didn't answer your phone, as usual. You should put on your raincoat. It's on top of your suitcase." I glanced at the pile of waiting bags. Quan's satchel was sitting on top, that awful patent law book poking out from one of the compartments. Six months' worth of resentment toward him bubbled in my throat like acid as I un-zipped my suitcase and started digging through it. "Where are my journals?"

"Oh. I don't know—"

"And my photos? What about those?"

"Go grab them, but be quick. We gotta go," he said impatiently.

"And the letter from my mom. And my postcard!"

"What postcard?"

"The one Weylyn gave me when he lived with wolves."

"Wolves? What the hell are you talking about?"

Before I could stop myself, I was shouting. "I lived with a wolf pack! I watched one of them get shot and die. It was the second-saddest thing that's happened to me after losing my mom, and you would have let all that wash away!"

Quan was obviously shocked. He put down his keys like they were a gun and I had another pointed at his head. "Mary. I don't know what you're talking about, but I do know that we have to leave. Now. So why don't you grab your journals and postcards or whatever and let's get out of here."

I thought about it for a full minute, pacing back and forth, toward the door and away. Quan watched me closely, a pained expression on his face. Finally, I answered, "I can't."

"What?"

"I'm not leaving."

"Are you serious?" Now he was angry. His jaw was so clenched I thought it might come unhinged. "What's his name?"

I guess my secret life wasn't so secret, after all. "Whose name?"

"The guy you've been cheating on me with?"

"I'm not cheating on you, Quan."

"Even if that's true, he's the reason you're staying, isn't it?"

He was the reason, but not because I wanted to die with him. This wasn't some morbid love story. I wanted to watch him and Merlin save the people of this town. I wanted him to save me. "Yes."

Quan had told me he loved me before, but there must have been something about the way he said it that didn't convince me. I loved him, too, once, but his lackluster debut performance had stayed with me, gnawing slowly at my heart and sabotaging every "I love you" he shared with me after that. Maybe he hadn't meant it that first time, but that doesn't mean he didn't love me the second or third time or that he didn't love me now. In that moment, I had no doubt he loved me. The pink drained from his cheeks, leaving a sallow mask behind, his eyes bulbous and shimmering with the promise of tears.

"I'm sorry," I added, too late.

"I hope that everything they're saying about this storm is wrong . . . for your sake," he said and handed me a letter. "It came this morning." The return address on the envelope read, *The Canis Fellowship*. By the time I looked up, he was already gone.

## 29

### BOBBY QUINN JR.

I woke to the shrill ring of my phone and rain hammering on the roof. The person on the other end of the line was no doubt my dad, calling to tell me—yet again—how badly I had fucked up. I didn't need him to remind me because outside, my mistake roared. Never before had my incompetence been so hard to ignore. It was usually the kind of incompetence that got drunk and napped in places it shouldn't, not the kind that flooded city streets and downed power lines. I had really outdone myself this time.

I buried myself deeper under the covers and waited for the phone to stop screeching. Two rings later, the machine picked up. "Bobby? Bobby, are you there?" It wasn't my dad. It was Lacey, and she sounded scared. "Bobby, please pick up!"

I jumped out of bed and ran to the phone. "Lacey? What's wrong?"

"My water just broke! I need to get to the hospital."

"Wait . . . you didn't leave town?" The day before I had told her to evacuate, but she clearly hadn't listened.

"No, I'm at my apartment," she said, panic rising in her voice. "Can you come get me?"

———

Traffic was slow because of the storm, bumper to bumper all the way to Pascagoula, where the closest hospital was located. All the while, Lacey cursed at the cars in front of us and lamented her decision to call me instead of an ambulance. "An ambulance would've had to get through all this traffic just to get to you. You would have had the baby on the ride back," I reasoned.

"Better than having it in your dirty, piece-of-shit car!" she shrieked.

I was kind of hurt. I loved my car. It was the only thing I owned that cost more than $200.

"Just hold on. Everything's gonna be fine." The doubt in my voice was obvious, but I think Lacey was in too much pain to notice.

By the time we got to the hospital almost an hour later, the storm had really picked up steam. Palm trees bowed like bendy straws, and cars skidded on the inch of water that coated the road. Part of me would rather have been in my dad's swimming pool with that alligator than watch the world I knew slowly drown.

A nurse helped Lacey into a wheelchair to take her to the maternity ward while I parked the car. The garage was full, so I had to park on the surface lot and walk through the downpour to get back to the emergency entrance. Lacey's overnight bag was drenched, and so was I as I wandered the halls trying to find where the nurse had taken her.

When I finally found her, she looked upset.

"Hey. What's wrong?"

She was close to tears. "The doctor says it's too late for drugs! I gotta start pushing when he gets back."

I sat down next to her on the bed. "It's okay. You're gonna be great."

Thunder clapped and the lights flickered. Lacey's eyes were as big as clay pigeons. "I'm scared, Bobby," she whimpered and grabbed my hand.

"Don't worry. I'm gonna keep you safe."

She nodded, reassured, then cried out in pain as she had another contraction. "Get the doctor!"

I ran out of the room to find a doctor and heard something tapping against the window at the end of the hall. A tree branch was whipping itself against the glass, *whack whack whack whack*, like it might break through at any moment. I imagined glass shattering and water flooding in like through the porthole of a sinking ship. I imagined the whole hospital underwater and motionless bodies floating in white coats and gowns, already dressed for the next part of their existence as angels.

My dad was right. Weylyn was a fraud, and so was I. Instead of taking realistic steps to build a levee, I had put my faith in a delusional man and his pet pig. If I made it through the night, I would resign from office effective immediately.

There was a loud *crack*, and all the lights went out. Doctors and nurses stumbled over each other in the dark and threw around the word *generator* in panicked voices. I could hear Lacey wailing in the other room.

"Doctor!" I grabbed the nearest one I could find. "My baby's coming."

## 30

# MARY PENLORE

I put on my raincoat and rubber boots and walked to the boardwalk in the heavy rain. I found Merlin wandering alone in front of a boarded-up tiki bar. "What are you doing here alone?" I asked him, rhetorically of course. I scooped up the little pig in my arms and headed toward the water.

The beach was transformed. It no longer bore any resemblance to the place I knew. It had turned into the heaving, rancorous thing of sailors' nightmares. A monster that danced on a graveyard of ships. I found Weylyn under the dock, standing as alert as a soldier. He looked shocked to see me. "What are you doing here?"

The rain beat so heavily on the boards above it sounded like machine-gun fire. I had to shout over it, "Because I believe you!"

Weylyn's mouth twitched briefly into a smile, then disappeared. "You shouldn't be here. It's dangerous," he said. "And what's Merlin doing here?"

"I found him on the boardwalk—"

"I told him to wait in the concessions building," he said curtly and snatched the pig from me. "You should really go."

"No! I'm part of whatever this is whether you like it or not."

Weylyn studied me like a drill sergeant evaluating a new recruit. I must have passed, because he turned silently back to the army of waves that were storming the beach.

"How much longer?" I asked.

"Not long," he said, holding Merlin tight to his chest so the tide wouldn't grab him. The pig watched the stormy sea, and I watched the pig. I didn't want to miss the moment when it happened.

It wasn't long before we were wading in almost a foot of water that would catch my legs every time a wave rolled in. "It's getting worse," I said nervously. A strong wave rocked over my knees, and I lost my balance. Weylyn reached out and steadied me before I could fall. "Hold on to this." He guided me to a cross section of two support beams. I wedged myself between them.

"Take Merlin," he said and handed me the pig. "Keep him safe."

"What? Why?"

"Please?" he pleaded.

Weylyn stepped out from underneath the dock. I shouted after him, "Where are you going? Weylyn!"

Weylyn didn't answer. He lifted his knees high and trudged through the waves that plowed against him, toward the ocean. The rain parted like a curtain as he walked through it, then closed behind him.

Now the water reached my hips. I looked down at Merlin, who was grunting anxiously. "Aren't you going to do something?" I was almost screaming. "You can make this stop! Why don't you?"

The pig looked up at me helplessly. I climbed on top of a horizontal beam and crouched there, holding Merlin in one arm and the vertical post in the other. Weylyn was nothing but a fuzzy shape now. *What was he doing out there?* I was furious at him, furious that he'd left me alone. Merlin was squealing now, probably because he saw Weylyn, too. "If you're so worried about him, then help him!" I was crying now. I had made a terrible mistake.

Then something completely inexplicable happened. It was subtle at first, so subtle I thought my eyes were playing a trick on me. The rain appeared to slow, as if the gravitational pull of the Earth had grown weaker. And it continued to slow until each drop became a liquid marble suspended in midair. I couldn't believe it, but I had to.

I could see Weylyn better now. He staggered from the force of the waves, but he held his ground. Above him, the clouds circled like sharks.

The wind died down. The tide sucked back toward the ocean like a turtle hiding in its shell, and the clouds stopped circling. Weylyn was hunched over, his body shaking like he was supporting a tremendous amount of weight, like Atlas holding the world.

Then came the storm's last stand. It let loose the only thing it had left—lightning. A dozen bolts dropped from the sky in one brilliant flash. The crack of thunder that followed rattled my bones. When the spots in my eyes had faded, I saw a clear sky, a calm sea, and Weylyn's motionless body on the sand.

## 31

## BOBBY QUINN JR.

"I had to hold the flashlight." I laughed and took a swig of beer. It was happy hour at Crableg Joe's, and I was feeling generous. I had bought the whole joint a round of beers and popcorn shrimp buckets to celebrate my good fortune. "Then Lacey screamed, 'Dammit, Bobby! You're pointing that thing right in my eye!'"

My friends who had gathered around laughed, and my little girl, Carly Jade Quinn, squawked at me from her carrier. That was the seventh time she had heard the story, so I couldn't blame her.

"So, I heard a rumor," my buddy Jake began, "that you were the one who brought that guy to town. The one they found on the beach."

Everyone watched me expectantly. I squirmed, uncertain of how honest I wanted to be. Talk of Weylyn had spread like wildfire since the hurricane, but I had mostly managed to stay out of the conversation until now. Supposedly, multiple people had seen Weylyn on the beach fending off the hurricane with his bare hands before he was struck by lightning. According to these eyewitnesses, the storm simply disintegrated the moment he hit the sand. I wasn't sure how much of this story was true—I hadn't heard from Weylyn since that day at city hall—but I liked to think that he kept his promise that day. Even if it was just fantasy, it was a hell of a story.

I scanned the faces of my friends, trying to decide what answer would result in the least amount of public humiliation. Carly Jade watched me intently over her fuzzy pink blanket, waiting to see whether her daddy would chicken out or not. I drew a deep breath, winked at her, and said, "His name's Weylyn, and yeah, I asked him to help us."

Instead of ridiculing me, my friends all looked at each other and shrugged. "Well, whatever the hell it was that you did, I guess it worked, 'cause we all still have homes to go back to tonight," Jake said, then clapped me on the back and raised his beer over his head. "To Bobby!"

"To Bobby!" my other friends toasted.

I clinked my beer bottle against Jake's and breathed a fermented sigh of relief.

"That was some storm," said a man's voice. I turned and saw my dad peering at Carly Jade from his wheelchair. For a moment, I wasn't sure whether he was addressing her or me.

"Yeah, it was," I said carefully.

"Teddy told me you've been working hard on storm cleanup. He said you've really stepped up to the plate."

"He did?" I said, surprised.

"I couldn't believe it myself," he answered, gently pinching my daughter's tiny toes.

"Would you like to hold her?"

He nodded. I pulled Carly out of her carrier and sat her in his lap. Then, for the first time since my dad's stroke, I saw him smile without any pretense, just simple joy. He looked from my daughter to me and said sincerely, "Congratulations, Mr. Mayor."

## 32

# MARY PENLORE

Weylyn had been unconscious for two days. He was lying in a room at Mercy Hospital with tubes coming out of his nose and arms like extensions of his veins, just like Mom had before she passed. I couldn't smell disinfectant without seeing her blue, cracked lips and the air that wheezed out of them.

I stayed with him most of the day, only taking breaks to go home and feed Merlin, who hardly ate what I gave him, anyway. I wasn't eating much, either, or sleeping. I kept dreaming about that day at the beach, or some version of it, but the beginning and end were always the same. It started with the sun bursting through the clouds, like it was coming up for air, and ended with me bent over Weylyn's still body, howling over the sound of the waves that lapped at his feet.

On the fourth day, I smuggled Merlin into Weylyn's room in a duffel bag, in hopes that the sound of the pig would somehow bring him back. When the nurse left the room, I sat Merlin on the bed. The pig sniffed his hair and grunted softly. Weylyn didn't respond. I lifted Merlin down and petted the velvety flesh of his ears.

The clothes Weylyn was wearing when he was brought in had been laundered and folded by hospital staff and were sitting in a pile on a chair by the bed. I noticed the corner of a piece of paper poking out from his pants pocket. I pulled it out. There were multiple pages, all wrinkled from moisture. Most of it was illegible, as the ink had run, but I did make out a few words at the top of one of the pages. The top-left corner was torn off, but I already knew what that piece said. It read:

> *[Mary] looks very pretty with her hair down. I considered mentioning that she wear it like that more often, but was worried she might think I don't think she's pretty when her hair is up. Maybe I should just tell her that her hair is pretty no matter what its configuration.*

I smiled to myself and tried to read the rest of the pages, but the ink was too smudged, so I folded them and put them back in his pants pocket.

I took Merlin home and came back that afternoon. When I arrived, Weylyn was conscious. "Weylyn? You're awake."

The young nurse who was tending to him looked at me sharply. "He isn't really in a condition to do much talking yet. I'll give you a moment, but I'd keep the chitchat to a minimum."

"May I ask your name, Nurse?" Weylyn croaked.

"Amanda."

"Amanda, I didn't think I was ever going to see this woman again. I doubt we will be discussing the weather or gossiping about celebrity misfortunes, so you need not worry about us 'chitchatting.'"

The nurse huffed and took her leave. I sat down on a chair next to Weylyn's hospital bed and said sternly, "I think we *should* talk about the weather."

"You're angry with me," he stated.

"What happened, Weylyn?"

"I was struck by lightning."

"Yes, but *why* were you struck by lightning?"

He gave a coy smile and fiddled with his hospital wristband. "I don't know, Mary. I don't control the weather."

"Don't you?" I insisted.

Weylyn let out a short laugh that launched him into a coughing fit. When he had recovered, I continued, "I think *you* stopped that hurricane. Not Merlin. I don't know how, but I think you did." I felt ridiculous just saying it, but the high of surviving a massive hurricane will make you do and say all kinds of ridiculous things. "Am I right?"

"You usually are, Mary Jane," he said; then he took my hand in his and closed his lids over the silver coins of his eyes. But I had one last thing to say before he drifted into sleep. "Weylyn, I left Quan . . . and I'm leaving in two weeks to study wolves out west."

Without opening his eyes, he said, softly yet assuredly, "And I'd like to come with you."

*book 4*

THE FOREST FAMILIAR

MELTWATER, MONTANA

1998

*33*

DUANE FORDHAM

There was only one set of tracks that led from my cabin. I used to fantasize about a second set of tracks, a woman's, ones she made walking to the yard to split logs or the coop to feed the chickens, two sizes smaller than mine with treads that left star-shaped impressions in the snow. But there was no woman.

But I did have Primrose. Every morning, I'd bring my cup of coffee with me to check on her. She was a Scottish Highland cow, a breed that bears little resemblance to the typical dairy cow. They are shaggy, prehistoric-looking creatures with mops of hair that fan over their faces. Margot, my ex, would joke that she looked like she had put her wig on backward.

Primrose was dun colored, with horns almost as big as a bull's. Despite their size, she never used her horns for anything other than scratching the occasional itch. She didn't even protest when Margot trimmed them with tinsel for Christmas.

She was about to mother another calf. Her belly hung low, and her udder was bagged with milk. It was only a matter of days before the calf would arrive, and I was as anxious as if it were my own kid. The real father was a seventeen-hundred-pound bull from Butte whose owner I paid to bring him up to Meltwater. After the deed was done and the trailer pulled out onto the main road, I couldn't help but feel the slightest bit angry, like that bull was some deadbeat running out on his family.

"Mornin', Mama." Primrose greeted me at the fence, and I patted her snout. Her breath was warm and humid against my palm and smelled like the hotel room Margot and I had shared on a trip to Florida that was supposed to save our relationship. I could tell it wasn't going to work when she reserved a room with two double beds.

Primrose used her nose to lift my hand, something she did when she was hungry. I usually just let her graze, but the winter had been a harsh one and didn't leave much in the way of vegetation. Plus, Primrose was eating for two. "I know, Rosie. I'll feed you after I drink my coffee." Only I never got the chance. Primrose butted the mug out of my hand, and I watched the brown liquid melt the snow at my feet. "All right," I said. "Message received."

I left a bale of hay for her in the barn, collected four eggs from the hens, and made an omelet with them for breakfast. Rosie was saving her milk for the calf, so I had to make the hour-and-a-half round-trip to Glacier Mercantile. I got bacon while I was there and chatted with Ellen, who ran the place. She was a pleasantly curvy woman, midthirties, with crisp, northern blue eyes. Her pupils contracted to the size of pinholes in the sun, which allowed her to stare straight into it for almost a minute without them watering. The second she showed me that trick, I was smitten.

"Heya, Duane! How you doing?" Ellen said as I walked in. She was wearing a low-cut sweater and jeans tucked into a pair of furry boots. Her blond hair was swept over one shoulder in a messy braid, and her cheeks glowed like she'd just come in from the cold. I wanted to take her to Florida, get a room with one king bed and an ocean view, and watch her eyes take in all that sunlight.

"Better now that I'm here with you," I said in my usual flirty fashion.

"Pshht! I bet you say that to all the ladies."

"Only my cow."

Ellen laughed, bringing her left hand up to her mouth. That's when I saw the ring. "Is that . . . an engagement ring?"

She wiggled her fingers as if I hadn't already noticed it. "Yep!"

"When did that happen?" I said like she'd just been diagnosed with some terminal illness.

"Last night. Moose had a fire going, and we were roasting marshmallows. He put the ring on the end of his stick and held it out and was like, 'Ellie, will you marry me?' I've never been so happy."

This was the first time I'd ever heard of Moose. I'd never even asked her if she had a boyfriend, probably because I'd hoped she secretly had feelings for me. Maybe if I had asked her out six months ago when I met her, before she went to whatever dive bar or truck show she met this Moose person at, she would have said yes.

"Wow. How long have you known . . . Moose?"

"Three months."

*Dammit.*

"I know that sounds fast, but when you know, you know."

"I'm happy for you. Really."

"Thank you." She looked down at her diamond, and I could swear her pupils contracted a little from its shine.

I grabbed my milk and bacon and got out of there as fast as I could. On my way out, Ellen told me to be careful. There was a big snowstorm coming and I was to call her if I needed anything and she'd bring it to me. I stopped at Rudy's General Store down the street and stocked up on enough canned soup and beans to last me all winter.

Eighteen inches. That's what was supposed to fall that night on top of the six that already sat fat and happy on the frozen earth. I made sure Primrose had enough feed for the next couple of days just in case I couldn't get more out to her. The snow was falling in huge, feathery clumps like God had ripped open a giant pillow. They clung to Rosie's coat, and she wandered into the barn looking like some kind of fairy-tale snow beast. I brushed the snow from her bangs, then headed back inside to a bottle of Southern Comfort and a crackling fire.

## 34

## MARY PENLORE

I was pretty certain I was falling for Weylyn Grey, but the moment I realized it for sure was not when he saved me from drowning or when he lay in that hospital bed after being struck by lightning. It was in a little roadside diner in South Dakota. After a goopy plate of biscuits and gravy, Weylyn and I ordered two pieces of blackberry pie. "Someone worked really hard to make this," he said, pointing to his slice with his fork. That's what sealed it for me, that simple appreciation for something that most of us take for granted. When he said it, I choked on my Cherry Coke and coughed violently for a minute straight.

"Mary! Are you okay?" Weylyn rushed around to my side of the booth and rubbed my back until I had finished hacking my lungs out. *Yes. I'm okay*, I thought. *I am very okay.*

I had accepted the Canis Fellowship, and Weylyn and I were driving the twenty-three hundred miles north to Mammoth National Park, Montana. Weylyn was still a little weak from his stay in the hospital, but overall, he was recovering nicely. It was early March, so we'd get to the park before the Canadian geese showed back up for spring, returning from Mason-Dixon Line states like Kentucky and Missouri. We'd tell them how far we'd traveled and watch their beady black eyes fill with respect.

"How much longer do you think we have to go?" Weylyn said after I had caught my breath.

"A day and a half. Still plenty of time for you to explain everything," I said and took a bite of my pie. It was still warm. "Mmmm. This is really good." I looked across the table to see Merlin bent over Weylyn's plate, his face covered in pie filling. "Apparently, Merlin thinks so, too."

"Merlin! No!" Weylyn reached across the booth to grab him, but the pig squealed, jumped out of his reach, and hid under the table. Weylyn sat back down on his side of the booth and looked sadly at his empty, blackberry-smeared plate. "I've told him a hundred times that all he has to do is ask and I'll share with him."

"I think it's the sharing he has a problem with."

"Yeah, I guess . . ." Weylyn eyed my piece of pie. It was so warm that the whipped cream was melting and sliding off the side. "Do you think you're going to eat all of that?"

"I dunno. Do you think you're going tell me what happened on that beach?" I shoved my fork through the golden, flaky crust and lifted a giant piece to my lips.

"I told you. I don't know," he insisted and tentatively reached for my plate. I pulled it out of his reach.

"Yes, you do," I said, chewing.

Weylyn scowled. "You're the scientist. Shouldn't *you* be telling *me*?"

I took another big bite. He whimpered slightly. "I don't know what *you* saw," I continued, "but what *I* saw defied the laws of physics."

"Now you're just being dramatic."

I started shoveling pie into my face faster than I could swallow. Weylyn watched in horror. "Okay, okay! I'll tell you. Just leave me a bite. Please?"

I laid my fork on the table and washed the rest of my bite down with soda. "Okay," I said. "Start from the beginning."

Weylyn heaved a sigh and peered out the window at the desolate stretch of highway. "The weather . . . ," he spoke quietly. "It's tied to my emotions, I think. If I'm in a bad mood, it rains. If I'm in a good mood, it's sunny. And then there's the damn rainbows."

I looked out the window and saw a rainbow hovering over the I-90. "What's wrong with them?"

"I can't eat a piece of cake or laugh at a joke without one of those ridiculous things showing up."

"You're making that up," I said and turned back to Weylyn, who was lifting a forkful of my pie to his mouth.

"Hey!" I was about to snatch the plate from him and finish it off myself, but my stomach hurt from scarfing down the first two-thirds. "This conversation is *not* over," I said. Weylyn grinned back at me, his lips purple with blackberry syrup.

That rainbow followed us all the way to Billings, Montana, where trails of snow snaked across the highway. I hadn't driven in snow in years, not since I left Michigan, so it made me a little anxious. I could tell it made Weylyn nervous, too.

"It's too bad you *don't* have magic powers," I said, half jokingly, "or you could take care of all this."

Weylyn didn't find it funny. "I don't joke about snow," he said brusquely, pulling up the fur-trimmed hood of his coat and closing his eyes.

Five hours later, we arrived in Meltwater, a small town on the west end of Mammoth National Park. We had been set up in a log cabin just north of town at the foot of the Elders, the three highest peaks in the park. I could tell Weylyn immediately felt at home in this wild place. He didn't even wait until the car had stopped before he jumped out and ran into the trees to gather firewood. "Why don't you wait until we've looked inside?" I called after him, but he was already darting around, scooping piles of dead branches into his arms. "How about you, Merlin?" I asked the pig in the backseat. He grunted in affirmation and followed me into the cabin.

The interior was plain, but cozy. It had the most basic Western comforts: a wood-burning stove, running water, electricity, bed. The only adornment was a century-old quilt that hung on the back of the sofa, depicting wolves running through trees after fleeing deer. Stitched on the top left corner was a solitary wolf howling at the moon. I imagined that quilt had probably been there since the cabin was built, long before anyone really studied wolves in an empirical sense, back when wolves were something men wrote poetry about, not reports.

The door swung open and Weylyn came bustling into the room, his arms heavy with kindling. He was out of breath with excitement. "This place is incredible! I found three types of edible mushrooms and dozens of raspberry bushes. It'll be a few months yet until we see berries, but imagine the kind of summer we'll have! We can have cake with raspberry syrup every single day!" He dumped the pile of wood at the foot of the stove. "Do you have matches? I'll get a fire going."

His enthusiasm was so infectious that I let out a small laugh.

"What? Did I say something funny?" he asked.

"No," I said, smiling. "I'm just glad you're happy."

"You seem rather happy yourself."

I thought about it, smiled shyly, and nodded. It was quite possibly the happiest I'd ever been.

There was only one bed, and Weylyn insisted I take it. "I used to sleep in a cave with a wolf as a pillow. I have no problem taking the couch." *The bed is big enough for both of us,* I wanted to say, but was afraid of sounding too aggressive.

I had never been very good at flirting. My sexy voice usually came out sounding slightly angry, which I think was some kind of unconscious defense mechanism. Quan once compared it to a dog. "They wag their tails when they're happy and when they're mad. How are you supposed to know the difference?" He quickly learned the difference when I grabbed his coffee and dumped it down a sewer drain. I liked Weylyn, and I didn't want to scare him off, so I decided to play it cool and let things happen in their own time.

## 35

## DUANE FORDHAM

I woke up on the couch the next morning with a headache, only it wasn't really morning. It was just past noon, and it was freezing. I yanked my afghan around me and wandered over to the thermostat. I had the heat cranked all the way up, but it was only fifty-five degrees. Out the window, I could see the snow had stopped falling, but it lay in steep drifts that were probably up to four feet deep. My front porch looked like one lumpy mass of freezer burn. The thermometer hanging outside the window read twenty below.

After coffee and a hot shower, I pulled on thermal underwear, two pairs of sweatpants, a sweatshirt, a fleece pullover, and wool socks. To go outside, I added a fur-lined parka, waterproof pants and boots, leather gloves, and a wool hat. The front door required a bit of a shove, but I managed to open it without too much snow spilling back inside the house. I grabbed a shovel and went to work carving a path for myself down the porch steps, around the side of the house, and down the hill to the barn. I had drunk three cups of coffee, but my head was still pounding. There was a time in my life when I could drink half a bottle of Southern Comfort and go mountain climbing the next morning. At forty-one, those days were long gone. If country music has taught me anything, it's that getting drunk probably isn't the best method of dealing with heartbreak. But I'm a traditionalist.

I was halfway down the hill when I heard a low, mournful bellow coming from the barn. I wasn't unfamiliar with the sound. Primrose had bawled like that after I had sold her last calf to a neighboring rancher.

I ran. Or tried to. It was more like plowing the snow with my legs. I dug in there with my hands to loosen it up, but it was slow going. Rosie's heartsick song continued until I finally managed to reach the door. I shoveled the nearly five feet of snow that was holding it shut out of the way and shoved it open.

Primrose stood in the middle of the barn standing over the body of her newborn calf, its coat still sticky with fluid. It didn't move or appear to breathe. Then I saw the wolf, a young male. It was lying on its side with a huge, gaping wound in its abdomen. I approached Rosie slowly so as not to spook her and noticed red on her right horn, not red tinsel or ribbon, but blood, cracked and crusted like it had been there all night. I bent over the calf and Primrose bellowed again, this time like she was pleading me to save it. But I couldn't. The calf was dead—Maisy, that's the name I had picked out for her. Maisy was a beautiful calf, coal black with round eyes that were wide with fear. I found myself crying. If I had only been sober, maybe I would have heard the attack and stopped it before it was too late. Rosie had done the best she could without me.

I left Maisy where she was to give Primrose a little more time to say good-bye, wrapped the wolf's body in a tarp, and dragged it to the far end of the pasture. The ground was too frozen to bury it, so I left it in a snowdrift, hoping it would act as a warning to the rest of its pack. If they decided not to heed it, then they'd have me to answer to.

## 36

## MARY PENLORE

I woke at the stinging hour of 4:00 A.M. to meet my fellow researchers. Hitchhiker's Road was closed for the winter, so instead of meeting at the main outpost, we met at an old brick building on the bank of a hot spring called Roslyn's Cauldron. Vapor rose from its glassy surface like exorcised spirits searching for a new place to haunt. There I was met by three strangers, two men and a woman, cocooned in green parkas. Apparently, my reputation preceded me. "This must be the Lobo Girl!" said a bearded man, early fifties, who I knew as zoologist Kurt Dobbs. He was famous in the scientific community not for his research but the three fingers he lost in an altercation with an alpha female. Wolves rarely approach humans, so Dr. Dobbs must have done something to provoke her, although he was all too quick to let the wolf take the blame.

"People usually call me Mary," I said firmly and held out my gloved hand. For someone with only a thumb and index finger, Dobbs's grip was surprisingly strong.

"Impressive," he said condescendingly. "Most feral children never learn to speak."

"Self-taught. Imagine what I could have done at the school you went to."

Dobbs's eyes burrowed into mine. "You should know, I wasn't in-cluded in the selection process. If I had been, you'd still be picking bugs out of swamps." He turned to the other male researcher. "You attach the toboggan to the Vmax?"

The other researcher nodded.

"Good. I need a cigarette. Meet me out there in three."

When Dobbs left, it wasn't just me who sighed with relief; so did the other woman. "I was hoping he'd get here late so I could warn you. He's been in a bad mood ever since he lost his fingers."

"But that was years ago."

"I know," she said wearily. She had long, inky hair and a cinna-mon complexion. Her high cheekbones suggested Native American heritage. I guessed Flathead because the reservation was not far from the park. "I'm Elka, by the way."

"And I'm Griffin," the male researcher cut in. He was late thirties or maybe early forties with peppered hair that most people his age would dye. He had the perpetually windburned face of a professional skier without the physique and wore glasses that probably fogged up every time he walked indoors. "So. Is it true?"

"Is what true?"

"Your story. Did you really live with wolves?" They examined me skeptically.

"Only for a few weeks," I said, now embarrassed. "I went to public school. My dad was a butcher."

Griffin laughed. "You don't have to convince us. Just him." He nodded out the window at Dobbs, grabbed his pack, and headed toward the door. "Welcome to the team, Lobo," he added. Outside, the two men jetted off on their snowmobiles, Griffin pulling a large sled behind him.

"What's the sled for?" I asked Elka.

Her eyes landed on a picture of a wolf taped to the wall. Out of the nine pictures that hung there under the heading *Nomad Pack*, this wolf was the biggest, almost certainly the alpha male. "It's for Amarok," she said with the reticence of a woman in mourning. "Come on. I'll take you to meet the family."

I was assigned to the Nomads, one of five packs that called the park their home. It was a two-hour hike to where Elka's tracker said the pack was located. "Normally, we'd take one of the snowmobiles, but Dobbs doesn't like sharing," she explained as our boots dragged through over a foot of powder, leaving tracks that looked more like skis than feet. The sun flared over the tremendous glacial peaks that rose on either side of us, artifacts of an ice age long gone. Every summer, a little more of the ancient ice tumbles down the mountainside to melt in puddles like common snowmen. As the glaciers slowly vanish, the forest grows: red cedar, cottonwood, hemlock, lodgepole pine—whose bare trunks extend a hundred feet or more before their branches bear needles. I craned my neck to see the underbellies of branches that cradled soft bundles of snow. It was likely the only green I'd see until the May thaw.

The pack had settled in a valley near Compass Lake. Elka said they had a fresh caribou kill and would likely spend the next day or two sleeping it off and coming back for seconds. When they did relocate, it would probably be to one of the park's other lakes. "We call them our swim team," said Elka. "When they settle, it's never farther than eight hundred meters from a lake."

I could see why. Compass Lake was a perfect coin of cerulean glass in the purse of five snow-swaddled peaks, a blue gem in a white crown.

Elka's GPS led us the next two miles to the Nomad pack. When we reached them, they were sprawled out on the snow, bloody, like victims of a massacre, only the blood was that of the caribou carcass that lay hollowed out next to them.

"Wow. That's a big girl," Elka said, meaning the caribou. "Timber probably took her down. She's the fastest." Elka pointed the wolf out to me. She was small, a natural sprinter with long, muscular hind legs. She lifted one and licked at the matted blood.

Quill, a female with a black-tipped tail, lounged next to her. Her three nieces were tugging on her ears and tail to get her to play. She snapped at them, clearly not in the mood. "Quill is Amarok's sister. And that's Astrid, Wisp, and Rabbit." Elka tried pointing to the right pups as she said their names, but they were wiggling too much for me to tell which was which.

"And that old girl over there is Cinder." Cinder's once jet-black coat was white around the muzzle and neck. Her eyes blinked lazily as she watched the pups. "She's the grandma, Amarok's mother. She used to be the alpha female before Amarok's father died, but the other wolves still hold her in high regard."

A coal-colored wolf with amber eyes paced back and forth next to the carcass. "That's Amarok's brother, Peat, the omega. He's not allowed to eat until the others are finished." Peat tried his luck and crept toward the carcass, but a large female snarled at him and he backed off. She was light gray save a dark patch that extended from the beginning of her snout to the base of her ears like a veil. "That's Widow," Elka explained, "the alpha female. She probably thinks Amarok is coming back, so she's making Peat wait." Peat sulked away from the rest of the pack, his skin stretching against his bones as he walked. He sat down, keeping his eyes on the caribou and panting heavily.

"How long will it take them to realize Amarok's not coming back?" I asked.

"Tomorrow, I'd guess. Widow will take it hard. As far as alphas go, they were very close."

"Do you think Peat will transition into the alpha role?"

"I doubt it. He's an untouchable, an omega for life." Peat rested his chin on his paws, his bony shoulder blades spreading like gargoyle wings behind his head.

We had been standing for only twenty minutes before the cold started to gnaw through my parka. I had already lost feeling in my fingers and toes, and my bottom lip was cracked and bleeding. Elka noticed me trembling. "Don't worry, Mississippi. You'll get used to it."

"Mississippi . . . Tell Dobbs I like that better than Lobo."

"Tell him yourself. He finally stopped calling me Pocahontas just last week."

I closed my eyes briefly and imagined wiggling my toes into warm, yellow sand.

Hours later, I arrived back at the cabin. Weylyn was curled up on a quilt by the fire with a stack of papers in front of him. He looked up at me and smiled. "Welcome home! I figured you might want a bath, so I turned on the hot water heater. And there's coffee in the pot."

"Thanks," I said through chattering teeth. I walked to the kitchenette and tried to pour myself a cup, but my hand shook so badly only half of it made it inside the ceramic wall. I didn't care. I gulped it down, nearly burning the roof of my mouth.

"Why don't you join me by the fire and get warm?" Weylyn scooted over to make a spot for me next to him on the quilt. I took off my boots and lay down with my toes precariously close to the flames.

"How was your day?" Weylyn asked.

"Cold," I said as my toes tingled back to life. "And kinda sad."

"Sad?"

Before I left for the day, I had seen Griffin drag Amarok's body back to camp. He had a three-inch hole in his side, gored to death by the horn of his prey. "Hey! Where's the cream filling?" Dobbs mooed and looked right at me. I said nothing and went inside to fetch a tarp.

"The alpha male of my pack was killed by cattle. They found him lying just outside a pasture," I elaborated.

A familiar expression crossed Weylyn's face, like a door closing on a memory. "That's a shame."

"Yeah." I expected Weylyn to ask more questions about the wolves—he was practically part wolf himself, after all—but he didn't. He just went back to scrawling something on a piece of paper in his lap as if I had never brought up the subject.

"What are you writing?" I asked, trying to hide my disappointment that he hadn't been more curious about my work.

"Well, first I wrote my name. I don't have a phone number, so I skipped that. Now I have to write my address. What *is* our address?"

"I mean, what are you filling out?"

"Oh! A job application for a logging company." I must have looked surprised, because he followed it up with, "It's time for Weylyn Grey to make an honest living. I even listed it in my 'skills' section just so there was no confusion." He proudly held up what looked like a résumé and pointed to his list of "special skills." *Honesty* was one of them, along with *positive attitude* and *punctuality*.

"I'm not sure those count as special skills, Weylyn. Those are qualities they just expect you to have."

Weylyn lowered the résumé, disappointed. "Then what qualities do I have that they *wouldn't* expect?"

"Weather manipulation?"

Weylyn looked unamused. "I'll just put *wilderness skills*."

"Fifteen Glacier Road West. That's our address."

"Thanks," he said and copied the address with the careful penmanship of a man with something to prove.

"I don't think I've ever been this tired in my whole life," I groaned and closed my eyes. My whole body ached, and my thawing fingers and toes felt like they were on fire. It was possible my toes *were* on fire, but I was too tired to sit up and check. As I drifted to sleep, Weylyn gently pulled the wet socks from my feet and carried me to bed. After he tucked me in, I could swear I felt him kiss me lightly on the forehead, but I may have already been dreaming.

I woke that night to a deep, subterranean silence. At first, I thought I had gone deaf, but a quick cough eased my fears. Out the window, snowflakes drifted softly, emitting a faint bluish glow like embers of a dying star. I pulled another blanket over me, my fourth, and was about to close my eyes when I saw something move outside.

The markings on her face were unmistakable. It was Widow. She stood as still as a statue, hot puffs of air jetting from her nostrils, her eyes fixed on the cabin. I thought she was looking at me, then realized she was peering into the next window over, Weylyn's.

The next morning, I decided it was a dream. Weylyn was still fast asleep when I left, so I made sure to lock the door behind me. My dreams would have to find another way in.

## 37

## DUANE FORDHAM

/

"You got a permit?" asked Gus as we sat on a felled tree to eat our lunches. It was one of those days that looks like summer from the tree line up even though there's snow on the ground. Supposedly, it was meant to stay like that all week. Lindsay, the owner, said he wanted one hundred loads of lumber before the next snow.

"A permit for what?" I asked as I popped open a Coke.

"Wolf hunting. State issued over three thousand just last month." He peeked inside the sandwich his wife had made for him. "Shit. Tuna. You like tuna? I'll trade ya," he said, waving his sandwich in the air like a flag.

"Sure. Why not?" I said and traded my sandwich for his.

"You're one helluva guy, Duane. Thank—what the hell is this?" Gus parted the two pieces of bread to reveal a creamy lump of tuna salad.

"You didn't ask what kind it was."

"You son of a bitch." Gus sloppily mushed the sandwich back together and shoved it back at me. "Tomorrow, pack turkey on rye. And a pickle."

Gus and I started working at Blackroot Timber on the very same day eighteen years ago. On that first day, I saved his leg from getting caught in a choker, and he tackled me out of the way of a tree after I made a bad cut. It was for that reason—maybe the only reason—I called him my friend.

"I thought hunting wolves was illegal."

"Used to be. Then they started spreading like wildfire. Now they're 'bout as endangered as house cats." Gus ripped into a piece of beef jerky. "I got mine back in November. Haven't used it yet. If you get one, we could make a weekend of it. A little hunting, a little camping, a lot of drinking."

I wasn't thrilled with the idea of spending time alone with a drunk, armed Gus, but I didn't say no. I had never really thought of wolves as a threat. I sometimes saw them in the woods, gliding over the snow like shadows, but as soon as they saw me, they'd bolt in the other direction. I even liked listening to their howls at night. The eeriness of the sound soothed me, like a train whistle or a roll of thunder. But it was different now. They'd taken Maisy from me, from Primrose, and I'd be damned if I'd let them take her, too. "Where do I get one?"

"Moody's has 'em. Do me a favor and pick me up some Coyote Cologne. The little shits love the stuff. Should work for wolves, too, since they're basically just big coyotes." *Wolves are nothing like coyotes*, I thought, but if Gus wanted to spray himself with coyote piss, who was I to argue?

I had been assigned a greenhorn to train the second half of the day. He had spent the morning with the fallers, and now it was my job to show him the ropes—or rather, the cables—of yarding logs. When I saw him loping down the hill like a happy, dimwitted animal, I knew it was going to be a long afternoon. "Whoa, buddy! Where's the fire?"

"Fire?" He looked over his shoulder in case a blaze had crept up behind him.

I sighed, already frustrated. "There's no fire. Jesus Christ. What's your name?"

"Weylyn Grey," he said and handed me a small card. It was white with his name typed in black ink at the top. Underneath, he had handwritten *Logger* in pencil. I stared at it for a second, baffled, then laughed out loud. "What the hell am I supposed to do with this?"

He smiled confidently and said, "The guys this morning all called me greenhorn. That card is so you don't have to."

I gave the kid credit. He had balls. "Okay. Here's the deal: You pay attention to everything I say. You memorize every word, every breath, every fart. You do that, and I'll call you by your real name. Deal?"

"Deal. What should I call you?"

"King of the Goddamn Mountain."

He wasn't as dumb as he looked. It only took him two tries to properly set the choker. I didn't even have to tell him to clear out when the lines were set. When we were at a safe distance, the carriage dragged the first of the logs up the hill and successfully deposited them on the landing. Same with the second load. Weylyn set the next three chokers with mechanical efficiency, like he had been doing it his whole life. He was all business until the logs began their ascent; then he'd take a moment to admire his work as they danced through the air like chimes caught in the wind.

By the end of the day, our crew had twenty-two loads headed to the mill. "Is that good?" Weylyn asked as we made our way up the rugged hill.

"That's good for a summer day. In winter, we don't usually count on more than sixteen. You worked hard today. Good job, Weylyn."

He smiled at the sound of his name.

"But that doesn't mean you get to slack off now. There'll be days harder than this one, I promise you that."

"I'm here to work," he said, tapping on his hard hat with his fist.

"That's all it takes. Hard work and not being a dumb-ass." I pointed to Vince Desoto, who was standing on a pile of felled trees smoking a cigarette. "See anything different 'bout that guy over there?"

Weylyn squinted. "Is he missing an eye?"

"Yep. One day he overloaded the carriage and the cable broke. Got him right in the eye." Vince noticed us staring and flicked us off.

"Don't be a dumb-ass," I repeated and slapped Weylyn on the back. "So, where are you from?"

"Michigan, Oklahoma, Alabama, and Mississippi," he rattled off without missing a beat.

"That's a lot of places."

"Yeah. I've moved around a lot. Not always by choice. I'd like to stay here for a while, though. The forests remind me of my home in Michigan."

"Oh, did you live near a forest?"

"No, I lived in one."

Before I could ask him what he meant, out of the corner of my eye, I saw a flash of fur through the trees. "Did you see that?"

"See what?"

I stopped to get a better look, but all I saw was trees and brush. "Never mind."

As we followed the skyline the rest of the way up the hill, I could swear I heard the faint padding of paws on the snow.

## 38

## MARY PENLORE

When I was young, my mom read me fairy tales. One in particular stuck out in my mind, "The Death of the Good King." He was beloved by all his subjects, and he left behind three daughters: Farwynna, Fionella, and Fahn. They grieved for nine straight days, and on the tenth, they were visited by the ghost of their father.

"Oh, good and just king, our father!" Farwynna, the eldest, cried. "I have done nothing but mourn for you for ten days! My garden is wilted because I do not tend to it. Wise king, what, pray tell, should I do?"

The good king held his eldest's hand and said, "Fairest Farwynna, do not mourn for me, for I am with you in your garden. I am the buds on the flowers and the fruit on the trees. I am the roots that bring it water and the sun that gives it life. I *am* your garden."

Farwynna's tears stopped running. "Thank you, Father!" she said and went outside to tend to her plants.

Next, Fionella, the middle child, spoke up. "Oh, good and just king, our father! I, too, have mourned for ten straight days, and I do not have the stomach to eat a single crumb. I miss the breads and meats that lay in our pantry, but I cannot eat out of love for you. Wise king, what, pray tell, should I do?"

"Fairest Fionella, do not mourn for me, for I am in the foods that fill your belly. I am the flour in the bread and the blood in the meat. I am the yeast that causes the dough to rise and the heat that cooks it. I *am* your food."

Fionella kissed the good king on the cheek. "Thank you, Father!" And she ran off to the pantry.

Finally, the good king's youngest and indisputable favorite, Fahn, hesitantly approached her father. "Oh, good and just king, my father. I have mourned for as many days as my sisters, but I fear I will mourn for many more. I do not have a garden to tend to, and I do not have the same love for bread as Fionella. Serving you and the kingdom was my only love. Wise king, what, pray tell, should I do?"

The good king pulled his daughter close to him. "Fairest Fahn, if you must continue to mourn, do it not for me."

"Then who shall I mourn, good king?"

"Mourn for the kingdom. For I have no sons."

It was then I'd ask my mom, "Why is he sad he doesn't have a son?"

"Because he can't leave the kingdom to his daughters. If he had a son, he'd know the kingdom was in good hands, but since he doesn't, he's worried a bad king will take over," she'd reply patiently and pull my blanket over me.

"Poor king . . . ," I'd mumble before wandering into a dream.

Amarok had no sons. His three pups were all female, so there was no one to pass his throne to, no one to carry on his name, so to speak. The kingdom mourned for him, and we mourned for the kingdom.

It was Widow who found the blood. She had gone off on her own to find him and caught his scent. For days, Widow led the funeral procession through the woods, wind picking up the hairs on her face like the flutter of black netting. The other wolves howled for their friend in minor keys, their voices shaky and flat. Widow was silent. She would need to find a new alpha, but until then, she had to lead.

I tried to talk to Weylyn about Widow but was met with the same polite indifference that he'd shown the night I'd told him about Amarok's death. It was strange to me that someone who'd spent the better part of his childhood with wolves wasn't more curious about the ones that practically roamed his backyard. Granted, that was a long time ago. He'd been living among people for almost twenty years now. When I met him, he was more wolf than man, and now he was more man than wolf. Maybe I had imposed a little of my own nostalgia for that time on him. If so, it was unfair of me to expect his undivided attention every time I uttered the word *wolf.*

And yet, it didn't feel right that my life with the wolves and my life with Weylyn were kept separate. I wanted to show him my world just as he had shown me his many years ago. "Hey, Weylyn," I said.

Weylyn looked up from his crossword puzzle. "Yeah?"

"I want to show you something."

Weylyn moved through the forest with such ease that I sometimes forgot I was the one leading us. While I glanced down at my feet to make sure I didn't trip, Weylyn peered up at the chandeliers of ice-covered spruce needles that sparkled like crystals. Occasionally, he would reach up and run his fingers across them as if they were glass chimes that needed to be played. As he did, loose snow would shake free from the boughs above, hissing gently as it caught the wind that whipped down from the mountain.

"I can't wait to see this place in the summer," Weylyn said over the crunching of our boots in the snow. "We could go hiking and fishing, or we could pitch a tent and camp out somewhere."

"Since when do you need a tent?"

"Oh, it's not for me."

I tried to picture myself sleeping in a tent while Weylyn slept outside my nylon door, but I couldn't. Instead, I imagined the two of us curled up in the same sleeping bag under a spray of stars. "I'd rather sleep outside," I said.

By the way Weylyn looked at me then, you'd think he'd read my mind. I could feel my skin grow hot beneath my parka and quickly looked away. "We don't have a tent, anyway," I added tersely, but I could still feel Weylyn's eyes on me.

"Outside it is, Mary Jane," he said. I could hear the smile in his voice.

We walked for another twenty minutes or so before we saw the Nomad pack about a hundred yards away on the bank of a frozen creek. Weylyn stopped dead in his tracks. "Is that your pack?"

"Yes! Come closer. I want to introduce you." I grabbed his hand and led him to the edge of a rocky outcrop that overlooked the ravine where the wolves were resting. "This," I said, proudly, "is the Nomad pack."

Weylyn's reaction was not what I'd hoped it would be. He looked uneasy the way most people would if you dragged them into the woods to look at wolves. But Weylyn wasn't most people. Weylyn *was* a wolf, or at least, he used to be. "What's wrong?" I asked.

"Nothing," he said, although it was painfully obvious he was trying to spare my feelings. "I'm just . . . surprised."

"Sorry, I should have said something."

"No, it's fine. I just never thought I'd be this close to a pack again."

"I thought you missed being around them," I said, gesturing to the wolves.

"I do. I think about them every day. But I like my new life, too, you know. I have a job. I have a home. And I get to see you every day."

I felt like a total idiot. I'd made Weylyn hike an hour in the snow just to try to re-create some childhood fantasy I had of him, when all he wanted to do was hang out with me in our tiny cabin and play cards. "You mean you aren't bored?"

Weylyn laughed a little too loudly, causing some of the wolves to turn their heads in our direction. "Look around, Mary. How could I be bored in all of this?" He scanned the towering tree-trimmed peaks before his gaze settled on me softly like silt. "And like I said. I have you."

I blushed, flattered to be considered in the same category as forests and mountains. "How about we head back and make some hot chocolate?" I said.

Weylyn nodded, but before we could turn to leave, something caught his attention. I looked down into the ravine and saw Widow watching us intently. I turned back to Weylyn, who met her gaze with his own sharp silver stare, and the two of them studied each other cautiously for several moments before Weylyn broke the trance. "Let's go," he said abruptly, and we followed our own footprints back the way we came.

## 39

# DUANE FORDHAM

I stopped at Moody's after work and was helped by a man behind the gun counter who introduced himself as Moose. He was like a white trash Frankenstein's monster: huge and badly constructed with arms of different lengths and a large forehead that looked like it was built for ramming males of the same species. "Ellen's Moose?" I asked.

"How do you know Ellen?" he returned suspiciously.

"Oh, I shop at her store sometimes," I said, as blasé as I could, considering my heartsickness.

He smiled, apparently sufficiently convinced I wasn't screwing his fiancée. "What can I help you with?"

"I need a hunting permit. For wolves."

"No problem, man," he said and retrieved paperwork from behind his counter. "Just need to see your ID." I handed him my driver's license and started filling out the paperwork. He pointed to a taxidermy wolf head mounted on the wall, his eyes twinkling with pride. "That one's mine." I looked up at the wolf, its lips pulled back into a snarl, white teeth gleaming in the fluorescent light.

"Impressive," I said despite being a little disgusted. Moose had clearly just killed that animal for shits and giggles.

"Got her right in the heart," he crowed.

I nodded politely and continued writing. What Ellen saw in this guy I had no idea, but I doubt it was the wolf head that did it.

I got home and went to check on Rosie. It had been a few days since the attack, and she still wasn't eating much. I had been leaving her hay because I kept the barn locked when I was gone and she couldn't graze. She had barely touched it. I could even feel her ribs through her coat, something I would have never been able to do before. "Don't worry, girl," I cooed and ran my fingers through her hair. "I'm gonna make this right."


I agreed to go hunting with Gus on the condition that he let me have the first shot. "No problem, man," Gus said, smoke jetting from his nostrils. We were sitting in the back of my flatbed on our cigarette break. I didn't smoke, but Gus smoked enough for the both of us. "I'll tell you what: I'll give you the first two."

"Thanks, man," I said.

Gus nodded and flicked ash over the side of the truck. "You got a score to settle. I'll help you in any way I can even if that means killin' the fucker with my bare hands!" He mimed breaking the wolf's neck, whimpered like a dog, and laughed.

I shook my head. Gus could be a real prick sometimes.

Then something caught his attention over my shoulder. "What're *you* lookin' at, greenhorn?"

I turned to see Weylyn standing there, awkwardly holding an un-lit cigarette between his thumb and index finger. One of the guys must have given it to him because he clearly had no clue what to do with it. "Nothing. You talking about wolves?" he asked, taking a few steps forward.

"Yeah. What about it?" Gus snapped.

"Gus, shut up," I said, then turned back to Weylyn. "You need a light?"

Weylyn glanced down at the cigarette pinched between his forefingers. "Oh. No, thank you. I don't smoke."

"Do you drink?"

"On occasion."

"I'm asking 'cause me and the crew are going out for beers at Cutters after work. You're welcome to join."

I could hear Gus open his mouth to protest, so I continued before he had the chance to speak. "We're going straight there once we wrap for the day. You in?"

"Yeah. That would be great," he said, pleased.

"Great. See you later, then."

"See you. Oh, and here . . . you'll probably get more use out of this than I will," Weylyn said as he handed his unused cigarette to Gus. Then, just before leaving, he added, "You know, wolves are really gentle animals if you get to know them. And I wouldn't try to kill one with your bare hands unless you're prepared to lose both of them."

As Weylyn walked away, I stifled a laugh. "Oh, you think that's funny, do you?" Gus said, tossing the cigarette in the dirt. "Why'd you invite that little piece of shit?"

"Because the crew's going out, and he's on the crew. What's your problem with him, anyway?"

"I dunno, man. He just pisses me off. Like how he's smiling all the goddamn day. Fuck the wolves. I'll use my bare hands to slap that stupid grin off his face."

I didn't bother responding. When Gus started on one of his rants, it was best to just let him talk until he got bored of listening to himself. Plus, I knew we were never going to see eye to eye on the whole Weylyn thing. I thought he was an all right kid, a little peculiar maybe, but he was a hard worker and a fast learner. As his boss, that was all I could ask for.

While Gus continued to list all the ways Weylyn had offended his masculine sensibilities, I noticed something moving in the brush fifty feet away and leaned in to get a better look.

"Hey, man," Gus said. "Are you even listening?"

"Sorry, it's just . . . I thought I saw something moving over there." My ax was leaning against the back window of the cab. I grabbed it.

Gus's eyes widened. "You think it's a wolf?"

"It's *something*," I said, swinging my legs off the tailgate. "You coming?"

Gus, of course, chickenshit that he is, didn't move. "I don't have my gun." *So much for killing a wolf with his bare hands*, I thought.

The pile of brush flinched as I walked toward it. I imagined a wolf crouching beneath it, its hungry, amber eyes glowing from behind a tangle of gnarled branches. Slowly, I poked it with the head of my ax. Nothing happened. I took a step closer and pushed some of the branches out of the way, holding my breath as I waited for the wolf to pounce.

But there was no wolf. Beneath the brush was a fresh, green sapling, not much taller than my knees. "What are you doing under there?" I said and bent down to take a closer look. As I did so, a green bud burst open and a glossy, new leaf unfurled right in front of my nose. I had never seen anything like it. It was as if time had momentarily sprinted forward, a short spike in an otherwise steady current. I touched the leaf, and as I did, the sapling trembled and spat out another one.

*I need to quit drinking*, I thought. I walked back to the truck, popped two aspirin I found sitting in the cup holder, and returned to work.

Cutters was the best and worst bar in town. It had been converted from a nineteenth-century log cabin into a place where loggers could come in out of the cold and drink themselves warm. Like at any good dive bar, the floor was perpetually sticky, and every square inch of the wooden booths was carved with people's names or their favorite curse words. In the back corner sat one sorry-looking, ripped pool table that most people used as a coffee table as evidenced by the dozens of ring marks on its rails.

I grabbed my usual seat at the corner of the bar next to the jukebox and ordered a pitcher of Coors. The rest of the guys filled in the seats around me, groaning about their bad backs and the snow they'd have to shovel when they got home. Weylyn was the last to wander in. He tentatively looked around the room for a place to sit, so I flagged him over and gestured to the empty seat next to me.

"The first one's on me," I said as he hopped onto the wobbly stool. "What're you having?"

Weylyn stared thoughtfully at the liquor bottles lined up behind the bar. "What do you suggest?" he asked.

"Two Jim Beams, neat," I told Al, the bartender, who nodded and pulled out a couple of highballs. I turned back to Weylyn. His expression torqued as something over my shoulder caught his eye. I turned to see what he was looking at and saw Gus glowering in our direction.

"Don't worry about him," I reassured. "He's just mad 'cause he only shits once a week."

Weylyn laughed. "And here I thought it had something to do with me."

"Well, you definitely got under his skin today, that's for sure."

Al passed us our drinks. Weylyn took a cautious sip and shivered slightly as he swallowed. "It's good," he said, unsuccessfully masking his disgust. The kid didn't smoke, and he clearly didn't drink, either.

"So, how'd you end up here in Shitsville, Montana?" I asked.

"Mary got a job here, and I decided to come with her."

"Mary, huh?" I said. "That the old lady?"

He looked mildly perturbed. "She's not old. It's her thirtieth birthday tomorrow."

"Oh, yeah? What you got planned?"

A worried look crossed Weylyn's face. "Well . . . I hadn't really thought about it."

"You're telling me you didn't plan anything?" You'd think the kid had never had a girlfriend before. "Man, she'll expect you to do *something*. Take her out to dinner. Buy her the fanciest thing on the menu, and don't forget the flowers. What's her favorite flower?"

Weylyn thought for a moment. "I know she likes daffodils."

"Daffodils. Perfect. Get her a big bouquet of daffodils while she's at work and leave them somewhere where she can see them as she walks in the front door. Trust me. She'll think it's super romantic."

"Okay," he said awkwardly. I may have overstepped a bit. It was clear he liked this Mary girl, although I got the impression that he hadn't told her yet. I knew exactly how he felt.

"So," I said, changing the subject. "Is it just you and Mary out here, or do you know anyone else in town?"

"Well, there's Merlin."

"Merlin?"

"My pig."

"You have a pet pig?" Of course he did. I couldn't imagine Weylyn with a normal pet like a dog or a cat. A pig was just weird enough to make sense. "I have a cow."

Weylyn's face lit up. "Really? What's his name?"

"Her name is Rosie. She just might be my best friend," I said. "Is that pathetic? That my best friend is a cow?"

"Merlin's my best friend, too. Although I've always gotten along better with animals than people," he said, eyeing Gus, who was now heckling a group of people playing darts. "Animals are more honest. You never have to second-guess their motives."

He had a point. I also preferred animals to most of the jerks I worked with. However, with Weylyn, I got the impression that the company of animals wasn't so much a preference for him as it was a way of life. I wasn't sure what made me think that. Maybe it was the way he checked for squirrels before felling a tree or how he would sit by himself during his lunch break and watch birds flying overhead. Whatever it was, there was something not quite human about him, like he belonged outside in the forest instead of sitting at a bar drinking shitty whiskey with me. I had the urge to *White Fang* him—shout, *Go on! Get outta here!* as I threw bar nuts at his back—so he could go be with his "own kind."

Then I thought, *Maybe that's the problem.* Maybe Weylyn had had enough people in his life telling him to "go on" instead of helping him to fit in. Maybe all he really wanted was someone he could have a drink with.

"Well, I guess we have that in common," I said, raising my glass. Weylyn raised his, too, and we toasted to not quite fitting in.

## 40

## MARY PENLORE

Spring was here, although it was hard to tell. Based on the amount of snow that fell that morning, it might as well have been the middle of January. Both Griffin and I decided to stay at base camp that day and type up our notes from the previous week, while Dobbs cut his toenails and listened to a hockey game on the radio. It was distracting, to say the least.

"Come on, Orlowski, you pussy!" he shouted at the radio. I didn't know who Orlowski was or what made him a pussy, and I didn't care. I just wanted Dobbs to shut his mouth so I could get some work done. "Hey, Kurt?" I said.

Griffin shot me a wary look and shook his head, but Dobbs didn't even look up. He clipped his big toe, and I could hear a soft *tink* as the nail bounced off the glass of the coffeemaker we all shared.

"Kurt!" I said, louder this time.

Dobbs's attention snapped to me like a shark spotting a seal. "What is it, Lobo?"

"Do you think you could turn the radio down? I'm finding it hard to concentrate." A quick gasp escaped Griffin's mouth. I kept my eyes locked on Dobbs, who was silently calculating his next move. Then he smiled wide and said, "How are you and Widow getting along?"

"Fine." The smile unnerved me. I had never even seen Dobbs's teeth since I started working there.

He stood up and turned off the radio. "Do me a favor, Lobo, and clean that up, will ya?" he said, pointing to the pile of nail clippings he had left on the floor. He pulled on his shoes and coat.

"Why was he asking about Widow?" I asked Griffin after he had left.

"You don't know?"

I shook my head.

"Dobbs' hand was Widow's handiwork."

"Seriously?"

"Yeah. The Nomads were his pack before the attack. That was the last time he was seriously out in the field."

"Have you ever gotten close to her?"

"I keep my distance," he said and went back to his notes. "Can't play baseball without my hands."

"Good thing I don't play baseball."

Griffin shot me a warning look. "There are two kinds of people who get themselves killed out there: stupid people and eager people. Don't let your eagerness make you do stupid things."

He was right. I almost drowned the last time I acted impulsively, and I liked my hands. I'd earn Widow's trust, I thought. But I'd have to be careful.


I finished work early that day, just in time to catch what was left of the sun setting behind the cabin. Weylyn cut me off outside the front door. "We're going out!"

"Tonight? Why?"

He looked at me like I had gone mad. "Because it's your birthday."

*My birthday!* I had completely forgotten. "Wow. You're right. I guess I'm just not used to snow in April, yet."

"Well, we shouldn't let a little snow stop us from celebrating," he said. "But first, I have a surprise for you. Close your eyes. No peeking," he said as he led me by the arm around the side of the building. When we had stopped, Weylyn said, "You can look now, Mary Jane."

I opened my eyes and saw yellow, a whole garden of daffodils. There must have been hundreds of them nestled in the white snow, their necks craned forward under the weight of their golden crowns. It was beautiful, but impossible. "But . . . how?" I stammered. "The ground is frozen."

Weylyn smiled. "I guess they were just sick of waiting."

I looked at him, hoping to find an answer somewhere in the gray pools of his eyes, but I couldn't detect a single ripple.

"Thank you," I said. Then I saw the tiniest splash, like the flick of a minnow's tail on the surface of a pond, and suddenly I knew there was a lot more hiding beneath the surface of those waters than I was ever likely to know.

There were only two restaurants in town—Mr. Pig's, a barbecue joint, and Glacier Lodge, a swanky restaurant that was part of the hotel. We decided on Glacier Lodge because even the mention of Mr. Pig's seemed to distress Merlin. I pulled on a clean pair of jeans and a sweater and was about to leave the bedroom when I had a sudden realization. *Weylyn asked me out. To dinner.* I looked at myself in the mirror, at my messy hair and old sweater that had pearled from too many washes, and decided I couldn't possibly let him see me like this, not if there was a chance that this night was going to be our first official date.

I opened my wardrobe and pulled out the only somewhat nice piece of clothing I had brought with me to Montana, a yellow cotton dress with tiny white flowers. I threw on some mascara and a pearl drop necklace and opened the door.

When Weylyn saw me, he looked at me in a way that felt entirely new. "You look exceedingly pretty, Mary."

My skin bloomed with reds and pinks. "Thanks. You look nice, too."

*Nice* wasn't the right word. He looked positively handsome in his gray slacks and royal-blue button-up. His hair was clean and slicked back. Even his teeth seemed a little whiter.

But something didn't feel right. It all seemed too . . . normal. I imagined Weylyn and me walking into that fancy restaurant and no one noticing. No one gawking or shaking their heads. No one whispering things like "Did you see that couple?" or "What are folks like that doing in a place like this?" Instead, we would place napkins on our laps and order a bottle of the house red without attracting so much as a glance in our direction. No one in that restaurant would have any idea just how special Weylyn really was.

I wanted us to throw a hunk of meat over a fire and watch the juices fizzle in the flame. I wanted us to eat with our hands and throw the bones in the fire and laugh as loud as we felt like laughing and howl at the stars.

Weylyn must have read my mind. "You don't want to go out."

"I'm sorry," I said. "I want to have dinner with *you*. It's just everyone else I'm not so crazy about."

"Good. Then we'll make our own," he said, pulling at his cuffs. "I haven't worn an outfit like this since Mrs. Kramer made me sing in the church choir."

"It looks pretty uncomfortable," I said as I helped him unbutton his sleeves. As I did so, his gaze rolled down my neck like beads of sweat. "Mary . . . ," he began.

"Yeah?"

"I'd still like this to be a date, if that's okay with you."

I nodded. "It's okay with me."

———————

We built a bonfire outside, emptied everything from the refrigerator into a cast-iron pot—beef, potatoes, onion, black beans, tomatoes, garlic, rice—and let it stew over the open flame. We crouched over our stew like Vikings, hair falling into our bowls, scooping it up with chunks of bread and slurping the rest. When we had had our fill, we crawled closer to the flame and drank coffee spiked with rum. The fire spat, catching the ends of our hair like they were wicks, and we took turns pinching them out with our fingers.

"I'm not afraid of fire," Weylyn said as he wet his fingers and extinguished the flame that had caught the end of my scarf. "I should be. I know that. But there are things I'm more afraid of." A shadow crossed over his face.

"What things?" I asked tentatively.

Weylyn reached down and grabbed a fistful of snow.

"You're afraid of snow?"

"I'm afraid of what it could be," he said and tossed the flakes into the fire.

Then I remembered something he told me years earlier. "Your parents died in a blizzard."

He nodded solemnly, flickering fire reflecting in his eyes. "I have this dream that I'm conjuring a huge storm. Blinding snow. Ice shooting from the clouds like bolts of lightning. Someone, a woman, is shouting my name, begging me to stop, but I can't. I'm both powerful and powerless." His voice sounded thin and torn like snakeskin.

I touched his cheek, drawing his gaze away from the dying fire. "You aren't powerless."

Before the cold had a chance to grab us, I pressed my lips against his and felt warm sand fill the spaces between my toes. Soon, we were miles away in a place that never snowed.

## 41

## DUANE FORDHAM

"Duane, you gotta see this!"

It was 6:00 A.M. "What is it, Gus?" I grumbled, in no mood to talk.

"Just get over here!"

I grabbed my thermos of coffee from the truck and followed him, wishing I were still home, asleep. It was a particularly cold morning, too, the kind you feel in your bones. A group of guys were all standing at the edge of the landing, looking downhill and mumbling among themselves. Gus and I joined them.

"Mornin', fellas," I croaked. None of them acknowledged me. They were all too engrossed in whatever lay at the bottom of the hill. I followed their gaze, and it didn't take long to see what was wrong with the picture: trees. The hillside was thick with them, the hillside we had left mostly barren the day before.

"I don't understand," I said, bewildered. "Are we in the wrong spot?"

One of the men, Bruce, shook his head. "That Yarder is right where I left it." The Yarder is a monstrous machine built for hauling in logs. The skyline cable runs from the top of the Yarder to a point at the bottom of the hill. It's a logger's north star.

"You sure someone else didn't move it?"

Bruce pulled a set of keys from his jeans pocket. "Unless someone broke into my house, stole the keys, then put 'em back in my pants without me noticing, I'd say no."

I remembered the sapling I had found the day before, the one that had sprouted leaves like magic. "Trees don't just grow back overnight," I said, faltering a little.

"Well, then, we all must be batshit crazy." Bruce slapped his helmet on his head. "All right, boys! Let's try this again."

The men dispersed, most heading to grab chainsaws so the trees could be felled for a second time. It had to be bad luck, I thought, to cut down trees that magically grew overnight, but none of us could afford to be superstitious, not in this economy.

Out the corner of my eye, I saw Weylyn walk to the edge of the hill and peer over.

"Got any theories?" I said.

Weylyn shrugged casually like I had just asked him the time and he wasn't wearing a watch, then hoisted his ax and made his way down the hillside.

"It all started after that kid showed up."

I turned around to see Gus still standing next to me.

"And just what do you think he's doing? Sneaking out here in the middle of the night with a hose and some Miracle-Gro?" I scoffed.

Gus lowered his voice and leaned in so I could smell his hot tar breath. "I saw him."

"Saw him do what?"

"Yesterday, we were felling together. I made a cut, then stepped off to piss. When I got back, the cut I made was gone."

"Sounds like you forgot which tree you cut."

"No. I knew it was the same one 'cause there was a green scar where I'd made the cut. The kid said the same thing as you, that it was different. I told him I've been in this business for twenty goddamn years, and I never forget a tree."

"So, what are you saying?"

"I'm saying that tree got *fixed* somehow, and he's got something to do with it."

I waved him off. "Sounds like you've been watching too much *Twilight Zone*."

"I'm telling you, man," Gus said, jaw set. "Something's not right about that kid."

I hated to say it, but he might have been right. Weylyn didn't even flinch when he saw those trees. He just went to work as if it was business as usual, and maybe for him, it was.

## 42

MARY PENLORE

Weylyn was all I could think about over the next few days. He kept me warm on my long treks out in the snow and kept me feeling safe as I trailed the Nomad pack on their caribou hunt. I didn't even care when Dobbs used my coffee mug as a spittoon for his sunflower seed shells. I was so happy that I rinsed out the mug myself and did everyone else's dishes for them, too. Dobbs watched me warily, as if I might snap at any moment.

Widow was not quite so lucky as I was when it came to her love life. A week after Amarok's death, the pack was visited by a lone male I called Dorian. He was a handsome wolf with cast-iron eyes and a honey-colored snout. He was bold, too, strutting right into the pack's camp without so much as an investigative sniff. Needless to say, Widow had little tolerance for the intruder. She gnashed her diamond-cut teeth and chased Dorian off, his tail between his legs.

Two other males had auditioned themselves that spring but were treated with similar disdain. They were both physically ideal candidates, more than capable of leading a pack. My only theory was that now that Widow had her crown, she didn't want to give it up. I didn't blame her. Being a wolf was kind of a man's game.

Then a week after my birthday, Dorian returned. He obviously harbored some resentment and wasn't about to take no for an answer twice. Widow snarled like a hellhound, but Dorian didn't back down. She lunged at him, but he was too quick. He whipped around and sank his teeth into the back of her neck. Widow yelped and twisted out of his grasp. The rest of the pack chased her attacker into the woods while Widow caught her breath. I could see her wound from where I was standing. It was deep and probably needed sutures. I had to get closer to know for sure.

I took a step toward her. She watched me evenly, like she'd been expecting me. I inched forward carefully so as not to spook her. The closer I got, the bigger and fiercer she looked. I got so close I could smell her breath, dank and musty like air inside a tomb, and her eyes the color of polished brass locked on to mine. My heart drummed against my ribs so hard I thought they would break. I unsheathed my trembling left hand from my glove and reached toward her neck slowly. The noise that escaped Widow then was no junkyard dog growl. It was the grinding of tectonic plates. I had barely brushed the hair of her coat when I felt the pressure of her jaw on my fore-arm. I staggered back, more out of shock than pain, and edged away, keeping a wary eye on her. She didn't follow.

When I was safely out of her sight, I pulled back my coat sleeve to examine my arm. I had ten puncture wounds. Luckily, they all missed major arteries and looked to be only a quarter of an inch deep. I sud-denly felt ridiculous. I had touched a highly aggressive wolf without tranquilizers. This was a warning bite. Next time, she'd take my whole arm.

I wrapped it in the gauze from my pack and headed back toward camp. It was still early in the afternoon, but I needed to tend to my wound, and I had an hour's hike ahead of me. I pulled the hood of my parka tight, ripped open a pack of hand warmers, and shoved them into the toes of my boots.

I had only walked a mile or so when I began to feel light-headed. Brown spots swarmed my vision, and I stumbled into a snowbank.

Blind and scared, I remained on my knees, waiting for the dizzy spell to pass. My arm throbbed as my heart pumped more and more blood to it, robbing the rest of my body of much-needed heat. As I raised it above my heart to slow down the flow of blood, I lost consciousness.

## 43

## DUANE FORDHAM

For four straight days, we plowed through that same damn hill, yarding nearly twice our average load size. We were raking it in, for sure, but every morning we'd wake to find the hill even thicker than the day before. The trees shot up like weeds, their branches twisting around each other until the canopy was so rank, you could barely see the sun. Wes Garrity even swore he saw a branch grow two inches in two minutes. He didn't come into work the next day.

By the fifth day, the trees were so densely packed it was hard to get a full swing of the ax, and even if you got a tree to fall, it would just end up leaning against the tree next to it. It was like playing the world's most dangerous game of dominoes.

The longer this went on, the slower we moved and the tenser the crew got. "They keep gettin' hung up!" Gus threw down his hard hat, exasperated, as the carriage struggled to pull his load through a snarled thicket. "It's like the goddamn Amazon down there!"

"Who you hollerin' at, Gus?" I said, too exhausted to raise my voice.

"Those asshole trees! That's who!"

"They're just trees," I said unconvincingly.

"No, they ain't! They're goddamn demon trees."

"What do you want me to do about it?" I shouted back, exasperated.

"What you should have done weeks ago!" he spat back. "It's him or me, Duane. You choose."

I heard a snapping sound as the carriage yanked the load free and started sliding back up the hill. "Get back to work," I ordered Gus, who glared at me, then stormed off to receive the new logs and unbale the chokers.

I spotted Weylyn watching from the edge of the forest. When he caught me looking at him, he quickly went back to working on freeing a line that had gotten tangled in some gnarled branches. I headed down the hill toward him. When he saw me coming, he froze.

"All right, Weylyn, if there's anything you want to tell me, now would be the time," I said frankly.

He didn't look up from the knot he was untying. "I don't know what you want me to say."

I wanted him to say he had nothing to do with it—that we were all crazy and we could go screw ourselves—but he didn't. He hadn't even batted an eye when that first crop of trees had shown up, and even today, when the rest of the crew were losing their goddamn minds, he was strangely calm. *Is he doing this just to mess with us?* I wondered. *Did he think it was funny?* I found myself getting angrier the longer I watched him. Rather than say something I might later regret, I turned and walked back up the hill to think.

I didn't see it happen, but I heard it: a loud *crack* followed by the unmistakable groan of falling timber and a series of consecutive thuds. Six. That's how many trees were felled at once. The only safe number is one. I marched down the hill to see what had happened and found Weylyn standing over one of the trees, his left arm wagging slowly like an angry dog. "What happened here, Weylyn?"

"I'll tell you what happened," Gus cut in. "Greenhorn here was trying to be a hero." A crowd had gathered. Weylyn squirmed under the heat of their stares.

"That true, Weylyn?" I asked.

"No, it's not," he said, indignant. "I didn't touch them."

"That's not what I saw," Gus countered. "You coulda killed someone with that slipshod shit."

Then one-eyed Vince threw his hat in the ring. "I saw him, too!"

"You *both* saw him?"

They nodded.

"That's not true! I was over there." Weylyn pointed downhill. "I ran up here as soon as I heard the noise. Same as the rest of you."

"Liar!" Gus shouted.

"Gus! For once in your goddamn life, shut up and let me handle it," I barked. Nonplussed, he set his jaw and crossed his arms in front of his chest.

I turned back to Weylyn. "Why are people saying they saw you fell those trees?"

"I don't know what they saw, but it wasn't me!" he shouted. A brisk wind caused the trees above to sway and groan. Then, through a small hole in the canopy, snow began to fall, creating a swirling, white column around Weylyn that was somehow both angelic and frightening all at once. Out of the corner of my eye, I could see a few of the other crew members nervously take a step back.

The truth is, I believed Weylyn. He was careful and smart, which was more than I could say for half the guys I worked with. He hadn't felled those trees. He had *grown* them and the thousands of others that strangled the hillside. I didn't know how he did it or why, but I knew what I had to do next. "Sorry, kid. You haven't left me much of a choice. I'm suspending you for a week without pay until we can get to the bottom of this."

Weylyn looked like he'd just been punched in the stomach. "I thought we were friends," he said bitterly, stepping out of the mound of snow that had gathered at his feet and handing me his ax.

*I thought we were, too,* I thought.

Weylyn started his lonely trek up the hillside. By the time he reached the top, the snow was so heavy that he disappeared from my sight altogether.

The snow was heavy enough that we had to suspend work for the day. It had to be some kind of world record: nine inches in an hour. On my way home, I had to pull to the side of the road because all I could see was white. Between each swipe of my wiper blades, snow piled so quickly you'd think it had been there all night. I even had to dig out my tires after only having been stopped for five minutes. By the time I got home, the snow had stopped and the sky was clear and blue like Ellen's eyes. There were a few hours of daylight left, so I grabbed my rifle and headed into the woods to clear my head.

As I wandered, so did my brain. I couldn't stop thinking about the expression on Weylyn's face when I had told him to leave. It wasn't the look of someone who had been caught playing an elaborate prank. It was the look of someone who had been betrayed. I suddenly felt stupid. I had let Gus convince me that the kid was some kind of evil magician who went around sprouting forests when no one was looking. Like White Fang, I had cast him out, only it wasn't for his own good. It was for mine.

It was three o'clock, and the light was sideways and orange. I hadn't seen a single animal worth a bullet, so I started my walk back. Then suddenly, I froze in my tracks and shouldered my rifle.

About a hundred yards away, a beautiful wolf with dark-gray coloring around its eyes watched me intently. The wolf, unfazed, took a step toward me. I took aim. Here I was, staring at a vicious predator who had probably killed calves just like Maisy, but something kept me from pulling the trigger.

The wolf turned sharply to the right and started walking. I followed it with my scope down into a ravine where it stopped by what looked like a parka buried in the snow. I lowered my gun and walked to the edge of the embankment to get a better look. Then I saw the blood. It had stained a small patch of snow next to the parka like syrup on a snow cone. The wolf looked back at me, then disappeared into the forest.

I scrambled down the embankment, dug the parka out of the snow, and flipped it over. Inside was a woman, no older than thirty with teacup skin and tiny fingers. Her eyes were closed, but I guessed they were green. She was unconscious, and her left hand was shiny with blood. I lifted her like a doll and carried her toward the road as fast as I could.

When I got back to the truck, I called an ambulance, but the operator said response time was slow because the roads weren't yet plowed from the storm. The girl had a pulse, but her breathing was shallow. I pulled up her sleeve to look at her arm. The bleeding had stopped, but her bandage was soaked through. I removed the old bandage and washed the wound with a bottle of vodka I'd been saving for later. Once I'd wiped away the excess blood, I saw what clearly looked like a bite mark. It was big, nearly the full length of her forearm. If we were in Florida, I would've said she'd crossed the wrong alligator. I redressed the wound with a clean bandage I found in my glove compartment and tucked her arm back inside her parka.

An hour and a half later, the girl was admitted into the ER with mild hypothermia. The doctors wrapped her in blankets and started her on a round of antibiotics for her bite wound while I hovered in the corner of the room, trying to stay out of everyone's way. Not long after the nurses and doctors had cleared the room, her eyes fluttered open. I was right about them. They were leaf green, and they looked at me with guarded relief.

"Hi . . . Who are you?"

I jumped up from my chair. "My name's Duane. I found you passed out in the snow," I answered.

"I'm Mary," she said, taking in her surroundings. "How did they let you in here?"

"I told them I was your husband."

The girl—Mary—raised an eyebrow.

"Sorry. I just wanted to make sure you were okay."

"I appreciate that," she said, smiling wearily.

"So, what were you doing out in the woods?"

Mary sat up slowly. "I'm a researcher. I study wolves." She caught me staring at her newly bandaged arm and frowned. "It's not a big deal."

"It looks pretty bad to me. What happened?"

"I don't really feel like talking about it."

"You should be more careful."

Mary narrowed her eyes at me. "Excuse me?"

"Around wolves. They're vicious predators."

"I know what they are," she said, indignant. "And they're not always vicious. They can be very loving, too."

"Let me guess. You think it was your fault you got bit?"

"Yes."

*And I guess it's Maisy's fault she got attacked, too,* I thought, fuming. "Well, you obviously know what you're doing," I said patronizingly.

"You're right. I do," she said, defiantly.

Then it hit me just how awful my behavior was. I was in a hospital yelling at a patient for getting hurt. She deserved an apology. "I'm sorry. That was totally out of line," I said, shaking my head ruefully. "It's been a long day."

Mary considered my apology, then said, "It's okay. Thanks for helping me. I could have died out there."

"Yeah. I could barely see you under all that snow."

"What do you mean 'under'?"

"There was a sudden blizzard this afternoon. You must have already been passed out."

"How sudden?"

"I mean it literally came out of nowhere. Dropped a record-setting amount of snow."

Mary's face contorted with worry, and she sucked in a short breath. "I hate to do this, but I need your help again."

So, this was Mary, *Weylyn's* Mary, and now she was asking me to give him a ride to the hospital. "We share a car," she said. "It's still parked at my work." I agreed, leaving out the part where he worked for me, and also the part where I'd effectively fired him several hours earlier.

When I pulled into the gravel drive in front of Mary's cabin, Weylyn—who had been waiting by the window—ran out the front door. His face dropped when he saw it was me. "Oh. I thought you were Mary," he muttered, then turned back toward the cabin.

"Mary asked me to come get you," I said. "She's at the hospital."

He spun around to face me, his eyes wide with fear. "What happened?"

Mary had asked me not to tell Weylyn what happened because she wanted to tell him herself, but I couldn't lie to him, not after the way I'd treated him earlier. "She got caught in that freak blizzard. I found her in the snow."

"This is exactly what I was afraid of," Weylyn said solemnly and tilted his head back. I followed his gaze into the night sky and saw snow falling for the second time that day, beautiful, silent, dangerous snow.

"What do you mean?" I said. Weylyn didn't answer, and I didn't need him to. Before I left the hospital, Mary told me something about Weylyn that a few weeks ago, I would have said was impossible, but after what happened with the trees, I'm not sure I believed anything was impossible anymore. When Weylyn lowered his gaze to me, he was no longer the goofy kid I had met weeks before. He looked small and frightened, like an animal cowering at the back of a cage after it knows it's done something wrong. "We'd better leave now," he said. "Before it gets worse."

Weylyn and I piled into my truck and sped off into the smothering snow.

The second blizzard was even worse than the first. The fir trees lining the highway were my only guide as I drove blindly through the unrelenting snow. I even blew through several intersections for fear that I wouldn't have enough traction to get my truck going again if I stopped. Weylyn's jaw was clenched, and his fingers bit into the armrests so hard they turned white at the tips. "You all right?" I asked him.

"I hate snow," he said through gritted teeth, which was ironic if he was in fact somehow responsible for it falling to begin with.

"I owe you an apology for today," I said after he had relaxed a little. "I was freaked out by everything that was going on, and I took it out on you."

"It's okay," he said, staring blankly out into the white abyss. "You did what you had to do."

"I know you didn't cut down those trees."

"That's not what I'm talking about."

I nodded. I guess Gus had been right about Weylyn, or about the trees, anyway. "So," I began awkwardly. "Does stuff like this happen a lot?"

"The trees or the weather?"

"Weather, I guess."

"Usually not snow. Mostly rain. Sometimes, heavier storms. Once it was a tornado."

"Holy shit." Surprised, I tapped the brake a little too hard, and the truck fishtailed. Weylyn cringed and clamped his eyes shut. "Sorry," I said, straightening us out.

Weylyn opened one eye and then the other. "Don't worry. I stopped it before anyone got hurt."

I pointed out the window at the snow whipping past us. "If you can stop it, then why are we driving through a blizzard right now?"

"I don't know," Weylyn said, agitated. "Before I came here, a hurricane hit the town I was living in. I tried to stop it and ended up in the hospital. I think it made me . . . tired."

"Tired?"

"I feel less in control. Getting it going is easy. Stopping it takes more effort, especially with snow," he said, distant. Then he closed his eyes, shutting out me, the snow, and the rest of the world. "I really hate snow."

# 44

I pulled my hospital blanket tight around my shoulders as I watched snow plummeting past my window in heavy, wet clumps. I had asked Duane—the man with the face like knotty pine who had found me in the snow—not to say anything, but he must have ratted me out. I guess I couldn't blame him. I'm sure Weylyn was worried sick, and he was probably just trying to reassure him that I was okay. I closed my eyes and hoped that they got here safely.

Forty minutes later, I woke to a soft knocking at my door. I looked up and saw Weylyn walk into the room, his hair and clothes slightly damp, face drawn. My ghoulishly blue lips smiled at him. "Hey."

Weylyn stopped at the foot of my bed. "Hey," he said, avoiding my gaze. "How are you feeling?" His voice sounded strained.

"A little tired, but other than that, pretty okay."

"Good." He stared out the window at the snow that had slowed to a gentle drift. "I knew it was only a matter of time before someone I love got hurt."

Someone he loved.

Still, there was a distance between us. "Come here," I said softly so as not to spook him.

Weylyn tentatively sat next to me on the edge of the bed. "I need to tell you something," he said, tracing the edge of my bandage with his thumb. "The night my parents died . . . the snowstorm didn't even show up on the radar. It happened so fast. It was like it was never there, like my parents died from something that never even *existed*." Weylyn's left hand reflexively began to flick back and forth, a remnant of the wolf he had once been.

"The worst part of it is I don't remember anything about that day. How do you not remember the worst day of your life? How do you not remember what you were doing? How you were *feeling*? I think about that day and all I see is white."

I grabbed his left hand to steady it, but I could still feel his fingers nervously tapping against my clasped palm.

"I've spent most of my life trying to convince myself that it was just a horrible coincidence, that I had no hand in it. I try to do good. I try to help people. Then I feel myself losing control, and I wonder if I'm fighting a losing battle. Maybe I'm this way for a reason."

I squeezed his hand tighter. "Weylyn, listen to me. None of this is your fault. Not your parents, not me."

Weylyn looked down at my hand and studied it for what seemed like hours. He and I both knew I was lying, but what else could I have said? I had never seen him look this tormented before, and I would have said anything to ease his mind, even if only for a second. When he finally looked up, his eyes were gauzy and dull. "Get some rest, Mary Jane," he said, standing up. Then, just as he was turning to leave, he added, "I'm glad you're safe," his words as wooden as the expression on his face.

That night, I drifted in and out of sleep like waves on a beach. I dreamed about Widow and her penetrating stare. I dreamed about teeth sinking into my peachy flesh and the ruby-red blood that stained them when they pulled out. Each time, I'd wake up with a thumping pain in my arm and a vague feeling of dread. Dread of what, I didn't know.


Saturday morning's sun threw itself against my hospital room window, creating a glowing golden box on the opposite wall. I watched shadows of birds flitting between silhouettes of tree branches like a puppet show and was reminded of Plato's Allegory of the Cave: how the shadows against the wall were perceived by the prisoners as truth, when in reality, there was a world they couldn't see that was creating those shadows. Everyone who saw that freak storm yesterday only saw the shadow of it. I had seen the other side of the fire. I had seen the truth.

I got a ride home that afternoon from Duane. He said he hadn't seen Weylyn since he dropped him off at the hospital the previous night. I thanked him for the ride and opened the door to the cabin.

No one was home. The coffeemaker puttered away on the kitchen counter, and Merlin sat on the back of the sofa like a cat, staring intently out the window. "Where'd Weylyn go?" I asked.

Merlin acknowledged me with a quick glance, then turned back to the window. *He's probably out gathering more firewood*, I thought as I looked at the dwindling pile on the hearth. The coffeemaker gave one last cough, and I set out two mugs and a loaf of bread. Then I grabbed milk, eggs, and butter from the fridge. Weylyn would be back soon, and we'd have coffee and french toast.

An hour went by, and the coffee was cold. I was beginning to worry. Merlin paced back and forth in front of the door, grunting anxiously. I fed him a piece of toast to calm him down.

Then I saw the postcard. It must have slipped off the kitchen counter, because I found it half-hidden under the bottom cabinets. On the front was a picture of a snowy peak. He must have picked it up at the park gift shop because the words WELCOME TO MAMMOTH

NATIONAL PARK were written in all caps at the bottom. On the back, in Weylyn's handwriting, it read:

*Dear Mary Jane,*

 *You are the best human I have ever had the pleasure of knowing, and that is why I must leave. If I had known then what I know now, I would have stayed in the shadow of the trees where I belong.*

 *I hope that you will take care of Merlin for me. Pigs are intelligent animals, him especially, but he will probably not understand.*

 *Forgive me for both my coming and going.*

 *With love,*

 *Weylyn Grey*

I read the letter three times silently, then once aloud. Merlin stopped pacing and listened, solemnly. Weylyn's words sounded wrong on my tongue, like swimming against a current. He thought he was doing what was best for me, but he was wrong. He wasn't getting off the hook that easily.

I ran to the phone and dialed. The person on the other end picked up. "Elka, I need to borrow one of the snowmobiles."

## 45

## DUANE FORDHAM

After I dropped Mary off at her house, I went to check on Rosie. I hadn't seen her since before the blizzards, and I wanted to make sure no other wolves had sneaked into the barn without my knowing. When I slid open the door, Rosie happily trotted over to me, bangs flapping against her forehead. "Hi, girl," I cooed as she nuzzled into me. "You won't believe what happened to me yesterday." I barely believed it myself. I hoped that once I got a good night's sleep, I'd convince myself I dreamed the whole thing.

I cleaned Rosie's stall and replenished her hay and water before heading into the house. By that time, I was so tired I could barely bend down take my shoes off. I was just about to crawl into bed with what was left of the vodka I had stashed in my truck when the phone rang. I groaned and dragged myself to the kitchen to answer.

Mary was on the other end. She sounded panicked. Apparently, she didn't know where Weylyn was and she wanted to know if I would help her look for him. I stared longingly at my warm bed with its layers of cozy wool blankets and said, "I'll be right there." Then I took one long swig of vodka before heading back out into the cold.

"It's my fault!" I shouted above the noise of the engine. I was behind Mary on the snowmobile, my hands around her waist, her hair fluttering over both our shoulders. The snowy landscape pinwheeled past us in stripes of white and green. "None of this would have happened if I had just kept my damn mouth shut!"

"No, it's not!" Mary yelled back.

"Then why'd he take off?"

"Because"—her voice cracked slightly—"he thinks he doesn't belong here, and he's wrong."

*Or maybe he's right*, I thought sadly. She knew him better than I did, of course, but it seemed as if Weylyn had made his wishes pretty clear. "Do you know where he might have gone?"

"I have an idea."

A few minutes later, Mary slowed the sled to a stop. "This is as far as we can ride. We'll have to do the rest on foot." She pulled out what looked like a GPS device and studied it for a moment. "East. About two miles."

"What did you do? Implant a tracking device in him?"

"I'm not tracking *him*. Come on. Let's go." She started walking. I didn't move. "Wolves. You're tracking wolves."

Mary nodded.

"And when were you planning on telling me that? I would have brought my rifle."

"You don't need a gun. They won't hurt you."

"Oh, yeah? Tell that to the mother of the calf I just buried."

The lines in Mary's face softened. "I'm sorry. Was he yours?"

"She. Maisy. I woke one morning to find her and the wolf dead in my barn. Primrose tried to save her . . . Well, she got revenge, anyway."

"Amarok."

"What?"

"That was the wolf's name," she mused. "Nature can be unkind."

I considered this for a moment. "Yes, it can," I said, then took a deep breath and followed Mary into the woods.

I tried not to speak so Mary wouldn't hear the tremor in my voice. Four fierce-looking adult wolves stood fifty feet away on the opposite bank of a river, pacing excitedly back and forth. What they were excited about, I couldn't tell; I just hoped it wasn't the smell of me. "I don't see Widow," Mary muttered, more to herself than to me.

"Who's Widow?" My voice wavered slightly, but I didn't think she noticed.

"The alpha female. The one who bit me."

I looked over my shoulder to make sure there wasn't a wolf sneaking up behind us. Luckily, the coast was clear.

"Wait! There she is." Mary pointed to a wolf moving out of a bank of trees and into the clearing. This wolf was bigger than the rest with dark-gray coloring around her eyes, just like the wolf I had seen the day before. Then out from the same bank of trees stepped Weylyn. Mary rushed forward.

"Whoa! Wait a minute," I said, grabbing her arm. "What are you doing?"

"I just need to get a little closer. Don't worry. They're terrible swimmers," she assured me and walked toward the riverbank.

I followed her against my better judgment.

## 46

## MARY PENLORE

I crept forward to get a better look. Weylyn was soon surrounded on all sides by curious wolves that sniffed him tentatively. Widow stood back and watched. She had already accepted him. Now, it was up to her family to back her up. Soon, the inquisition was over, and the wolves lost interest in the newcomer and wandered off.

Then Widow did something I'd never seen her do: she groveled. She crouched by his feet, ears down, and rolled onto her back. It then dawned on me what was happening. She had chosen a new alpha. She had given her crown to Weylyn.

As he bent down and scratched her behind the ears like she was a harmless dog, I felt a sadness more acute than anything I'd ever felt before. Weylyn Grey didn't belong in my world. He belonged in theirs, and there was nothing I could say to convince him otherwise.

My suspicions were only confirmed when he finally looked up and saw me. There was freedom in his face, relief mixed with sadness. In that moment, I could feel sand between my toes, water on my skin. I saw the sun melt into the water until everything was starry and purple. I held Weylyn one last time in that dark place, then turned and walked back into the bright white snow.

47

DUANE FORDHAM

The snow was melted by the next morning. As I lay in bed, I listened to huge chunks of ice break off, skid down the roof, and shatter on the ground below. Outside my window, water gushed from the gutters into my already overflowing rain barrel, then ran in rivulets toward the street. Our annual spring thaw, a process that usually took a couple of weeks, had happened all in one night.

I imagined Mary wading through the slush in a pair of rubber boots, searching in vain for wolf tracks. My heart went out to her. She had definitely gotten the raw end of the deal, although I felt sorry for Weylyn, too. He had tried his best to fit in. He moved out to the middle of frozen nowhere, got a job, and put up with Gus's bullshit all because he wanted a life with her. I still didn't know exactly what happened in those woods, but the romantic in me believed that Weylyn had grown that forest for Mary, the forest I had helped cut down.

After getting up and realizing I was out of coffee, I drove through the very shallow river that used to be Route 728 to Glacier Mercantile. The sleigh bells hanging from the door announced my entrance, and a pretty Hispanic woman behind the counter looked up. "Hi! You're the first customer we've had today. Wha'd you do?

Swim here?" She chuckled. Her laugh was warm and earthy, like cello music.

"No, I'm a terrible swimmer. I came here on water skis." I smiled as the woman laughed again. "I haven't seen you here before."

"Oh, I'm Sophia. I'm filling in for Ellen. She's on her honeymoon."

"Oh, yeah. She mentioned something about being engaged," I said, feigning disinterest.

"Yeah. To a guy named *Moose*. Can you believe that?"

"Actually, yes. I've met the guy. His name fits him perfectly."

Sophia laughed. Clearly, we had better taste in people than Ellen did. I snuck a glance at her left hand and noticed she wasn't sporting a ring of any kind.

"Hey, you don't happen to work for Blackroot Timber, do you?" she asked.

"I do. Why?"

"Because people have been coming in here telling these stories about a forest that keeps getting cut down and growing back overnight. You know anything about that?"

"Yeah. I was there."

Sophia's lips parted in amazement. "So, it's true?"

I nodded. "I know it sounds crazy."

"I like crazy stories," she said and leaned across the counter, her long black hair spilling over her shoulders.

"Actually, it's kind of a love story."

Sophia raised her eyebrows and smiled sweetly. "Even better."

*third interlude*

WILDWOOD FOREST, OREGON

2017

# ROARKE

"If Ruby were my girlfriend, I'd never break up with her," I said, licking grease off my fingers. "Especially not for a bunch of stupid wolves." Boo raised one eyebrow and growled, then went back to licking the dried cheese clumps off Weylyn's plate.

"I agree," said Weylyn. "I made a terrible mistake. One I've had to live with all these years." He walked my plate over to the sink but didn't set it down. Instead, he just stood there staring out the window with that plate in his hand, as if he had forgotten it was there. An uncomfortable silence followed, but instead of changing the subject like a considerate human being, I said, "It doesn't make sense. If you lived with the wolves and Mary was studying them or whatever, wouldn't you guys see each other all the time?"

Weylyn turned on the faucet and began wiping the plate with a wet rag. "My pack and I left the park. Walked all the way to Canada."

"Why'd you leave them?"

"I was chased out by another male."

"You ran away?" I laughed. "Why didn't you fight him?"

"Because he was a wolf. He had teeth that could cut steel cable, and mine can barely chew a caramel without choking."

"What about Mary? Did you ever try to find her?"

"I tried once."

"What happened?"

Weylyn hesitated, as if he was deciding between telling the truth and telling me what he thought I wanted to hear. "It's a long story," he said, choosing neither.

He set the wet plate in the drying rack and turned off the water. "The first coat will be dry by now. We should get back to work."

We applied the second coat of mud and straw in silence. I could tell Weylyn's mind was somewhere else, probably snowed in with Mary in their cabin in the woods, sitting by the fire and counting snowflakes as they drifted past the window.

Unsurprisingly, none of my friends believed me. "He had me in his web! I had to cut myself out with a knife," I told Mike on Monday as we stood in line for lunch. Ruby, who was ahead of us, giggled and whispered something to her best friend, Olivia, while the lunch ladies spooned creamed corn onto their trays with a sickening *plop*. Giggling girls usually meant one of two things: either they liked you or they thought you were stupid. It was impossible to tell the difference. Feeling self-conscious, I looked away.

"Yeah, right. I bet there wasn't even anyone in there," Mike said dismissively.

"How would you know? *You* ran away," I said, quieter this time. "He was a crazy old guy who said he'd feed me to his wolf if I told anyone where he lived."

Mike raised his voice so the whole lunch line could hear him. "Dude, that's just a stupid story for babies. I can't believe you bought it in the first place." I heard Ruby giggle again from the end of the line.

"He's real," I said as I ate one of his french fries. Stealing food was how my friends and I displayed dominance over each other. The less of an appetite you had at the end of the school day, the stronger you were.

"Then prove it," Mike said, stuffing a whole handful of my fries in his mouth and washing them down with a swig of my chocolate milk.

When I knocked on the front door of the cabin, no one answered. I waited a minute before trying the doorknob. It was open. "Weylyn?" I said as I stepped inside. There was no sign of Weylyn or Boo aside from the faint smell of burned cheese. I sat down at the kitchen table to wait and pulled out my mom's digital camera that I had borrowed under the guise of a "class project." I figured I'd take a bunch of photos of leaves and tell her I was supposed to identify which types of trees they came from.

A few minutes later, I heard voices outside. I listened closely and realized it was just one voice, Weylyn's, but it sounded like he was arguing with someone. I poked my head out the door and saw him about thirty feet away crouched down next to a raccoon with a stumpy tail. I couldn't hear very well, but I thought I heard him say, "Are you sure?" The raccoon squeaked something in response, and Weylyn nodded as if he understood.

As I stepped out of the door, the raccoon scampered up a tree and out of sight. "Roarke," Weylyn said, surprised. "What are you doing here?"

"Just wanted to say hi," I said, tucking my mom's camera into my back pocket. "What's with the raccoon?"

He shifted his weight awkwardly. "Oh, that's my friend Matilda. She's helping me with something."

"Cool. I wish I had animals to do my chores for me. I once tied a duster to my dog's tail, but she ate all the feathers."

There was something off about Weylyn today. He seemed distracted and anxious. Even his hair and clothes were a little more unkempt than usual. *Perfect for the photo*, I thought, then cringed a little at my own shamelessness.

"Are you okay?" I asked. "You look kind of . . ."

"Bedraggled?"

"Yeah." I wasn't sure what *bedraggled* meant, but it didn't sound good.

Weylyn tried running his fingers through his hair, but they got stuck partway. "I haven't seen my own reflection in months."

"Here," I said, pulling my mom's camera out of my pocket and snapping a picture of Weylyn before he could protest. I looked down at the screen, disappointed. His eyes were half-closed, and he looked more confused than scary. If I showed Mike this picture, he'd just think it was some random homeless guy.

"Can I see it?" Weylyn asked. I hesitated, then handed the camera to him. His face sank. "It's worse than I thought."

"It's not *that* bad."

"I have actual twigs in my beard," he said, pulling one out and tossing it on the ground. "I've never been one to obsess over my looks, but this is a new low, even for me." He handed the camera back to me. I tapped the little trash can icon on the screen and deleted the picture.

I may not have had a scary picture of Old Man Spider, but Weylyn helped me stage a few action shots with Boo to impress my friends. My favorite was one of Boo mid-yawn with my head dangerously close to his open mouth. It was kind of blurry, but you could see the fangs really well, which is all I cared about, anyway.

Weylyn invited me to hang out for a while, so we tossed the leftover straw from the roof in the fireplace along with a few pieces of wood, and Weylyn showed me how to light a fire. Once we had a flame going, he cracked open a bag of sunflower seeds, and we took turns spitting the shells into the fire.

"Nice one!" I said when one of Weylyn's shells knocked over a charred twig. "I thought I was the best spitter I know, but looks like you got me beat."

Weylyn laughed. "I've never been complimented on my spitting before."

"I guess wolves don't really do spitting contests, do they?"

"No, not so much. Although sometimes they bet each other on

who can howl the longest. I usually lost, but I had the disadvantage of being human. Different lung capacities, I guess."

I spat out another shell. "Don't you ever miss being around people? I mean, wolves are cool, but they can't spit or climb trees or anything like that."

Weylyn chewed as he considered my question. "I miss some people. Not everyone, of course, but I like to think I still have friends out there."

"Like . . . What was her name again? Your foster sister?"

"Lydia."

"Do you ever see her?"

"I visit her every now and then, although it took me a while to get up the courage to go."

"Because of what happened with Mary?"

He nodded thoughtfully.

"What finally made you decide to go?"

Weylyn's eyes flitted around the mostly empty room. "I was tired of being alone."

*book 5*

FIREFLY KEEPER

FAIRWEATHER, PENNSYLVANIA

2011

## 48

## LYDIA KRAMER BARNES

Bill and I put down roots in Mouse Country. I had a baby inside me and an irrational notion that I had to give birth to my child in a wheat field so that in the event he jumped out of me too quickly, he'd have something soft to break his fall. I had Micah in a hospital, of course, but I had a very acceptable view of a wheat field from my window.

Bill called the Pennsylvania countryside Mouse Country because there are mice everywhere, literally. Name a place you wouldn't think you'd find a mouse, and we've found one there: the toaster oven, a shampoo bottle, Micah's potty. At first, I tried laying traps and I caught a few of them that way, but Pennsylvania mice are smarter than Oklahoma mice. They quickly learned how to get the piece of chocolate without tripping the spring. I had effectively set up an open candy bar.

I shouldn't have been surprised. It was an old farmhouse, after all, yolk colored with white shutters and a wraparound porch, the kind of place that made you want to throw open the windows and set pies on the sills for the neighbor boys to steal. Previously owned by generations of Amish, the house didn't have a single outlet, so we hired an electrician to wire the place. Supposedly, it had lived through the Civil War, although I couldn't confirm if it had seen any actual combat. There's a hole in the fence I like to pretend was made by a musket ball intended for Ulysses S. Grant. Thanks to the soldier's poor aim and an iron codpiece, Mr. Grant lived to tell the tale, but the fence wasn't so lucky.

We had a garage that I used as my studio—I had moved on from body art to more salable goods: paintings. I sold them at art fairs and local shops and used the profits to make scary art that was only allowed in the house at Halloween: leather gargoyle masks with teeth growing out of their wagging tongues; dolls' heads with scorched hair floating in bowls of oatmeal; a portrait of my mother wielding a bloody stake entitled *Clara Kramer, Vampire Hunter.* Daddy thought it was hilarious, but I didn't show it to Mama. Somehow, I didn't think she'd find it funny.

I made these things not because I was living out some sick fantasy but because they made me laugh. No one else did, so I painted cute animals, too.

We inherited one unexpected asset with the property: a bee colony. Neither Bill nor I knew anything about bees—Bill thought they were the same as wasps—but we hired a beekeeper named Rodger who not only knew the difference between bees and wasps but also could identify all twenty thousand species. We built a fence around the beeyard to keep Micah from wandering into the hives, and Rodger brought us honey every Friday, which I sometimes traded with my neighbors for muffins or pies.

At age seven, Micah decided he wanted to be a beekeeper. From his bedroom window, he'd watch Rodger in a cloud of bees, gingerly sliding frames of crispy, golden combs from their hives; then he'd beg me to let him help. "I'm not a baby anymore!" he'd shout, his miniature fists balled and shaking. "I'm seven years old!" He was so cute when he was angry.

My voice was calm. "Let me ask you something. When was the last time you saw a seven-year-old keeping bees?"

"A couple of days ago," he said confidently.

"Really? And where was that?"

"At the place where they let kids work."

"Oh, you mean the Third World!"

He nodded. "Yeah, that one."

"You should have said that in the first place. We'll go get you a passport tomorrow and put you on a plane."

"A plane?" he said, bunching his eyebrows.

"Yeah, you'll have to fly across the ocean, far away from me and Dad. But you'll be fine 'cause you're seven now, and you can take care of yourself."

Micah's face whitewashed with fear. "No! I don't want to go far away!"

"Then talk to me again in another seven years; then we can talk about you helping Rodger." I figured by that time, he'd be too interested in girls to care about bees, anyway.

Minus the occasional bee-related outburst, Micah was a really good kid. His teachers were always telling me stories of how sweet and kind he was: how he helped up Bethany H. when she fell on the playground; how he stayed in during recess to help clean the chalkboards; how he always raised his hand before speaking. I knew behind all those sweet stories there was something they weren't saying. I saw it in the occasional bruise on his chin or rip in his backpack. Micah was picked on. He was slightly chubby, like me, and would rather be inside reading fantasy stories than playing sports. I gave him my old Wandering Wizards books for his tenth birthday, and he read the whole series in only three months. He started calling himself Tarquist the Unseen and testing "potions" on the cat. I had to wash her frequently to get the dried cranberry juice out of her fur.

We had another son two years Micah's junior named Clay. The two of them couldn't have been more different. Clay loved sports, Transformers, and eating contests. He had lots of friends and loved being the center of attention. I must have had meetings with the elementary school principal every week because I have every inch of that office memorized: a brass nameplate with one screw missing; a picture of her kids—two girls, one boy, and a labradoodle—in a five-by-seven-inch frame on her desk; a candy dish that was always full of Reese's Pieces. I even had a preferred chair—the one with the teal upholstered back—because it was more comfortable than the one with the faux-leather back.

Her name was Nancy, and even though Clay was disruptive, she liked me because the angel, Micah, had also come through her school, so it was obvious I wasn't the problem. "How do you do it?" she asked the day Clay jumped on his desk and broke it. "How do you live with two boys? One is enough to drive me crazy."

"I grew up with four sisters," I said. "I'd take a fraternity over a sorority any day." And like a frat, the boys were constantly fighting, stuff was always getting broken, they threw up and peed the bed and passed out on the floor. In some ways, it was scarier than a frat because their behavior didn't require a single drop of alcohol.

It was a strange life we had built for ourselves, my boys and I, and it only got stranger the summer we found Weylyn in the beeyard.

It was the first day of the boys' summer vacation. It was eight in the morning, far too early for them to be awake yet, so I used what valuable quiet time I had to get some art done. I opened the garage door to let in the warm June breeze and started by coughing up one of my cutesy dog paintings. I had made one of a Labrador retriever in a bathtub that started a bidding war between two old ladies at the County Arts Fair. Everyone kept asking me if I had more, so I made it a series. The one I was currently working on was a pug in a washbasin.

Bill pulled into the driveway, back from a trip to the nursery to buy some gardenias for the side yard. "You smell that?" he said as he hopped out of the truck, his nose wrinkled with disgust like the snout of that stupid pug.

"Smell what?"

"You really don't smell that?"

I shook my head and pointed to the trash cans on the other side of the garage. "It's your turn to take out the trash. I did it the last two times, three if you count cleaning Micah's invisibility potion off the ceiling."

"I'm not talking about the trash." Bill circled his truck, inspecting the tires. "It's my goddamn tires! I drove through eight steaming piles of Amish horse shit on the way home, and I'm supposed to take it to Hartlaub's in an hour for a tire rotation!"

"Then hose them down first," I said, indifferent, and cleaned my brush in a jar of mineral spirits.

"I shouldn't have to! That's the point. I swear they do it on purpose to piss me off." Bill was a paranoid person. He genuinely thought that most people had it out for him. I wanted to tell him to stop worrying because our Amish neighbors didn't care about him enough to plot against him, but I think the paranoia made him feel important in a world that said he wasn't. *Why do you have to believe that the government mistakenly put you on the terrorist watch list for you to feel good about yourself?* I wanted to say. *You're important to me. Isn't that enough?* Instead, I occasionally told him I heard a clicking noise during a call so he could think maybe someone had bugged the phones.

"Remind me why we moved out here again?"

"To get closer to nature."

"Well." He sighed. "I'm gonna go hose nature off my wheels." He grabbed the coiled hose from its peg on the garage wall, then looked over my shoulder at my canvas. "Cute painting," he said and kissed me on the head.

"Thanks," I said, pleased. "Oh, and will you take a look at those beekeeper applications today? Rodger said we shouldn't leave the hives unattended for more than a week, and it's almost been two."

Bill hooked up the hose to the spigot. "Bees were making honey long before man knew what honey was. I think they can manage another few days without our help."

"I'm just saying . . . he's the professional." I packed up my paints and left the garage door open so my oils could dry in the fresh air. While Bill hosed off his tires, I heard the morning bumps and shouts from the boys inside the house and felt the first prick of a headache. It was only the first day of summer.

## 49

## MICAH BARNES

You won't read about Tarquist the Unseen and his Wand of Fortitude at your local library. If you want to hear about the time he vanquished the Fell Witch of Roch, you'll have to ask me, because I'm the only one who knows. I am the mighty Tarquist, born from the belly of a blue whale where my mother was trapped by my nemesis, the Warlock Zephidas. First birthed by my mother, then by the Great Whale, they also call me Tarquist the Twice Born. I have over one hundred names, but most people know me by my lay name, Micah Barnes.

It was finally summer. I had spent nine months scratching days off in my calendar, leaping out of my desk at the sound of the bell one hundred and eighty times. I had watched leaves fall, then snow, then flowers bloom through my classroom window. Yesterday was my last day of the eighth grade, and while my classmates hung around in hallways signing yearbooks, I ran straight for those double doors and hoped that none of my "friends" caught me. That's what Ms. Mahoney called them when she saw Josh Peck shove me into a trash can. "Micah! Tell your friends that we don't roughhouse in the halls!" To be fair, I was the only one whose name she knew, and calling them my friends was better than calling them my bullies.

I didn't really have any friends in the traditional sense. I considered my parents my friends, though I wouldn't have dared to say it out loud. Clay, my brother, was probably my best friend. Or at least, he used to be. In the last year, we had drifted apart. He started playing soccer while I played wizard, and slowly we had less and less in common. When we weren't fighting, we ignored each other. If I'm being honest, I preferred the fights, because at least we were talking. It was the silences I hated, because it meant we had stopped trying.

I would most likely spend the summer alone, but that was okay. I'd rather be alone than surrounded by five hundred other kids and Josh Peck. My freedom was temporary, that wasn't lost on me, but three months seemed like a long time back then. The summer stretched out in front of me like the road to some strange and distant land. All I had to do was keep my wits about me and keep walking.

"When are you gonna quit that wizard stuff? It's really stupid," Clay said while practicing kicks in the backyard.

"It's not stupid," I snapped back. He had interrupted my training with his soccer practice. I was having trouble concentrating on my immobilizing spell with the sound of that stupid ball smacking against the back fence. "Can't you do that somewhere else?"

"Can't you do your lame magic tricks somewhere else?" he said as he kicked the ball in my direction, hitting the fence next to me with a deafening *whap*!

"Stop it or I'll . . ." I pointed my wand at him threateningly.

"Or you'll what?" he said, amused. "Turn me into a rat?"

I was really angry now. I marched toward him, wand outstretched. "I'd do a lot worse than that."

Clay laughed. "Then do it, Frog."

Frog. That's what the kids at school called me. It started when Andy Jarvis found me practicing my water manipulation spell in the bathroom and called me Finneas Frog after the main character of the Wandering Wizards book series. Finneas is brave, selfless, loyal, and one of the best wizards in all the Seven Earths. I know it was meant as an insult, but I took it as a compliment.

Except this time. Clay had never called me that before. He was friends with kids that did, but he had never stooped to that. Maybe that's why I hit him.

My wand struck him on the cheek, barely missing his eye. A glossy red comma appeared on his skin and with it came a pause while Clay considered how the next clause would read. He snatched the wand out of my hand and launched it over the fence into the beeyard. "Fetch!" he shouted gleefully. I lunged for his soccer ball, planning to throw it over the fence, too, but he was too fast. By the time I pulled myself up off the grass, he was already at the back door to the house.

I turned toward the gate. It was unlocked. *I'll just run in, get my wand, and run out,* I thought. Plus, I was fourteen and two months, older than Mom said I needed to be to help Rodger. I pulled the beekeeping helmet out of the utility shed and put it on. It was too big, but it would have to do.

I swung the gate to the beeyard open and stepped inside. The hives were bright white, assembled in neat little rows like a military graveyard. Each had a set of three filing cabinet–style drawers and a flat wooden top. I could hear a soft, steady *buzz*, but I didn't see any bees, not even one returning to the hive, furry with pollen. I figured they were all inside their boxes making honey for my Sunday morning pancakes.

The Wand of Fortitude was only a few feet away, but my curiosity about the bees got the better of me. I walked up to the first hive and lifted the top. No bees flew out. I pulled out one of the honeycomb frames, expecting to see a few crawling around in the tiny hexagons, but I only saw pools of fresh, gooey honey. I ran my finger across it and sucked at the ochre syrup. It was warm and sweet.

I returned the file to its drawer and continued along the rows. The *buzzing* got increasingly louder. Then I saw the beating of tiny, wafer-like wings from behind the last of the hives. I ran to the end of the row, then stopped abruptly in my tracks. Behind the last hive there were bees, thousands of them, but it wasn't the bees that surprised me; it was what they were hovering over. A man lay on the ground, still as death, with long limbs and a tumbleweed of hair. The bees didn't swarm him or crawl into the folds of his crumpled clothes, but they hung in the air around him like a force field.

I stayed a second too long, because that's all the time it took between the first bee noticing me and the attack that followed. They descended upon me like a mushroom cloud, jabbing every inch of exposed skin on my arms and legs with their stingers. "Moto Finalus!" I shouted and swatted at them, but that only seemed to make them angrier. I started crying, I'm pretty sure of that; then I got tired of fighting and curled into a ball on the ground while my attackers stuck me over and over like needles in a pincushion.

Then I heard a voice. "Stop!" I looked up and saw the bees reluctantly retreating, and the man I thought was dead was looming over me. Without a word, the stranger bent down and lifted me over his shoulder. I was too shocked to object. It was the first time Tarquist the Unseen had ever lost a fight, but it was also possibly the first time he had encountered real magic.

## 50

## LYDIA KRAMER BARNES

I was in the kitchen, on hold with the phone company, when Weylyn burst through the back door with Micah slung over his shoulder like a sack of potatoes. I dropped my phone on the floor, causing the battery to pop out, and my first thought was, *Shit! I lost my place in line.* Thoughts like *Is my son okay?* and *What is my estranged brother doing in my kitchen?* came shortly after. "Weylyn? What are you—"

He skipped the pleasantries and cut right to the chase. "Is he allergic to bees?"

"Micah? No. We had him tested," I answered, addled.

He unloaded Micah onto a kitchen chair and pulled the beekeeper's helmet off his head. His arms and legs were covered in swollen red bumps. Thankfully, his head and neck were normal. I ran to him. "Micah! Shit! Are those bee stings?"

He shrugged. "I have to go back. My wand—"

"You're not going anywhere," I bristled.

Weylyn cut in, "Do you have a pair of tweezers? We need to pull out the stingers."

"Down the hall, last door on the right. In the medicine cabinet."

Weylyn hurried off to fetch the tweezers.

"You know that man?" Micah asked.

"He's your uncle Weylyn."

"*That's* Uncle Weylyn? He looks like a homeless person."

"Don't talk about your uncle like that!" I scolded. I then added quietly, "Although he does look pretty homeless."

Micah lowered his voice also. "He was sleeping in the beeyard. I thought he was dead. And the bees were all over him, but he just kept sleeping or whatever, like he didn't even notice it. It was weird."

"You shouldn't have been in there," I said sternly.

"But you said when I was fourteen—"

"That you could *help*. Under *supervision*. But Rodger isn't here," I corrected. "And what's this I hear about you hitting your brother?"

"He called me 'Frog' like all the other jerks at school," he whimpered pitifully.

"That was a crappy thing to say. I'll talk to him about that, but you're old enough to know you shouldn't hit anyone ever for *any* reason."

Micah nodded solemnly. This kind of behavior wasn't like him. Clay had provoked him, that was obvious, but Micah was usually so even tempered. I was worried.

Weylyn came back with the tweezers and bent down next to Micah. He turned to me. "Do you mind?"

"No. Go ahead."

Weylyn addressed Micah. "This might be a little uncomfortable." Micah nodded and watched Weylyn, transfixed, as he pulled the stingers out one by one. "I recommend an oatmeal bath," Weylyn said when he was finished. "It will help with the itching."

"Go upstairs and start the water," I instructed Micah.

"But—"

"Now."

Micah muttered something under his breath and sulked up the stairs. I turned to Weylyn, finally getting a good look at him. He was taller than I remembered and older, of course—forty-three by my count. But under the grubby clothes and earth-smeared skin, he was still as handsome as the last time I saw him. I didn't know where he had been those last fifteen years, but he looked forgotten, like a pressed flower in the pages of a book.

Before I had the chance to ask him one of the hundreds of questions that were tumbling over each other in my mind, he spoke. "I'm sorry. I've made a terrible mistake."

He went for the door, but I grabbed him by the arm, stopping him. "Where do you think you're going?"

"I shouldn't have come."

He tried to yank his arm away, but I held fast. "Weylyn Grey! If you think you're going to come into my home after fifteen years and leave after fifteen minutes, I will punch you in the nuts so hard you won't be able to walk straight for a week! Now . . . Sit. Goddamn. Down."

Weylyn sat tentatively in a chair like a shamed child. "That's better," I said and sat in the chair next to him. "Fifteen years . . . What the hell happened, Weylyn?"

"I prevented a hurricane from destroying a town, accidentally grew a forest that indirectly caused a blizzard, became alpha of a wolf pack, was kicked out of the wolf pack, and wandered the country until I found your address," he said by rote like a bored schoolboy reciting the alphabet.

Then he added, "Oh, and I think the bee attack on your son was my fault."

I couldn't tell if he was joking or not. I guessed the part about the wolves was probably true, but the stuff about hurricanes and forests sounded like something out of one of Micah's books. "You always did have a weird effect on animals."

"I'm sorry. I shouldn't have been there."

"If you weren't there, he'd be in the hospital right now," I said. "I *am* mad at you, though."

"Why?"

"I think it's bullshit that in *fifteen years* you never called."

"Sorry. For most of that time I had really bad reception." I decided not to ask what he meant by that because I already had a pretty good idea.

"Why'd you come here?"

"Because you're the only family I have left. And I missed you."

"I missed you, too." I gathered him in a hug. He smelled like wet mushrooms, but I didn't care. "Micah says you were sleeping back there?"

"Yeah, I got here early this morning and didn't want to wake you, so I took a nap." He ran his fingers delicately over the curved arm of the chair. "It's been a long time since I sat in an actual chair."

"Are you sure you don't want a crate?"

Weylyn laughed. "I'd forgotten about that. The look on your mother's face . . ."

"You'd think a drag queen had come to dinner."

Weylyn laughed again, but in a weary sort of way. "How is Dad?"

"Good. Seventy-eight years old and still preaching. He worries about you."

"Really?"

"You should give him a call."

"I will."

Weylyn self-consciously rubbed the back of his dirty hand with his thumb. "There's another bath off me and Bill's room," I said. "I'll run you one."

"Thank you," he said, abashed.

I ran a bath and set out a towel, soap, and a clean set of Bill's clothes for Weylyn to wear. I sat on the edge of the tub, listening to the roar of the water and thinking about my brother who wasn't really my brother. Even accounting for his obvious concern over Micah, I knew from the moment Weylyn walked in the door that morning that something was wrong. He had the pained look of a man who had wandered for so long that he had forgotten what he was looking for. My heart broke for him, but I was also kind of glad that his wanderings had led him here. He would stay here as long as he needed, I decided as the steam fogged the mirror above the vanity. I wasn't going to lose him again.

I turned off the faucet and shouted down the stairs, "Water's ready!"

## MICAH BARNES

From the top of the stairs, you can hear everything that's being said in the kitchen. That's how I knew about my surprise birthday party last year, and that's how I knew Uncle Weylyn was a wizard. My jaw dropped when I heard him list his powers: talking to animals, controlling the weather, growing forests with his mind! Maybe he was trying to be funny, but it didn't sound like a joke. It was real. It had to be.

I heard my mom start up the stairs, so I darted into the bathroom and turned on the water. A minute later, she brought me oatmeal for my bath and examined my stings again. "I know it's itchy, but try not to scratch. Scratching only makes it worse." I nodded and she left, closing the door behind her.

The oatmeal water looked like puke, so instead of climbing in, I sat on the toilet fantasizing about the adventures my uncle and I were about to have and the spells he'd teach me. I wrote a list of all the things I wanted to learn on a piece of toilet paper, then wetted my hair and unplugged the drain.

## LYDIA KRAMER BARNES

I made spaghetti with meatballs for dinner—from what I could recall from our childhood, it was Weylyn's favorite. Bill arrived home from his errands and joined me in the kitchen. He seemed flummoxed. "Clay's face is cut, Micah looks like he has smallpox, and there's a stranger in our house wearing my clothes."

"He's my brother," I said while draining the noodles.

"The adopted one that you haven't seen in years?"

"That's the one." I divided the spaghetti between five bowls.

Bill gave a lazy, noncommittal nod. "What about the boys? What happened?"

I ladled sauce and meatballs onto the nests of noodles. "Clay and Micah got in a fight. Micah was stung by bees, and Weylyn saved him. I think we should offer him a job. Will you help me take these to the table?" I gestured to the bowls on the counter.

Bill picked up two and carried them to the kitchen table. "A job?"

"We need a new beekeeper."

"Does he have any experience?"

"He's always been good with animals," I said, trying not to smile.

Bill thought for a moment. "If you think it's a good idea, it's all right with me."

"Great. Now go get the boys. Dinner's ready."

"Okay. Oh, and your *brother* told me to tell you he's not hungry."

"Oh?"

"When he told me, I thought he was just some homeless guy, so it threw me off a little."

"Where is he now?"

"On the porch. Want me to tell him dinner's ready, anyway?"

"No," I said, remembering the crate Daddy had given Weylyn to sit on at the dining room table when he was a kid. "He'll come in when he's ready."

## 53

## MICAH BARNES

I woke with the long yawn of sunrise, with the birds and the beasts and the Sunday school teachers. I must have woken before my parents, because I didn't hear the clink of spoons in coffee mugs or the smell of burned bacon. Parents slept in, too, sometimes, I reminded myself.

I fanned my toes like a deck of cards and peered bleary-eyed out my bedroom window at the beeyard below. There was Weylyn, barely more than a shadow in the dim morning light, moving from hive to hive like a ghost looking for his own headstone, hoping that someone had left flowers. He reminded me of a character from the *Wandering Wizards*, Magnus Thunderblood. He was a great wizard that lived in a shack on top of the highest peak in Wist. His only friends were the eagles that lived on the sides of the cliffs and brought him fresh fish and news from the cities below. Magnus was the most powerful wizard in all the Seven Earths. A single sneeze could sink a whole armada. It was because of this power that he isolated himself from the rest of mankind, lest he bring it to ruin.

I crept downstairs and out the back door. The cuffs of my pajamas soaked up the morning dew as I crossed the yard to the utility shed. Inside hung Rodger's beekeeper's suit. My skin still burning from the day before, I gingerly pulled on the too-big suit and made sure it was properly zipped before stepping into the beeyard.

Uncle Weylyn saw me straightaway. "Your mom said I'm not allowed to let you in here."

"I'm just here to get my wand," I said as I bent down and picked up the birch twig. "What are you doing out here this early?"

"The bees are less active at this time of day."

"But that shouldn't matter to you."

"Oh? Why is that?"

"Because you're magic." He shifted his weight, obviously uncomfortable with my accusation. "It's why you don't have to wear a suit. I'm in training, so I still have to wear one."

"I don't wear a suit because I don't react to bee stings," he said coolly.

"I heard you and my mom talking. I know about the hurricane and the wolves and all that."

"Did it occur to you that maybe I was joking?"

"You don't look very funny."

"A story, then."

"I guess it could have been . . ."

"Well, there you go. Mystery solved," he said dismissively and went back to his work.

"Only . . . that doesn't explain how you stopped the bees from attacking me."

Weylyn looked up from the hive, exasperated. "I don't know what you're talking about."

"I want you to teach me."

"Teach you what? How not to get stung by bees? Start by avoiding the back end. It's the pointiest."

"Here's a list," I said and pulled out the piece of toilet paper I had written on the day before. "I figured we'd start with invisibility, then move on to levitation, but I'm open to suggestions."

I handed him the note, but he had no more than glanced at it before he held it back out to me. "I think you should go back inside before your mother finds out you were here." He glowered at me with his piercing gray eyes. Magnus Thunderblood could set a man on fire by raising his left eyebrow. I decided not to take my chances.

"Mom makes pancakes on Sundays. I like mine with honey," I said defiantly and turned back toward the house.

If he wasn't going to tell me the truth, I'd have to hide in the shadows and wait for him to show his hand. I was Tarquist the Unseen, after all. You didn't know I was there until it was too late.

## 54

## LYDIA KRAMER BARNES

Sunday was Pancake Day. It sounds like a holiday, an awesome one where you wake up, eat a fat stack of pancakes, then sleep till dinner. That's pretty much what it is, unless you're the one making them: two hours over a hot stove, pouring giant Frisbees of batter while people shout their orders at you:

*"Blueberries!"*

*"Chocolate chips!"*

*"Raisins, coconut, banana, walnuts!"*

By the time everyone else is fed, there's a puddle of batter left at the bottom of the bowl, just enough to make yourself a small saucer of a pancake. Every week, you up the amount of batter you make to adjust for this disparity, but the outcome is somehow always the same. "They're growing boys," I tell myself as I pour syrup over my co-medically small breakfast.

This particular day was a Sunday, so I hauled myself out of bed and headed down to the kitchen. I had barely started the batter when Bill stomped into the room carrying a sledgehammer. "Damn mice," he growled.

"Why are you carrying a sledgehammer?" I asked, trying not to sound concerned.

"Damn mice have chewed through all the wiring in the house and killed the power!"

"The power's out?" I tried the light switch, and sure enough, nothing happened. *If only I had an electric stove*, I thought. *Then I wouldn't have to cook.*

Clay came crashing into the room. "Moooooom!" he cried. He was still wearing his soccer ball pajamas and his hair stuck straight up like a Muppet's. "*Super Punch Ninja* is about to start and the TV won't turn on!" That was his favorite show. It was rated TV-PG for "animated scenes of kicking and punching."

"The power's out," Bill explained.

"What?" Clay shrieked.

"What makes you think it was the mice?" I asked Bill.

Bill walked over to the toaster and held up the power cord. It was frayed like it had been chewed on. "I caught the little guy in the act, but he got away."

"Moooom—" Clay tried to interject.

"He was probably just a decoy to distract you from the larger plot."

"I'm serious, Lydia."

"How am I s'posed to watch *Super Punch Ninja*?" Clay shouted and punched my blender, knocking it off its base and onto the counter.

I turned to him, exasperated. "Dammit, Clay! You're not going to be watching any *Super Punch Ninja* if you keep punching my appliances!"

This infuriated Clay even more. "It's not fair!"

"Neither is the corporate tax code, but the world keeps spinning."

I turned to Bill to back me up, but he had his ear up against the wall. "There's a scratching sound . . ."

"It's a power outage, Bill!" I had lost all patience. "Let me call the electric company before you start demo-ing my walls. And you!" I said, pointing at Clay. "Go to your room. I'll call you when breakfast is ready, and you'd better have calmed down by then or no pancakes."

Clay heaved a childish groan and headed back up the stairs while Bill slinked out the back door.

Finally alone, I closed my eyes, sucked in a deep pocket of air, and let it slip out of my lungs in a slow stream like a crowd filtering out of an auditorium. When I opened them, Weylyn was standing in front of me. I jumped. "Weylyn!"

"Sorry. Did I scare you?" he asked.

"No . . . yes, but it's okay. Is that honey?"

He held up the golden jar with a faint smile. "Micah said he likes it on pancakes."

"He does. Thanks," I said, taking the jar. "I wasn't expecting honey on your first day, but then again, you're . . ."

"Full of surprises?"

"Yes. Definitely." I put the jar on the counter and got to work on the pancake batter. "You want some?"

Weylyn shuffled his feet awkwardly. "No, thank you. I should get back to the bees."

I pointed my spatula at him menacingly. "I wasn't really asking. You're eating breakfast with us, and it's going to be terrible."

"Terrible?"

"You'll see." I put my spatula on the counter and turned back to the batter. The look on Weylyn's face when he sat down at the kitchen table was the same one Clay wore when I told him to go to his room. It had been a long time since he sat down for a meal with a family, so I understood his hesitance, but I had to break him back into human life, and that wasn't going to happen if he spent all his time with bees.

When the batter was ready, the rest of the boys filtered in, and the terrible, horrible, clamorous breakfast began. Weylyn fidgeted in his chair as Clay and Micah flicked blueberries across the table at each other and Bill rattled on about the empires that mice have collapsed. Weylyn didn't know what he wanted on his pancake, so I made a smiley face with chocolate chips and banana slices. When I sat it in front of him, he stared at it blankly, then ate one of the banana slice eyes warily. Minutes later, I heard him yell over my shoulder, "Banana-chocolate face!"

I smiled to myself and sliced up another banana.

That wasn't the first time we'd had a power outage that year, or even that month. It was all over the news. POWER OUTAGES PLAGUE RURAL PENNSYLVANIA was the headline on just about every media outlet. The last four summers had been some of the hottest on record, and the severely outdated power grid couldn't handle the additional demand. Sometimes we'd be in the dark for a week or more, but we usually read about it in the paper before it happened so we could prepare: COUNTY-WIDE OUTAGE EXPECTED WITH NEXT WEEK'S HEAT WAVE.

After two years of this, I offered up a portion of my land to the city to build a windmill. The project was barely under way when Councilman Marcus Beattie, whose father was CFO of Heartland Coal, filed an injunction on the basis of "unknown environmental and economic consequences" and stopped construction in its tracks. Three years and twenty-six blackouts later, no new energy projects had been entertained by the council, and we still had a partially built windmill on our property.

When I called Central Pennsylvania Power later that day, I expected to get the same automated message I usually did: *Due to an energy shortage, service has been disabled for [insert number here] days. We appreciate your patience during this time.* Instead, I got through to a customer service rep. "There was no scheduled blackout. Yours is the only home that's out. The transformer at the bottom of your drive experienced a power surge."

"What caused it?" I asked.

"You tell me, ma'am. It came from your house."

Over the next few weeks, Weylin began to open up. He wasn't quite himself yet, but he ate all his meals with us, and even if he didn't say much, I could tell he appreciated the company. Every morning he brought us honey—Rodger had only produced a jar a week—and soon we had so many jars that the pantry door wouldn't close. I tried to use it up by making honey butter, muffins, cornbread, and cake. I put it in my tea and on my toast, but it still accumulated faster than it was consumed. I started giving it away to the neighbors I liked, then the neighbors I didn't like just to get rid of the stuff, but it just kept coming.

Three extra pounds and a diabetes scare later, I asked Weylin if there was some way he could slow the process down. He thought for a moment, then said, "Maybe I'm not right for this job."

"No, no!" I quickly backpedaled. "The Honey Festival is coming up. I'll just sell a bunch of it there."

Despite his improvement, I could still sense something wasn't quite right. One night, after I had sent the boys upstairs to bed, I found Weylin on the front porch swing, watching fireflies play hide-and-seek in the grass, lost in his own thoughts. "Room for me out here?" I asked. He nodded and I sat down on the swing next to him. *Wuthering Heights* was open on his lap. "What do you think of it?" I gestured to the book.

"Oh, it's theatrical nonsense, but it was on the library's list of 'One Hundred Books to Read Before You Die.' It was listed last, probably because you get so fed up after reading it that you croak."

I laughed. "Maybe you should stop before you get hurt."

"Now you mention it, I have a bit of a headache." He shut the book with a satisfying *thwap*! "Ridiculous love stories have that effect on me."

"Wow. Who made you so bitter?"

Weylin looked up at me hesitantly, unsure of whether to continue. "After my parents died, when I lived with my wolf family, I played this game where I'd pretend to have a problem and someone would fix it for me like . . . I would lose my favorite postcard and then some kind-faced couple would happen by and help me find it. You know, just simple stuff. I never fantasized that they wanted to adopt me and take me back to their horse ranch with a swimming pool and a trampoline or anything crazy like that. I was just so tired of having to figure everything out for myself that I wanted someone to help me, even if it was with some stupid, insignificant problem I was having.

"Then I met this . . . girl. She would sit with me and we'd talk, and she taught me how to read. I loved my wolf family, but she reminded me of how good it feels to connect with another human being."

The fireflies had migrated from their hiding places among the grass to the flowerbed at the foot of the porch. Weylyn watched them while he gathered his thoughts, then continued, "I ran into her again, years later. I had a chance to have a real connection with another person, and not just any person, *Mary*. I must have known I was in love, but . . . well, I know it now."

A firefly landed silently on Weylyn's shoulder.

"What happened?" I asked.

"She got caught in a snowstorm that I started. She could have died. If Duane hadn't found her . . ." He trailed off, then turned back to me, a grave expression on his face. "I'm dangerous, Lydia. Maybe not as much as I used to be, but still . . . I came here, anyway. What does that say about me?"

"It says you care. About people. About me." I took his hands in mine and squeezed. "You have all this good inside you, but you give it all away. You don't keep any for yourself. Why is that?"

The fireflies bobbed up the stairs and circled Weylyn in a beautiful, lilting halo. I gaped at them, astonished. Weylyn hardly seemed to notice. He squeezed my hands back. "Because it's not safe with me. Nothing is."

## 55

## MICAH BARNES

Using a pair of binoculars my parents got me for my tenth birthday, I had been watching Weylyn from my bedroom window for three weeks without anything significant to report. I was beginning to think I had made a mistake. Maybe I had misheard him that day in the kitchen. Maybe he was just a regular guy who told weird stories.

I asked my mom what she thought about it. "Your uncle is just odd, that's all," she said dismissively. "And stop spying on him. He deserves a little privacy."

So, I let it go. I was disappointed, of course. I had been looking forward to having a teacher so I could do real magic, not just pretend stuff. The binoculars went back in their case, and I concentrated on more realistic goals. Specifically, I wanted to win this year's Honey Run.

The Honey Run is an event held the last weekend of every June at the Honey Festival. The runners have to slog through a fifty-meter trough filled with a honey-esque concoction of sugar, water, and gold food coloring that comes up to your knees. It is a relay, so the first team member has to run twenty-five meters, then pass the honey dipper to his partner so he can finish. The winning team of each age group receives a trophy, T-shirts, and their picture in the paper.

Clay and I had been a team for the last three years, and we won every year. Despite being bad at most sports, my size gave me an advantage in the Honey Run because it gave me momentum. As I plowed through the sticky goo, I'd look over and see my skinny competitors wriggling in place like bugs on flypaper. Clay was skinny, too, but he had the explosive thighs of a sprinter that allowed him to leap across the honey like a skipping stone. Those were the only trophies I'd ever earned, and I kept them on a special shelf in my bedroom.

I biked over to the fairgrounds the day before the festival and went to the sign-up tent. "Micah and Clay Barnes, returning champions," I said proudly to the woman behind the table.

"I'm sorry, but it looks like there is already a Clay Barnes signed up for that event," she said and held the roster out to me. Sure enough, Clay's name was on the list next to his idiot friend Gunner. I felt tears coming on and turned to leave. "Do you still want to sign up?" the woman called after me, but I was already on my bike, letting the air evaporate my tears and carry them into the clouds. If I was lucky, they'd fall with the rest of the rain at 2:00 P.M. the next day, canceling the Honey Run.

When I got home, Clay was sitting on the couch watching TV like nothing had happened. I thought about how great it would feel to throw my big, fat fist into his little bird face. How satisfying it would be to kick his feet out from under him and sit on his neck till he cried. Better yet, I'd cast a paralyzing spell so he couldn't run or play soccer or even tie his shoes, but to do that, I'd need Weylyn's help.

That night, I saw Weylyn sitting on the front porch alone. I was about to go out there and beg him to help me when my mom beat me to it. Instead of getting ready for bed like she had asked, I went up to my room and cracked the window so I could hear their conversation. I couldn't make out most of what they were saying, but I did hear Weylyn mention a girl he loved named Mary, who he thought he had put in danger somehow.

An hour later, I woke with my face pressed up against the cool glass of my window. I sat up, leaving behind a greasy smudge the shape of my nose and cheek. It was nighttime, and the crickets and frogs were playing Marco Polo from their hiding places in the tall grasses. The moon was either a waxing crescent or a waning—I could never tell the difference—and the landscape was a collage of Rorschach inkblots, save one small patch of light.

It came from behind the thicket at the far end of the beeyard, a soft, pulsing, green-yellow glow. I grabbed my binoculars and suctioned them to my eyes to get a better look. I couldn't see the origin of the light, just the leaves on the trees changing color—black, green, yellow, green, black. I watched and waited for a few minutes, then went in for a closer look.

When I crept downstairs, Mom and Dad were busy watching something on PBS with British people wearing pants that looked like they had been put on backward. Whatever it was, they were completely engrossed because they didn't notice me slip out the back door.

The bees probably weren't out at this time of night, but I figured I'd put on the beekeeper's suit just to be safe. I opened the door to the gate slowly so it wouldn't squeak, and I headed toward the light.

As I made my way across the yard, my mind flooded with things it could be: an alien spaceship, a luminescent specter, a radioactive cheeseburger ready to bestow superpowers on the first person to take a bite. I once learned in school that a mouse has a resting heart rate of up to seven hundred and fifty beats per minute. That's what my heart felt like as I crept closer to the pulsing glow, trying to match the sound of my breathing with the air around it so I wouldn't be noticed by whatever lay beyond those trees.

I stepped inside the tree line and held my wand out for protection. Even if I couldn't do any magic with it yet, I could still use it the old-fashioned way. The light was coming from behind a cluster of walnut trees. I found a hiding spot among them and peered around their trunks.

I had to suppress a gasp when I saw it. The light was the work of thousands of fireflies, blinking gently like earthbound stars. Wey-lyn stood in the center of their galaxy, peering into a white bee box that glowed like pirates' treasure. He gingerly reached into the box and pulled out a honeycomb file, its mesh dripping in a luminescent goo. Weylyn turned the file in his hands, admiring it, then held up a mason jar and tipped the file so the honey—or whatever it was—ran inside.

I leaned in to get a better look, lost my balance, and tumbled out from my hiding place in plain view of Weylyn. He looked at me ca-sually as if he'd been expecting me. "I figured you'd eventually see the light," he said, a hint of amusement in his voice.

I scrambled to my feet, embarrassed by my performance. "You knew I've been watching you?"

"Of course. I can see your window from the beeyard."

I felt like an idiot. I couldn't even live up to my name, the Unseen, with a pair of damn binoculars! How was Weylyn ever going to take me seriously?

"I don't blame you. I'd be curious, too, if I'd overheard what you did. Unfortunately, I've never eavesdropped on anything of much interest. Last week, I overheard a couple arguing in the gro-cery store over what jam to buy. I made the mistake of offering my opinion, and the man told me to go choke on a strawberry. He didn't intimidate me so much as put me in the mood for straw-berry jam."

It was more words than I had heard him speak since he'd arrived. I gaped at him, not knowing how to respond. "While we're on the subject"—he held out the jar with the bioluminescent honey—"would you like a taste? It basically tastes like sugar but with a slight electrical shock." I shook my head, my tongue tingling just thinking about it.

"Suit yourself," he said and screwed the cap on the jar. "It doesn't stay in solid form for long. In a few minutes, it will be nothing but pure light. See?" He fetched a second jar that burned like a light-bulb.

"B-but . . . h-how?" I stuttered.

Weylyn shrugged. "You believe in magic, don't you?"

I nodded emphatically.

"Of course you do. I read the list you gave me, but I'm not sure I can be of much help to you."

"Why not?"

"Because I can't do any of those things. Even this"—he pointed at the jar—"wasn't my doing."

"So, you're *not* magic?"

"I can't *do* magic. I'm not like those wizards in your books that can wave a wand and turn a turnip into a train car."

"Can't you do *anything*?" I'm sure I sounded rude, but I was fourteen. I hadn't yet perfected the art of diplomacy.

Weylyn didn't seem to take my tone personally. "I can't deny that strange things seem to happen around me. Like that power outage a few weeks ago. I stubbed my toe really hard on the doorjamb and *poof*! No power. That's enough to make any man reevaluate his perspective on the world."

I was angry, angry that Weylyn could possess such awesome power and not only deny it but waste it on a stubbed toe! He didn't have the discipline to train himself to control it. I had the discipline. I had the dedication. Weylyn just made jokes and put magic in a jar like it was some trinket at a gift shop. He couldn't teach me anything because he wasn't willing to learn. "Yeah, I guess you couldn't be a real wizard because wizards train really hard to hone their powers," I snapped.

Weylyn's left hand flinched like he was swatting away a fly. "Some things are out of our control," he said evenly, putting his left hand in his pants pocket.

Then I did something I'm not proud of. "What about Mary?"

Weylyn's eyes narrowed. "How do you know about her?"

"I heard you and my mom talking. You said she could have died. Was that because of you?"

He didn't answer. I felt a drop of rain on my forehead and continued, "All I'm saying is that maybe if you had trained properly, that wouldn't have happened."

Weylyn gave me an icy stare, and for a moment, I was afraid. Then a sadness passed over him like a shadow, and the rain fell in a cold, wet sheet. I turned, too ashamed to look at him any longer, and ran back to the house.

The rain lasted into the next day, and the Honey Run was canceled. I couldn't help but think that it wasn't just my words that upset Weylyn but the fact that I was cruel enough to say them in the first place.

I tried my best to avoid Weylyn over the next few days. I pretended I was sick and ate meals in my room. I occasionally saw him out the window in the beeyard, but I left my binoculars in their case. On day four of this charade, my mom caught on that I wasn't sick and insisted I leave my room. I went straight to the garage to get my bike and spent most of the day cycling in circles around the neighborhood. By the time I got home, I was dehydrated and sore, giving me a legitimate excuse to hide out in my room.

I must have fallen asleep, because I woke up to a knocking sound. "Micah?" said Weylyn from the other side of the door. I contemplated crawling out the window onto the roof or hiding in the closet, but both options seemed so cowardly. I decided to face my problem head-on.

I opened the door. Weylyn was standing in the hall, waiting for me. He didn't look mad like I thought he would. In fact, he was smiling. "Your mom asked me to come get you. Dinner's ready."

"Yeah, okay," I said groggily. I was about to slide past him when he stopped me.

"I'd like to talk to you about something first, if that's okay."

I nodded, uncertain.

"I was thinking about what you said," he began. "Even though I can't teach you anything, maybe you could help me instead."

"Help you with what?"

"I could use an assistant. I thought you might like to help me with the bees and"—he paused, deciding whether to continue—"I could use a training partner."

"*Really?*" I nearly shouted.

Weylyn hushed me. "Yes, really. Your mom said it was okay as long as you were careful. With the bees, I mean. She doesn't know about the second thing, and we probably shouldn't mention it just yet."

He didn't have to ask me twice. I accepted my assignment and reported for duty the next day.

## 56

## LYDIA KRAMER BARNES

Bill and I were the embarrassing parents. I found this out from Clay's friend Gunner, the one with the gap teeth and the peanut allergy. I was asking Clay what snacks I should bring to his soccer tournament coming up, and the little twerp turned to me and said, "You know, Mrs. B., you and Mr. B. might want to cool it on the snacks and T-shirts and team spirit shit." He actually said *shit*. "It's embarrassing." For the rest of the season, I brought peanut butter cookies so I could see the look of disappointment on his face when he couldn't eat my "embarrassing" snacks.

But his words got me thinking . . . maybe I *was* embarrassing. Bill, definitely. He refused to sit on the bleachers with the rest of the parents, preferring to stand on the sidelines with the coaches. He was loud, but he only shouted words of encouragement, unlike some of the subtler parents who waited until they were in the car to tell their kids how much they sucked.

I guess I was just as embarrassing, only in a different way. No one asked me to bring snacks. The other parents hadn't asked me to make PARENT PEP SQUAD T-shirts or organize team pizza parties. I had done that all on my own, and no one had offered to help. I told myself it was because I loved my kids more, but maybe it was because the other kids told their parents what Gunner told me and the other parents had listened.

Clay played in a summer soccer league in a snooty nearby suburb, and it was the day of their big rivalry game. I insisted Micah come along, and he threw a fit. Clay had been giving Micah a hard time lately, and I blamed it on Gunner and the rest of his crew of under-parented misfits. Clay had always been rambunctious, but never hurtful or spiteful, and he and Micah had mostly gotten along. I only hoped he wouldn't push Micah so far that he could never get him back.

I asked Weylyn to come along, too. He and Clay had kicked a soccer ball around in the backyard a few times, and he seemed to really enjoy it. I also thought it would be good to get him out in society again, even if the soccer parents were a bunch of snobs and alcoholics. He had been in a particularly good mood the last few days—excited, even. I asked him what his new attitude was all about, and he answered in typical cryptic Weylyn fashion, "I'm in training." I asked him what he meant, and all he did was wink at me and walk away with a little bounce in his step. I had no idea what this "training" of his was, but as long as it didn't involve natural disasters, it was fine with me.

The forecast said it was supposed to be sunny that day. When we arrived at the field, a foreboding wall of clouds was rolling in, and the other parents were suggesting postponing the game. After five minutes of bickering, the parents and coaches finally agreed that they would allow the kids to play but would suspend the game at the first sound of thunder.

I had brought a cooler filled with lemonade and ice cream sandwiches topped with—you guessed it—peanuts. I wore my PARENT PEP SQUAD shirt, and Weylyn wore the matching hat and cheered even louder than Bill when Clay's team scored. Micah had his face buried in a book and only looked up when Weylyn spoke to him. The two of them had been spending a lot of time together in the beeyard and seemed to be getting along really well. Micah needed someone in his life other than Bill and me, especially since his and Clay's relationship had become strained. It was good for Weylun, too.

"What an accurate kick!" Weylyn exclaimed as Clay passed the ball halfway downfield to an open teammate. I had to hold back laughter. While the other parents shouted stock sayings like "Go, Urchins!" and "Nice shot!" Weylyn offered much more specific commentary. "Excellent maneuverability!" he cried as Clay dribbled the ball around an opponent, then turned to me. "Has he ever considered dance lessons? He's very light on his feet."

"I doubt it. He cares way too much about what the other kids think of him." Weylyn looked confused, as if he couldn't see any reason why dancing would embarrass a twelve-year-old boy.

"Atta boooy, Claaaaaaaaaay!" Bill's voice boomed, rattling the bleachers.

"Why does Dad have to yell so loud?" Micah grumbled from behind the pages of his book.

"At least he's not reading a book when there is an exciting sporting event right in front of him," Weylyn half teased, half reprimanded.

"It's not exciting. It's boring."

"Your uncle is right," I jumped in. "Put the book away and watch your brother."

"Why should I watch his stupid soccer game when he ditched me at the Honey Run?"

"Because he's your brother," I said, then added, "and he hasn't noticed his cleats are untied, so there's a good chance he might trip."

Micah gasped. "You're not going to tell him?"

I shrugged. "Boys like your brother need to fall on their face every once in a while. It reminds them they're human." I handed him an ice cream sandwich. "Here. Eat this and look happy." He pretended to be reluctant about taking it, but ate it with the happy urgency of a dog under the dinner table.

It was only five minutes into the second half when Clay fell, but not because of his shoelaces. He was kicked in the shin by one of his own teammates—number thirty-seven, Gunner!

Before I had time to process what had happened, Micah was running down the bleachers and onto the field. "Micah!" I called after him, but he didn't look back. I turned to Weylyn. "What's he doing?"

Weylyn shook his head.

Clay lay on his back, rocking and clutching his shin. Bill and Clay's coach went to check on him, but Micah headed the other direction, toward Gunner. He had his stick—I mean, wand—held out in front of him and was mumbling something I couldn't hear.

Weylyn stood abruptly. "I'll be right back," he said, then trotted down the bleacher stairs.

"Wait! Weylyn, where are you going?"

He pretended not to hear me and disappeared behind the bleachers.

I turned back to the field to see Micah waving his stick in little circles and chanting. All the kids were laughing, Gunner especially. "Micah!" I called after him. *Don't give them another reason to tease you!*

Then Micah's voice rolled like thunder above the laughter, "Electro Spectrum!" There was a sound like a whip cracking, and a bolt of lightning struck the tree behind Gunner, causing him to nearly leap out of his skin. The other parents gasped.

Gunner backed away from Micah, his eyes wide with fear. A few of the tree's branches had caught fire, and the ref squirted it with his Gatorade bottle to put it out.

Bill rushed Clay off the field, and I ran to the sidelines. "Clay? Are you okay?" Clay nodded, looking mildly stunned.

When Micah joined us, none of us knew what to say, mostly because none of us knew what had just happened. Clay was the first to speak. "Thanks, Micah. That was awesome." Micah nodded, embarrassed, then sat back on the bleachers and reopened his book.

When Weylyn returned a minute later, I noticed a distinct limp in his right leg. "What happened to you?"

"Nothing," he said. "Just stubbed my toe."

"Uh-huh . . . ," I said, watching him closely.

Micah kept his eyes on his book, but I saw the slightest hint of a smile cross his lips.

## 57

## MICAH BARNES

The rest of that summer was the best I've ever had. Clay and I started spending more time together, riding bikes and building forts like we used to. He said his friends were all scared of me now. They really thought I had magic powers. "I'm sorry I made fun of you for all that wizard stuff. It's actually kind of awesome," Clay admitted as we ate ice cream on the front porch. "Now no one can mess with either of us!"

Weylyn and I never spoke about the lightning. There was no need. We both knew what had happened and there was no need to belabor the subject. I showed my thanks by helping him in the yard for a few hours every day. During the day, I harvested honey. At night, I harvested light. Weylyn called the latter our training sessions because together we were learning how to harness the power of the fireflies in a safe and controlled way. I wasn't doing magic, but I was in it, surrounded on all sides by incredible, beautiful things. It made me feel like a wizard even though I wasn't one, even though I could never be one.

We kept the light in jars, just as Weylyn had shown me on that first night. I pulled out the files and poured the firefly honey—as we started calling it—into the jars, making sure the seal was nice and tight. "Just don't open them up once they're sealed," Weylyn explained as he screwed one on himself. The jar made a *popping* noise, completing the seal. "We wouldn't want any light escaping."

Soon, we had so many jars that the thicket lit up like a Christmas tree. To avoid being conspicuous, we dug a hole that we kept the jars in and covered it with a tarp. The fireflies must have thought we were crazy, burying all their precious light, but we were saving it. I asked Weylyn what we were saving it for, and he said, "For a rainy day."

"Wouldn't tickling your feet be easier?" I said.

He held a jar of light under his chin like a kid telling a ghost story. "You're assuming that I enjoy having my feet tickled. Maybe I hate it and you tickling them would end the world as we know it." He was probably right. I decided not to test his theory.

After a few weeks of training, however, I started to get bored. Every night was the same thing: put firefly honey in jar; make sure jar is sealed; put jar in hole; repeat. I wanted something new. I began to wonder what would happen if I opened one of the jars. Would the light fly out like a shooting star? Would it evaporate into a shimmering cloud? Would it explode? My curiosity gnawed at me. Every time I looked at one of the jars, I felt the urge to smash it on the ground and see what happened. It was reckless, I know, but for the first time in my life, I felt like I had power, and I wanted to see where it would take me.

On one of those nights, the power was out in the house—it had been like that for a few days—so I spent most of the day outside where the air moved. Weylyn had gone inside to fetch more empty mason jars, and I held a full one in my hands. It was warm to the touch and brighter than most of the others. *One jar can't hurt*, I told myself. I hadn't even finished the sentence in my head before I broke the seal.

The glass shattered in my hands. Something heavy landed with a leaden *thump* on my toe. I hollered and staggered back. There, on the ground, lay a sphere of light, the size of a baseball. I reached out my hand toward it and felt a zap of electricity. Whatever this thing was, it was charged and ready to shock.

"Stay back!" Weylyn dropped his pallet of jars and rushed at me, eyes flashing beast-like in the dark. I scrambled out of his way as he began digging a new hole.

"What're you doing?" I asked.

"Go home!" he barked, not looking up.

"Not until you tell me what you're doing."

We locked eyes. I squirmed under the heat of his stare. "I told you not to open it," he said, livid. "We don't know what this stuff is or what it can do. What if you had gotten hurt? Or worse?"

I had messed up bad. How was Weylyn ever supposed to trust me again when I couldn't resist opening a stupid jar? I looked away and tried not to cry.

He sighed and sat back on his haunches. "Sorry," he said, his voice softening. "I shouldn't have yelled at you like that. It's just . . . I've seen what happens when this kind of stuff gets out of hand. You said it yourself: powers need to be honed. If they aren't, people can get hurt. Do you understand?"

I nodded silently.

"Good." Weylyn shoved the glowing orb into the new hole with a stick and kicked dirt over it. He wiped his hands on his pants and turned back to me. "The power's back on. You should go inside."

I sulked back to the house, tail between my legs. When I got inside, the power was back on as Weylyn had said it would be. As I walked up the stairs to my room, I heard my dad talking to my mom in the kitchen. "We're lucky. Rest of the county's still out."

58

## LYDIA KRAMER BARNES

It was the worst blackout in our county's history, and the state government couldn't get their story straight. One minute it had to do with failing transformers; the next minute they blamed it on budget cuts. The power had been out for almost two weeks, and there was no end in sight.

Except for us. Our home had only been out for three days before the power inexplicably came back on. At night, I used as few lights as possible to not attract attention. I didn't want strangers knocking on my door asking to charge their cell phones. I wasn't unsympathetic, though. I made fifty pounds of ice in my freezer and distributed them between the retirement homes and day care centers. I gave them honey, too, but mostly because I needed to get rid of it.

Twenty days into the outage, I heard a knock at the door. I reluctantly opened it to find Elliot Wharton, my kids' pediatrician, looking pale and anxious. "Dr. Wharton?"

"Hi, Lydia," he said feebly. He looked past me into the house at the TV show I had been half watching. "So, it's true," the doctor said matter-of-factly.

"Yes," I said, chagrined. "Do you want to come inside and cool down?"

"That would be wonderful. Thank you." He walked inside and paused for a moment under the vent, letting the air push his thin, wispy hair back from his sweat-beaded forehead. "Lydia, I feel embarrassed even asking this . . ."

"What is it?"

He wiped his brow, then continued, "My friend from the retirement home said she saw you dropping off ice, and I figured I had to come see for myself. The hospital's been running on the back-up generator for over three weeks now, and we're almost out of fuel." He paused, then continued, "How are you getting your power?"

I shrugged. "I honestly don't know."

"The whole grid's down. And I don't hear a generator."

"We don't have a generator. Honestly, Elliot, I don't know what to tell you."

"Okay," he said, his voice thick with disappointment. "I hoped you might know something we didn't."

I was a little insulted now. "Don't you think if I did, I'd tell you?"

"Yes. You're right." He angled toward the front door. "Sorry to have disturbed you." Dr. Wharton vanished back into the dark the way he came.

I turned off the TV and sat listening to the silence. Then I heard faint footfalls on the wooden floor behind me.

It was Weylyn. "I think it's time I showed you something."


Jars of light. Hundreds of them buried in a hole in the ground in my backyard. I turned to Weylyn, whose face glowed an eerie shade of green. "What is this stuff?"

"We call it firefly honey."

"We?"

"Micah and I."

"Micah knows about this?"

Weylyn nodded sheepishly. "He found me out. I wasn't prepared to share it with anyone yet . . . not until I knew what it was."

"You let my kid keep something like this from me?"

"I'm sorry. I should have included you."

"Damn right you should have!" Once I had blown off a little steam, I took a deep breath and looked back at the jars of light. "What are they?"

He walked over to another tarp on the ground and pulled it back. It was another hole with one small sphere of light sitting in the center. "I think it's the reason your house has power."

"Holy shit, Weylyn! Do you know what this means? You discovered a new energy source!"

Weylyn snickered to himself.

"What's so funny?" I asked, slightly annoyed.

"I may have eaten a very small amount of my great *discovery*."

"You *ate* it?"

"It looks like honey when you first harvest it. Don't worry; if I'd poisoned myself, I would have known weeks ago."

"What about this?" I pointed to the ball of light. "Is it dangerous?"

"You wouldn't want to play a game of catch with it, but other than that, I think it's mostly harmless."

I thought about Dr. Wharton and the hospital and the hundreds, possibly thousands of people sitting in their dark, steamy homes praying for a miracle. I once asked my dad if he believed in magic, and he said he believed in possibilities. I liked to think I felt the same way. Call it a miracle, call it magic, call it whatever you want, but I was looking right at it.

"All right, Weylyn. What do we do with this thing?"

I couldn't borrow Bill's truck without telling him what I needed it for. "I want to load it up with a bunch of jars of energy and drive them

out to the windmill site so we can open them and end the blackout."
Bill's reaction was not what I was expecting. I thought he would laugh
and ask what I really needed it for. Instead, his eyes bugged out with
intrigue. "I knew they weren't telling us the whole truth."

"Who?" Now I was confused.

"The government."

"I still don't get it."

"You found the secret energy source the government has been
keeping from us! Come on, Lydia. Keep up!"

"I hate to break it to you, honey, but this has nothing to do with
the government."

"No?" he said, his enthusiasm dampened.

"No. But if you want to get back at them, you can help us move
these jars."

Of course, Micah—the little spy that he is—heard the whole
thing, and he and Clay hopped in the truck with us. Between the five
of us, it only took half an hour to load all the jars and drive them
over to the windmill site. Weylyn rode in the back of the truck with
the jars, carrying the ball of energy himself with a pair of oven mitts.
"Be careful over those bumps!" he shouted to Bill as the jars jostled
and clinked against each other.

The windmill site was distinctly windless that night. The air was
so still and black it felt like we were in a vacuum. The steel base of
the windmill only added to the effect, as it looked like a discarded
piece of a space station whose mission had been cut tragically short.

The base was hollow with a small oval door, so we agreed inside
it would be the best place for the jars. "That way it won't draw too
much attention," Weylyn reasoned.

It took another half hour to load all the jars into the base. By the
time we were done, it had started to drizzle, but we still stood back
to admire our work. A beam of light poured out of the open top of the
base, making it look like something alien.

Weylyn picked up the sphere of light in his mitted hands and nodded to me. I nodded back, trying not to wear my nervousness on my

face. "Come on, guys. We have to clear back." I prodded my boys back toward the truck.

"But what about Weylyn?" Micah said.

"I'll be fine," Weylyn answered. "Your mom wants you to clear back so you can get a better view."

"A better view of what?" Micah asked warily.

"I'll see you in a minute," Weylyn said and walked toward the light.

I loaded the kids into the truck, and Bill pulled out. We were almost at the house when the earth shook beneath us and the sky flashed green. I tried to get the kids to look away, but they wouldn't. I saw it in the side mirror: the terrible bright light, the shards of flying metal. The kids screamed, and so did I. I couldn't help it.

Bill slammed on the brakes and motioned for me to take the wheel. "Take the kids back to the house."

"Where are you going?" I said, panicked.

"To look for your brother." Bill ran back toward the light, which was still billowing in the sky like a mushroom cloud.

I jumped into the driver's seat and drove home as fast as I could. I rushed the kids inside the house and ran to the living room window. The explosion had subsided, and the light had transformed into a bright sphere the size of a small house, suspended in midair like a second moon.

Down the hill, I saw our neighbors' lights blink on.

I switched off all the lights and sat in the dark, rocking my children as their tears formed wet rings on my clothes. Weylyn had told me not to worry. He knew what he was doing, he said. He would be fine, he said. Our conversation from earlier that summer rang in my head:

*Because it's not safe with me. Nothing is.*

I closed my eyes and prayed for the first time in twenty years. Then I heard a familiar voice behind me. "Who died?"

I snapped around to see Weylyn standing behind me, his clothes and hair a little tousled, but otherwise fine. "Oh my God!"

"Weylyn!" Micah leaped out of my arms and into his.

"I found him in a goddamn tree," said Bill, who stepped out from behind him and pulled Clay and me into a round hug.

"That's so cool!" Micah was practically yelling with excitement. "What happened? Did you fly? I thought you said you couldn't fly!"

"Micah, honey. Will you give me and your uncle a second?" I asked.

Micah looked disappointed. "But—"

"He can tell you all about it tomorrow," Bill said and escorted the boys into the other room.

"Dammit, Weylyn!" I slapped him across the face.

Weylyn grinned stupidly while his left cheek turned pink. "It's good to see you, too, Lydia."

I grabbed him and squeezed him tight. "You idiot. Don't you scare me like that ever again."

Power for the whole county came back on that night. It didn't take long before I started getting calls from neighbors who noticed the giant glowing orb near my house. Did I know what it was? How did it happen? Was it dangerous? My answer to most of them was: *I don't know.* When I woke the next morning, the orb had dissolved into nothingness, leaving behind an unexplained energy source and wild rumors about what had happened that night. By the time word of a mysterious stranger and a truckful of glowing jars reached the local news station, Weylyn was long gone.

We were sitting at the kitchen table, drinking coffee and watching birds sing from the branches of the dogwood tree in the backyard, when Weylyn handed me his letter of resignation. "I'm sorry, Lydia, but I have to resign from my duties as beekeeper. I have more work to do, and I'm afraid I can't do it here." Then he added, "You probably think I'm running away again."

"No, I don't," I said sadly. "I wish you didn't have to leave, but I understand why."

Weylyn looked surprised. "You do?"

"You have to find Mary."

Weylyn smiled and looked out the window at the swaying ears of corn in the field beyond ours. Mary had to be somewhere in that impossibly vast everywhere, and if anyone was going to find her, he would. "I'm not ready yet," he said wistfully.

I squeezed his shoulder. "You'll get there."

He left early the next morning, while we were all still asleep. It was Sunday, and I had planned on making him a pancake breakfast before he left. Instead, I found a postcard with his handwriting on the kitchen counter next to a jar of honey.

*Dearest Lydia,*

*I didn't want to wake you. I gathered the honey this morning. You should have less of an issue with volume now that I'm gone. I know I have no say in the matter, but I think Micah would make an excellent candidate for my previous position as beekeeper.*

*Also, please tell Micah I did a little research on your computer, and apparently, arrowroot is rumored to have some magical properties. I don't know if there's any truth to that, but it might be worth looking into.*

*You can tell Bill that I talked to the mice, and they agreed to find another place to take up residence. I found an abandoned shed a quarter mile from here that might fit the bill, so I offered that up as a possibility.*

*I should also mention how grateful I am. I feel more hopeful than I have in years, and it has everything to do with you and your family. My wolf brothers and sisters have a saying (or a howl) that goes, "Don't leave anything you can't come back to." I know I can come back here and I will be welcomed, and that brings me more comfort than anything else in this world.*

*Your favorite brother,*

*Weylyn*

I put the postcard in a box where I keep other objects that are precious to me and started cooking. Soon the Sunday morning rumpus began and pancake orders were hurled at the back of my head like fastballs. As I bent over the hot stove, my tears left salty impressions in the batter like the ghosts of blueberries past.

Weylyn Grey was always welcome in my home. He continued to visit me long after the kids had left and Bill had passed. He even delivered the eulogy at Bill's funeral when I didn't have the courage to do it myself. He added his own little joke about mice at the end that no one else understood but brought me to tears (in a good way).

Most of the time he'd show up unannounced, usually in some peculiar way—I once found him on top of the garage helping a family of birds build a nest. We'd make pancakes and talk about the adventures he'd had and the people he'd met along the way. He came here when he needed a break, a sanctuary, a friend.

He wasn't really my brother, but he was my family and one of the best friends I ever had.

## 59

## MICAH BARNES

*Tarquist the Fire Starter was the name I was given after I set the tree ablaze that was the goblin Gungrot's home and life force. As the tree withered and burned, so did he, and the Prince Clayborn was saved.*

*"Let this tale be a warning to the rest of the goblin kingdom!" I cried from atop the pile of ashes. "Tarquist the Fire Starter does not play with fire—he commands it!"*

*But then the pile of ashes became a new foe more terrible than Gungrot and all the goblins in the kingdom. Its name was Darkness, and it blotted out the setting sun. I commanded the fire to set the beast ablaze, but Darkness swallowed the flames whole and jetted them from its nostrils.*

*All seemed lost; then there was a faint glow from behind a bank of trees. Out stepped Greylord, Keeper of the Light, and his staff, Firefly. Greylord swung Firefly against a rock, smashing its glowing glass bulb. A brilliant flash of green light filled the sky, and Darkness howled with terror. The creature crumbled back into ashes, revealing a starry sky and a great, glowing boulder of light floating where its black head once was.*

*"This is my gift to you," said Greylord, Keeper of the Light. "May it keep darkness away when the sun cannot."*

*Then the wolves made sounds at the sight of it, a long train of Os with a soft beginning and ending. That was their name for it, so we called it Moon, also.*

I looked up from my notebook and scanned the bored faces of my classmates. I guess fantasy wasn't for everyone.

"That was wonderful, Micah!" my teacher, Mr. Nickels, gushed. "Keep writing like that, and you'll be an author someday."

He was right. I kept writing and rewriting that silly little story until seventeen years later, it was the first of a series of published novels with my name printed in Gothic-style lettering on the cover. Beneath my name, standing between two beautifully illustrated gray wolves, stood a man with silver eyes and a knowing smile.

*fourth interlude*

WILDWOOD FOREST, OREGON

2017

## ROARKE

All the blood seemed to drain from Ruby's face. "Is that a *wolf*?"

"Yep. A mean one, too." A group of kids had crowded around me at the bus stop to gawk at the photographic proof of my battle with a vicious wolf.

"Are you hurt?" Ruby said, gently placing her hand on my wrist as if double-checking that I still had a pulse.

"Never been better," I crowed and glanced over at Mike, who was leaning against a stop sign, pretending he didn't hear me. It was the first time in my life I had ever truly been able to render him speechless.

It went on like that for the rest of the day at school. Kids would ask to see the pictures, and I would recount the whole grisly tale: how Old Man Spider had tried to feed me to his wolf, and how I had made my escape by blinding the beast with my camera flash.

My mom didn't find it quite as amusing, however. In my haze of glory, I forgot to delete the photo from her camera before handing it back to her. A few minutes later, I heard a piercing scream from the kitchen. Unsurprisingly, I was grounded and forced to look at pictures of victims of animal attacks until I was queasy.

A week later, my grounding was lifted, and I joined my friends in the patch of woods behind our school's soccer field for another round of Truth or Dare. My run-in with Old Man Spider had garnered me a status bump among my peers and a new nickname. "Hey, Wolfman," Ruby said with a coquettish flick of her ponytail as I dropped my backpack in a pile with everyone else's. I winked at her, which sent her and Olivia into an adolescent giggle fit. Mike snorted in disgust, then dared me to stick my hand inside a burrow and hold it there for thirty seconds (presumably to give whatever animal happened to be inside ample time to bite me).

Normally, I loved a good dare, but my heart wasn't in it that day. As I lay on my belly with my arm in that dank hole, worms wriggling between my fingers, I thought about Weylyn. For someone who had spent his whole life having adventures, his present circumstances were pretty dismal: living alone in a run-down cabin covered in cobwebs with only his pet wolf to talk to. I imagined him standing at the kitchen sink, staring out the window with a vacant expression as spiders spun webs around him. Eventually, he was just another forgotten thing in that house, something that had gotten stuck and left behind.

"Roarke!" someone shouted, jolting me out of my thoughts.

"What?"

"It's been like two minutes," Ruby said, pointing to my arm that had, by this point, fallen asleep.

"Oh, yeah," I said, pulling my arm out of the hole and shaking it back to life. Mike looked disappointed that I still had all my fingers. "I have another dare for you," he said, handing me a rock.

"But I just had my turn," I protested. "What's the rock for?"

Mike pointed to a raccoon with a stubby tail, rummaging inside a dead tree stump. It looked a lot like Weylyn's friend Matilda. She was probably out running Weylyn's secret errand for him, the one he had acted so squirrely about a couple of weeks earlier.

"You want me to *hit* the raccoon?" I said. Ruby let out a horrified gasp. This was low, even for a jerk like Mike.

"Sounds like you're scared."

"No. I'm just not cool with hurting animals."

"But I dared you."

"I don't give a shit!"

"Fine!" Mike snatched the rock from me. "If you won't do it, I will." He pulled his arm back to throw.

"No!" I shouted and shoved him as hard as I could in the chest. Mike hit the ground, and the rock tumbled out of his hand. Ruby gasped again, this time covering her mouth and candy heart nose with her hands.

"Asshole!" Mike groaned and rolled onto his side, clutching his shoulder in pain. I turned to Matilda, who was now intently watching the whole episode from on top of her tree stump. She blinked in a slow, deliberate way that I interpreted as a show of gratitude, then scampered off. Rather than see if Mike was okay, I ran after her.

"Hey!" Mike yelled. "Roarke! Get back here!"

I ignored his cries and followed the raccoon to the outskirts of the woods, where I saw a little house on a quiet street surrounded by fir trees. I hung back as Matilda darted across the road and squeezed under a hole at the bottom of the cedar fence.

I pulled myself onto the branch of a nearby tree to get a better view, but I couldn't see the raccoon anywhere. I was about to leave when the front door swung open. Out walked a woman, late forties, wearing jeans and a light sweater. There was something familiar about her, and while she checked her mail, I tried to figure out what it was.

Then it came to me. It was from a picture in my yearbook, one of a lady from the zoo who had visited my classroom with her wolf puppy, the same lady who had tried not to laugh when her wolf peed on Mike's backpack. In the picture, she was bent over, holding on to the pup's hindquarters as it curiously sniffed the toes of my classmates. *The Wolf Lady*, I thought. *Could it be?*

"What are you doing here?" said a voice.

I jumped, nearly losing my balance and falling off the branch I was sitting on. I steadied myself and looked down to see Weylyn glowering back at me, trees casting menacing shadows across his face. "Weylyn? Geez, you scared the crap out of me."

"What are you doing here?" he repeated.

I turned back toward the house, but the woman had gone inside. "Did you see her? It's *Mary!*" I scrambled down from the tree. "Mary's the wolf lady!"

"Wolf lady?"

"The one from the zoo!" I said. "I told you about her. She came to my class."

"Oh. Right."

"I saw her! She lives in that house over there."

Weylyn cast a nervous glance at the house but didn't look surprised.

"Wait . . . ," I said, finally putting the pieces together. "You already knew she lived here, didn't you?"

He sat down on a fallen log and nudged a pinecone with his foot. "She's the reason I moved here."

I stood there, confounded by his nonchalance. "But . . . if you know where she lives, why haven't you gone to see her?"

"I have seen her."

"You *have?*" Now I was pissed. This whole time, I thought Mary was some long-lost love when, in reality, she was never really lost at all, just temporarily misplaced like loose change beneath couch cushions.

"Well, only from a distance," Weylyn said, almost too quietly for me to hear.

"What do you mean, 'from a distance'?"

"I mean that I haven't actually spoken to her."

"Why not?" I said curtly.

Weylyn looked longingly at the little house across the street. "Because I was waiting until I was ready."

"What do you mean, 'until I was ready'?"

"I had to make sure she'd never get hurt again."

"So, are you?"

"Am I what?"

"Sure?"

"I don't know. Maybe," he said tentatively. "It's hard to tell."

"Well, there's only one way to find out," I said pointedly.

Weylyn stole one more nervous glance at the house. "I can't," he said, then jumped to his feet and disappeared back into the forest.

I shook my head. What Weylyn needed was a confidence boost. He needed to be reminded of the man he was before the blizzard, the one who stared down hurricanes, not houses. As his friend, it was my job to help him.

"You are persistent, I'll give you that," Weylyn said when I showed up at his door for the ninth day in a row. My last eight attempts at getting him to see Mary had failed, but I was nothing if not stubborn. This time, I had brought supplies.

I shoved past him carrying a large green suitcase.

"Why do you have a suitcase?" he asked. "You're not expecting to stay here, are you? Boo is prone to night terrors, and believe me, you do not want to be in the room with him when he has one of his nasty spells."

"It isn't for me," I said, unzipping the suitcase to reveal a wrinkled pile of men's clothing.

Weylyn pulled out a checkered dress shirt with a small ketchup stain on the collar. "You brought me clothes?"

"My dad was donating a bunch of stuff to charity, so I stole a few things. I thought you should have something nice to wear for when you go see Mary."

He dropped the shirt back into the suitcase, annoyed. "That won't be necessary."

"Come on," I whined. "At least take these." I held out my dad's electric hair clippers and razor to him. "You said it yourself, you need to shave."

Weylyn eyed the clippers, combing his knotty beard with his fingers. "It would be nice to feel my face again . . ." He mulled it over a little longer, then took them from me reluctantly. "This doesn't mean I'm agreeing to anything."

"Of course not."

"I just really need to shave."

"Sure."

Weylyn shot me one more leery glance, then disappeared into the bathroom. Half an hour later, he reappeared clean shorn with a dozen little cuts on his chin and neck. I laughed. "You look like you lost a fight with a cat."

He gingerly dabbed at his chin with a tissue and winced. "I'm a little rusty."

"It looks good, though. You know, minus all the blood and stuff."

Weylyn checked out his reflection in a copper skillet that was hanging from a web that had trapped most of his other kitchen utensils. "You think so?"

"Definitely. Mary will love it."

I could see Weylyn's pained expression in his reflection in the copper pan before he turned back to face me wearing a cordial smile. "Thank your dad for letting me use these," he said as he handed the clippers and razor back to me. "And I appreciate the clothes, but I won't be needing them."

"Why not?"

Weylyn tensed up. Boo must have sensed it because he ran to his side and stared me down, daring me to continue. "Roarke. We've been over this. *Many times.*"

"Yeah, and it doesn't make sense. You love her, right?"

"Of course I do," he snapped.

"Then *talk* to her!"

A deep growl resonated from Boo's throat. "It's not that simple," Weylyn said, teeth clenched.

"You won't talk to her because you're a coward," I spat. *Coward* was the word Mom used when my dad wouldn't tell Grandma to "mind her own goddamn business." It had made him so angry once that he punched a hole in the living room wall.

The word had the desired effect on Weylyn. His eyes narrowed, and a big, juicy vein popped out of his right temple. I had him where I wanted him. He just needed one final push. "I guess if you won't talk to her, then *I* will."

Weylyn's eyes flashed like someone had struck a match behind them. "No, you won't!" he bellowed.

A powerful gust of wind whipped through the front door and threw me flat on my back. From the floor, I watched the wind rip cobwebs off the ceiling, and all around me, things started falling: frying pans, toasters, shovels, shoes, books, the handlebars of a bike. Then I saw my knife—the one that had gotten stuck in the web weeks before—break loose and plummet toward me. I rolled under the kitchen table as the knife pierced the floorboards where my body had been a moment before.

I poked my head out from under the table and witnessed a side of Weylyn I'd never seen before. He was no longer a silly man with sticks in his beard. He was the man from the stories, the one with the dark, wild hair and eyes of molten silver. Hurricane vanquisher; keeper of the light; wolf. He drew one deep breath and, as he exhaled, the wind subsided.

"W-was that you?" I stammered. I was glad Ruby wasn't here so she didn't have to see the shine of unfallen tears in my eyes. I wasn't sure if I was crying out of fear, because I had gotten a face full of cobwebs, or both, but either way, it was not one of my proudest moments.

Weylyn rushed over to help me up. "Oh, Roarke. Are you okay?" he said, pulling me to my feet.

I quickly wiped a tear from my cheek. "Yeah, I'm fine," I said casually. "I was just surprised, that's all."

"Are you sure?"

"Yeah, it's no big deal."

"Okay, then . . ." Weylyn's words tapered off into silence. He sat down on a kitchen chair and buried his face in his hands. Boo emerged from the bathroom, where he had been hiding, and sat next to Weylyn. He whined softly and nuzzled into his neck. "Now you see why I can't be around Mary," he said, his voice muffled.

I sat down next to him. "Yeah, I mean, the wind was pretty spooky. But you stopped it."

He lifted his head, and I noticed that his eyes were watering slightly. "It doesn't matter. I still let it happen."

"So what? You had it under control in like five seconds. No harm, no foul. It was pretty awesome."

"You think so?"

"I mean . . . it would have been cooler to see you stop a hurricane, but I'll take it."

Weylyn laughed the way adults do after they've been sad (when their mouths realize they're happy before their eyes do). "Next time, I'll whip up something a little more interesting."

"Cool."

We settled into a comfortable silence while Weylyn's brows slowly unknit themselves. When they had finally relaxed, he looked at me and said, "Tomorrow's her birthday."

"Mary's?"

He nodded. "Matilda says she's planning on celebrating alone."

"That sucks," I said. "I'd be really mad if no one showed up to my birthday party."

"What if someone showed up that you hadn't invited?"

I shrugged. "That would be okay, I guess. It would mean he was a better friend than the ones who were invited and didn't show."

"You're probably right," he said, bending over and yanking my knife out of the floorboards.

"You're not gonna let her have a crappy birthday, are you?"

Weylyn hesitated.

"I can go with you if you're scared."

He opened his mouth to say something, but no words came out.

"Come on," I said, playfully poking him in the arm. "I *dare* you."

Weylyn relaxed a little and smiled nervously. "Will you help me with something?"

"Sure."

"I need you to pick me some flowers. Daffodils," he said. Then almost to himself, "It has to be daffodils."

book 6

OLD MAN SPIDER

WILDWOOD FOREST, OREGON

2017

## 60

## WEYLYN GREY

My name is Weylyn Grey, and I'm near-sighted, allergic to ragweed, and my feet are flat. I can't cast spells, I don't grant wishes, and I'm not sure if I can turn a frog into a prince, but I have no intention of finding out. Some people like to think I can affect the weather, but I'd still recommend a good, old-fashioned umbrella for keeping the rain off. It's also been said that I can talk to animals, but if you want me to teach your dog to speak English, I'm sorry. You're out of luck.

When I was a boy, my kindergarten teacher asked the class to draw a picture of what we wanted to be when we grew up. The other kids drew pictures of astronauts, cowboys, and princesses. They wanted fame, fortune, adventure. I wanted none of those things, so I drew myself wearing a sensible suit and a briefcase.

"What are you supposed to be, Weylyn?" my teacher asked.

"A man with a job," I said, satisfied.

But the universe had other plans for me.

I remember one of the boys in my class, Gregory, drew himself as a wizard fighting a dragon. I ran into him ten years ago at a Boise bus station. He now works for H&R Block.

I've been called magic, but I wouldn't use that term exactly. I like to think of myself as always being in the right place at the right time, or the wrong place at the wrong time. Very rarely am I simply in an acceptable place at a generally convenient time. That said, I find those rare occasions very pleasant, mostly because they give me time to work on my crosswords.

Mary never called me the M-word. She was skeptical and practical and delightfully cynical. Despite her pragmatism, Mary had a big heart. One time, when Merlin had a dreadful cold, she sat with him all day, feeding him apples and singing sea shanties (Merlin loved sea shanties). She even let him sleep in her bed, which I'm sure afforded her very little sleep of her own—if you've ever heard a pig with a cold snoring, you'd understand. I pretended to also be sick so she would sing me sea shanties, too, but I couldn't fool her. She sang to me, anyway.

I have no doubt that Mary took excellent care of Merlin after I left. I wouldn't have trusted him with anyone else.

I searched for her for five years. It's harder to find a person than you might think, especially when that person has a common name like Mary and has changed her last name. I never met her husband, although I saw him once, watering their garden and wearing a pair of lemon-yellow galoshes. He seemed like a respectable fellow, although respectability is hard to judge when you're hiding in a tree.

I wanted to make sure he was taking care of her, so I enlisted the help of my neighbors. In the mornings, my feathered friends checked up on her, singing songs outside her kitchen window while she and her husband ate breakfast. The squirrels and rabbits would take turns dropping in on them in the afternoons when they were most likely to be working on the garden together or reading on the back patio. And in the evenings, the raccoons would shuffle down their chimney like little burglars and watch Mary and her husband from behind the ceramic fireplace logs. They watched TV at night, but lately, the husband wasn't there, the raccoons reported. He hadn't watched TV in over three months.

Or worked on the garden, according to the squirrels.

Or eaten breakfast, according to the birds.

I asked my friends how Mary looked. Was she okay? Was she sad? They confirmed the latter.

I had lived less than ten minutes from Mary Jane for over nine months, and I had left her alone. She had the man in the yellow galoshes. She didn't need a fool like me with cobwebs in his hair and nothing to comb it with. At least that's what I told myself.

But if I'm being honest—which I almost always am—I was scared. What if she didn't recognize me? Or worse—what if she didn't want to see me? I certainly didn't deserve her forgiveness. Then again, I never really thought I deserved her love, either. The man in the yellow galoshes probably deserved her love. I bet he never almost killed her with a snowstorm and ran off to live with wolves. Men who wear yellow galoshes don't really get involved in that particular sort of mischief.

But now the man, her husband, had left, and I couldn't bear the thought of Mary being alone.

Not again.


Roarke and I hid behind a crop of fir trees across the street from Mary's. Hers was a little, square house; neat, like a perfectly wrapped package. The lawn was trimmed, and the brick path that led to the front door was lined with red flowers.

"I still can't believe Mary is the Wolf Lady," said Roarke as he handed me the bouquet of daffodils he had picked earlier. "That's so cool." I imagined Mary holding a wolf pup up by the armpits for the children to see, like the baboon in that movie with the cartoon lions. Mary probably even showed the older kids her scar from when she got bit—Widow had felt very sorry about the whole thing. She'd had a bit of a temper.

"So . . ." Roarke stared at me expectantly.

"So, what?" I answered, knowing full well what he was referring to.

"So, go!"

"Sssh!" I hissed. "She'll hear you."

"Hurry up and do it already," he said, scratching his arm. "I'm getting a ton of mosquito bites out here."

"Fine! Just give me a second." My stomach churned, and I was positive I was going to experience that morning's breakfast in reverse all over Roarke's father's hand-me-downs.

"How do I look?" I asked the boy, smoothing out the wrinkles in my shirt.

"Good, I guess," he said, shrugging.

I wasn't reassured. "Well. Wish me luck."

"Good luck. Tell Mary I say happy birthday."

"I will," I said, then sucked in a deep breath and stepped out from behind the trees into the midmorning sun.

Crossing the street was the easy part. The hard part came when my foot hit that brick path. My courage fizzled and doubt took over, hatching a dozen little spider eggs of fear in my mind. The spiders crawled around on the spongy surface of my brain, whispering things like: *Go home. She doesn't want to see you. She'll never forgive you.* I stopped dead in my tracks, like the bricks had magically come apart and built a wall in front of me.

I would have married her. And I would have had kids if she had wanted them. Sometimes, I daydreamed about them riding Boo around the backyard like a horse and eating warm sponge cake that Mary had just made, their fat little faces sticky with raspberry syrup. I tried to limit my time spent in those fantasies. They had a tendency to make me sad afterward.

By all accounts, I've led an extraordinary life, and I'm sure that is part of what drew Mary to me in the first place. But I like to think that I could have been Man with a Job and she would have loved me all the same. If I had been Man with a Job, Mary wouldn't have been caught in that blizzard.

I wondered if Mary the Wolf Lady could love Old Man Spider. I hoped she hadn't heard the same ghastly stories that Roarke had heard about me. I wouldn't expect her to believe them, but still, it wasn't the first impression I wanted to make after all these years.

"Hey!" I heard Roarke hiss from behind me. "Don't stop!"

Something whistled. I looked up to find a captive audience—the birds, squirrels, and raccoons—perched in the tree above, leaning forward on their branches in anticipation. I didn't want to let my friends down, so I took another deep breath and continued.

I made my way down the path, nearly crushing the bouquet of daffodils in my clenched fist. As I walked, the garden on either side of me began to change. The cropped grass grew and grew until it was long and shaggy and leaning. The flowers leaped out from their beds and spread across the brick like flames until the path was a long red carpet of petals. Other, wilder species of flowers burst from the ground, sending clumps of earth flying. Their stems grew taller than the grass, taller than me, and when they were done climbing, their buds fireworked into star-shaped blooms of every color imaginable.

At the time, I barely noticed the transformation. All I could focus on was Mary's front door getting closer and closer to me. Thick swaths of ivy crawled up the front of the house, and by the time I reached the stoop, the door was nearly hidden from view. I grabbed hold of the brass knocker just as a green tendril was wrapping itself around it.

I knocked.

I'd stared down tornadoes and hurricanes, and yet, I'd never been this uncertain in all my life. My heart fluttered like moth wings, and my knees trembled. I was sweaty, dry-mouthed, nauseous, and slightly faint. I considered leaping into the tall grass and hiding there until Mary went back inside to grab her Weedwacker.

Thirty seconds had passed. *Maybe she isn't home*, I thought.

I had used up all my courage with the first knock. I didn't have any left for a second, so I continued to wait.

Sixty seconds. *She's not home*, I thought. I glanced over at Roarke, who was peeking out from behind a tree. He looked almost as disappointed as I felt. We both knew I wasn't brave enough to come back another day and try again.

Then the door opened.

Mary's chestnut hair was pulled back into a graceful bun, save one silver tendril that curled over her right temple like a sweet birch leaf. Her eyes hadn't dulled with age. They were still a bright, eager green, and the lines on her face didn't look carved out by time, but rather like they had been drawn on with a fine lead pencil. But it wasn't just her appearance that made her lovely. It was the tiny, wristwatch movements in her lips and chin. The gentle sighing of her breath. The lavender scent of her clothes.

I thought she wouldn't recognize me, but the moment she opened the door, she said, "Weylyn Grey," like she'd been expecting me.

"You don't seem surprised," I said, slightly disappointed.

Mary glanced up at my friends in the tree, and they scattered. "I haven't used my fireplace in over six months because there's always a raccoon in it. I figured you probably had something to do with it."

She looked past me into the small jungle I'd accidentally grown for her. "I like what you've done with the garden."

"I'm sorry, Mary Jane. I didn't—"

But before I could finish apologizing, she wrapped her arms around me, and I wrapped mine around her in return.

And there we stood until the years we'd spent apart felt like minutes.

## 61

## MARY PENLORE

"Somewhere warm," Weylyn said when I asked him where he wanted to go. It was September, and we were sitting on the back porch, watching a skein of geese point the way south. It had been five months since Weylyn had shown up on my doorstep, and for five months we'd filled our days with long, lazy breakfasts, walks in the woods with Boo, and visits to the wolf sanctuary that I owned and still worked at part-time. It was a peaceful, unassuming life scored by birds in the morning and crickets in the evening, and because it was precious to us, we handled it with care. Some days, the sun would shine and on others it would rain, but Weylyn swore he had nothing to do with either. "I prefer to be surprised these days," he said one afternoon as we watched a summer shower from the comfort of our bed.

"Me, too," I agreed, although I knew he wasn't only talking about the weather. I had noticed the far-off look in Weylyn's eyes as we watched TV together, the way he looked past the screen and through the window at willow fronds that danced like wind chimes in the breeze. Once, I came home from work and found him on the back porch, pacing back and forth like a caged animal. When I asked him what was wrong, he said he was just walking off a cramp.

Weylyn wasn't the only one feeling restless. The need for adventure tugged at my tendons, and at night, I'd toss and turn, imagining Weylyn and me trekking through mossy rain forests and sandstone plateaus or floating down a river on a raft we'd built ourselves. Inevitably, we'd wander off course and discover we'd been walking in circles, but it didn't matter. We weren't really lost as long as we were together.

So, on that cool September evening, as we sat watching the sun set one minute earlier than it had the night before, I said, "Somewhere warm sounds nice. I've always wanted to see the desert."

"The desert, huh?"

"Yeah. We should go."

Weylyn's silver eyes studied me, trying to figure out if I was serious or not. He knew how much I loved my little house with the fir trees in the front yard, and a desert was the furthest thing from it. "Are you sure?"

"Not for good," I was quick to add. "Just until we feel like we've seen what we need to see."

Weylyn flashed me one of his wraparound smiles, then watched the last of the geese vanish behind the tree line. "When do we leave?"


The next morning, we packed up the car with a few essentials and hit the road. Weylyn asked that we drive west first until we hit the coast, then south toward California. "It's about time we saw the ocean again," he said, eagerly unfolding the road map and tracing his finger down the red line that denoted the 101.

Weylyn's face was glued to the window as we snaked along the Pacific Coast Highway. On our left towered ancient redwood forests, and on our right, azure waves tumbled and crashed into craggy cliff faces. Weylyn pointed to an exit for a nearby beach. "Let's stop and stretch our legs."

"Good idea," I said, pulling into the exit lane. "I could use a break."

I parked the car and let out Boo, who loped wildly toward the ocean. Weylyn laughed. "I think he likes it."

We took off our shoes, sat in the sand, and watched the waves roll ashore like we had when we were still young and almost in love. The low-hanging sun burned deep orange, and sea spray burst out from behind the rocks like embers. It looked just like a postcard I had been given many years ago by a strange boy, a boy who met a sad girl and tried to make her happy the only way he knew how. Once again, Weylyn had wandered into my life at just the right moment, and now he was wandering off. Only this time, I was going with him.

What happened next wasn't extraordinary in any way. The waves didn't suddenly rise, and the clouds didn't magically part. Weylyn Grey simply took my hand in his, and we watched the sun melt into the ocean until it was just the two of us under the great starry purple.

*epilogue*

# WILDWOOD FOREST, OREGON

## 2028

## ROARKE

My mother once said, "You get to take one big risk in your life, Roarke. One. So don't waste it." She said this to me when I was sixteen after I begged her to let me go on a white-water rafting trip. I'm not sure where she had found this statistic—my guess is she heard it in a movie and filed it in her brain under *Aphorisms to Drive Roarke Crazy*—but I took her at her word. So, according to my infinitely wise mother, I was allowed one near-death experience, and I chose to use it on my twenty-first birthday by climbing Mount Campbell, the twelve-thousand-foot peak that loomed over the forest I had played in as a kid.

Two of my friends from college agreed to join me on my adventure, and we spent the weekend climbing, drinking, and eating mostly stale trail mix. On the second night, I lay in my tent staring up at the stars through the plastic skylight, my head buzzing with booze and half-formed memories of a strange man who lived in this very forest. For years, I had convinced myself that only some of what I remembered from that spring was actually real. The wolf, the spider's web, the plants that sprang from the ground like magic; those were all just figments of a young boy's active imagination, the product of too many cartoons and too little common sense.

I had barely closed my eyes when I heard a howl. The sound wasn't close, but it wasn't distant, either. Whatever animal had made the noise couldn't have been farther than a quarter mile away. Cautiously, I crawled out of my tent and stood up. My eyes adjusted to the dark as I scanned the surrounding woods. It was a balmy night, especially for three thousand feet. The fireflies were out, blinking on and off like tiny lamplighters trying to set fire to the ferns and tall grasses. One drifted past me, and I gently cupped it in my hands. Greenish light pulsed between the cracks in my fingers as I carried the tiny creature to edge of the clearing.

I unthreaded my fingers, and the firefly floated into the trees. I was about to head back to my tent when I noticed several other fireflies flying in the same direction. At first it was just a few, then a dozen, then a hundred bobbing beacons on what appeared to be a pilgrimage of some kind. I watched in awe as they began to congregate around something deep in the forest.

A figure . . . or maybe two.

Or possibly nothing at all.

## ACKNOWLEDGMENTS

I want to thank everyone who took a red pen to this book—all the family, friends, and colleagues who spent their evenings reading my novel instead of whatever was on their nightstand—and to my parents, who provided me with the opportunity to study what I loved.

I'd also like to thank my agent, Andrea Somberg, for making my first publishing experience a positive one, my editor, Peter Wolverton, for his invaluable notes, and the rest of the team at St. Martin's Press.

Lastly, I'd like to thank Max, whose love, support, and insight made this book—and so many other things—possible.

Reading Group Gold

# BEASTS OF EXTRAORDINARY CIRCUMSTANCE
by Ruth Emmie Lang

*A Reading Group Gold Selection*

## About the Author
• A Conversation with Ruth Emmie Lang

## Behind the Novel
• Running with Wolves

## Keep On Reading
• Recommended Reading
• Reading Group Questions

Also available as an audiobook
from Macmillan Audio

For more reading group suggestions
visit www.readinggroupgold.com.

 ST. MARTIN'S GRIFFIN

## A Conversation with Ruth Emmie Lang

### What was your inspiration?

The idea for *Beasts* started with an image I had in my head of a beekeeper leaning over a glowing beehive. At first, I thought it would make a cool illustration, so I attempted to draw it. After realizing that my artistic skills weren't quite up to par, I decided to write a short story instead. That one story became a series of tall tale–style stories, and at some point, I realized they could all be part of a larger narrative. I guess you could say I wrote a book by accident!

*"I drew a lot of inspiration from the great outdoors."*

While writing, I drew a lot of inspiration from the great outdoors. I have a deep personal appreciation for all things wild and would happily spend all day outside if I could (although, I'm a redhead, so that's probably not the best idea). I think magic and nature complement each other because so much of the natural world is yet to be explained, and magic, by definition, is unexplainable.

### Have you ever met a wolf in real life and what was it like?

I did! It was one of the coolest experiences of my life. She was a gorgeous gray wolf from a sanctuary in Ohio. When we were introduced, the first thing she did was rub up against my leg and kiss me. I grew up with a dog, so I was surprised by the similarity in their mannerisms. She even liked getting her belly pet! This was months after *Beasts* had already been released, so I was relieved to know that my descriptions, while a little on the fantastic side, were not that different from the real thing.

*What made you decide to tell Weylyn's story
through different points of view?*

I chose to tell *Beasts* from multiple perspectives
for several reasons. First, I liked the idea of Weylyn
as a mythical figure who leaves stories behind
wherever he goes. Someone living in Oklahoma
and someone else living in Oregon could each hear
an urban legend about Weylyn and never know
it was about the same person. Second, I consider
*Beasts* not only to be a story about Weylyn, but
also a story of how he affects the lives of the people
he meets. In that way, each character becomes a
part of Weylyn's mythology. Third, I think telling
the story through other people's eyes makes the
fantastical elements more believable. No narrator
is 100 percent reliable. They all have their own
beliefs and biases, which undoubtedly influence
their interpretation of the events that take place.

*How do you push through writer's block?*

I am no stranger to writer's block. I've found
that if I wait until I *feel inspired* to write, I never
get anything done. What works best for me is to
have a set writing schedule. I force myself to write
anything—even if it's terrible—for at least one
to two hours most days. I find that if I stick to
a schedule, eventually I'll get into a rhythm and
the ideas will flow more naturally. I have many
drafts of stories that live on my hard drive and will
never see the light of day, but I don't regret having
written any of them. Like panning for gold, you
have to sift through a bunch of bad ideas before
you get to the good ones!

*What research did you to do write this book?*

I am not a zoologist, or a logger, or a beekeeper, so I can't speak to any of those topics with any authority. I did, however, do research in order to make those chapters of the book read in a believable way while still leaving room for fantastic embellishment. For the logging chapters, I researched the key vocabulary and watched hours of documentary footage about the logging process. Obviously, a forest growing overnight is far from realistic, but I tried to ground the logging crew in reality, so the reader wouldn't have to work as hard to suspend their disbelief.

As far as the wolf chapters go, I definitely took some artistic license, but only after watching various documentaries about wolf behavior. Mary's glassworm research in the beginning of book 3 was based on research my sister was doing at the time while completing her master's degree, so she was a great resource. Again, I tried to strike a balance between telling a good story and including enough relevant scientific detail that Mary felt convincing as a zoologist.

*Do you have a favorite scene from* Beasts—*why that scene?*

My favorite scene in *Beasts* is when Weylyn leaves Mary to go back to live with the wolves. It was a hard scene to write, because I hated pulling them apart, but it felt right. Weylyn was torn between two identities: that of a wolf and that of a man. He never felt quite at home in society, despite his best efforts to belong, and when his powers put Mary's life as risk, he decides that the human

world is maybe better off without him. I knew that ultimately I would bring them back together, but I didn't yet know how, so it was a sad scene for me to write—I *may* have even teared up a little. As a writer, I get really attached to my characters, which is probably the reason I like to give as many of them happy endings as possible!

*About the
Author*

*Running with Wolves and other things I wrote about while relearning how to walk*

When I started writing *Beasts of Extraordinary Circumstance*, I didn't know it was a book yet. It was a short story, or maybe a collection of short stories, or a series of illustrations that I didn't have the adequate artistic talent to execute. So, if you had told me when I was sitting around in my pajamas drawing amateur wolf doodles that I would have a publishing deal in three years, I wouldn't have believed you. I also wouldn't have believed you if you had told me that the day my editor made the offer, I would be in too much pain to walk.

I used to be pretty good at walking. In fact, I could walk so fast that I called it running, and I'd run for an hour, sometimes two. For twenty-eight years, I was lucky enough to be able to take my feet and my body for granted.

Then in the fall of 2014, my luck ran out.

"What is it that's wrong with you again?" I got this question a lot from well-meaning friends who, understandably, were confused by my situation.

"I don't know," I felt like saying, because, for a long time, I had no idea what was happening to me and neither did many of my doctors. My medical history was one huge, terrifying Rube Goldberg machine, each ailment comically stumbling into the next while I sat by with my feet propped up on a pillow, helplessly watching it happen. For over a year, because of what seemed to be circulatory problems in my hands and feet, it was too painful for me to walk, go out in the sun, or even tie my shoes.

*"I used to be pretty good at walking."*

Several months and one postponed wedding later, my pain had escalated to the point where I barely slept, and when I did, I'd wake up every hour or two. One night, I dreamed that a cat was biting and clawing at my feet, then I woke to the kind of tremendous pain that such an attack would illicit, only there was no cat, only my own body clawing at me from the inside. The next morning, Max, my fiancé, made me chocolate-chip pancakes with raspberry syrup, and when I was finished eating, I broke down in tears. Not because the pancakes were bad (they were delicious), but because they were the only thing I was looking forward to that day or the next or the next, and now they were gone.

One trip to the emergency room and many doctor's visits later, the mystery of what was causing my pain was mostly explained. Due to an extended period of immobility, the veins in my legs weren't working efficiently as they should, and my poor shoulder posture was causing my muscles to compress my nerves and possibly the vasculature of my upper extremities. In the fall of 2015, I began down the long, frustrating road to recovery—literally. I ditched my crutches and hobbled in small circles around my apartment, trying to flex the stiff muscles of my puffy, red Muppet feet. I swallowed my screams, gritted my teeth, and listened to a lot of *This American Life*. I imagined Ira Glass narrating my story someday, his matter-of-factness a soothing balm on my emotional burns. I hoped for a day when I could tell my own story with the dispassion that comes with time and distance. I also hoped that I wouldn't blow what could be the biggest opportunity of my life.

*Behind the Novel*

Writing is hard on a good day. You can sleep in, eat a balanced breakfast, take a long, hot shower, then open your laptop and not write a single word. Now imagine trying to write on a computer whose keys feel like they are made of overturned thumbtacks. I've never walked on hot coals, but the goal was essentially the same: do it as fast as possible. This was how my hands felt during the first set of revisions for my editor. Max kindly offered that he type while I dictate, like I were an aging novelist hermit and he, my eager apprentice, but I said "no." I needed to see my words on the page to know if they were the right ones, so I took a deep breath and danced my fingers across the coals.

*"I took a deep breath and danced my fingers across the coals."*

Courage is defined not as the absence of fear, but the willingness to do take action despite being afraid. By that definition, I guess I must have been brave, because I was terrified 90 percent of the time. My worst fear—that my illness had rendered me incapable of writing about anything other than my own sadness and boredom—thankfully did not come true. In fact, what happened was exactly the opposite. Once I started putting words on the page, words I was happy with, I could feel myself relax. It was the perfect escape. For a few hours a day, I got to pretend to be someone else, someone who could do all the things I couldn't. I hiked through forests, swam in the ocean, and ran with a wolf pack before collapsing in front of a warm campfire to rest my feet, which were sore from the day's adventures, not illness.

Some of my favorite chapters were written during these months of pretending, and also, some of the saddest. The protagonist of *Beasts of Extraordinary Circumstance*, Weylyn Grey, has strange abilities that he struggles to control. On good days, his gift is a magical oddity, but on bad days, it's dangerous and debilitating to himself and the people he loves. I know how he feels—well, not the magic part, but the being-out-of-control-of-your-own-body part. We had something in common, Weylyn and I: a fear of ourselves. Both of our bodies had betrayed us and we struggled to be able to trust them again. We isolated ourselves. We waited for our luck to change. Sometimes, we waited too long. I'd been hurt and so had he, and so we suffered together in the way only a writer and her hero can. And then, we said good-bye.

Every time I finished a round of revisions, I'd slip into what I'll refer to as my "Airbnb funk." If you don't know what that is, it's when you're so restless that you spend hours on Airbnb and plan vacations you can't go on. After my first round of revisions, I planned a trip to the Pacific Northwest. After the second, I planned a trip to the American Southwest. By the third round, I decided enough was enough, and I rented an actual cabin in the actual woods for a night.

It wasn't a vacation per se, but it was the first time in two years that I'd spent the night anywhere other than my own bed. By that point, I was walking again—albeit slowly—and was able to hike the rough three-mile trail through the park's caverns. After our hike, Max and I retired to our log cabin, ate dinner, and huddled under the same blanket as we roasted marshmallows. As I listened to the crackle of the dying fire, I pulled out my last set of revisions for *Beasts*, and wrote the final sentence.

I wish I could say this essay is my Ira Glass moment. The moment when I tell you that what happened to me is all in the past and I've moved on with my life, and for the most part, that would be true. I've started running again, and although I still get nerve pain in my hands, with physical therapy, I should make a full recovery. I'm no longer forced to cancel plans because I misplaced my only pair of comfortable pants, and I (almost) never cry while eating pancakes anymore. I still haven't had a wedding yet, but thanks to the good people at the Franklin County Courthouse, I have a husband, and that's the important part, anyway.

And I have a book, one that by some miracle, I was able to finish despite my circumstances. I'm not Weylyn, but telling his story helped get me through the worst part of mine, and for that, I am forever in his debt.

*"I'm not Weylyn, but telling his story helped get me through the worst part of mine."*

 # Recommended Reading

### St. Lucy's Home for Girls Raised by Wolves
Karen Russell

This collection of short stories is what made me fall in love with magical realism. Each story is beautiful in its strangeness, exploring some of the weirdest and wildest corners of Florida. If you like the story "Ava Wrestles the Alligator" and want to read more, Russell penned a novel with the same setting, *Swamplandia!*

### Wild
Cheryl Strayed

Odds are, if you haven't read this one, you have at least heard about it. It is an incredibly popular book and for good reason. I listened to it on audio during my daily commute, and there were times when I would arrive home only to sit in my car for fifteen minutes until the chapter I was listening to had finished. I love hiking, so listening to Cheryl's journey made me feel like I was out there with her, blisters and all.

### The Name of the Wind
Patrick Rothfuss

*The Name of the Wind* is, in some ways, a traditional high fantasy story—boy who realizes he has a special power and enrolls in a magical school to master said power—but its execution is by no means typical. Kvothe, the hero, is one of the best written characters I've read in years. He's charismatic, witty, bold, and plays a mean lute!

### *The Gentleman's Guide to Vice and Virtue*
Mackenzi Lee

This romping YA is part high-stakes adventure, part coming-of-age, and part love story. Similar to the *The Name of the Wind*, *The Gentlemen's Guide to Vice and Virtue* stars a mischievous protagonist whose hubris is both his tragic flaw and part of his charm—think: a young Hugh Grant. Despite his rakish reputation, Monty has a heart of gold that makes it easy to forgive his transgressions.

### *The Particular Sadness of Lemon Cake*
Aimee Bender

Have you ever eaten a sad piece of cake? Rose Edelstein has. She can taste emotions in all kinds of foods, an ability that is occasionally thrilling, but more often, burdensome. I listened to this book on audio during a road trip to Virginia, and by the time I got to my hotel, I really wanted lemon cake. Although I recommend this book, I wouldn't suggest reading it on an empty stomach.

### *Atlas Obscura*
Joshua Foer, Dylan Thuras, and Ella Morton

*Atlas Obscura* is proof that the truth is sometimes stranger than fiction. This book is basically a catalogue of every strange and obscure roadside attraction on the planet, ranging from crystalized skeletons to hair museums to gardens made entirely of poisonous plants. In their first-ever print book, they highlight the best oddities their website (and the world) has to offer.

### *The Snow Child*
Eowyn Ivey

This melancholy book about a couple living in
the snowy Alaska wilderness is part fairy tale, part
family drama. Jack and Mabel always wanted a
child, and finally get one when the little girl they
build out of snow comes to life. It's a heartbreaking
book, but the language is lovely, and the setting
will make you want to cozy up by the fire.

### The Lord of the Rings Trilogy
J. R. R. Tolkien

I'm recommending these classic books not because
I think you haven't heard of them, but because
I would be remiss if I didn't mention the story
that made me want to become a writer. I don't
read much high fantasy, but to me, The Lord of
the Rings is the perfect embodiment of the genre
(and storytelling in general). If you don't want to
commit to reading the whole series start to finish,
the movies are wonderful, too.

 *Reading Group Questions*

1. Weylyn's story is told through the perspectives of the people he meets throughout his life. In your opinion, was this an effective way to tell Weylyn's story? Did you feel like you got a chance to know him or did you wish you had more chapters from his point of view?

2. Weylyn's powers allow him to affect parts of the natural world. If you could have a power that affects the natural world, what would it be and why? What possible repercussions could there be for using said power?

3. On page 163, Mary says "Without beauty, we'd be bored. Without science, we'd be dead." Do you share her sentiment? How significant a role do you think beauty—or more specifically, the arts, literature, and the natural world—plays in our lives?

4. Many of the characters in *Beasts* are missing some form of human connection in their lives. Do you think this feeling is universal? Do people inherently need other people to be happy and fulfilled?

5. Weylyn spent much of his childhood with wolves, but in many ways, he defies the stereotype of the withdrawn "feral" child. Why do you think the author chose to write him this way? In what ways could his upbringing have contributed to his gregariousness?

6. On page 315, Weylyn writes, "My wolf brothers and sisters have a saying (or a howl) that goes, 'Don't leave anything you can't come back to.'" Do you think it's possible to pick up where you left off with a loved one after many years have passed? If you were in Lydia's or Mary's shoes, would you haven forgiven Weylyn for disappearing?

7. What does the title, *Beasts of Extraordinary Circumstance*, mean to you?

8. Many of the narrators in the book don't fit in socially with their peers. Even Weylyn, to an extent, wants to find a place where he can belong. To what degree, if any, should we change ourselves to fit in?

9. In chapter 61, Mary notices a far-off look in Weylyn's eyes. They are torn between the home they've created for themselves and the need for adventure. Which would you choose? Cozying up at home or exploring a new place?

10. The characters in *Beasts* are witness to incredible natural events. Have you ever had any amazing or strange experiences in nature yourself? If so, how did you react?

Scottish-born RUTH EMMIE LANG currently
lives in Cleveland, Ohio, with her husband.
Visit www.ruthemmielang.com to learn more.